MW01136691

CITY IN CHAINS

HARRY TURTLEDOVE

aethonbooks.com

CITY IN CHAINS
©2025 HARRY TURTLEDOVE

Aethon Books
www.aethonbooks.com

Print and eBook design and formatting by Kevin G. Summers.

Published by Aethon Books LLC.

ALSO BY HARRY TURTLEDOVE

City In Chains

~

Want to discuss our books with other readers and even the authors?

JOIN THE AETHON DISCORD!

I

Winter in Lutesse had been hard and cold, and felt all the harder and colder because wood and coal were so hard to come by for most people. Now, with the sun getting up early and staying out late, they'd mostly forgotten the black days, forgotten the frozen fingers and the three layers of woolen socks, one atop the other, that warded against frostbitten feet.

Malk Malkovici watched the sun go down behind the Obelisk from his bedroom. He lived over his shop and office, where he sold old broken things to whoever might want to buy them. *Malkovici Brothers – Junkmen*, the sign above the entrance declared. That was what he'd paid the painter to put there, anyhow. He couldn't read or write himself. The sign brought in business, so he supposed the man had done it right.

Broken tables? Pillows with horsehair sticking out through the upholstery here and there? Five mugs, one with a broken handle, from a set of six? Pots of tinned copper with enough of the tin worn away to make them dangerous for cooking? Rusty iron lampstands or skewers?

My stock in trade, Malk thought with a smile. He was in his late thirties, his greasy black hair pulling back at the temples, his swarthy cheeks plump. In Lutesse these days, that plumpness made him a man to note. Three years after the Chleuh marched into Lutesse, few here had enough to eat, much less too much.

He'd watched them parade down the Boulevard of Dreams after the surrender. Like everyone else who'd lined the grand avenue, he couldn't believe what he was seeing. The invaders became conquerors became victors became occupants, holding Lutesse and the whole Kingdom of Quimper in iron chains.

How quiet it had been that day! *Just about this time of year, too,* Malk remembered. No one who'd stood on the sidewalks had said a word. He couldn't prove anyone had even breathed. Only the rhythmic thumps of the Chleuh's brown boots and the louder rhythmic thumps of the drums that beat a cadence for them broke the stillness.

No, there'd been one thing more. Here and there in the silent crowd, as softly as she could, a woman sobbed. That day, watching his adopted homeland humiliated, Malk Malkovici had wished he could sob himself. And Malk the Junkman was about as sentimental as a parsnip.

Sunset turned the clouds the color of candyfloss, the color of smoked salmon, the color of blood. Before that march on the Boulevard of Dreams, lamp starters would have gone through Lutesse to hold night at bay. Now . . . Now you could hear Chleuh underofficers bawling in accented Quimperi: "Douse 'em, people, or you'll be sorry!" They patrolled in pairs to keep from being sorry themselves.

Since Malk had no lamps shining, he didn't worry. Before he started any, he would make sure to close his dark curtains. He did business with the Chleuh; if he hadn't, he likely would have died by now. He didn't want to offend them in any small way.

And he didn't want a dragon swooping down on his building and setting it ablaze because a careless lamp invited it. No matter what Quimper had thought when she rolled over and showed the Chleuh her belly, the wider war went on. Not all of it went the way the occupants wished it would, either.

Which was one of the reasons Malk also did business with people who cared for the Chleuh not very much at all. Was it the biggest reason? Not being a man in the habit of examining himself, the junk dealer didn't worry about that.

He was pouring himself a brandy—a bottle saved from before the war, not the horrible rotgut they made these days—when his wife walked into the living room. "Hello, Efa," he said, and poured her one without missing a beat.

"Thanks," she told him. They clinked and drank. Smooth fire ran down his throat. Efa smiled and smacked her lips. Yes, she also appreciated quality. Malk smiled, too: sardonically, for what went through his mind was, *She married me anyhow.*

She was small and slim and clever. Except for his brother, Sarmel, she was as much family as he had. They'd met as children in a Nistrian orphanage at the far end of the continent from Quimper, and been together ever since.

"Any news?" she asked him now.

He shrugged. "I haven't heard anything. Not many people downstairs, not much trade. It's been a quiet day."

"By all the gods, we deserve a few of those!" she said.

"I don't want what I deserve from the gods, mine or anyone else's. I want mercy instead," Malk said. "Getting just deserts is for holy men. I'm not holy, and all the gods know it. I'm alive, though. I'd like to stay that way."

"Well, I've had a mutton roast cooking all afternoon, with mushrooms and turnips. Cornmeal mush on the side. However we go, we won't starve."

"Cornmeal mush!" Malk made a wry face. That was what the kids in the orphanage had got most of the time; it was what Nistrians ate when they ran out of everything else. These days, it was also what people here ate when that happened. He still didn't hate it, though he couldn't have said why. It did, however, remind him of a land that hadn't wanted him.

Spooning on mutton juices improved the mush—no doubt of that. Malk hadn't gone hungry for years now. Oh, yes, in Lutesse that made him one of the lucky few. Unlike a lot of those people, he had the sense to know it.

He and Efa washed dinner down with a decent red wine. After they finished, she tidied up. Malk closed the dark curtains that fronted all the windows in the flat. Then he fed scraps of mutton to the lamp salamanders. They shone happily, spreading a warm red glow through the place.

He happened to know the lamp starters had fed the salamanders on the tall poles at streetcorners with dead rats. He could have done the same; his cats and the traps he set downstairs didn't catch all the rats that skulked through the heaps and stacks and piles of this and that downstairs, but they caught a good many. He was a man who watched his coppers. Life in the orphanage taught you that in a hurry, if you ever got any coppers to watch. Somehow, though, he felt the fire elementals who lit his home deserved better.

Efa's uncle had fed mice and rats to his household salamanders. For all Malk knew, old Ory still did. He'd taken Malk and Sarmel into the junk business when they came to Lutesse with Efa. He'd thought of them as hired hands, as hired backs. He'd never dreamt they would take the business from him, but inside five years they did. Half as smart as Ory thought he was would have made him twice as smart as he really was. Malk still sent him food and silver every now and then. He got never a word of thanks, which would have bothered him more if he'd expected any.

He'd just coaxed light from the little salamander on the nightstand by his side of the bed when that Chleuh underofficer shouted again: "An hour after sunset! Curfew's on! We catch you prowling around outside, we'll throw whatever's left of you on the pyre!"

Efa came in then, with a bit of mutton in one hand and a romance with a gaudy cover in the other. As she got her bedside lamp going, Malk pointed to the book and asked her, "What's this one about?"

"Great King Clovsi and his wives," she answered.

Malk grunted. Two centuries earlier, Clovsi's Quimperi armies had overrun most of the continent. They'd even marched through far-off Nistria, though they hadn't stayed. But Clovsi'd had more trouble with him women than any one man deserved . . . and he hadn't been able to hold on to all he'd seized. He'd died fighting. Wags said that, if he hadn't, his wives would have.

Efa said, "I can teach you your syllables, you know. It isn't hard. If I could learn them, I know you can. They might help you in the business . . . and reading's a good way to make time go by on long nights when nothing else is going on."

"Maybe," Malk Malkovici said, by which he meant *no.* It wasn't that he thought his wife was wrong; he suspected she was right. But his life held too many complications as things were. Reading would only add another he didn't need. After a moment, he added, "Too many nights lately when nothing else is going on. We must be getting old."

She set the romance down. "Do you want to do something about that?"

He considered. A yawn interrupted the considerations, which told him what he needed to know. Efa laughed. That didn't make Malk angry; after a moment, he laughed, too. She understood him better than anyone else in the world did—better, he often thought, than anyone else had any business doing. *It must be love* went through his mind. As always when that happened, the idea surprised, delighted, and scared him in about equal measure.

Guisa Sachry stared at his wife in horror. "My best friend?" he yelped. "And my best friend's *dog*?"

Vonney smiled back at him, one eyebrow lifted. “Nobody’s perfect,” she said.

“You *bitch*!” he howled, clapping his hands to the sides of his head.

The theatre exploded in guffaws and clapping. The lighting master and his helpers tossed snacks to the salamanders that lit the house. As Guisa went offstage with Vonney so they and the rest of the cast could come back for their bows, he sneaked a look at the audience. He always did. Even more than most actors, he had to know right away that he’d been liked.

He had been tonight: no doubt of that. Everyone who mattered in Lutesse was out there laughing and applauding. Well, almost everyone; a few stubborn souls still kept their distance from the Chleuh. Guisa couldn’t understand that. They’d won. They were here. They’d been here for three years, and he didn’t think they’d be leaving any time soon. An artist had to be *seen*, or he ceased to exist.

The Chleuh were out in force tonight. King Kangen’s minister was here, front row center. A row behind him sat the garrison commander and his chief lieutenant, both with a charming, , smiling companion. Another row back? The military constable and the spymaster; each of them also had . . . a friend. More blue-gray uniforms, less elaborately decorated than the grandees’, salted the audience’s Quimperi civilian garb.

Out came the cast: lesser players first, as was the custom. The Chleuh whooped for the dancing girls. Well, Guisa’d put them into the play to be whooped at, and plenty of his own countrymen called out, too. The hands other players drew might sometimes have been more heartfelt, but were definitely less raucous.

At last, it was the stars’ turn. A few people—including, Guisa proudly noted, Vurk the minister—stood up to cheer Vonney and him. Guisa bowed to his wife (they were married in real life as well as in the play). She took half a step forward and curtsied to the house. Then she drew back and curtsied again, this time toward him.

He stepped forward a full pace and bowed low, basking in the applause that washed over him. It was, he felt, less than he rated; every hand he'd ever got was less than he rated, at least to him. But it was also a more potent drug than any the wizards created in their alchemical alembics. He'd tried most of those, and given them up one by one. This warm noise, this reminder of how much he was loved, never failed to delight.

Guisa had to make himself straighten, had to make himself wave to the ensemble, spreading some of his acclaim to men and women who deserved it so much less. It put him in mind of feeding salamanders. They were useful, so you had to do at least some of what they needed.

One last bow or curtsy from everyone, and the cast left the stage as the curtain came down. They'd get out of their stage finery, clean off most of their makeup—leaving a little on to tell the world they were performers—and return to whatever ordinary clothes and ordinary lives they had away from the theatre.

Being truly husband and wife, Guisa and Vonney shared the best dressing room. As she splashed water on her face, he said, "You were very good tonight, my sweet." He even mostly meant it. They'd been married only a few months, and she had only half his years: the glow was still on her.

Before Vonney, he'd married two other actresses the same way. To be fair, he'd done what he could for their careers, just as he was doing what he could for hers. They'd thrown him over anyhow. One of these days, he suspected Vonney might do the same, but not while he could still be useful to her.

He'd paid her a compliment, and she hadn't even heard him. From behind the cloth she used to scrub off powders, she said, "What was that, dear? I was cleaning up, and I missed it."

"I said, 'You were very good tonight,'" Guisa repeated, less warmly this time. He couldn't help adding, "I myself was even better." People called him *Imy* because he said *I myself* all the time.

They didn't do it to his face, but he knew about it. That didn't break him of the habit.

Vonney's jaw set. She was going to say something they'd both regret—Guisa could see it in her eyes, which seemed to change from green to flinty gray at a speed a chameleon would have envied. Before she could, though, someone tapped at the dressing-room door.

With more relief than he cared to show, Guisa opened the door. A nervous-looking stagehand stood in the narrow hallway. "Please excuse me, sir," he said, "but Count Vurk presents his compliments and asks if you and your lady would do him the honor of seeing him for a moment."

That was most correct. As King Kangen's ranking civilian official in Quimper, Vurk could have walked into the dressing room unannounced. Who would have been in any position to tell him otherwise? But he asked leave, as politely as if he were a guest in Lutesse, not its viceroy.

"Yes, of course," Guisa said quickly. "Tell his Excellency it is always the greatest honor to receive him."

The stagehand hurried away. Guisa quickly washed and dried his own face. No sooner had he set down the towel than another knock sounded. This one seemed more authoritative than the stagehand's, but Guisa knew he might be imagining that. Pasting a wide smile of welcome on his face, he opened the door again. Vonney seemed frightened till she remembered she needed to smile, too.

Count Vurk was nearer seventy than sixty—a good ten years older than Guisa—but still not a man anyone sensible would care to trifle with. Despite gold-rimmed spectacles, in his fancy uniform he put Guisa in mind of nothing so much as an old bandit chieftain playing dress-up. No doubt he knew what to do with the shortsword on his belt.

He bowed stiffly, first to Guisa, then to Vonney. "Thank you both for an enjoyable evening of nonsense," he said in grammatically perfect Quimperi with a throaty Chleuh accent. "Nonsense, especially enjoyable nonsense, is hard to come by these days." The lightning war that had crushed Quimper hadn't ruined all of Chlé's foes, as everyone here had been sure it would three years earlier. Kangen still swore his kingdom would conquer, but . . . .

Even thinking such things was dangerous. Guisa knew it. Without missing a beat, he answered, "To amuse you, your Excellency, is always my dearest hope."

"And mine," Vonney chimed in behind him. Yes, she knew where power lay.

"I am glad to hear it," Vurk said dryly. "I hope you will both do me the honor of attending a small entertainment I've laid on at my residence."

"Your servant, sir!" Guisa exclaimed. His wife made a wordless noise of agreement. For one thing, refusal would have been a deadly insult. For another, the Chleuh minister always set a good table, even in times as hard as these.

"Splendid!" The count's smile made him look more predatory than ever. "I shall be sure to let the staff know you are expected." He bowed once more to Vonney and Guisa, then withdrew. By *staff*, he meant *bodyguards*. Anyone who showed up unannounced at a gathering of his was liable to come down with a sudden case of loss of life.

"I wonder who will be there," Vonney said as she started to put on clothes that suited the street, not the stage.

"So do I." Guisa changed, too. As he put on an ordinary tunic and trousers, he added, "I wonder if we'll meet anyone new who's worth knowing." He meant *anyone new we can use*, but one didn't say such things so openly, even to one's wife. Vonney would understand him.

When they left the theatre, the night shrouded them in its thick black veil. In peacetime, Lutesse had a name for bright lights. No more, alas, no more. Guisa could have found his way home with his eyes closed. Now he and his wife turned right, not left, walking up the street rather than down it. He'd often visited Vurk's residence before, but his feet didn't automatically find their way there.

Before long, his eyes adapted. The stars blazed bright on their deep blue velvet ground, while a moon, a couple of days past full, was climbing in the east. Yes, once you got used to this, you could see well enough.

"A dragons' moon," Vonney said incautiously.

"Bite your tongue," Guisa snapped, and went through every small ritual he knew to turn aside bad luck. People called him superstitious. He didn't think of it that way. What he did might not help, but he didn't see how it could hurt.

A Chleuh sentry with his crossbow cocked stepped out of the shadow that had hidden him. He'd have a partner who still lurked back there, maybe with a tarncape that turned him next to invisible. "Halt! Show pass!" he barked in rudimentary Quimperi.

Guisa and Vonney had them; as performers, they were allowed out after curfew. The sentry slightly unhooded a lantern to examine the paper. As he did, Guisa said, "Count Vurk himself has invited us to his dwelling."

The Chleuh only grunted. Maybe he didn't care; maybe he just didn't understand. But the passes satisfied him. He closed the lantern, gave them back, and said, "You go on."

On they went—for another half a block. Then bells began clanging all through the city: the warning that dragons were overhead. A searchlight—a big salamander suddenly fed a lot, with a curved reflector under it to focus its light—stabbed an orange beam up into the sky, trying to spot the raiders. Other lights quickly joined the first.

"Now look what you went and did!" Guisa exclaimed.

"I'm sorry," Vonney said, as if it really were her fault.

A dragon swooped down and belched fire at buildings between the theatre and the grand mansion Count Vurk had appropriated. "I think his Excellence will just have to do without us tonight," Guisa said. He took Vonney by the elbow and steered her back the way they'd come.

More dragons dove on Lutesse, some flaming, others dropping barrels full of oil and naphtha with wicks that would set them ablaze when they hit the ground, still others sending down great jars full of sorcerous energy that sprang forth in fiery gouts when they smashed below.

Giant arrows, some purely material, others also powered by wizardry, did their best to knock the dragons and the Hontermen who flew them, out of the sky. Once upon a time, the island realm of Honter had fought alongside Quimper against the Chleuh. After Quimper yielded, Guisa—like almost everyone else in his kingdom—had expected Honter would soon surrender as well. It hadn't happened yet. That embarrassed some Quimperi. Guisa didn't care.

He did care that, when he and his wife got back to their block of flats, it still stood and wasn't on fire. The doorwoman let them in. "Everyone's down in the cellar," she told him. "Just in case."

"I believe it," he said. He and Vonney hurried downstairs.

Most people down there were in their nightclothes. It was crowded and dark. Guisa and his wife did the ending of the play over again, to give his neighbors something to laugh at. Laugh they did, maybe harder than the fancy crowd in the theatre had not long before. They clapped loud and long, too. Guisa soaked in the sound like a sea sponge soaking up salt water.

When the bells rang the all-clear, he and Vonney went up to their flat. He murmured the charm that brought the crystal to life so he could hear what the authorities in Lutesse had to say about the raid from the air.

Instead of the authorities, he got Erol Paki. The little man—Guisa had met him, and knew he was just over five feet tall—had been a journalist before the war. These days, he used his resonant tenor voice to say what the Chleuh wanted to hear. By the way he sounded, he enjoyed saying it, too.

"We'll get through this," he was shouting now. "We will, and

Honter won't! Because I tell you, the same way I tell you every night, Honter must be destroyed! I'll talk with you again tomorrow night."

Honter must be destroyed had been his signature phrase since he started going out over the ether. It was how he ended his nightly talks, even if the prospect seemed less likely than it had three years before. Music began to come out of the crystal. Guisa silenced it. He wasn't in the mood.

The morning air stank of smoke when Malk Malkovici walked to the corner kiosk to buy a news sheet for Efa. The old woman who ran the kiosk shouted out the headline—today, "Air pirates murder Quimperi!"—the way she always did. Malk rolled his eyes. She wasn't telling people anything they didn't know, not this morning.

She must have heard him from almost as far away as he heard her. The soles of his shoes were wooden, and clattered on the sidewalk slates. Unlike most people in Lutesse, he could have afforded to repair them with leather. He hadn't, though. Looking as if you had money was always risky, never more so than during wartime.

He bought a sheet and started to turn away. As he did, a senior Chleuh underofficer ambled up to the kiosk. Senior indeed: by the gray in his whiskers, he was older than Malk. The old woman sold news sheets to occupants as well as to the occupied. She held out her hand for the underofficer's coin.

When he gave it to her, she passed him the sheet. "Here you go, you big pussy," she said, more fondly than not.

He nodded and walked off reading. He didn't know any Quimperi, didn't know she'd insulted him—insulted him twice, in fact, since she'd used the intimate pronoun as if he were a child or a dog. Malk had watched her do all this many times before, ever since the Chleuh marched into Lutesse.

He almost turned back to ask the old woman what she'd do if the Chleuh underofficer ever learned enough to know she was giving him the glove. But she'd probably just say something like *I'll take care of it.* He'd give the same kind of answer that wasn't really an answer if anybody asked him that sort of snoopy question. Better to keep quiet about things that were none of your business.

He tipped his battered cap to a constable who passed him on the street. The patroller lifted his own uniform cap. "How goes it?" he asked.

"It goes," Malk answered. After a moment, he added, "I hope everything that came down last night missed the people you care about, Bezen."

"We're all right, thanks," the constable said. He'd walked this beat for at least five years before the Chleuh came. Except for holidays and a bad spell of the grippe, he hadn't missed any time since. His own job hadn't changed a bit; what had changed was who gave his captain orders and who saw the reports that senior officer wrote.

"Gods curse the Hontermen," Malk said. King Kangen's dragons carried destruction across the Narrow Sea to Honter, while the islanders avenged themselves on the Chleuh in Quimper, which was easier for them to reach than Chlé itself.

"Gods curse them indeed," Bezen replied, though he couldn't keep one eyebrow from quirking ever so slightly. Malk's gods were not the same as his. Malk and Efa clung to the Old Faith. Most people in Quimper, in Chlé, in Honter, in Nistria—most people everywhere, when you got down to it, though the Muos out in the boundless east were schismatics—followed what they called the True Faith.

What Malk and Efa and others who belonged to the Old Faith called the folk who followed the True Faith, they kept to themselves. People who believed in the True Faith often called those who kept to the Old Faith stubborn fools, devil-lovers, demons in human shape, and other such endearments. Because there were so many more of them, they could say whatever they pleased, and say it as loud as they cared to.

They could do more, and worse, than calling names, too. King Kangen blamed followers of the Old Faith (and the gods—or demons—they worshipped) for everything that had ever gone wrong in Chlé since the beginning of time. The Chleuh cheered when he did. Why not? Blaming other people was always easier than blaming yourself.

In Quimper, it had been easier for those who belonged to the Old Faith: not easy, but easier. That was why Malk and Sarmel had got out of Nistria and come northwest as soon as they could. The Nistrians had a long history of putting on hobnailed boots before they stomped the Old Faith. So did the Chleuh and the Muos. So did Quimper, but not so much lately.

"If you're smart," Bezen remarked, "you'll watch yourself when you go talking about the gods."

"If I were smart . . ." Malk Malkovici spread his hands and let it go right there. The constable laughed, clapped him on the shoulder, and strolled down the street.

Bezen wasn't a dangerous man. Unlike some constables Malk knew, he didn't do anything vicious for the fun of it. Of course, if his captain got orders from some high-ranking Chleuh, Bezen would follow them, even if that meant turning into a crocodile and biting down hard. He *might* try to tip off some people he liked beforehand. He might, but then again he might not. You never knew till things went bad.

Since the surrender, every shrine to the Old Faith in Lutesse was closed and locked. King Kangen hadn't done that. He hadn't even ordered the Quimperi to do it. They'd got the idea themselves, and carried it through to curry favor with their new overlords.

Just because Quimper hadn't put on hobnailed boots to jump on the Old Faith for a while didn't mean the kingdom had forgotten how. Some things, evidently, nobody ever forgot. Men and women who believed as Malk did had disappeared from Lutesse. The Chleuh had grabbed some of them. The Quimperi seized the rest and handed them over to Kangen's men.

Not one of those vanished believers had come back to the capital: not one Malk knew about, anyhow. So he smiled and made small talk with Bezen, but kept an eye on him just the same. *I've still got eyes to keep*, he thought.

He paused a moment to get his pipe going. The harsh, nasty mix he smoked these days was what you could buy with ration tickets. He could have afforded better from the black market, but, as with the soles of his shoes, he didn't. Someone who followed the Old Faith and showed he had money was doubly in danger.

Back to his shop he went. He unlocked three locks to get in, then locked them behind him and took the news sheet up to Efa. A couple of minutes later, he unlocked them again to open for business. He trusted no one these days. Not constables, not thieves, not Quimperi, not Chleuh, no one.

He'd only just stashed the keys in his belt pouch when a Chleuh, whose silver-embroidered shoulder straps proclaimed him a colonel, strode in. Malk took off his cap, as anybody who belonged to the Old Faith was supposed to do when face-to-face with one of King Kangen's warriors. "Good morning, sir," he said, bowing his head. "How may I serve you today?"

"Oh, never mind that nonsense when it's just the two of us," the colonel said impatiently. His name was Tebron. He could say such things if he wanted to. He could also forget them if he wanted to. He was an occupant, after all, not one of the occupied. After a beat, he went on, "How much brass do you have?"

Malk looked up. "I have enough for all my ordinary needs," he replied with dignity, thinking, *I'd be long dead without it.*

Colonel Tebron's chuckle was more than half a bark. "Good to hear you admit it!" he said. "How much do you have that I can cart away, though? How much can you get your hands on in the next few days? By, say, the turn of the week?"

"What I have is here." The junkman pointed to piled-up ewers and door furnishings and ornaments and other scrap. "You can take it away at the usual rate."

"I can take it away for nothing." Yes, Tebron remembered he held the whip hand.

"Of course you can. But if you drive me out of business, where will you go the next time you need a lot of brass in a hurry? Or anything else? And if you want my brother and me to go out and buy for you right away, you know I'll have to pay a premium. I'll need cash up front to do that."

"Will you? You've likely got more socked away than I'll ever see." Tebron wasn't wrong, but Malk would never admit it. The Chleuh muttered to himself. "All right. I'll take what you've got now—I'll send wagons for it. As for the other, how much can you grab and how much will you have to shell out? You'll give back whatever you don't spend, of course."

"Of course, sir!" Malk exclaimed: he was the image of innocence.

They haggled more or less good-naturedly. Unlike some Chleuh, Tebron understood he was spending his kingdom's coin, not his own. When they agreed, he clasped Malk's hand, something he didn't have to do. "My men will pay you when they pick up your stock here," he said.

"Fair enough, sir," Malk said. Tebron turned and marched out. Malk nodded to himself. He'd do pretty well for himself if he could get what the occupant required, and he thought he could. And, while he was getting it, he might run into some people who'd be interested to learn that Tebron wanted it.

Guisa Sachry frowned as he scooped salt from the saltcellar to spread it on his poached trout. The frown was—couldn't help but being—theatrical. "Why are we using this pottery thing? And the pepper mill, too?" he added, noticing. "They're nothing but cheap trash! Where's the nice brass set?"

"A junkman came by yesterday. I sold it to him," Vonney said. By the way she didn't look at Guisa, she'd hoped he wouldn't notice, or at least not so soon. Defensively, she went on, "He paid well. I didn't give them away."

"How much?" Guisa asked. When she told him, he blinked. "Well, you could have done worse. Still, I myself liked the shine the brass gave the table."

She looked down at her plate and didn't answer. Guisa had seen that before, from other wives. Apologizing without apologizing, was what it was. *Fair enough*, he thought. The world wouldn't end if they got their salt and pepper from pottery. He understood that as well as Vonney did. He'd also at least started to understand that you couldn't argue about everything all the time, not if you hoped to stay married. At the moment, he did.

When Vonney saw a storm wouldn't blow up over the saltcellar and pepper mill, she asked, "Dear, do you believe what the stories say about the people who follow the Old Faith?"

"Which stories? People have been telling stories about them for the past thousand years. Longer, probably."

Vonney made an impatient gesture. Guisa noted it with an actor's eye, and a playwright's. He knew just where she could drop it into their play. Then she said, "Not *those* stories. The ones you hear around Lutesse these days, the ones about how the Chleuh are sending them off . . . off *somewhere*, and they aren't coming back."

He looked around before he answered. They had no servants, though he could have afforded some. He had trouble trusting his wife with the details of his private life, and wives were supposed to love you, or at least act as if they did. Trusting someone you just paid . . . He shook his head. He didn't want to do it.

There were no other ears inside here, then. The building was old, and boasted thick walls. Nobody could possibly have overheard. Guisa nervously looked around just the same.

After some thought, he said, "I myself try not to listen to stories like that. I don't know whether they're true or not. I don't want to find out. The less I know about such things, the better off I am. The same goes for you, my darling. Believe me, it does."

"Why don't you want to know?" she asked.

Her being young and at least seemingly innocent was part of

what had drawn him to her. Now, though, he spoke to her as if she were a child, and not a very bright one at that: "Because if I know such things, I may make the mistake of showing some important Chleuh official that I know. I don't think I can get away with making that kind of mistake. I may be wrong, but I don't want to have to find out."

"Oh." Vonney paused, too. She nodded slowly. "That makes more sense than I wish it did."

"Yes, I myself think so, too." Guisa raised an eyebrow. "What made you ask the question, anyway?"

"The junkman. Sarmel, he called himself. If he didn't have the Old Faith written all over his face, I've never seen anybody who does."

"Some people do, I'm afraid. But some people who aren't have that look, too, so you can't always be sure." Guisa Sachry sighed dramatically—he hardly knew any other way to sigh, since there was barely a moment in his life when he wasn't acting. "If he looks that way and he truly follows the Old Faith, I'm afraid that's nothing but hard luck for him."

"He talked with an accent, too," Vonney said. "I thought by now we'd given the Chleuh all the foreigners who belong to the Old Faith."

"Hmm. Come to think of it, I thought so myself. Didn't the General do that so we wouldn't have to give them such people whose families have lived in Quimper as long as anyone can remember?"

The General had run Quimper as a Chleuh marionette since the surrender. King Dalad had been fleeing to Honter when a Chleuh dragon flamed the small boat that carried him and his whole family. A brigadier in the fleeing fleet, a beanpole named Char Tubis, made it across the Narrow Sea and vowed to carry on the fight against Chleuh. Except for a few woodsrunning raiders, no one in his homeland paid much attention to him.

Quimper, these days, was a kingdom without a royal family, which happened to be the least of its worries. The General had been a hero in the last war. Well past eighty now (and well past it, too), Petli Philtain gave Count Vurk and King Kangen someone who would follow their orders.

Vonney said, "However the junkman does it, he's still here."

"You wouldn't think anybody in that line of work would have enough money to pay people off." Guisa shrugged. "Not my worry. I myself am also still here. So are you, my dear, of course."

II

Malk Malkovici's junk wagon looked like, well, junk. The front wheels didn't match the ones in back. Some of the planks that made up the bed and sides were painted, others not. Some bare boards looked like recent repairs and patches (they were). Some, pale, warped, and grainy, might have been as old as Lutesse.

So might the ancient, swaybacked horses that pulled the wagon. Malk counted himself lucky to have them just the same. The Chleuh had bought or stolen—requisitioned, they called it—most of the horses and donkeys and mules in Quimper to use for themselves. The agent who'd come to examine Malk's animals had taken one look, laughed himself silly, and let the junkman keep them.

And so they plodded along now, down the street next to the big train station in the eastern part of town. Malk spotted a garbage-can lid in the gutter. It would be tin-plated iron, but that was part of his stock in trade, too.

"Whoa!" he called, and pulled back on the reins. The horses' mouths were as hard as King Kangen's heart, but they got the message. He hopped down, grabbed the lid, and chucked it into the back of the wagon.

A train pulled into the station. It was a Quimperi train, which meant the dragon that heated the boiler was as old and decrepit as Malk's horses. All the younger, stronger, hotter dragons powered Chleuh trains hauling soldiers from one part of their overstretched domain to another. King Kangen might have bitten off more than he could chew, though no one would have thought so when his men strutted into Lutesse.

No sooner had that thought crossed the junkman's mind than another train left the station, heading east. It was longer than the local that had just arrived, and picked up speed fast. Every compartment in every car was full of Chleuh soldiers. None of them looked happy.

Chlé had thought the war against Muosi would be the same kind of walkover the attack on Quimper had been the year before. Thinking something true, though, didn't make it so. Not even Kangen's mightiest mages could go against that ancient, obvious truth. And so the fighting in the east dragged on and on and on.

Warriors came to Lutesse to unwind, to get away from their endless, grinding struggle for a little while. Then they went back to it. Out in the east, not many prisoners got taken. Malk wouldn't have wanted the Muos to capture him, anyhow. Nor the Chleuh, if it came to that. Nobody in the east fought clean.

The junkman lifted his hand to wave to the departing soldiers. One or two of them waved back. If they wanted to think he was wishing them luck, they could do that.

He flicked the reins. The horses ignored him; they were perfectly content to stay where they were for a while. Malk had a whip, too. He snapped it a foot above their backs. He couldn't remember ever touching their bony flesh with it. One of them turned and gave him a rheumy, resentful stare even so. He snapped the whip again. The horses got going.

"About time," Malk said, as if the animals could understand. The snorts he got back argued that they could, and that they were as sardonic as most of the people he knew.

They didn't go any faster than they had to. Shopgirls and secretaries slid past them on scooters. Trams and the underground didn't run anywhere near so often as they had in peacetime. Cabs? Malk snorted as disdainfully as the horses had. Cabs were a fond but distant memory.

Everyone used scooters these days. Shopgirls, secretaries, lawyers, bakers; even Chleuh soldiers on leave rode ones they hired. Men said the women in Lutesse were uncommonly leggy now. Malk enjoyed glimpses of tanned, muscular legs himself. He hadn't talked about that with Efa. He didn't intend to.

When he pulled up at a rubbish tip, he gave the old fellow who kept an eye on things there a couple of small silver coins. The man sketched a salute. He and Malk had an understanding. Malk would have been within his rights just to go on in: within his rights before the war, anyhow. These days, he took no chances on the man ratting him out to the Chleuh. Smarter to keep him sweet.

He got down from the wagon, set the brake, and gave the horses feed bags. Then he put on stout leather gloves. He didn't care to guddle around in the trash without them. He wished he could protect his nose, too. The rubbish tip stank.

Metal, pottery, glass, wood . . . Into the wagon it went. Somebody would find a use for the stuff. Malk frightened a couple of rats that scurried deeper into the holes and crevices in that field of garbage.

Once he'd got enough to satisfy himself, he untied the feed bags from the horses' heads. To show him what they thought of that, they went even slower on the way out. "See you soon!" the old man said.

"Take care, friend," Malk said. He knew every tip guard within a day's travel of the city. If doing his job meant helping to keep them in brandy or tobacco or the nasty, sour-smelling bread the bakers sold these days, he didn't mind.

If you can't get along with people or be useful, you'll never make it, no matter what you do, he thought. After the Chleuh started running Lutesse, he'd managed to find ways to make himself useful to them. Three years later, they still found uses for him. Men who didn't understand called him lucky. He shrugged. They could call him whatever they pleased.

He knew the underofficers who controlled traffic where big streets joined, too. Most of them were overage and overweight. By now, they looked almost as shabby as the Quimperi. But Lutesse was a dream come true for them; they lived in fear of getting on one of those eastbound trains and going off to fight the Muo hordes. One by one, they waved him along. He nodded and smiled every time. Making them happy didn't even cost him money.

He pulled to the edge of the street in front of a shop that sold secondhand clothes and scraps of cloth. He was a junkman, not a ragman, but the two trades had a good deal in common. No one gave him the side eye when he walked into the shop.

The man behind the counter had a sour, sharply pointed face that could have belonged on one of the rats Malk had scared. Seeing Malk didn't make him seem any happier. Affecting not to notice, Malk asked, "How does it go, Evets?"

"How do you think it goes? It goes not at all. It's fornicating terrible." The rat-faced man sounded as disgusted as he looked.

"I'm sorry to hear that. I hope it gets better soon." Malk laid sympathy on with a trowel. Down where it didn't show, he was relieved. Had Evets told him everything was going fine, he would have said quick good-byes and done his best to get away. Odds were his best wouldn't have been good enough.

"Ahh, that's what you say." Evets lit a black, twisted cheroot. The smoke that came from the glowing coal smelled so vile, Malk was surprised the Chleuh hadn't tried to asphyxiate people with it. Or, for all he knew, they had. After a couple of puffs, the ragman asked, "So what d'you know that's new, you clapped-out son of a whore?"

"I love you, too," Malk said mildly.

"Don't give me that. You only love yourself." Evets' pumping gesture showed how he meant that. He added, "Nobody else would put up with you, anyhow."

"It could be. So what *do* I know?" Malk rubbed his chin. Whiskers rasped under his fingers; he hadn't shaved lately. "I talked with Gare the baker before I got here. He told me he'd baked thirty-one fresh muffins, every one of them chock full of raisins." It wasn't much of a code, but he supposed it was better than coming out and talking about train cars and soldiers.

Evets' mouth twisted. "Gare's a gods-cursed liar. Where's he going to get that many raisins in stinking times like these? Next thing you tell me is, he fixed up his muffins for a bash by the Obelisk." You could see the tallest monument in Lutesse not just from Malk's bedroom window but all over the city. Like other things in their conversation, it held a different meaning here.

"That's where I think he was going, all right," Malk said. "As for the raisins, I saw them with my own eyes."

"Some people are prophets. More are liars." The ragman waved toward the door. "Get out of here, you dumb cow. You've wasted enough of my time."

Malk gave back a two-finger reply more often used in Nistria than in Quimper. He wasn't surprised when Evets recognized it and blew harsh smoke at him. Out he went. What news he had, he'd given. Evets would pass it along. To whom, Malk didn't know, or want to know. What he didn't know, the Chleuh couldn't tear out of him.

"Come on, my beauties," he told the horses. "Let's go home." He played with anyone who would play with him. If some of the people he played with found out about the others . . . He didn't like to imagine what would happen then.

~

Count Vurk's receptionist was a Quimperi, one young and decorative enough for Guisa Sachry to notice. When Guisa walked into the minister's antechamber and announced himself—he always announced himself—she smiled a bright, professional smile and said, "Please do take a seat, sir. I'll let him know you're here."

The chairs for waiting visitors looked to be of Chleuh army make. They were no more comfortable than they had to be: maybe even a little less. Guisa sat all the same; he was nothing if not polite.

A writing machine and a crystal sat on the receptionist's desk—everything there was as modern as next week. She bent low over the crystal to recite the activating charm. She said it in a whisper, and brought a hand up to her mouth so Guisa couldn't read her lips. He hadn't intended to, but she couldn't know that.

Light flared inside the vitreous globe. After a moment, it formed into Count Vurk's image. The receptionist spoke to him in Chleuh. With an actor's practice, Guisa hid his distaste. He admired the occupants, but not enough to care to learn their barbarous jargon. He would sooner have coughed up a lung. Given the way Chleuh sounded, he didn't think there was much difference between the one and the other.

Vurk answered in his own language. The receptionist nodded, then covered the crystal for a moment with the palms of both hands. As soon as it went dark, she seemed to remember Guisa was there. Returning to Quimperi, she said, "Go right in. He's looking forward to seeing you."

"Thank you so much," Guisa said.

The chairs inside Vurk's sanctum were of a kind a human being could use with pleasure. The minister's desk had to be a couple of centuries old; it was a small masterpiece of ornate Quimperi woodworking. "Good of you to join me today," he said after clasping Guisa's hand.

"I am sorry to have missed the entertainment the other night. Desolated, in fact. But . . ." Guisa let his voice trail away.

"Yes. But." Count Vurk shrugged: not quite the way a Quimperi would have, but expressively even so. "The war goes as it goes, not always as we wish it would go. We hit the Hontermen. Whenever they find the chance, they hit us back."

"They're treacherous beasts, burning and killing in their ally's metropolis." Like a lot of Quimperi, Guisa looked down his nose at the Hontermen for not yielding to Chlé as soon as his own kingdom did. At the time, he'd thought King Kangen would put his knee on their necks in short order. But here they were, three years later, and the fighting went on. It made him wonder about Quimper's choices . . . and his own.

One of Vurk's bushy eyebrows twitched. "We have a saying. In your language, it would go something like 'That animal is treacherous. If someone attacks it, it defends itself.' It is one of the things that happen."

It hadn't happened in Quimper, not for very long. Six weeks after the Chleuh stormed in, the General ordered the warriors still in the field to lay down their weapons, and accepted King Kangen's armistice demands. That was fine when you remembered how many soldiers and ordinary people would have died had he refused them. When you reminded yourself that Honter hadn't had its neck wrung like a chicken after all, though, you did ask whether everything really had worked out for the best.

Guisa didn't like asking questions like that. He'd been all for the armistice—anything to stop the disaster. Thinking he might have been mistaken made him wonder about his own good sense, which he didn't care to do. To keep from thinking such uncomfortable thoughts, thoughts that did to his mind what the chairs in the antechamber did to his back, he asked, "What can I do for you today, your Excellency?"

Vurk smiled. Guisa didn't find it his best expression. It made him look like a wolf licking blood off its muzzle after a big bite of elk. All he said, though, was, "There is someone I'd like you to meet."

"I would be honored, of course," Guisa said. "A countryman of yours?"

"No, as a matter of fact. A Quimperi. Let me see if he's here." Vurk was as careful activating his crystal as his receptionist had been with hers. Her image sprang to life in it. Vurk spoke to her in Chleuh. When she answered, the smile the minister gave seemed less . . . less carnivorous than the one he'd used before. He spoke to her again, then broke the connection and looked up at Guisa. "He just arrived. She's sending him in."

A moment later, the door opened. In walked a stocky man of about forty. He wore a gray-blue uniform. It wasn't quite the same color or cut as Vurk's, but it came close. It was nothing like the dirt-brown uniforms Quimperi soldiers used. The man saluted Chleuh-style, too, with a clenched fist over his heart. "Victory to King Kangen, your Excellency!" he said loudly.

"Victory!" Vurk said, and then, "Odrio, this is Guisa Sachry, the famous performer, writer, and director. Guisa, here we have Odrio Cazh, who is the Leader of the Quimperi Popular Party."

"My privilege, sir," Odrio Cazh said, extending his hand. "I've enjoyed your work for many years."

"Thank you," Guisa said automatically. As automatically, he clasped the proffered hand. Afterwards, a considerable part of him wished he hadn't. Afterwards, of course, was too late.

"You will know that, as Leader of his party, Odrio Cazh aids in the coordination between Quimper and Chlé," Count Vurk said to Guisa. *Coordination* was what the Chleuh called getting Quimper to do what Chlé wanted.

"I do know that, yes," Guisa said. He had done well for himself since the Chleuh marched into Lutesse. He'd done well by cozying up to them, yes. What else could he have done? They were here. They'd won. Some people ignored them, or even cut them. Those people wore lean and hungry looks, for they didn't find much work. To Guisa Sachry, falling out of the public eye felt too much like dying.

Cozying up to the Chleuh was one thing. The Quimperi Popular Party was something else. Odrio Cazh and his followers wished they *were* Chleuh, and acted as much like the conquerors as they could. The Leader and some of his men had even gone east to fight the Muos. Guisa noticed that one of the decorations on Odrio's uniform was a Chleuh wound medal.

"I asked the two of you to join me here today because Odrio told me he would like to seek a favor of you," Vurk continued.

"Isn't that interesting?" Guisa said tonelessly. There were limits to how close to the Chleuh one should get. He knew that. But the count, being a Chleuh himself, might not.

Sure enough, Vurk nodded to Odrio Cazh. The Leader (Leader of a small faction, a faction cordially despised by most Quimperi) said, "That's right. In a week's time, my Free Guards will stage a march down the Boulevard of Dreams. I will review them as they pass the Obelisk. I would be more honored than I can easily tell you, sir, if you would join me on the reviewing stand."

In something not far from despair, Guisa looked at Count Vurk. The Chleuh minister's welcoming smile again suggested blood dripping from his canines. *This is what it comes to,* Guisa realized. Yes, he'd done very well for himself since the Chleuh laid hold of Lutesse. His plays got produced. He performed in them. He and Vonney had plenty to eat, and what they had was good. He hadn't worried about the price for all that. But here it was.

"I–I may have a rehearsal that day, and—" he began.

Smiling still, Count Vurk slashed the edge of his hand through the air like a knife. "Oh, let your stand-in take the rehearsal. You're so good, so reliable, everything will be fine for the performance."

Guisa didn't like the way he said *reliable.* Odrio Cazh said, "Do please come, sir. Your presence would honor us, honor our righteous cause, and honor the great, the ever-victorious King Kangen."

He sounded polite to the point of seeming obsequious. That didn't mean he didn't know who held the strength here. *If I say no . . .* Guisa thought. He wasn't sure exactly what would follow if he did. But he was sure his life would become less pleasant. How much less pleasant? Did he really want to find out?

He'd done so much better than most of Lutesse. Did he want to be hungry and cold? Did he want to find out what a cell in the old castle King Kangen's watchdogs used, was like? Everything had a price, yes, even prosperity.

"It would be my privilege," he said to Odrio Cazh in a voice like ashes.

The Leader beamed. "I thank you so very much!" he exclaimed. Count Vurk . . . smiled.

Malk Malkovici's wagon clopped along a side street. They were coming to Lutesse's most famous, most important thoroughfare, so he would have reined in anyway to let traffic to by before he tried to cross. Today, he reined in because a Quimperi constable held up a white-gloved, imperious hand to order him to stop.

"What's going on?" Malk asked. Constables didn't usually mind traffic on streets so narrow.

"Parade coming by," the man said, in the tone officials used when they meant *You're stuck with it*. "You'll have to wait till it passes."

He looked as if he hoped Malk would get angry. Malk didn't. If he had to wait, he had to wait. The horses would be delighted. As far as they were concerned, standing around beat working any day. "Can I edge forward enough to watch it properly as it goes by?" he said.

"Yes, come ahead," the constable answered grudgingly. He sounded as if he worried Malk would try to gallop the team across the avenue, which only proved he was no judge of horseflesh.

Up went the wagon. The horses stopped at the edge of the intersection. Back on the driving bench, Malk still couldn't see very much. There didn't seem to be very much to see. A few people waited on the sidewalk, but only a few. "Not a great big crowd," he remarked. "What kind of parade is it?"

"A battalion of Free Guards recruited from the members of the Quimperi Popular Party will be reviewed by the Leader and other important personages." The constable's voice held nothing at all. Were the wind able to talk, it would have been no more expressive. Whatever the man thought of the Quimperi Popular Party, he kept it to himself.

"Well, well." Malk kept his voice as empty as the constable's.

Letting other people know how you felt had been dangerous in Lutesse these past three years, and grown more so as time wore on.

A moment later, he heard the sound of an approaching band: thumping drums and then trumpets and fifes or flutes or whatever they were. No sign of the men banging out the military march, not yet. Lutesse was a quiet city these days; sound carried a long way.

"They're playing the Great King's march," the constable said. Again, no one could have guessed what that meant to him. Malk remembered Efa's romance. Great King Clovsi had seized about as much of the continent as King Kangen of Chlé ruled now. He hadn't been able to hold it. Whether Kangen could . . . The scales were still bobbing up and down about that.

Before long, the rhythmic thump of booted feet echoed along the Boulevard of Dreams. The flagbearers were the first men to appear, one with Quimper's green-and-white banner, the other with Chlé's red one. *The bloody sheet*, Quimperi had called it, until it flew from the top of the Obelisk.

Seeing Quimperi in Chleuh sallets instead of their own crested iron skullcaps was a jolt. So were the Chleuh-style swallow's nests on the shoulders of the bandsmen's uniforms. Flagbearers, bandsmen, the hard-faced ordinary fighters behind them: they all looked very sure of themselves. Malk supposed you would have to be sure of yourself to take up arms for your own kingdom's conquerors.

To take up arms . . . The Chleuh shouldered crossbows one way, Quimperi another. The soldiers from the Quimperi Popular Party might be going to war for King Kangen, but they still carried their weapons in their own kingdom's fashion. Noticing that, Malk Malkovici didn't know whether to laugh or weep.

He did know that the Popular Party seemed none too popular. Soldiers who'd marched through Lutesse on their way to fight the Chleuh when the war was new had been cheered, and sometimes hugged and kissed, as they tramped along the streets. Now? Now a man let out a shout, followed a few seconds later by a woman's call of "Victory!" If anyone clapped, the sound of boots on stones drowned it.

Behind the men, horses—better horses than Malk's, not that many were worse—drew death-spitters on wheeled carriages. Two or three warriors feeding quarrels into the death-spitters, working the cranks that operated them, and replacing bowstrings as they broke could shoot as fast as a couple of squads of ordinary crossbowmen. Distilled infantry, wags called the devices.

The rattle of the wheels' iron tires on stones faded away. The constable stepped out into the Boulevard of Dreams and looked left and right. He nodded to Malk. "The way's clear. Go ahead and cross."

"Thanks." Malk flicked the reins. For a wonder, the horses moved forward before he had to remind them of the whip.

His head swung to the right. The battalion from the Quimperi Popular Party looked much less impressive from behind than it had from the side. Ahead of it stretched the broad boulevard, at the end of which stood the Obelisk. King Kangen's red flag fluttered above the monument, as it had for the past three years. The Chleuh wanted to remind Lutesse under whose boots it lay.

Near the base of the Obelisk stood a reviewing stand. Malk shaded his eyes to get the best look he could at who stood on it. It was too far away to let him make out much. Some of the men wore that almost-Chleuh uniform; others were in civilian dress. He couldn't recognize anybody.

One of the women who'd been watching the soldiers march by turned her head to stare at Malk. She pointed his way. "You're one of *those* people, aren't you?" she exclaimed.

"No. Not me." He could come out with that much Quimper without letting her hear his accent, but not a whole lot more. He flicked the reins again, and snapped the whip above the horses' backs. The last thing a man of the Old Faith wanted was to be recognized by Odrio Cazh's fanatics. If they stomped him for the fun of it, what would the constable across the street do? Nothing—Malk knew Lutessian constables too well to imagine otherwise.

The horses moved a little faster, but not nearly fast enough to suit him. The woman said, "You are so! Look at you, out there in the open like a real man!" More of the Popular Party people did look. A man started to step out into the street.

Malk whipped his team, first one horse, then the other. They neighed in angry astonishment, but they sped up. He hadn't known they had that much left in their legs.

The Popular Party man trotted purposefully toward him. He used the whip again, offhandedly, as if by accident. It caught the Quimperi in the face. He reeled back, clutching at himself.

If the others came after Malk . . . The wagon reeled around a corner, almost tipping over. Along with the whip, Malk had a knife on his belt. He knew how to use it, but one against a mob made bad odds. He took another corner, even more recklessly than the one before.

After that, he risked a glance over his shoulder. They weren't following. Maybe all the brave ones had volunteered to fight for the Chleuh king. The rest might be good for noise and bullying, but precious little else.

He let the horses slow. Some of the metal and wood he'd gathered had spilled during their wild dash, but he wasn't going to worry about that. Right now, he was just glad neither of the old nags had fallen over dead.

"Wait till we get home, lads. Oats and hay till a little before you burst," he said. Only after the words were out of his mouth did he realize he'd spoken in Nistrian. He shook his head. He hadn't done that in years except with Efa and, every once in a while, with Sarmel. On the streets of Lutesse, he always used Quimperi. Except today he hadn't.

You haven't come so close to dying or getting your face kicked in on the streets of Lutesse till today, he thought. He was lucky he wasn't lying on one of those streets, bleeding and calling in Nistrian for the mother he didn't even remember.

He was lucky the Chleuh hadn't grabbed him and taken him

away. They'd taken away a lot of people who belonged to the Old Faith. The Chleuh who were stationed in Lutesse didn't want to go east. The fighting in Muosi ground up men like a millstone. Malk didn't know what happened to people who followed the Old Faith when they went east. Whatever it was, he didn't think it was anything good.

The sun shone brightly. It was warm. A blackbird hopping on some grass chirped. Since the people from the Popular Party weren't chasing him any more, everything seemed peaceful—everything except his heart, which still thuttered in his chest. The horses plodded along. He steered them toward his shop and home.

Except for a couple of minutes, it had been a good day. He didn't think he'd tell his wife about those couple of minutes.

Another fine performance. Guisa Sachry didn't think he'd ever been better, in fact. Somehow, though, he'd won fewer laughs than he thought he deserved. He scratched his head as he and Vonney went offstage to wait to come out again for their bows.

Up came the house lights: the lighting master and his assistants fed the salamanders their treats. Out came the lesser players. The applause they got seemed about right to Guisa. He wondered if he'd been imagining things.

Then he and Vonney stepped out again. He gestured to her. She curtsied. The audience gave her a loud hand. She was young and pretty and shapely; she danced and acted . . . pretty well, anyhow.

Smiling happily, she waved to him. He bowed deeply. He got a decent round of applause, but he was sure he deserved better than that. As he straightened, he looked out at the audience.

As usual these past three years, it was divided between Chleuh and Guisa's countrymen. The occupants seemed as enthusiastic as usual—they came to the theatre to have a good time, and they did. The Quimperi, on the other hand . . . Well, some of them were clapping. Others, though, had faces that might have been carved from the basalt of the Obelisk.

Guisa bowed again, a sour taste in his mouth. Word must have got around. Cozying up to the Chleuh was one thing. Every Quimperi who'd watched the play cozied up to the Chleuh to one degree or another, most often to one degree and another. But cozying up to Odrio Cazh and the Quimperi Popular Party, especially to the Free Guard recruits who'd go fight for King Kangen, was something else again.

I crossed a line when I did that, Guisa realized miserably. He'd known it when Odrio asked him to go up on the reviewing stand. Yes, he'd known, but it wasn't something he could safely explain to Count Vurk. Maybe he might have if Odrio Cazh weren't standing right there. Vurk made sure the Popular Party's Leader was, though. Vurk might be a Chleuh, but he was a damned clever Chleuh.

One last bow from the whole company, and then they trooped back to the dressing rooms. As Guisa and Vonney cleaned up and changed into ordinary clothes, she said, "I don't think they gave you your due tonight."

"Really? I myself noticed nothing strange," Guisa said.

Vonney gave him a look, the kind of look wives give when husbands spout nonsense. They hadn't been married long, but she'd got it down pat. "You *always* notice how the crowd takes to you," she said, so he was less subtle about it than he'd thought. Quickly, she added, "What artist doesn't?" That helped a little—not enough.

He sighed. "It's politics, my dear. The ingrates who sat on their hands are no purer than I am. They only think they are."

Before Vonney could say anything to that, someone knocked at the door. A stagehand: he called, "You decent in there?"

Since Guisa and Vonney were, he opened up. The stagehand looked nervous. No, he looked scared to death, doubtless because of the uniformed man behind him. Voice wobbling, he said, "Colonel Nardand would like to compliment you on your performance."

Not seeing anything else to do, Guisa stepped back. Sep Nardand strode into the dressing room as if it belonged to him, not to the stars of the show. Who was going to argue with the head of the Watchmen? No one with any sense; no one with any sense of self-preservation.

"I myself enjoyed the play tonight," Nardand said.

"Th—Thank you very much," Guisa said. He would have answered the same way had the officer told him he hated it. You didn't want to anger King Kangen's top Quimperi police official. Guisa didn't even let on that he'd noticed Nardand mocking the way he talked.

"You're a funny man. You're a clever man. You're a man who wants to take care of his nice-looking young wife." Sep Nardand's hard gaze turned toward Vonney for a moment. She looked down at her hands, as if meeting his eyes might turn her to stone.

"Thank you for the compliments, sir, and yes, I do. Of course I do," Guisa said, more alarmed than ever.

When Chleuh left the big cities in Quimper and went out among the farms and villages, woodsrunners would sometimes bushwhack them. Every now and then, the woodsrunners would sneak into the cities, even into Lutesse, to murder and set fires and steal. The Hontermen and Muos, who wanted the occupants here to have an unquiet time, gave them what help they could. So did the Anadans, Honter's overseas allies.

Nardand's Watchmen fought the woodsrunners for King Kangen. Some of them were veterans like him, some toughs who'd sat in cells till he scooped them out, some harebrained youngsters who just wanted to punch and kick and shoot anybody who got in their way. Their private war with the men who harried the Chleuh was fought with no quarter on either side.

So if Nardand decided cutting Guisa's throat and carrying Vonney off to death or what they called a fate worse than that would do King Kangen's cause a copper's worth of good, no one would stop him. No one would even talk about it, except very quietly with the closest, most trusted friends. *Shame about old Guisa,* they'd say then. *Glad it wasn't me.*

"Good. That's good," Nardand said now. "I was happy to see you get up there with Odrio Cazh and show everybody where you stood."

Guisa wasn't happy about it himself, and never had been. He stood in the dressing room wishing he could sink through the floor, wishing the many mirrors show no more reflections of him than they would have of a vampire.

Sep Nardand seemed not to notice he was getting no response. Whether he did or not, Guisa was much less sure. His face, tough and shrewd, revealed very little. In his own way, he was an actor himself. He said, "I would like you to do me a favor, though."

"What kind of favor? I'm not particularly young. I'm not particularly brave, either," Guisa said.

"Oh, I know that." Nardand's casual agreement flayed, as it was no doubt meant to do. After a nicely time pause to let the sting build, the Watchmen's chief went on, "But you're a smart fellow. I already said that. You must be, or you wouldn't do so well for yourself. So now you can put that smart pot of yours to work for King Kangen and victory." He rapped the side of his head with scarred, knobby knuckles to show what he meant.

"I don't understand what you want." Guisa Sachry didn't want to understand, either.

"No? I'll spell it out for you, one syllable at a time. Give us a play that makes the murderers and ambushers look like a pack of stupid fools, so everyone will laugh at them walking out of the theatre. I don't care if you make them out to be villains or not. That doesn't matter. Make them out to be idiots, funny idiots. Nobody wants to have anything to do with people like that."

No, he isn't stupid, Guisa realized. That made things worse, not better. He tried his best: "You must understand, sir, that with performing and with preparing other projects already contracted for, I don't know how I could possibly find the time for this soon, no matter how worthy it—"

"Cancel everything else," Nardand said flatly. "You won't lose money on it, that I promise you. Money is easy. This is for Chleuh and Quimper." That he put Kangen's kingdom ahead of his own told everything that needed telling.

"Cancel everything else?" Guisa Sachry said in genuine horror. "But in that case I myself wouldn't go on. It is not possible!"

Nardand had a dagger on his belt. For a moment, Guisa thought he'd use it. But then he chuckled. "All right, strut around if you must. Cancel the rest. We'll keep you happy—as long as you produce. So long." He nodded stiffly and left.

III

Bells woke Malk Malkovici in the middle of the night. Till the war came, he'd never paid much attention to bells. They called members of the True Faith to prayer. Priests who served the Old Faith weren't allowed to make that kind of unseemly racket. If their followers didn't know when services were, too bad for them.

These days, though, bells meant danger. Malk rolled over and nudged Efa. "I'm awake," she said. "I was just about to poke you."

"We'd better get down to the cellar," he said.

"How much difference will it make, if a dragon decides to flame right here?"

Malk thought about that, not for the first time. "Some. If the building falls down, I'd sooner it falls down on the ground floor and doesn't squash us in the ruins."

"By now, I hardly care any more. What do you think of that? If the Hontermen and the Anadans don't kill us, the Chleuh will. I want to see what's going on, not hide underground like a mole."

"Hold on for a moment, then." A tiny salamander let out a faint red glow from a little glass-and-metal fixture on Malk's nightstand. He got out of bed, picked up the night light, carried it into the next room, and closed the door behind him as he came out. Then, moving slowly and carefully because the bedroom was very dark now, he went to the window and pulled back the black curtains. He did the same in the living room.

The moon was rising, so a little light came in. That was all right. But if a Quimperi constable or a Chleuh night warden spied light spilling out from a window, he'd shoot a crossbow bolt into it without warning.

Searchlights powered by big salamanders sent their orange spears of light into the night sky, trying to impale dragons on them. As always, Malk had mixed feelings about that. The dragons flew from Honter to harry the occupants, who held Lutesse in chains of iron and who would have disposed of him like an old snotrag if he hadn't made himself useful to them. Then again, the dragons were liable to do for him, too, as Efa'd pointed out.

She came and stood beside him, her shoulder brushing his. He put his arm around her and pulled her closer. Her warmth against his side comforted and reassured him. Frightened puppies might huddle together the same way. *Down under everything else, we're just animals*, Malk thought.

Somewhere off to the east, dragons swooped low and gave forth with tongues of flame. For a moment, Malk clearly saw his wife's face. "What do you think they're going after this time?" she asked.

"The train station, maybe," he said. "If they can damage it or wreck it, they kick the Chleuh where it hurts most."

He felt her nod. She said, "It's a shame they didn't come when those Popular Party fighters were boarding there."

"Shh!" he said. They were speaking Nistrian, as they mostly did when it was just the two of them. All the same, he knew the danger that someone down on the street might overhear and understand.

"It will be all right," Efa answered serenely. "They should all grow like onions—with their heads in the ground."

Whatever the dragons had flamed over there, they'd started fires whose glow lit up the horizon almost like sunrise. Fire brigades would be rushing to douse the blazes if they could. Malk had watched them in action before. Fighting fires fascinated him, as it fascinated almost everyone.

Big horse-drawn tubs of water were one thing. Water elementals were something else. Seeing mages call them up, watching them move against the heat of flames antithetical to their very essence, was a spectacle that never grew old or stale. And in a city like Lutesse that had a river running through it, evoking them and bringing them into action against fire was easier than it would have been in many other places.

These days, most of the firefighting wizards were Chleuh. Their Quimperi counterparts had been sidelined; the occupants trusted only the ones who belonged to the Popular Party or some of the other movements of that kind. Malk had to admit the Chleuh did their jobs well enough. Their wizards wanted to burn up no more than anyone else did. The only ways to tell them from the locals were the language they used to cast their cantrips and the helmets on their heads: they wore sallets much like the ones Chleuh warriors used.

A moment later, Malk's thoughts snapped back closer to home. He heard the heavy beat of dragon wings in the air not far away. Looking up, he saw the dark shape silhouetted against the stars.

Snapsnapsnapsnapsnap! A death-spitter in a nearby square shot quarrels into the night sky. Malk expected nothing from that. Death-spitters hurled bolts with mad abandon because, in the nature of things, most of them missed. Most, yes, but not all, not tonight.

Flame gouted from the wounded dragon's mouth. So did a great bellow of anguish, a bellow that made Malk's hair stand on end as if it were the bottlebrushed tail of a scared cat. Every sorrow the world had ever known might have been boiled down to a pint and poured straight into his ears. Tears stung his eyes.

And the dragon crashed to earth on the shop and the flat above it right across the street. In an instant, the building began to burn. Malk ran for the stairway before he consciously realized what he was doing. Jevon the mason wasn't just an acquaintance; he was a friend. If Malk could do anything for him, he would.

He'd got halfway down the stairs before he noticed Efa was only a couple of steps behind him. "What are you doing?" he said over his shoulder.

"The same thing you are," she answered. He shut up.

He opened the front door without hesitation. Any constables or Chleuh wardens who were close by would have run away. A body lay in the street. No, not a body—the man moved. For a moment, Malk thought it was Jevon or one of his sons. Then he saw the man wasn't in his nightshirt, but wore dragonrider's harness instead.

Grabbing the fellow under the arms, he dragged him back into the shop. "Do what you can for him, sweetheart," he said as he straightened again. "I'm going back out to see if anything's left of the poor mason and his family."

This time, he closed the door behind him. If anyone looked in and saw that Andanan or Honterman, he was a dead man. He got as close as he could to Jevon's building, but that wasn't close enough. The heat was so savage, he prayed his own place wouldn't catch on fire, too.

More neighbors came out. They passed buckets of water from hand to hand till the water went onto the flames. Malk worked in the bucket line, but he knew it was as pointless as pissing into a furnace. He just hoped the dying dragon had smashed Jevon and his kin and that they hadn't roasted as their place burned.

"May the gods keep them," said Danat Reblen, the carpenter who lived two doors down from Malk.

"May it be so," Malk agreed. His gods weren't the same as Danat's. At the moment, it hardly seemed to matter. And, at the moment, with his mouth and nose full of smoke and with his face about ready to blister, Malk had trouble believing in any gods at all.

Danat tried to call up a water elemental as luckless Jevon's house fell in on itself. He failed, of course. Since he was no wizard, things might have gone worse had he succeeded.

As the other men started back toward their homes, Malk crossed the street himself. No one could say he hadn't done everything anybody could do. He opened the door quickly and closed it behind himself. "How is he?" he asked.

"He's alive. He's got a lump on his head and some burns." Efa looked up from the dragonrider. "You're burned, too!" She had a bowl of water and some rags she'd been using on the man from across the Narrow Sea. Now, she sprang to her feet and used them on Malk's face and hands.

The cool water felt wonderful. The rags came away black; he must have been covered in soot. "Does he talk Quimperi, or even Chleuh?" he asked.

"I don't know," Efa answered. "He's not quite here yet. He's just mumbling, not talking. Why? What difference does it make?"

"We'll put him down in the cellar for now. But we can't keep him. You know that. If we do—" Malk drew a thumb across his throat. "Moving him will be easier if he speaks the language. If he has to keep quiet all the time, we're in trouble in case we get stopped."

Efa made a face. "Well, you're right," she said, something Malk didn't hear from her every day.

"Let's get him down below. We'll worry about everything else after sunup," he said. Hooves and wheels clattered in the street. Alarm sluiced through him—had someone noticed him bringing in the dragonrider and squealed to the Chleuh? He slid the downstairs curtains back far enough to let him peek outside. Then he relaxed. It was a pumper, come too late to do anything much for poor Jevon's building.

Between them, Malk and Efa got the foreign dragonrider down the stairs and into the cellar. They laid him on an old sofa there: one more bit of junk Malk had brought back. Efa put a blanket over the man, who barely seemed to notice.

There was a subcellar under the cellar. The trap door down to it hid under a rug. It was where someone could hide if things *really* got hot. They'd stash the dragonrider there if they had to. Malk also had a crystal down there with which he could listen to emanations from Honter. That was dangerous; if a Chleuh wizard detected it, it could be a capital crime. Lots of people did it anyway. Sometimes you needed to hear things that weren't Chleuh nonsense and drivel, even if Quimperi voices came out with it.

Malk and Efa went upstairs. She started brewing roasted chicory. It would be getting light soon. They weren't going back to sleep, and they both knew it.

General Stulp was the Chleuh commander in Lutesse. Guisa Sachry had met him at the theatre, and at the various functions where the occupants and the Quimperi who got along with them gathered and ate and drank. Stulp, like Count Vurk, seemed uncommonly civilized . . . for a Chleuh, anyhow.

Guisa hadn't visited the chateau where the general and his staff did whatever they did before now, but had no trouble finding it. Since the Chleuh marched into Lutesse, a whole second set of signboards had sprouted in the city. The ones the occupants had put up were white, inscribed in black in the spiky Chleuh script, and had one end pointed to show direction.

At the chateau, Chleuh officers hurried in and out. Some had message pouches of oiled, waterproof leather on their belts. Others swung onto horses and trotted away with whatever orders General Stulp was sending forth.

At first, he didn't think the chateau was actually guarded. Then he realized the brickwork on either side of the doorway slightly changed its appearance with each step he took towards it. When the Chleuh attacked Quimper, they had more tarncapes whose magic bent light around them, and better ones than his own countrymen did. That was one reason Chlé had won so easily. They still seemed to have as many as they needed, which Quimper never had.

Watching the occupants, Guisa felt like a cat among mean dogs. The feeling got worse when the first two men he approached proved to have not a word of Quimperi between them. They eyed him as if he were mad for coming here. He wasn't so sure they were wrong, either.

But then an older, more senior soldier said, "What do you need?"

The fellow had a heavy accent, but Guisa Sachry wasn't inclined to be critical. "Sir, I have a problem I wish to bring to General Stulp's attention," he said.

"And who you are, that he should listen to you?" the officer asked.

"Sir, I myself have the honor to be Guisa Sachry, the performer and playwright."

"You do?" The officer stared, then said something in his own language that sounded pungent. Then he returned to Quimperi: "By the gods, you do! Fry me for a sausage, sir, but it's a pleasure you in the flesh to meet, you might say." He seized Guisa's hand and pumped it vigorously. "I have myself laughed silly over your antics more times than I can tell you. So what kind of business with the general you have got?"

"I mean no offense, sir, but that is a matter I would sooner discuss with him, if that be possible," Guisa said. "It is of some importance, though, or I would not have come here to talk about it."

"Well . . ." The Chleuh thought for a moment, then took Guisa's arm. "You along with me come. I will take you to him. If he wants you afterwards to throw out, that's his business. Guisa Sachry! I will to my wife write that I have you met!" Chuckling, perhaps at the memory of some performance he'd seen, he started down the corridor. Since he still had hold of Guisa's arm, the actor perforce followed.

Paintings, some of them two or three centuries old, hung on the walls. Tables equally old held statuettes of rose quartz and exquisitely shaped porcelain ewers. In the midst of all that elegance, the poster of King Kangen came as a jolt. The Chleuh monarch's fierce face scowled out at the world. His right finger jabbed out toward whoever stood in front of his image. His left thumb pointed back at himself. Underneath him was a legend in Chleuh.

"What does it say, if you don't mind my asking?" Guisa wondered.

"Eh?" The officer seemed surprised he couldn't read it. "In your language, it would be something like, 'You and I together, we'll win!'"

"Oh," Guisa said, and not another word. King Kangen—the Chleuh generally—always seemed terribly in earnest to him. That made them dangerous. It also made them laughable, though showing it did was also dangerous. Like most men terribly in earnest, they were ever so sensitive to scorn.

A couple of secretaries—to Guisa's disappointment, both Chleuh underofficers rather than pretty girls—did whatever they did in General Stulp's outer office. The officer whose name Guisa never learned, spoke to one of them in their native tongue. The underofficer went into the general's private chamber. When he came out, he nodded.

The officer gave Guisa a little shove forward. "Go ahead," he said. "The commander will you see."

"Thank you very much!" Guisa said.

General Berhard Stulp was younger than Guisa, probably still on the lively side of fifty. A lot of King Kangen's top officers belonged to that generation. Too many of Quimper's marshals were paunchy fellows with drooping white mustaches. Char Tubis, who'd got away to Honter, was an exception, but thinking about Char Tubis wasn't smart here. General Petli Philtain, who carried out Kangen's orders in the absence of the royal family, certainly did fit the bill.

Stulp rose from his chair and bowed, as if Guisa were an equal. "Good to see you again," he said in fluent Quimperi; they'd moved in the same circles since Chlé occupied Lutesse. "Take a seat, take a seat, and tell me what you think I can do for you."

"Thank you," Guisa said. He sat; so did the Chleuh general. Guisa explained what Sep Nardand wanted him to do.

"I see," General Stulp said when he ran dry. After a moment, he went on, "I still don't quite understand what you want me to do about it, though."

"You outrank Nardand, and of course you're from your kingdom, which of course he isn't." Unrehearsed, Guisa felt himself floundering, but he thought he'd got the idea across. "Would it be possible for you to, ah, persuade him that this is an unnecessary project?"

"But why? I think that kind of play would be excellent," the Chleuh commander said. "Give the Quimperi a reminder that their destiny remains with us, take their minds off the troubles of a long war . . . Yes, excellent!"

I don't want to do it! Guisa Sachry almost screamed out the words. If he had, everything that came afterwards would have been different. Not necessarily better, but different. That *not necessarily better,* though, paralyzed him like an adder's venom. He didn't have the nerve.

Instead, he said, "I don't think I can do it full justice, though, with all my current commitments. I wouldn't want to give anyone a shoddy piece of work. That would reflect badly on my client, and I myself would feel dishonored if I offered less than my best."

"Cancel everything else, then," General Stulp said, as Sep Nardand had before him. "Give this new play the whole of your attention."

"But that would require me to break several contracts!" If Guisa sounded desperate, that was because he was. He was desperate enough, in fact, to blurt out more of the truth than he usually did: "And it would mean I would go unseen for the gods only know how long!"

"I'll tell you what," Berhard Stulp said genially. "Let me talk to Count Vurk. As the ambassador, he has an easier time getting money on the left—"

"On the left?" Guisa didn't follow.

The Chleuh chuckled. “Sorry. I translated one of our figures of speech. It means *unofficially*. I’m sure he could arrange a stipend for you so you don’t suffer because of your work. You and we together, we’ll win.”

“I was not asking for money. Money is not the most important thing in life,” Guisa said.

“It will be unofficial. It will be discreet. I understand that not everyone here is always eager to seem too close to us.” Stulp looked pleased with himself, as if he’d solved all of Guisa’s problems for him.

And he had solved some of them, though a Chleuh’s ideas of discretion were unlikely to come up to Quimperi standards. “Money is not the most important thing in life,” Guisa repeated.

“What is, then?” Stulp sounded honestly perplexed. “What more do you need?”

“An audience!” Guisa blurted. “You are not a performer, so this may be hard for you to understand. But I myself, I myself do require one, as the ordinary man requires bread.” Even Guisa rarely doubled up the phrase that gave him the nickname he didn’t like.

“Can you act in one thing and still write at the same time?” Stulp answered his own question: “You must be able to, or you wouldn’t have turned out all the work you have. Do that, then. We’ll make sure it’s worth your while, and we’ll make sure you don’t land in hot soup on account of it.”

A native Quimperi would have talked of melted cheese, but Guisa got the meaning this time. And, like Nardand before him, Berhard Stulp sliced through his arguments as readily as the Chleuh had sliced through his kingdom’s defenses three summers earlier. Quimper had seen no choice but to surrender. Nor did Guisa Sachry now.

“I am your servant, sir,” he muttered.

The general shook his head. “By no means. No, by no means. You work together with me for the greater glory of Chleuh and of King Kangen. All over the continent, men work together with my folk to defend our lands against the greedy, gold-grubbing Hontermen and Anadans on the one hand and the savage, uncivilized, misbelieving Muos on the other. When we work together, we cannot possibly fail!"

By the way he said it, he believed it. He made Guisa want to believe it, too. Believing it had been easy three years ago, when the Chleuh entered Lutesse as if they were on their way to ruling the world. Guisa'd thought they had been, and made his choices accordingly. He still thought they might, though he was less sure now. He wished he had a way to hedge the bets he'd made then.

Since he didn't, he bowed his head as if an axe were about to come down on the back of his neck. He'd played enough defeated kings and traitor dukes to make the gesture seem natural to him. "I am your servant," he said once more.

"But no. Not at all," General Stulp answered. "As I told you a few minutes ago, you and we together, we'll win."

"Yes, just as you told me," Guisa said, and made the best escape he could. Things hadn't turned out the way he'd wanted. He had to hope the way they had turned out wouldn't be too bad.

He walked past the poster of King Kangen again on the way out. Kangen did look fierce and warlike—no doubt of that. But discreet? Guisa shook his head. None of the Chleuh soldiers or clerks or whatever they were who bustled along the corridors of the chateau would know why. All the same, what they understood of discretion wasn't all it might have been.

When Guisa got to the doorway, he looked left, ahead, and right before venturing out. No one he recognized saw him leave. One of the drawbacks to celebrity, though, was that people he didn't recognize were liable to recognize him. They were also liable to wonder why he was coming out of the occupants' military headquarters.

As he walked away from the chateau, he did his best to give the impression that he'd never been inside. He might have been doing a brisk morning constitutional. On the stage, his stiff back and long strides would have left the audience howling, Here, he just hoped they seemed convincing.

A skinny boy—he couldn't have been more than eleven—in a shabby cap and a threadbare jacket was hawking news sheets. "Chleuh moving forward against the Muos again!" he called. "Big battle in the south!"

Guisa fished a copper from his belt pouch and bought a copy. Only after he had it did he see it was *I Am Everywhere*. His lip curled in distaste. All Lutesse's news sheets, naturally, followed the Chleuh line these days. *I Am Everywhere*, though, almost seemed to run ahead of that line. It sounded more Chleuh than the Chleuh themselves.

He wondered what the bored wizards who used the law of similarity to turn one sheet into thousands thought of the stuff they reproduced. He wondered whether they thought of it at all or just did their jobs with the same offhand skill they'd shown before the occupants came. Most of the news sheets then had shouted about what a barbaric monster King Kangen was. The tune might have changed now, but the musicians stayed the same.

The story the little peddler had been shouting about said the Chleuh were smashing everyone in southern Muosi who dared stand against them. They'd won a lot of victories there the past two years, but they hadn't managed to knock the Muos flat. Muosi was a big place. Man for man, the Chleuh were found to be better soldiers. Man for two or three men? That wasn't so clear.

On the third page of the sheet were the theatre notices. Even when times were bad, or especially when they were bad, people went looking for the imaginary worlds they found on the stage. *I Am Everywhere*'s critics commonly liked what Guisa did, which made him take the rest of their opinions seriously, too.

Posters pasted to a wall urged men under forty who followed the True Faith to join the Watchmen. *Fight for Quimper! Fight against assassins!* they shouted in big green syllables. Guisa Sachry shivered. He feared the woodsrunners might murder him because he'd accommodated the Chleuh. Now he also feared the Watchmen might if he angered Sep Nardand. How could you live if both sides wanted you dead? *So unfair*, he thought. *So very unfair!*

A couple passed him on the street. His own clothes were old, but in good repair. He had to look his best whenever he went out in public. He'd spent more silver than he cared to think about keeping leather on the soles of his shoes. This man and woman walked past, clattering as if they wore horseshoes. His trousers were out at the knees; one patch was darker than the ground cloth, the other lighter. His jacket had seen better decades, too. The woman's jacket came down almost to her ankles, a style twenty years out of date. And it had seen hard wear in those twenty years; like the man's trousers, it was darned and patched and threadbare.

They both had pale, pinched faces, the faces of people who hadn't got enough to eat for a long time. Guisa Sachry hadn't seen, or at least hadn't noticed, faces like that for quite a while. People with such faces didn't come to his performances—or, if they did, they sat up in the back of the balconies where they weren't so obvious.

As he noticed their hunger, they noticed his double chin. Something in the man's expression made Guisa wish he were skinnier. He dug three or four silver half-crowns from his pouch and held them out. "Here," he said. "Till times get better."

The man's mouth narrowed. He was going to tell Guisa where to head in; the actor could read it in his eyes. Before he could, though, the woman grabbed the money. "Thank you for your kindness, sir. Even a little helps." She put the coins in her own pouch. It too had been repaired, but it would hold what went into it.

When the man started to say something, she fixed him with a glare that would have frozen a cave bear in its tracks. Men postured and made speeches; women did what needed doing.

Up the street they went. After a few steps, he managed a gesture. She slapped his hand away. Guisa made mental notes; if he could pull this kind of drama from performers, crowds would go wild.

When he got back to his block of flats, the doorwoman handed him a flat box wrapped in brown paper and twine. "Looks like a present," she said. "See—the return address says it's from 'An Admirer.'"

"That's very nice, Marsa," Guisa said, smiling. This wasn't the first time he'd got a gift from someone who liked his work. He hoped it wouldn't be the last. He tipped the doorwoman for giving him the box and not hanging on to it herself. If you didn't keep her sweet, things like that were liable to happen.

Up the stairs he went, much more cheerful than he'd thought he would be after walking out of General Stulp's commandeered chateau. He'd worry about that business later; the box was here now.

"What is it?" Vonney exclaimed when he walked in and showed her the package.

"I don't know. Marsa showed me it came from 'An Admirer.'" He showed his wife the return address, then used a pen knife to cut the twine and slit the paper under it. The box beneath was of cherry wood, with top and bottom fitting together so tightly, Guisa had to slip the knife blade between them to lever them apart.

The top popped off when he did. A horrible stench filled the flat. The box was full of dogshit. A note fluttered to the floor. He didn't look at it till he'd got rid of the disgusting present. Only then, as an afterthought, did he pick it up.

Dog turds for a Chleuh dog, it said. He disposed of it without showing it to Vonney. He didn't want to worry her. Every now and then, he'd wondered whether the woodsrunners thought he'd gone too far. He didn't wonder any more. Now he knew.

"Hey, Sarmel," Malk said when his brother walked into the junk shop.

"Hey yourself," Sarmel Malkovici said. He was three years younger than Malk, and a couple of inches taller. They looked very much alike, but Malk was the one with the drive that had got them from Nistria to Quimper and that had turned Efa's uncle's junk business into something bigger than old Ory'd ever imagined possible. Sarmel would have failed as a leader, but he made a fine follower. He asked, "Is he ready?"

"As ready as he's going to be," Malk answered. "I'm pretty sure he understands he's supposed to keep his mouth shut no matter what. That's the important thing."

"Think so, do you?" Sarmel said.

Malk laughed, for all the world as if it were funny. He set a hand on his brother's shoulder for a moment. "Come on. He's out back. Efa's keeping an eye on him."

They went through the junk shop and out the back door. The wagon stood behind the building, next to the stable, horses hitched and ready to go. For an assembly of ancient, mismatched boards with a leaky tin roof, that stable cost Malk a pretty penny: he had to pay off the building inspector twice a year, since it was illegal as could be.

Efa sat in the driving seat holding the reins. The wagon bed was full what what looked more like trash than junk. Most of it *was* trash; Malk didn't want to risk anything valuable on this trip--except his neck, of course, and his brother's with it.

Atop the trash sprawled the Honterman who'd flown the dragon. To look at him, you would have guessed he was trash himself. What covered him came closer to rags than clothes. Once they got out there on the street, he'd lie still, as if dead or blind drunk. The idea was that Malk and Sarmel were taking him back to his kin, and that he was in no condition to answer questions.

That was Malk's plan, anyhow. Whether the dragonrider really got it . . . Malk hoped so. They had no tongue in common, only gestures and playacting. If things went badly wrong, Malk was ready to give the Honterman to the Chleuh and say he'd meant to do it all along. He didn't want to, but he would.

Efa slid down. Malk squeezed her and kissed her before he climbed up onto the bench. "Be careful," she told him.

"If I were careful, I wouldn't have anything to do with such a stupid scheme," Malk answered. She made a face. It wasn't as if he were wrong.

When he got behind the horses, Sarmel handed him the reins. "Shall we try it?" he said, sounding more cheerful than any man in his right mind had any business doing.

"I guess we shall." Malk flicked the reins. The horses ignored him. He snapped the whip above their backs. That got them moving, and at an almost respectable clip. He'd actually had the nerve to touch them with it not long before. They hadn't dreamt such a thing was in the rules. They didn't want him doing it again.

The wagon hadn't gone farther than half a block when it rolled up to Bezen the constable. Malk and Sarmel both tipped their caps to him. The Honterman just lay there, his eyes mostly closed, a stupid smile on his face. He did understand what he was supposed to do, then. Good.

"Here's something out of the ordinary!" Bezen said. "Are you taking him to the rubbish tip?"

Malk laughed. Any joke a constable made was funny. "No, just back to his wife," the junkman answered easily. "We'll let her throw him out."

"You'd do him a favor if you took care of it yourself, I bet," Bezen said, but he waved them on and got back to walking his beat. One test passed.

Plenty of people noticed the unconscious-looking man in the wagon as they crossed Lutesse. Quite a few laughed and pointed and exclaimed and made the same kind of jokes Bezen had. Somebody asked how much Malk and Sarmel hoped to get for their passenger as scrap. The brothers smiled and laughed themselves. The more they looked like men who were doing an ordinary bit of work and enjoying themselves in the process, the less likely anyone was to do something unfortunate—poke the Honterman with a stick, for instance.

After a little more than an hour, the wagon pulled up in front of

Evets' shop. Malk had got the dragonrider's threadbare clothes from the man who dealt in them. He'd also warned the dealer he would be bringing the fellow by. Evets had connections with people who could hide downed air warriors from the Chleuh and sometimes even smuggle them back to Honter. As usual, Malk didn't know the details, or want to.

He turned to Sarmel. "You want the head end or the feet?"

"As long as you're asking, I'll take the feet," his brother answered.

They managed to get the Honterman down from the wagon without bouncing his head on the cobblestones. He was playing dead drunk with as much enthusiasm as Guisa Sachry would have put into the role; he made himself limp as a sack of beans. Malk and Sarmel had to ease him down to the sidewalk so Malk could open the door, then pick him up again.

A couple of customers were pawing at tunics and jackets that had seen better years. No chance to do this on the sly, Malk realized. Play it for laughs, then. "How does it go, Evets?" he said loudly.

"Rotten. It's always rotten," the ragman answered, so that was all right, anyhow. Evets didn't miss a beat, either: "What's that junk you've got there?"

"Your worthless cousin, you mean? It's what's left of him," Malk said.

"He got smashed again? I hope you didn't have to pay off the turnkey to get him back this time," Evets said, clapping a hand to his forehead in extravagant disgust. "By the gods, if he's not a dried-up pile of donkey dung, I don't know who is!"

They went back and forth like that for a while. One of the women who was trying to find a jacket that suited her chimed in, too. She had plenty of stories to tell about her cousin who drank too much. It was a shame the Honterman didn't understand what was going on; he might have enjoyed it.

Finally, Evets said, "Haul the stupid goose into the back room and throw him on the sofa, will you? When he comes round, I'll give him the kind of what-for he's never seen till now."

"And a whole fat lot of good that will do you," Sarmel said.

The ragman rolled his eyes. "Don't remind me."

The sofa was even more disreputable than the one down in Malk's cellar. He and Sarmel set the Honterman down while Evets shut the door behind them. As soon as it closed, the dragonrider came to life as if by magic. Evets spoke softly to him in nasal Honterese, then held a finger to his lips to warn the foreigner against making too much noise.

In a whisper, the Honterman replied. Malk and Sarmel looked at each other. If Evets could talk to the man, things were bound to go better.

"Well," Malk said in a voice meant to carry, "now that we've delivered your stupid cousin, we'll be on our way."

"I'm going to kick him from here to the Obelisk and back," Evets answered, also loudly. "Sorry he caused you so much trouble." In low-voiced Honterese back by gestures, the ragman made sure the dragonrider understood he needed to stay where he was. Then Evets went out to the front of the shop with Malk and Sarmel to see them off.

As the horses clopped away, Malk allowed himself the luxury of a long sigh of relief. His brother nodded. "That went better than I thought it would," Sarmel said. "One Chleuh who thought it was funny, but not the way you laugh at, and we'd have been standing on our heads in the cesspit."

"I know," Malk said, and then, after a moment, "I'm sorry I dragged you into it."

"Not the first time. Won't be the last, either," Sarmel answered. "We have to do whatever we have to do, that's all."

Malk got his pipe going. Even it didn't ease his nerves. "This gods-cursed war! Who would have dreamt it could go on so long? Not close to over yet, either."

"The Locusts never thought it would last, either," Sarmel said, using Lutesse slang for the Chleuh. Malk nodded. If anything gave him hope, that was it.

IV

By now, Guisa Sachry had learned to judge how things were going as much through silence as through words. As long as the news sheets and crystals pundits crowed about Chleuh victories like roosters announcing sunrise, he guessed things were going pretty well for King Kangen's men. When they stopped crowing . . . he drew his own conclusions.

He said nothing about those conclusions to anybody, even Vonney. That was something else he'd learned in the three years since the Chleuh paraded into Lutesse—somebody always noticed what you said. The only way to stay safe was to wrap yourself in silence.

When he couldn't help it, he made little feckless lunges at the play Sep Nardand wanted him to write. It didn't go well. Now he was sitting in the second row of the theatre where he was reviving an old comedy by Gorec Sembel and supposedly watching the rehearsal of a scene in which he didn't appear (there weren't many of those, but there were a few). In fact, he was scribbling notes for the other play, the play that would tear strips off the woodsrunners.

"Excuse me, sir?" The sweeping boy sounded scared to speak to the actor and director. The job he had wasn't much, but he might starve if he lost it.

"Huh?" Reflexively, Guisa spread a hand over his notebook. He didn't want *anyone* seeing what he was working on, though he wasn't at all sure the little sweep could even read. "What is it?"

"Sir, I'm very sorry to bother you, sir, but there's a gentleman in the lobby who says he's got to see you."

Something in the way the sweep stood made Guisa sure the "gentleman" had slipped him something to come down front with the message. Without a sweetener, the boy never would have dared. "What kind of gentleman?" Guisa asked. A Chleuh? A Watchman? The way things were, those seemed likeliest.

"A gentleman, sir. He dresses fancy, like you."

The Watchmen weren't gentlemen, not like that. Even Nardand would have been in uniform, not street clothes. Guisa wanted to tell the sweep to tell whoever it was to go away, but didn't have the nerve. Muttering to himself, he stood up. "Take five!" he called to the performers on the stage. He followed the sweeping boy up the aisle.

He wouldn't have said the man smoking in the lobby dressed like him. The fellow looked like a robber trying to seem like a gentleman and not having much luck. His jacket had too much silver thread, his trousers were too tight, and the bill of his cap was too long. A waxed chin beard partly hid a scar on his jaw.

"I'm Guisa Sachry, sir," Guisa said. "What can I myself do for you?"

The stranger's smile didn't reach his eyes. But he sounded friendly enough as he answered, "You can't do nothing, uh, anything for me." Yes, he came from the gutter, even if he didn't live there any more. He took a pouch from his belt and held it out to Guisa. "I can do somethin' for you, though. A friend o' mine asked me to give you this here."

"Uh, thank you." Guisa cautiously took the pouch, wondering if it held a scorpion or a tiny coiled venomous serpent. But no—it was too heavy for that, heavy enough to startle him. "Thanks," he said again, this time with some real warmth.

"Any time, friend." The man in the tough-boy outfit slipped away with a quiet haste.

Guisa disappeared, too, into the jakes just inside the front door. The smell of stale piss in there was strong enough to make his eyes water. He reminded himself to talk to the theatre manager. The audience deserved better, or they wouldn't come back. The comfort station by the dressing rooms was cleaner; the manager had to know the performers would tell him off if he let that one get so filthy.

When Guisa opened the pouch and held it upside down, goldpieces spilled into his other palm. He hoped they were goldpieces, anyhow. These days, sharps duped fools with lead counterfeits sorcerously plated with brass to give them the proper heft and shine. But when he bit a couple of these to test them, they yielded under his teeth the way they should have. Gold, sure enough.

This had to be General Stulp and Count Vurk quietly paying him off, as Stulp had said they would. Guisa swore under his breath. He wished the Chleuh officials had stiffed him. That would have given him an excuse to forget about the play Sep Nardand wanted. Now they'd expect some serious work from him. They'd be unhappy if they didn't get it, too!

He threw the empty pouch into the rubbish bin. He didn't want to keep anything that could connect him in any way to the men the goldpieces came from. If he'd had the stomach for it, he would have thrown the money after the pouch. But the goldpieces went into his own pouch instead.

He told himself Stulp and Vurk would know he'd got the payoff. The fellow from Lutesse's underworld would say he'd made the delivery, and the Chleuh would have ways to make sure he spoke the truth. No real point ditching the gold, then. And it would come in handy. Gold always did.

Shaking his head, he walked back to his seat in the second row.

He must have looked as gloomy as he felt: Vonney, who'd watched his return from the wings, called, "Is everything all right?"

"Yes," he said, and made himself nod. He had to hope he meant it. And he had to buckle down on that accused play. Well, not right now. He waved to the players relaxing on the stage till he finished his business. "Come on, my friends. Let's do it one more time from the top."

When he and Vonney walked into their flat, she remarked, "You hardly said a word all the way home. It isn't like you."

He took a deep breath. Instead of shouting at her for saying he talked too much, though—his first impulse—he let it out again. He unhooked his belt pouch and let the money inside slide out onto an end table.

His wife stared. "Where did that gold come from? We won't need to worry about . . . about anything for quite a while now, will we?"

"It came from the Chleuh. Maybe from Vurk, maybe from Stulp," Guisa answered. "They want to make sure I do that play for them."

"Oh." Vonney didn't say anything more after that for some little while. Guisa watched things spinning behind her eyes. At last, she came out with, "Well, I was wrong. We have worries after all."

He hadn't married her for her brains. A nice pair, a pert behind, long legs, a pleasant voice . . . Whether he'd married her for brains or not, he realized she had them. "You see it, too, then."

"Yes. Of course I do. If you finish that thing and they put it on with your name behind it all through the provinces, we won't be able to stick our noses out the door without bodyguards. And how will we know the bodyguards aren't sending word back to the woodsrunners, too?"

Guisa kissed her. He'd feared she wouldn't understand the problem. But she got it, perhaps more clearly than he did himself. He said, "I don't dare not write, but I don't dare finish, either."

"You have to be like Remar in the fable, weaving all day and then at night unraveling what she'd done." Vonney smiled. "It took the wicked landlord years to catch on. Do you think the Chleuh are that stupid?"

"I wish I did," Guisa Sachry said dolefully. "The woodsrunners will kill me if I deliver. The Watchmen and the Chleuh will if I don't. Or they'll throw me off the stage!" He wasn't sure sure which horrid fate would be worse.

"You'd better write some of it, anyhow, and show that to them," Vonney said after another pause for thought. "Enough to give them something to look forward to. *Then* have trouble. You'll buy some time that way."

He kissed her again. "You *are* smart!" he exclaimed. He wasn't sure he'd ever said that to a woman before.

She winked at him. "If you don't let on, I won't." She'd trusted him enough to let him see she wasn't just a pretty face and a nice shape. That meant . . . Guisa Sachry wasn't sure what it meant. Whatever it meant, he was grateful, an emotion he didn't feel every day—or every year, either.

Everybody told stories about the midnight knock on the door. Malk Malkovici told them himself. The best such tale he knew had the punchline *No, sir, he lives one flight up*. He never could get through that one without ruining the gag by laughing too soon.

Everybody told stories about the midnight knock, of course, because it could happen to anybody. Malk knew too well that it could happen to him. He had friends—business associates, anyhow—among the Chleuh and the Quimperi who followed them. And he had more among the woodsrunners and other people who wanted to see the Hontermen and Anadans drive King Kangen's soldiers out of Quimper. Who might sell him out to whom, then, was a question with many possible answers.

All the same, he didn't expect the midnight knock at his door. Even when you knew it could come, you never wanted to believe it would. But it did. He slept soundly. Whoever pounded on his front door, though, might have woken a dead man, let alone a sleeper.

Efa clutched at his arm. "Do you want to go out the back or hide down in the subcellar?"

Fresh banging from the back told him he couldn't go out that way. The subcellar . . . If they sniffed him out down there, he was trapped. And they could hang attempted concealment on him, too, along with whatever else they thought they had.

All that flashed through his head in an instant. So did fear of what they'd do to Efa if they didn't catch him. He sighed. "No, I'd better go down and let them have me. I think I'll be able to get loose."

"How?" she demanded—a much too reasonable question.

"I'll manage." He was shedding his nightshirt as he answered. He had a little money pouch he could hide in his armpit, with its elastic strap on his shoulder. They'd find it if they stripped him naked, but probably not if they didn't. He put the nightshirt back on and went downstairs in the dark.

The pounding hadn't stopped or even slowed. "Open up!" somebody out in the street bawled.

At a muttered command, the banging at the front door stopped, though it went on in back. "Watchmen!" whoever owned that voice answered proudly. "Open up in the name of King Kangen or we'll smash in the door and smash you, too."

Malk wondered whether having Sep Nardand's men take him was better or worse than being seized by the Chleuh. He'd find out. When he opened the door, one of the men on the sidewalk shone a bright, reflector-backed salamander in his face. Blinking, he asked, "What do you think I did?"

The fellow who'd ordered him to open up—he couldn't see the face, but recognized the voice—growled, "You're one of the filth who follow the Old Faith. And you had the crust to whip a member of the Quimperi Popular Party. Now you pay for it! Come on with us!"

As Malk came, one of the Watchmen hit him in the ear and

another kicked him in the rear. Head ringing, he staggered up the street. Every so often, one of them gave him another smack. He endured the thumping as best he could. They might have done worse. Had they known he'd passed along the Honterman, they would have. This was trouble, but he still had hope.

Their station was a few blocks away. When they got there, they patted him down, but they didn't find the pouch. They threw him in a tiny cell that held a lidless, stinking bucket, a straw pallet bound to be full of lice and fleas and bedbugs, and nothing else. The click of the lock on the closed door had a dreadfully final sound.

He sat down on the stone floor. He wanted nothing to do with that disgusting mattress. Chances were he'd end up verminous anyhow, and have to visit the public baths before he went home so he wouldn't bring pests back with him.

After a moment, he laughed, not that anything was funny. If thinking he'd be able to go home again wasn't the height of optimism, he didn't know what would be.

A couple of hours later, the cell door opened. "Malkovici!" a Watchman barked. Two more stood behind him. "Get up, you son of a whore!" the tough in front went on.

Painfully, Malk did. They frog-marched him down the hall and into an office. The chair they made him sit in had straps to bind his hands and feet. They used them to make sure he didn't leave.

On the other side of the desk sat an officer. He got up, came over to Malk, and slapped him in the face. "That's for making me work in the middle of the gods-cursed night," he said, his voice surprisingly mild. "It's also just a taste of what you'll get if you give me any trouble."

Malk tasted blood, but the open-handed slap hadn't loosened any teeth. He said, "Sir, I never give King Kangen's people any trouble."

"You just missed costing Briec Gourin an eye," the officer said. "The more you lie, the worse it goes for you. The Popular Party's the one good thing that's happened in this stinking kingdom lately."

"I deal with the occupants, sir," Malk said. "They buy from me. They have let me stay in Lutesse because I am good at my work and they know they can rely on me. That man did not know who I was. He and his friends would have hurt me or killed me if I hadn't kept him away. I am sorry I almost put out his eye—I didn't mean to do that."

The only lie Malk told was that he was sorry. *You deal with the occupants, too, you Watchmen,* he thought. *Don't you know I would long since have disappeared if they didn't think I was useful? That's what happens to people who belong to the Old Faith, especially if they weren't born in Quimper.*

He looked down at the floor just in front of him, sneaking glances at the officer from under lowered lids. The Watchman didn't get up and start slapping him around some more. That was something, anyhow. After a bit of thought, the fellow did growl, "Trying to feed us stories will only make it go harder for you, you know."

"I'm not telling stories!" Malk said. "You can check with the occupants yourself." He almost swore by the gods, but held off at the last instant. The Watchman would only tell him his were the wrong gods to swear by. Why give the fellow the chance to score a cheap point?

"No need to check with anyone," the officer said, his voice blizzard-cold. "We had orders from Colonel Nardand himself to lay hold of you, and lay hold of you we did. No one who follows his superior's orders can ever find himself in the wrong. It is not possible!"

What if your superior is a fool? Or a villain? The questions occurred to Malk right away. He didn't ask them; as with an oath, voicing them would only have made things worse. That the Watchman had got his orders straight from the leader of his force chilled the junkman, though. This Briec Gourin had to have clout, or Sep Nardand wouldn't have worried about what happened to him. Or maybe his belonging to the Quimperi Popular Party had made the colonel notice the case.

Nardand was no fool. He would have been less dangerous if he were. A villain? As far as Malk Malkovici was concerned, any Quimperi who served the Chleuh so well and so willingly couldn't be anything else. Nardand had fought the invaders till Quimper surrendered. Then he'd surrendered himself, body and soul.

"You will get what's coming to you, every copper's worth," the Watchman said. A moment later, he yawned. "You won't get it right now, though. I'm too cursed sleepy to give you what you deserve. Well, almost too sleepy." He came around the desk and slapped Malk again, harder this time. Shooting stars danced across the junkman's field of vision. The officer spat in his face. "Just a taste of what you'll see when we really start working on you."

He went to the door and called for Watchmen of lower rank to haul Malk back to his cell. Malk eyed him, again doing his best not to be obvious about it. He wanted to memorize the fellow's features. If his gods were kind, one of these days he might have the chance to repay a little of what he owed.

If his gods were kind, how had they let their worshippers fall into such desperate, deadly danger? Were they testing them to learn whether their faith was strong enough? Or had they been imaginary all along? Were the folk of the Old Faith perishing for nothing, perishing because the gods they reverenced *were* nothing?

Those three ordinary Watchmen came back into the office. They gave Malk something more urgent than philosophy to worry about, which might have been just as well. "Take this chunk of vulture bait back where you found it," the officer told them.

"To obey!" they chorused. They saluted fist over heart, as if they were Chleuh. One of them unfastened Malk's bonds. The other two had a cocked crossbow and a sword, in case he got frisky. He didn't. He had trouble standing, much less fighting. That second slap had rattled his brains, all right.

"Come on, you stinking hound! Off to your kennel!" the man with the sword said once Malk finally made it to his feet. The other two laughed. So did the officer. The Watchmen enjoyed cruelties large and cruelties small; enjoying cruelty was one of the things that made men join them.

Back to his cell Malk went. Anyone who tried to keep a dog in a room like that would have got in trouble with the the constables for heartlessness to brute beasts. Malk didn't say anything about that, no matter how true it was. He would only have given them another excuse to rough him up.

He made sure he stayed on his feet all the way to the cell, too. Had he stumbled or gone down, they would have been more likely to kick him for a while than to help him up again.

When the door thudded closed and the lock snapped shut, he knew an odd relief. If they weren't in there with him, they couldn't hurt him any more. He used the smelly bucket, then curled up on the floor as far from the pallet as he could go. That wasn't nearly far enough to suit him. He didn't think he'd be able to sleep, but he did.

He woke somewhere not far from dawn, stiff and sore. A little light leaked into the room from the small barred window in the door and the equally small barred window set into the wall at a level much too high for a prisoner who wasn't a human flea to reach. A prisoner who was a human flea would find plenty of company in that verminous pallet.

A little after the sun rose, a Watchman came into the cell with a pail of water and a bowl of swill. That was the only word Malk could find for it. It made what the Nistrian orphanage had fed its charges seem like a banquet Count Vurk would have enjoyed.

Ignoring it for the moment, he asked the Watchman, "Would you take someone a message for me?"

Before he could even add *I'll give you money*, the uniformed man —no, uniformed boy: he couldn't have been much above seventeen —said, "Go futter yourself," and slammed the door as hard as he could.

Malk reflected on how to win friends. Then he drank a little of the water, which tasted stale. He used a little more to try to clean his face. Only a little—he had no idea how long he'd have to wait for more. And then, after a curse aimed partly at the Quimperi Popular Party and partly at Sep Nardand, he ate the swill. It tasted worse than it smelled, which he wouldn't have believed possible. He ate it anyhow. It was what he had, so he tired to make the best of it.

After that, nothing. A lot of nothing. He sat in the cell, ignored. For all he could prove, the Watchmen might have forgotten he was there. Every so often, they'd walk down the corridor, boot heels thumping on stone. Once a prisoner in a cell not close to Malk's screamed, "Yngvi is a louse!" Who Yngvi was, the junkman had no idea.

By the tiny amount of air that got into the cell through the barred window, Malk guessed it was hot outside. The station's walls had to be thick, because it wasn't hot inside. *Good*, he thought. If he started baking in here, he'd have to drink his water faster. This way, he could stretch it out more.

He told time—guessed at time, really—by the way the gloom shifted. He used the bucket again, and wondered what would happen when he filled it. He didn't want to find out.

No one came in to question him him or to haul him away for a grilling all day long. When he thought it was getting on towards evening, the door opened again. Three men came in. One, who looked more like a trusty than a Watchman, grabbed the honey bucket. Wet noises from the hallway said he'd dumped it into a barrel. He brought it back and set it on the floor again.

The two proper followers of Sep Nardand took Malk's almost empty water pail. They did give him another one, though, with more water in it. And they doled out a new bowl of swill. Not a fresh bowl of swill—nothing could have made that nasty glop fresh.

Malk stayed in a corner and hoped they didn't beat him up to settle their own dinners, which were bound to be better than what they fed him. They paid him no more attention than they would have given to a sick sheep huddled there.

After the door slammed, the junkman swore softly. He'd had coins in his closed hand, ready to use to bribe a Watchman to carry word of his plight out of the station. But he couldn't bribe one man with two more watching. Like making love, corruption needed privacy.

He drank more water, and also splashed more on his bruised face. If they were going to give it to him twice a day, he didn't need to be too careful with it. And, with grim determination, he choked down the swill. It was as vile as it had been in the morning.

Would they haul him back to the officer's room in the hours before sunup for a fresh round of questions and smacks? He couldn't stop them if they did, so he tried not to think about it.

Sleep didn't want to come after a long day of doing nothing. The floor felt harder than it had the night before, too. He thought about going over to the pallet, thought about it but didn't do it. All too soon, he'd be lousy and bedbug- and flea-bitten anyway, but he wanted to put off the evil moment as long as he could.

When he did doze, bad dreams and his bruises kept waking him. He couldn't remember the last time he'd had such a dreadful night. If the Watchmen got him tired enough, he might tell them whatever they wanted to know. Like brandy, exhaustion loosened tongues.

He was dozing again when the lock on his door clicked open. He came from sleep to full alertness all at once, as if he were a startled cat. The coins were in his hand before the door swung wide.

In walked a Watchman with another pail of water and another bowl of what pretended to be food. Quick, softly, and urgently, Malk said, "I'll pay you if you tell the Chleuh quartermaster colonel named Tebron that I'm locked up here."

"Ha!" the Watchman said. "Pay me what?" Malk showed him the money. The way he gaped said he wasn't the brightest candle in the chandelier. He asked, "Where'd you get that?"

"Found it in the bucket," Malk answered, deadpan. More seriously, he added, "Once I'm out, I'll give you as much again if you come round my shop."

Without another word, the Watchman snatched the coins and made them disappear. Malk dared hope something would come of that. He didn't dare believe it would. Hoping for the unlikely was one thing. Believing in it was something else again.

Another day dragged by. He drank water. He ate the vile stuff in the bowl. It was enough to keep him alive, not enough to keep him from being hungry all the time. He noticed it was starting to taste better to him—not good, but better. He didn't think that was because the station cook had accidentally stewed up a palatable batch. More likely, he'd got to the point where anything resembling food seemed all right.

He slept as well as he could after darkness filled the cell: badly, in other words. He still wanted nothing to do with the pallet, though some of his itches said whatever lived in the moldy straw was interested in him.

More swill for breakfast the next morning. Except for feeding him twice a day and dumping the bucket once, the Watchmen might have forgotten he was there. No one questioned him after that first night. No one seemed to care at all. He worried about Efa and Sarmel. Worrying was all he could do.

Then, when his belly told him the supper bowl was a couple of hours away, someone undid the lock and opened the cell door. Alarm shot through him. He hadn't been a prisoner long, but long enough to realize breaks in routine were liable to mean bad news.

In strode an officer he'd never seen before. "You are Malk Malkovici?" the man demanded.

"That's right, uh, sir," Malk said.

The Watchman looked disgusted. The way his nostrils twitched had nothing to do with the stench from the honey bucket. "Get out," he said, as if the words were as disgusting as prison swill. "You're free. Go on, go."

Malk wore only the nightshirt they'd grabbed him in. By now, it was filthy. He didn't care. He got to his feet as fast as he could. If people on the street stared at him, then they did. "Thank you, sir! Thank you very much!" he said.

"It wasn't my idea. Thank your connections," the Watchman

answered. "Now leave, before I decide I don't care about who you know."

Malk left. Sure enough, it was late afternoon. His eyes needed a bit of time to get used to the blast of sunlight. As he'd thought they would, people gave him funny looks. He didn't care. He was able to walk away, and that was all he cared about.

The attendant at the door to the steam baths took one look, or perhaps one whiff, and threw his arms wide to bar the way in. "Sorry, but we've got limits," he told Malk.

The junkman didn't care about that, either, or not very much. He'd almost got home when he ran into Bezen the constable. "By the gods!" Bezen exclaimed. "What happened to you?"

"Watchmen," Malk answered economically.

"By the gods!" Bezen repeated, his eyes widening. "And you're *out*?" He sounded as if he didn't believe it, and who could blame him?

"I'm out," Malk said. The constable looked at him as if he were one of the True Faith's Sanctified, or even a heavenly messenger. Malk realized he'd become a man of consequence to Bezen. All things considered, he could have done without the honor. He walked on.

I Am Everywhere wasn't the only news sheet in Lutesse that reviewed plays. When they praised Guisa Sachry's writing or acting, he thought it no less than his due. When they had the gall to dislike something he'd done, he reminded himself that the sheets recruited theatre critics from homes for the feebleminded and the insane.

His father had been a performer before him, and greased the wheels of his rise to prominence. He'd never really had to worry about bad reviews. They irked him, but couldn't hurt him till now. He approached the Watchmen's headquarters on Auristo Avenue with feet that would rather have run away.

This was worse than meeting with the Chleuh commandant. General Stulp *was* a Chleuh, and blind to much that went on in

Quimper. Not Sep Nardand. He understood his countrymen, all right; that was part of what made him so valuable to the occupants. His talent for killing without worrying about it also served him well there.

"I would like to see your colonel, please," Guisa said to the tough in an underofficer's uniform, who sat behind a desk in the front hall.

"Who are you, and why should he give a fart?" the Watchman growled.

"I myself have the honor to be Guisa Sachry, and I've finished a job of work for him," Guisa said, trying to hide his fear.

Plainly, the Watchman didn't know his name. That always annoyed him. But the mention of work made the man wary. "Hold on. I'll check," he said, and sent an underling upstairs to do so.

The flunky came back and nodded. A trifle surprised, the underofficer waved Guisa forward. Forward Guisa went, wishing Sep Nardand had forgotten about him since they last saw each other.

"Well, well. You took a while, but here you are," Nardand said when Guisa was ushered into his office. He tried to sound genial, but that didn't seem to be in his character. He seemed more like a mean dog who knew his chain was too short to let him bite the man in front of him.

"Here I am," Guisa agreed, and then, trying to stay safe, he added, "This is a lovely chamber." The walls and ceiling were painted in the style of two centuries earlier, with heavenly messengers coming down to deliver benefactions to mankind. It was ornate and elegant and altogether unlike anything Watchmen did.

And the gambit failed. Nardand grunted and said, "I hardly even notice the place. I just work here." He held out a battered hand. "Give me the play now. Let me have a look at it."

Guisa passed him the pasteboard case that held the mansucript. He mostly used a fine leather one, but he wanted neither this play nor Nardand's touch sullying that. This case was disposable. At the moment, Guisa Sachry felt very disposable himself.

Before reading, Nardand put on spectacles. He frowned right

away. "'*Among the Villagers*, by Gorec Sembel'?" he said. "Why didn't you put your own name on it? Don't you want to be seen with us?"

"You misunderstand," Guisa said quickly, though the head Watchman understood only too well. "Gorec Sembel was a playwright of a lifetime ago, who made his name laughing at fools from the countryside. People still remember his works—I'm putting together a revival of one now. That was what gave me the idea for this piece. I've done it in his style, as best I could. It will seem familiar to provincial audiences."

Nardand looked at him over the tops of his glasses. *If you're lying, you're a dead man*, his eyes said. But Guisa wasn't lying. Getting the idea to ape Sembel's work had let him do the play at all. And that the older writer had a name that sounded a bit like his didn't hurt, either.

When Guisa didn't break down in shivers, Nardand lowered his head again and began to read seriously. He chuckled a couple of times, and smiled more. He wasn't a man who showed much, so Guisa took that for a good sign.

Nardand went through the pages so fast, he could only be skimming. When he looked up again, he nodded. "Yes, I think this may do," he said. "There are some bits that need fiddling with, but it's good enough. And now that I've got it, we need to put it out there in a hurry."

Guisa had put in those bits on purpose. He'd hoped the Watchman wouldn't spot them, but Nardand, though a barbarian, was shrewd. He saw where his men didn't look as good as they might.

As for putting the play out in a hurry . . . What little the Chleuh-controlled crystal talks and news sheets did say hinted that the fight in the east against the Muos wasn't going the way King Kangen wanted. Trying to put the best face on things, they talked about "straightening lines" and "consolidation" and "heavy defensive struggles."

The news-sheet writers no doubt hoped the people who read the sheets wouldn't understand what lay behind the words the wizards reproduced by the tens of thousands. But some of those same writers had written some of those same things when Quimper's soldiers fell back before the onrushing Chleuh. Readers had got their meaning then, and surely got it now.

Then, they'd talked about it. Now . . . Sep Nardand's face said talking about it now wouldn't be such a great idea.

"You'll get your last payment," Nardand said after a moment. "Clever, what the Chleuh pieced together to let you have it on the sly."

"Clever, yes." Guisa lied without hesitation. The gangsters who showed up at the theatres asking for him made everybody in his company look at him sideways, and everyone who worked in the building, too. General Stulp and Count Vurk seemed to know only two kinds of people in Lutesse: the upper crust and the scum.

"All right, then. If I need you again for anything else, I'll let you know," Nardand said, waving his hand in dismissal. Guisa got out of the inelegant killer's elegant office and out of the Watchmen's headquarters as fast as he could. Once he made it to the sidewalk, he took a deep breath. The air outside didn't feel free—what air in Lutesse did?—but it felt far freer than what he'd breathed inside.

V

The knock on the door came just before sunup: right after curfew lifted. It was soft and tentative, nothing like the banging and pounding the Watchmen enjoyed. Malk Malkovici had already finished paying off the Watchman who'd taken word of his troubles to Tebron, so he didn't worry much about them now.

And he was waiting for this knock, and opened up at once. "Master Kergrist!" he said. "Come in, come in! You don't know how glad I am to see you!" After a moment, he let out a sardonic chuckle. "Well, I take that back. You probably do."

"It could be," Batz Kergrist agreed with a wry smile that stretched his long, thin face in surprising directions. "The next person I meet who's fond of vermin will be the first, I'll tell you that."

"I believe you, yes I do." Malk had to fight the urge to scratch all the time. Even when he didn't actually itch, he imagined he did. He'd been lousy in the orphanage in Nistria; all the children mewed up there had been. Not after he came the Quimper, though, not till he spent some time in the Watchmen's cell. He explained that to the wizard, adding, "I couldn't even steam them away—the bathhouse man said I was too foul to let in. I can't say I blame him, either. And baths here haven't done the job."

"Once you have company, it can be hard to get rid of them," Batz Kergrist said. "I'll do my best. You'll want the spell to focus mainly on you, then, and after that on the building?"

"On me and my wife, mainly." Malk raised his voice: "Come down, Efa! Kergrist the pest-killing mage is here!"

"Good to see you, Master Kergrist," Efa said when she got downstairs. "Can I give you a roll or some coffee-that-isn't?"

"The rolls are top notch—she baked them herself," Malk added.

Batz Kergrist shook his head. "I thank you, but I broke my fast before I walked over." Because not many people in Lutesse had enough to eat, declining offered food was good form. The wizard's tunic and trousers flapped on him; he was skinnier than he'd been when they were new.

Recognizing as much, Malk said, "We've got plenty, we truly do."

"Well . . ."

That hesitation was enough. Efa hurried up to the kitchen and returned with two rolls on a plate and a streaming cup of chicory. "Here. Eat. Drink," she said in tones that brooked no argument.

"Well . . ." Batz said again, and then, "Thank you very much." The way the rolls disappeared made Malk think the mage had told a polite lie about his breakfast. Times were hard, and not getting easier. The wizard patted at his mouth with his sleeve. "Thank you so much. Those did hit the spot. Shall we go on now?"

"If you please, sir," Malk said. Efa nodded vigorously. Try as Malk had to rid himself of his vermin, now she had some new occupants, too.

"All right, then." Batz handed back the plate, which Efa set on the counter. The sorcerer rummaged in his battered leather case. He took out a brass brazier, a yellow powder in a glass tube, a spider that lived in a fatter glass tube with a perforated iron lid, and a tiny salamander in an asbestos box.

He poured some of the powder into the brazier. Then he fed the salamander a half-grown cricket he extracted from another jar whose lid had air holes. When the salamander began to glow, he picked it up with a pair of tongs and touched it to the yellow powder. A plume of gray smoke rose as Batz put the salamander back into its fireproof box.

Malk recognized the smoke's stink right away. "Brimstone!" he said.

"That's what it is," Batz Kergrist agreed. "Back before wizardry had come very far, they used to fumigate houses with brimstone alone. But the spell amplifies the effect. Now don't joggle my elbow, if you know what I mean."

He began to incant, first in Quimperi, then in the sonorous older language from which it had grown: the language followers of the True Faith still used for prayer. A Quimperi mage with a skill so minor as killing pests could still practice his craft without Chleuh supervision. The occupants didn't believe he could be dangerous. Malk wondered how wise they were.

Batz used a small wickerwork fan to spread the smoke far and wide. "I should have put the brimstone in a censer, but I couldn't find mine this morning," he said sheepishly. "This will also work, but it's less elegant."

"I worry more about how well the charm will work than about how pretty it is," Malk said.

"Good for you! That's a sensible attitude." Batz tipped the spider out of its jar and onto the counter near the brazier. After it scurried about for a little while, he caught it again, explaining, "Bedbugs and fleas and lice are insects. Symbolically, they have no fiercer foes than spiders. This next charm will tie the symbolic world to the real one."

"So it will be as if your spider is eating up all our vermin, then?" Efa asked.

"That's just right!" Batz Kergrist smiled his oddly engaging smile once more. "You understand what I'm doing, sure enough. A bit of study and you could probably do it yourself."

"She worked her magic on me a long time ago," Malk said.

"You're a pest, all right." Efa poked him in the ribs with a long-nailed forefinger.

Chuckling, Batz began the new cantrip. It had a rhythm different from the one before, a rhythm that put Malk in mind of the spider's many jointed legs. On and on it went. Every so often, Batz would wave toward the stairs, as if wafting his magic up to the second story.

"Send some down into the cellar, too, just in case," Efa said.

The wizard nodded and aimed passes that way, too. When he finished, he said, "This should take care of things. If it doesn't, you'll come back and tell me I don't know what I'm doing, and I'll have another go at setting things right. I do my best, but nobody's perfect."

He wasn't a fly-by-night; he'd had his little neighborhood trade for years. Malk didn't think he wouldn't be there if he needed to make a second visit. And not only was no one perfect, the times weren't, either. "What do I owe you?" the junkman asked.

"Oh, a couple of silver crowns ought to do it," Batz said.

"No wonder you're so skinny!" Efa exclaimed. "Malk—"

"I'll take care of it," Malk said. He paid Batz twice what he'd asked. The wizard tried to protest. Malk wouldn't listen. "Don't worry about it. Gods be praised, I'm getting by right now. I know things are hard. I won't starve for shelling out a little extra, and I'll help keep you from starving, too."

"You're a gentleman, sir," Batz Kergrist said.

"I promise you, you're the only one who thinks so. To most people, I'm a damned foreigner who talks funny and worships the wrong gods." Malk didn't usually show his bitterness to acquaintances, only to his wife and his brother. He knew breaking that rule could cost him everything. But he trusted Batz, even if it made him a fool.

"You're a gentleman," the mage repeated. Malk just snorted. He didn't usually show how pleased he was, either. Methodically, Batz packed up the tools of his craft. Touching a forefinger to the bill of his cap, he said, "I'll be off. Folks have been saying I'm off for a long time, but don't you listen to them. Gods give you a good morning, sir —and you, my lady."

Out he went, bringing his hand up to his cap again as he closed the door behind him again. "He's a nice man," Efa said.

"I hope you don't think he's *too* nice." Malk stuck out his tongue so she'd know he was teasing.

"Oh, stop!" Efa made a face back at him. After a moment, she went on in a different tone of voice: "Malk . . ."

"What?" he asked, alarmed. He knew she was going to say something important, but had no idea what. That alone scared him.

"I think I'm going to have a baby. I won't be sure till the moon goes halfway round again, but I think so."

Malk wanted to dig a finger into his ear to make sure he was hearing right. They hadn't used any sponges or sheaths or charms against conception for years now. He'd just thought they weren't going to have any children. Now . . . Now his knees didn't want to hold him up. He set a hand on the counter to steady himself. "A baby?" he whispered.

"That's right." Efa nodded. "I wish it weren't now, when we don't know whether they'll grab us and take us away, but. . . ."

"A baby," Malk said again, more firmly this time. "For us, I think any time is a good time for a baby. Maybe not for some other people, but for us." He managed a couple of steps forward and squeezed his wife.

As they clung to each other, his mind whirled like an air elemental whipping up a dust devil. In spite of his brave words, he had no idea how he could protect a baby if the Chleuh or the Watchmen did decide to lean him out. He'd managed to stay on the occupants' good side, or at least mild side, this long. Could he keep doing it till the baby came?

Would the Chleuh still be here nine months from now? He grimaced. They probably would. The way they acted in Lutesse, they never intended to leave. Of course, what they intended wasn't always what happened. They'd planned to lay hold of Muosi and fill it with people from their own crowded kingdom. The Muos, though, turned out to have plans of their own.

Life had never been simple. Now it got complicated in ways he hadn't even dreamt of. "We'll manage," he murmured in Efa's ear. "One way or another, we'll manage."

"I hope so," she said.

Now that he'd given Sep Nardand his play, Guisa Sachry was out and about more than he had been lately. But he soon began to wonder whether going out wasn't more trouble than it was worth. Count Vurk still set a fine table. So did General Stulp, to whose gatherings Guisa found himself invited more often than he had before. All the same . . .

Something had gone out of those soirees. Guisa felt it, but had trouble putting a finger on what it was. When he said so to Vonney, she gave him that look again. "I know what it is," she told him. "The Chleuh are worried, that's what. They don't want to show it, but they are."

"You're right!" Guisa gave her a look, too, one of admiration. "You *are* a clever thing. Once you point it out, it's obvious."

"Everything is, once somebody points it out," his wife said. Then she kissed him, so he didn't feel too very punctured.

If the Quimperi who helped the occupants hold on to their kingdom were also worried, they made a good game try at not showing it. They laughed. They danced. They drank—Count Vurk got the very best from all over Quimper. And they ate. There stood Erol Paki, going through a plate of steamed prawns one after another as if afraid they'd get snatched away in a few minutes.

Guisa wondered how much the Chleuh paid someone like Paki to shout on the crystal night after night that Honter must be destroyed. Not enough to keep him well fed, evidently. That was interesting.

The actor idly scratched the front of his own tunic. It was still snug against the belly under it. He enjoyed these feeds—he'd had some of the prawns himself, and they were very good—but he didn't depend on them the way some people did.

Off in a distant, dark corner of the room, the light didn't look quite right. Guisa frowned for a moment, but only for a moment. Even though the people at the gathering were their friends, the Chleuh had posted somebody in a tarncape to spy on them. They didn't fully trust Quimperi . . . and they probably had their reasons not to.

A harsh laugh made Guisa's head whip around. Yes, there was Sep Nardand, a glass of brandy in his hand, his face red enough to argue it wasn't the first one, or even the third. Guisa feared the commander of the Watchmen would come over to congratulate him on *Among the Villagers*. The fewer people who knew he'd had anything to do with that, the better.

But Colonel Nardand wasn't paying him any mind. Normally, that would have irked Guisa—he wanted everybody to pay attention to him all the time—but it came as a relief now. Nardand was trying his luck with one of the pretty girls who decorated the dining hall like the flower arrangements on the tables.

Guisa suspected the Watchman's luck would be good. Who'd have the spine to say no to someone who could order her jailed or tortured or killed if she did? She might not like doing whatever he wanted her to do, but that didn't mean she wouldn't. Oh, no.

She's a lot like me, Guisa thought. The room was warm, but he shivered anyway, as if a goose walked on his grave. Then he went over to the bar to get his own glass filled again. If you drank enough, you didn't have to think about why you were with the people you were with.

The young man who poured for him had a face absolutely empty of expression. Guisa knew better than to say anything foolish in front of him anyway. Blackmail was one worry. Another was that the barman reported back to the Chleuh . . . or to the woodsrunners. Guisa didn't know which would be worse. Both were bad.

"Ah, Master Sachry," someone said behind him.

He turned. As usual, a smiling Count Vurk was a frightening Count Vurk. Guisa bowed to the Chleuh ambassador. "I thank you very much for your kind invitation here, your Excellency," he said. His own face and voice gave away nothing. Acting for a living had its uses.

"It is my pleasure," Vurk answered. "Together, we will win, you and we. You must be proud. You are an ornament to King Kangen's magnificence."

"You do me too much honor," Guisa said. Vurk and Stulp and the other Chleuh here, who made some effort to understand Quimper, were almost acceptable overlords because they did. But the less Guisa had to do with King Kangen's magnificence, the gladder he would be.

"Together, we will build a new continent, one that will stand strong for lifetimes yet to come," Vurk went on. "The Muos' moves forward will fail when the fall rains turn their dirt tracks to mud, by the gods. And if the Hontermen and the Anadans try to land on these shores, be sure we shall kick them back into the Narrow Sea. Be very sure of it, for it is true."

"Of course, your Excellency," Guisa murmured. Even weeks ago, Vurk hadn't talked this way. He sounded like someone who needed to shore up his own confidence more than that of the person he was talking to.

He might even have realized as much. For a Chleuh, he was clever. His smile twisted a bit as he went on, "The merely difficult we do at once. The impossible? That sometimes takes a bit longer. As we are seeing. But fear not. We *shall* prevail."

"Yes, your Excellency," Guisa said. Vurk went off to talk with someone else. The performer drained his glass and turned back to the barman, which he hadn't intended to do before the ambassador buttonholed him.

He found himself in line behind Erol Paki. "Oh, hello. Good to see you," the little commentator said. "Been a while. They lay on a demon of a spread here, eh?"

"They do indeed," Guisa said. He could look down at the top of Paki's head and see how sparse his hair was getting. Paki had a provincial accent, too, one you didn't notice so much when his voice came out of the crystal. Maybe he tried harder to seem Lutesse-born and -bred when he was working, and let that slip while away from the oration room.

"Everything will work out fine. You wait and see. It will." Unlike Count Vurk, Paki sounded utterly sure of himself. He paused for a moment to tell the barman what he wanted and wait till he got it. Then he resumed where he'd left off: "King Kangen, he's a marvel. Even the Chleuh, they don't deserve him the way they should. As for us, we're just lucky to have him come and put this sorry place to rights."

People like Odrio Cazh talked the way Paki did. Guisa didn't think the Chleuh were such a blessing for Quimper; he only thought he had to accommodate himself to them once they'd got here. He didn't want to seem lukewarm, though, so he said, "You put it so well."

"You're too kind," Paki said. He wore a Chleuh-style ceremonial dagger in a yellow leather sheath on his belt. Guisa didn't think he'd ever seen a man less likely to be dangerous with that kind of weapon. After a moment, Paki stepped aside. "I do apologize. I'm standing between you and your drink."

"I won't die of thirst." Guisa moved up to the bar and gave the man behind it his order. When he got the glass back, he slid a quarter-crown across the zinc. With murmured thanks, the barman made it disappear.

Erol Paki raised his glass in salute. "Your health."

"And yours." Guisa clinked with him. They both drank. Yes, Count Vurk could still get his hands on liquor from before the war. He didn't serve the nasty stuff they made nowadays, aged an hour and a half in the flask and then funneled straight into a bottle with a label that looked old. Nothing but the best for Vurk . . . and his guests.

"We'll beat them all. You wait and see—we will," Paki said. "We'll clean out everybody who's left that still worships the wrong gods. Not so many of them any more, but we'll sweep out the ones who are. Nobody will miss them, either, not even a little bit."

"That's ambitious." Guisa Sachry remembered how Vonney had sold the brass saltcellar and pepper mill to one of those people. Even then, he'd been surprised to hear of them out and about.

"The Chleuh don't think small. That's what makes them so marvelous. They see something that wants doing, and they go ahead and do it," Paki said. "They'll give the uncivilized schismatics who worship the right gods the wrong way what's coming to them, too. You wait and see. They will."

"One may hope," Guisa said, though the news sheets still talked about defensive struggles and rectified lines. The Muos said the gods hated wealth unless everybody had it, though they didn't always practice what they preached. Their king and his court lived high on the hog, and they weren't too faithproud to throw in with Honter and Anada against Chlé.

"One may indeed. If you'll excuse me . . ." Erol Paki made his way towards one of the pretty girls, who were also part of Count Vurk's entertainments. Guisa looked away so Paki wouldn't see him smile. She stood half a head taller than the crystal commentator. *If he goes down on her later tonight, he'll be going up on her instead*, Guisa thought. He fished a little notebook from a jacket pocket and wrote that down. If he could sneak the line past the bluenoses, it would bring down the house.

Then one of those pretty girls came up to him and said, "I beg your pardon, but you *are* Guisa Sachry, aren't you? The performer, I mean."

"I myself am that man, yes," he said. His eyes slid around the room till he found Vonney. She was smiling at something Count Vurk was saying, and not paying any attention to him. He smiled himself, at the girl. "Is there something I might do for you?"

She curtsied to him, gracefully enough to show she'd had practice at it. "I hope there may be. My name is Xya Fulgine. I'm a dancer at the dive called Ridiculousness."

"Are you?" he said. He knew of the place. It was one of those joints where the girls either took their clothes off or came out naked to begin with and pranced around. Those places had done well for themselves even before the war. These days, Chleuh soldiers on leave from the grinding war against the Muos filled them to overflowing.

Xya Fulgine nodded. "That's right. And I'm sick to death of men groping me and yelling filthy things at me thinking I like them. I really do dance well, Master Sachry. I don't just show myself off. I was wondering if you could find me a place in your company."

"Isn't that interesting?" he said. "Things may not be so different there as you hope, you know. And, forgive me for saying so, but here you are at a gathering like this one."

"I don't expect men to be anything but men. I know better than that," Xya answered. Something in her tired smile said she had plenty of reasons to know better, too. "I only want them to try to be gentlemen and to listen to *no* every once in a while."

"You may be able to hope for that much. On good days, anyhow." Guisa didn't say no. He didn't say yes, either. He waited to see what happened next.

She looked at him. The smile stayed on her face, but bent even a little more. "It's going to be that way, is it?" she asked. Guisa still didn't reply. Xya sighed. "I'd do almost anything to get a spot in your chorus. I can do the job. I wouldn't be there just because . . . well, just because."

Guisa glanced over at Vonney again. She was still talking and laughing with the Chleuh ambassador. General Stulp and one of his aides had joined the conversation, too. They all seemed to be enjoying themselves. Guisa hadn't run around on her before, not even once. Then again, he also hadn't had an engraved invitation handed to him on a silver platter.

"Almost anything?" he said. She nodded. He'd yielded to temptation before, which was one reason he'd been married three times. He looked toward the door. "Shall we step outside for a bit, so we can talk about it without being overheard?"

"Talk about it," Xya echoed. She was younger than Vonney, and looked it—everywhere but her eyes. Her shoulders went up and down in a sigh. She had lovely, sculpted collarbones, Guisa noted. She said, "Yes, we can do that."

She'd played these games before; she didn't make it obvious that the two of them were leaving together. Guisa stood outside the exit, waiting for his eyes to get used to darkness after the brightly lit hall. When Xya Fulgine came out a moment later, she seemed to have no trouble. He wondered if she was part cat.

Gardens surrounded the Chleuh embassy. If you knew where to look, you could find quiet, secluded nooks. Guisa had taken Vonney to a couple of them before they got married. He set his hand on Xya's arms. "If you'll come with me . . ." It didn't occur to him till later that she probably knew those secluded spots better than he did.

Soft giggles and other small noises warned him away from the first place he led her to. He managed to find another one, not quite so good, a little farther down the graveled walk. "Well," she said when they stood under a small tree that might well have been planted there to shade such dalliances. It sounded like a complete sentence.

"Well . . ." Guisa didn't throw himself at her. She'd said she didn't fancy that. They'd made the bargain. Let her figure out how to keep it.

She stated it one more time: "I'll take care of you now. You take care of me later." Then, gracefully enough to show she was a dancer, she dropped to her knees.

Take care of him she did. He'd known better, but also a great many worse. He tried not to make uncouth noises when pleasure flooded him. Afterwards, as he was fastening his belt again, he asked, "Can I do anything for you now?"

"No, don't bother," she said coolly, so it was all business.

"All right. Come by in a day or two. If you don't fall all over yourself trying out, I'll put you in the chorus line."

Xya stood up. "Fair enough. I can do that. You should go back, before anyone makes something of your being gone."

"Yes, I should," Guisa said. She was cool indeed.

The Chleuh guards didn't look at him sidewise as he walked in again. They saw such comings and goings often enough. Being young and handsome, they probably went into the gardens with one or another of Count Vurk's pretty girls themselves every so often.

"Did you go to the jakes and fall in?" Vonney asked when he found her again.

"I went to the jakes. I got to talking with someone in there, and we stayed in the hall for a bit afterwards," Guisa answered; he had practice at this kind of thing. "A Chleuh publisher—he has hopes of getting some of my works translated."

"They wouldn't sound as good," Vonney said at once—the usual Quimperi attitude toward the occupants' language.

As a matter of fact, Guisa shared that attitude. "The money would be nice, though," he said. Since the publisher was fictitious, he wouldn't see any. But he knew he was mercenary. Vonney would wonder if he fell out of character.

He waited to see what kind of entrance Xya Fulgine made. When she didn't come back at all, he decided she'd got what she needed from the gathering. That was good; Vonney wouldn't try adding one and one and maybe coming up with two.

Xya turned up the theatre two days later. She acted as if she hadn't met Guisa before. "Somebody told me you might have an opening for a dancer," she said.

Guisa didn't even need to finesse that, as he'd feared he might. "We do," he said. "One of the girls sprained her ankle last night, so we're light. Tell me your name and then get up on stage and show me what you can do."

"I'm called Xya Fulgine," she said. She didn't seem frightened to audition. Well, if she'd performed at a place like Ridiculousness, nothing much would scare her. And she could dance, by herself and with others. Guisa wasn't the only one who watched her closely. Some of the girls who didn't just dance but were getting small speaking parts looked anxious.

"I think I'll take you on," Guisa said when she finished. "Two and a half crowns a day."

She looked disappointed. "I usually do better than that where I am."

"I'm sorry. It's the going rate for the chorus here," Guisa said, which was true. Other dancers' nods told Xya he wasn't out to gyp her—any more than he gypped them.

"I'll take it," she said after a moment's thought. "I may not get as much, but it will be more . . . more peaceable." That was as close as she came to talking about what she'd done before.

On the way back to their flat, Vonney said, "Didn't I see that new girl at Count Vurk's the other night?"

"You may be right. I think I noticed her, too." Guisa wanted to say he'd never set eyes on here before, but she wouldn't believe that. He knew she knew attractive women caught his eye. She didn't know Xya had done rather more than that. He didn't want her finding out, either.

"She has the moves, that's plain," Vonney said. "If she fits in with the other dancers, she's a good find."

"Yes, I thought so, too," Guisa said. His wife talked about something else. He smiled to himself. He'd got away with it.

"Brass, bronze—anything with copper in it. And iron. As much as you can lay your hands on," Colonel Tebron told Malk Malkovici.

"You will have heard the news out of the east. We're raising as many soldiers as we can, and they all need weapons."

"I am your servant, sir." Malk didn't just touch his cap; he swept it off and bowed to the Chleuh quartermaster officer. "I am your servant, and I am in your debt for getting me out of the Watchmen's cell."

"Oh. That." Tebron pulled a face. "Some of those people think they're more important than they truly are. They don't have free rein when it comes to harrying men who help King Kangen."

"I thank you very kindly." Malk knew plenty of Chleuh who would have let him rot in that cell or let Sep Nardand's hounds tear him into strips. For an occupant, Tebron was a decent fellow . . . or maybe Malk was just one of his pets, to be watched over and taken care of like a cat that enjoyed sitting in laps. The junkman went on, "I've brought in more brass and bronze since the last load you bought from me, and iron is still not too hard to come by, though it used to be easier."

"Yes, I was looking over what you have here. It will help. Everything we get hold of will help. How much for all your stock right now?" The colonel stiffened, as if braced to charge into battle against the Muos himself.

Malk waved at the piled-up chunks and bits of metal. "Sir, take it all, every bit. This time, it's yours."

"What?" Tebron looked and sounded as if he couldn't believe his ears. Most of the time, Malk haggled over every bent, useless nail as if it were made of gold. By all the signs, Tebron enjoyed those dickers, too. In that, he differed from a lot of Chleuh. Supply officer seemed the right slot for him.

"It's yours," Malk Malkovici repeated, not without pride. "I told you, I am in your debt. How can I pay you back except like this? When you come here next time, we can argue about what things are worth. Today? No."

The colonel rubbed his chin. "You're all right, Malkovici. You truly are." He rubbed it some more. "You know, there are some people who . . . who don't follow the gods my folk do to whom King Kangen has granted certificates of Chleuh-hood, so they don't need to worry about those complications any more."

Malk drew himself up, though he was still several inches shorter than Colonel Tebron. "Sir, I am what I am. If I took a paper like that, all my ancestors would think I was spitting on what they suffered for so they could keep it alive."

"It is said there is such suffering even now." Tebron chose his words with obvious care.

"Yes, sir. It is said." Malk shrugged. "What can one do?"

"One could seek a certificate of the kind I mentioned. One could. But if one has honor, not seeking such a certificate becomes easier to comprehend." Tebron made as if to put his right fist over his heart. He didn't quite finish the salute, but for a Chleuh even to start it to a member of the Old Faith was remarkable enough.

"I'm a junkman. What does a junkman know about honor?" Malk said. "Send your wagons by. They can pick up what I've got."

"I will, you stubborn polecat. And I'll send by some paperwork with them, so everything looks the way it's supposed to. I don't want anybody wondering why they gathered this load for nothing."

"Ah! Yes, I understand that." Malk wondered whether Tebron would just let the money he would have paid for the scrap metal fall into his own belt pouch instead. Quite a few Chleuh would have; taken all in all, they were no more honest than any other group of men Malk had dealt with. He liked to think better of the quartermaster colonel, though.

"Do you want to know something? You have not heard this from me, you understand. I will call you a liar to your face if you ever say otherwise."

"If you don't think you can rely on me, sir, keep quiet," Malk said.

"There is that, yes. Well, I've started, so I might as well finish. It occurs to me that the time may come when you can put in a good word for me, the way I put in a good word for you with the Watchmen. It may come sooner than you think, too."

"You'll understand, sir, that someone like me doesn't go farther than a day's travel from Lutesse. What happens on the coast of the Narrow Sea may as well happen on another world, as far as I'm concerned."

"Nothing is happening there now. You know that. If anything does start happening there, you may find out about it before I do," Tebron said.

"Sir, I have no idea what you could be talking about," Malk Malkovici said with dignity.

"Of course not. It doesn't matter one way or the other, not really, since in fact we aren't having this conversation at all," Tebron said. "I'll send over the boys—and the paperwork—this afternoon. Take care of yourself."

"And you," Malk said. If all the Chleuh were like the quartermaster colonel . . . the war probably never would have started to begin with.

When the Chleuh wagons came, the underofficer driving the one in front thrust papers at Malk. "You sign these," he said in rudimentary Quimperi as scrap metal started banging and clattering into the wagon beds.

Since Colonel Tebron had warned him about paperwork, Malk made sure Sarmel was there. His brother read Quimperi and could even puzzle out Chleuh. "Is everything the way it ought to be?" Malk asked.

Sarmel knew the Chleuh were getting this load for free. He also knew the papers wouldn't show that. He went through them carefully all the same, looking for hidden traps and snares. After finishing, he nodded. "I think we're all right."

"Good." Malk hadn't expected anything else—Tebron had saved his freedom, and probably his life—but didn't care to take chances. He dipped a pen into a bottle of ink that sat on the counter and made his mark on the proper lines. He'd seen lots of papers like these; he knew where to scribble. Then he handed the sheets back to the officer. "Here you are, sir."

The man checked to make sure he didn't miss any places. Chleuh had, and commonly deserved, a name for thoroughness. Once satisfied, the underofficer nodded. "Good. Is good," he said. He stowed the papers in a waxed-leather tube that dangled from his belt.

"Did you have to give them all that for nothing?" Sarmel asked after the wagons clanked up the street. The inside of the junkman's shop seemed empty indeed with so much gone.

"Did I have to? No. But what you do when you don't have to is what people remember," Malk said. "We aren't safe yet. We won't be safe till—" He broke off. In spite of what he'd heard from Colonel Tebron, saying *till the Chleuh are gone from Lutesse* seemed too dangerous, even here. His brother would understand the words whether he said them or not.

VI

Another after-show gathering, this one at the headquarters of what had been Lutesse's largest publishing house before the war. It still was, though these days a bright young Chleuh functionary named Artak Shmavon decided whose works would see the light of day. Shmavon published Guisa Sachry's plays, so naturally Guisa liked him.

He also published a wide variety of other playwrights, romancers, and poets. He had reason to make it seem as if King Kangen's hand didn't lie too heavily on Quimper. And, as far as Guisa could tell, he truly savored literature, whether his own kingdom's or the occupied one's.

Artak put out a nice spread—not so splendid as Count Vurk's, but still nice, especially in a hungry city. Some pretty girls came to his events, too, though again fewer than to Vurk's. A publishing official didn't have the clout or the budget the minister did.

Guisa wondered if Xya Fulgine would be part of the decoration at this gathering. When he didn't see her, he smiled to himself. One thing fewer to worry about.

A scholarly-looking man in his mid-thirties clinked wineglasses with Guisa. “I enjoy your work, sir,” he said. “It’s good to see you. Been too long.”

“Thank you for your kindness. I myself would agree it has been too long.” Guisa tried to slip away. Brasi Robillach was another one of those people even someone who accommodated himself to the occupants didn’t want to have too much to do with. True, he’d been a rising writing star before the war. Since then, though, he’d seemed to enjoy himself editing *I Am Everywhere*.

Robillach set a hand on Guisa’s arm now. “I have something in mind that may interest you,” he said.

“Oh? You do?” Guisa wondered how to take that. The editor hadn’t gone after any of the women Artak Shmavon had laid on. Guisa happened to know his tastes ran toward men instead. *Do they run toward me?* he wondered. He doubted it. He wasn’t young, and Robillach had to know he liked women.

Which meant this might be political. That was liable to prove worse, and harder to escape.

Behind his round-lensed spectacles, Robillach’s dark eyes were cool and watchful. “I do,” he said, and straightened the scarf he wore around his neck. He wasn’t the kind of man who, liking men, played at being a woman, but the gesture held a bit of that.

“Tell me what’s on your mind, then,” Guisa said resignedly. If it wasn’t anything he cared to go along with, he thought he could get away with telling Brasi Robillach no.

“Do you know Nea Ennogue?” the editor asked.

“The teacher? The writer? I’ve met him several times. I haven’t seen him in a while, though, much longer ago than the last time I saw you.” As often happened in Lutesse these days, Guisa talked around what he meant. Nea Ennogue was one of those stubborn people who refused to have anything to do with the Chleuh. That meant he and Guisa didn’t travel in the same circles any more.

“I still do, every now and then,” Robillach said. “He gets food once in a while from our kind of people, and he got some coal last winter, too. He doesn’t always know where it comes from. He might not use it if he did. If you know anything about him, you know how stiff-necked he is."

"Oh, yes." Guisa Sachry nodded. "As obstinate as they come, that one."

Robillach smiled. "He is. He really is. But I was thinking that we could have a chance to talk him around if we feed him a good meal, pour something nice down his throat. He isn't stupid. It would be good to bring him over to the right side, the side that sails with the tide of history."

Just after the surrender, who chose to make friends with the Chleuh and who didn't was often as much a matter of luck as anything. Some of the people who decided one way still kept up with those who'd gone down the other path. Defeat seemed much more complicated than victory would have. In victory, everyone sang the same tune. Not here, not now.

Slowly, Guisa nodded. "If he'll break bread with us, I'll break bread with him. It should be . . . interesting." He was sure Brasi Robillach wouldn't have proposed this without getting leave from Artak Shmavon or Count Vurk or some other prominent Chleuh. Going along with it wouldn't anger the occupants or, probably, the woodsrunners.

Robillach smiled a charming smile. "Excellent! Yes, it certainly should. I need to get hold of someone who can get hold of Nea and set things up. You'll hear from me when it's all arranged—or if it falls through." He drifted off to talk with someone else.

A few days later, Guisa did hear: one of *I Am Everywhere*'s critics sidled up to him after a performance and slipped him a note. *He has agreed to join us*, Robillach wrote, his script as elegant and refined as the rest of him. *Four nights from tonight at the Leaping Hare, which I'm sure you'll know. I'll see you then—Brasi.*

Guisa did know the Leaping Hare. Before the occupants marched in, theatre people had kept it hopping till the sun came up. These days, it was a popular dinner stop for Chleuh officers. Guisa wondered wondered what Nea Ennogue would think of that.

First things first. "Let him know I'll be there," Guisa told the man from *I Am Everywhere.*

The fellow touched a finger to the bill of his cap. "I'll do it, Master Sachry."

Brasi Robillach was forethoughtful enough to have picked an evening when the theatres were closed. Dressed in his most nearly new formal attire, Guisa made his way to the eatery.

About half the tables had Chleuh sitting at them, sometimes with their countrymen, sometimes with prosperous-looking Quimperi, sometimes with companions more feminine and more charming. Guisa saw Brasi and Nea Ennogue at a table near the back. The editor waved to him. He nodded back as he told the headwaiter, "There are my friends."

"Yes, sir. I hope you enjoy your meal with them," the man replied. "And let me tell you how much I enjoy you on the stage."

"Why, thank you!" Guisa said with well-practiced surprise.

Brasi Robillach stood up as Guisa walked over. So did Ennogue, stiffly. He was a few years younger than Guisa, with hair still dark and a bushy mustache. Guisa remembered he'd taken a war wound as a young man. "Glad you could join us," Brasi said.

"Glad to be here," Guisa said. He dipped his head to Nea Ennogue. "Very good to make your acquaintance again, sir."

"If you say so," Ennogue answered: not the most promising start.

"Let's be friends in spite of politics, at least till dinner's done," Brasi said.

"I'll try. I'm not the actor Master Sachry is, though," Nea said.

A waiter handed them menus and asked, "Something to drink?"

"Brandy for me," Robillach said at once. Guisa nodded; the evening might need lubrication. After a moment, Ennogue nodded, too.

After the waiter went off to get the drinks, Nea examined the menu. "The dishes haven't changed since I was here last. The prices have, though." He looked around the room. "The clientele, too."

"We were weak. We were corrupt. We got what usually happens

to the weak and corrupt when they face the strong and virile," Robillach said. A lot of men with his tastes had fallen for the Chleuh head over heels, politically and romantically. He seemed to be another one.

Nea looked at him—looked through him, really. "You could say that with a straight face three years ago. These days? Have you *seen* the Chleuh lately? Not the fine gentlemen here: I mean the underofficers and the common soldiers. They're about as shabby and threadbare and worn out as we are. And every one of them who has a job here dreads the order that will put him on the train to go fight the Muos."

"Even Quimperi recognize that the schismatics are a danger to the whole civilized world," Brasi said loftily.

"I saw posters slapped on a wall on my way over here," Guisa said. "Muo posters somebody'd sneaked in and put up overnight. They had a roasted capon with the General's face, and they said *Eat the Rich!* Forgive the pun, but I can't stomach that."

"The occupants' posters would say *Eat the Poor* or *Eat the Old Faith*. Is that better?" Ennogue returned.

Guisa's jaw dropped. He hadn't heard anyone talk that way since before the General surrendered to the Chleuh. Everyone was supposed to hate Quimper's enemy then. Now . . . Saying such things now, especially in an eatery full of important Chleuh, took more courage than Guisa would have wanted to give a character. It wouldn't have seemed believable to him.

Brasi Robillach looked as if he'd bitten down hard on a green persimmon. "You might have the sense to remember where you are, Nea," he murmured. "I didn't invite you here to see you—"

"To see me carted away by the Watchmen?" the writer suggested.

"Someone has to keep order," Brasi said.

Before Ennogue could reply, the waiter came back to the table and asked, "Have you gentlemen made up your minds?" That was bound to be just as well; no one wanted to keep going while the young man stood there and listened.

Guisa chose tongue stewed with onions and turnips, a dish he'd enjoyed since he was a boy. Nea Ennogue ordered pork ribs baked in a sauce full of spices. And Robillach asked for beefsteak.

"How would you like that, sir?" the waiter enquired.

"Rare. Blood rare," Brasi answered. The waiter scribbled and went back to the kitchen.

Ennogue lifted an ironic eyebrow. "You might have the sense to remember where you are, Brasi," he said. "Choosing a Honterese specialty here? If Nardand's heroes decide to keep order . . ."

Robillach's lips skinned back from his teeth in what seemed half a grin, half a snarl. "Nothing would make me happier than Honter sinking to the bottom of the sea," he said, and Guisa Sachry believed that. More calmly, the editor of *I Am Everywhere* went on, "I do like beefsteak, though, and the cooks here know that rare means rare."

"None of us took the capon," Guisa said. "I might have, if I hadn't seen those posters. I hope someone will have scraped them off by the time we head home." He sighed. "More will pop up, though, like toadstools after a rain."

"Why do you suppose that is?" Nea asked.

"Because the Muos aim to tear down everything that should be built up!" Robillach spoke before Guisa could. "Chlé shields the whole continent from their schismatic lunacy."

"'Schismatic lunacy.'" Ennogue tasted the phrase as if it were a new red wine. He slowly nodded. "Not bad. Maybe you should have been a writer yourself."

Brasi opened his mouth, then closed it again. After a moment, he said, "And you, sir, as well." Ennogue dipped his head to him. They might have been duelists, pausing to salute each other at a moment when they were both tired.

Before too long, the food came. Guisa gave it his full attention, which it deserved. Robillach seemed happy with his beefsteak, too. "If it were any rarer, it would kick me when I cut it," he said.

For some little while, Nea Ennogue concentrated on working meat off bones. In due course, he said, "This is the best meal I've eaten for quite a while. However much we disagree, Brasi, I thank you for the invitation."

"My pleasure, in more ways than one," Robillach replied. "However much we disagree, we're all Quimperi. We want our realm to prosper. That gives us a bond, even if the means we choose aren't the same."

"I myself would agree," Guisa said. "The more we can all work together, the better off we are."

"Perhaps to a degree, perhaps for a while." Nea Ennogue paused for a moment to clean his lips and mustache with a linen napkin as white as a tern's breast. "For a while, but not forever. Sooner or later, one side will win, and then pay back the losers. And that will also be among us Quimperi, as it were."

"I have confidence in King Kangen," Brasi said, and looked to Guisa for support.

Guisa wished he hadn't. But the choices you made on the spur of the moment, you had to live with later. If he said he'd suddenly gone over to the side of the woodsrunners, the Muos, and the Quimperi soldiers exiled in Honter, what would happen to him? Nothing he wanted to imagine. He couldn't say that, and didn't. He said, "The Chleuh are very strong."

"So they are," Robillach agreed.

"If the things you do, if the way you fight a war and the way you occupy the lands you win, if those things make everyone else hate you, make everyone else care for even the mad Muos more than you, what good does your strength do you in the end?" Nea asked.

"You're frank," said the editor of *I Am Everywhere*.

"The way things are these days, that's what I have left," Ennogue said. "Most of the time, I'm not even frank. But I dared hope you didn't invite me to this wonderful supper so you could turn me over to the occupants. The way things are these days, you wouldn't need evidence. Just whispering my name into the right ear would be plenty. Do you know the right ear, Brasi?"

"Quite well. The left one, too," Robillach said, and won a chuckle from Nea Ennogue. But then he continued, "You would do well to put yourself on better terms with those who hold the power these days. Truly, you would. I say that as a friend." He held up a hand before Ennogue could protest. "Yes, as a friend, even if I know you will say you are no friend of mine. But a little acceptance, just a little acceptance, would go a long way for you."

"So I could put my signature on something like *The Manifesto of the Wise Men of Quimper* the next time Count Vurk feels the need for it, you mean?" Ennogue said.

Robillach snarled again, this time more than halfway. Guisa Sachry winced; he couldn't help himself. That manifesto had come out the year before, and condemned the Hontermen for attacking Quimper to fight the Chleuh. Robillach's signature was on it, along with those of many other Quimperi writers and thinkers who backed King Kangen. At the time, Guisa'd been offended not to get invited to sign. Suddenly, he was glad he hadn't been.

"One of these days . . . One of these days, Nea, that viper's tongue will be the death of you," Brasi said. He didn't sound like a man who was joking.

But Ennogue only shrugged. "You knew who I am and what I think when you invited me. And you might take care that your poison pen isn't the death of you."

Trying to come back into a conversation from which the other two men had effectively excluded him, Guisa said, "We hoped this would be an evening of peace and reconciliation. Now is not the time to quarrel, but to come together. I myself am confident of this."

"You've done well for yourself these past three years. You can afford to say such things," Ennogue replied. Guisa's face heated as if salamander-scorched. The teacher and writer took his pouch off his belt. He asked Robillach, "And what do I owe you for the supper tonight?"

Brasi gestured for him to put the pouch back. “Don’t worry about it. I invited you, and I’ll pay the bill. Things we try don’t always work, that’s all.” Only a certain tightness around his mouth said he didn’t have every bit of his aplomb back.

“I thank you for that. You do remember when we both thought the same kingdom was the one worth fighting for, anyhow,” Nea said.

“We still do,” Robillach replied. “But Quimper had sunk so far into corruption and weakness that we needed someone to take us by the scruff of the neck and shake us straight.”

“Are we better now, straighter now, than we were three years ago?”

Guisa broke in again: “War is hard.”

“It should be. Otherwise, we’d get to like it too well.” Ennogue slowly climbed to his feet. He gave a stiff little bow. “A fascinating evening, gentlemen. I’ll see myself out.” Away he went, limping a bit from his old wound.

Malk Malkovici drove his wagon towards a rubbish tip in the southern part of Lutesse. He hadn’t been there for a while, so he dared hope the pickings would be good. He took his pipe out of his mouth, tilted his head up, and blew a smoke ring at the sky. The ring disappeared almost at once; the heavens were gray and gloomy. Autumn was here, and settling in to stay.

Sarmel sat on the bench beside him. He was smoking, too, though he never had learned to blow smoke rings. “Not a whole lot of scavengers like us left,” he remarked.

“I was thinking something a lot like that myself,” Malk said. “We must be brothers, or something.”

“So *that* explains what’s wrong with us! I knew there had to be something,” Sarmel said, and then, “How’s Efa feeling?”

Before Malk could answer, a constable stepped out into the

middle of the street and raised an imperious, white-gloved hand. "Pull over!" he shouted. Malk often thought men became constables for no other reason than that they liked telling other people what to do. "Pull over!" the fellow repeated. "You're blocking official traffic."

Looking back over his shoulder, Malk saw three big closed coaches coming up behind him. Their teams were larger and younger and fresher than his, so they were gaining. They could have gone around him; there wasn't much traffic on the avenue. These days, there never was much traffic in Lutesse. But Malk didn't argue. When you argued with constables, you lost. He pulled over.

The wagons rolled past. Chleuh soldiers drove them. More sat on their roofs, armed and ready for anything that might happen. The doors were locked and barred; boards had been nailed over the windows. No one inside could see out, and no one outside could see in.

But Malk had a good notion who the men inside were. They were singing, some the Quimperi royal song, others hymns sent up to the gods of the True Faith. That should have sounded discordant, but somehow didn't.

When the coaches had passed, the constable waved the junk wagon forward. "Go on, go on," he said impatiently, as if Malk had stopped by mistake instead of at his command.

As usual, the horses didn't want to get moving. Malk snapped the whip above their backs. They snorted in annoyance, then started walking. Little by little, the singing faded as the coaches got farther ahead of them.

"Another day in the park," Sarmel said. His voice sounded uncommonly grim.

"So it is." Malk's voice sounded the same way. The Chleuh used the park not far from the rubbish tip where he and his brother were going to dispose of woodsrunners and other prisoners who they'd decided needed killing. Sometimes the bodies just disappeared afterwards; sometimes the occupants mounted heads on pikes in a calculated show of frightfulness. Malk still didn't know which was worse.

The Chleuh had chopped down a tree in the park when they started executing people there, so the condemned men—and occasional women—could lay their heads on the stump while the axe fell. Before long, the headsman had plied his trade enough to splinter that first stump. Unless they'd cut down another tree without Malk's noticing, they were on their fifth stump now.

"That could have been you in one of those coaches," Sarmel said.

Malk shook his head. Feeling it go back and forth on his neck reminded him he was alive. *The best way to be*, he thought, and said, "No, the Chleuh don't let the Watchmen slaughter anybody in their special park. Nardand's lads have to do their murdering somewhere else."

"If they'd killed you, would you be any less dead?" his brother asked, which marched only too well with what had gone through his own mind a moment before.

Shrugging told him he was still alive, too. "Maybe a little," he said. "Not enough to matter."

Sarmel considered. "Yes, that sounds about right."

Before long, their path diverged from the coaches'. Malk knew a certain amount of relief. If he didn't see and hear the condemned men going to their fate, he didn't have to think about them . . . quite so much. In spite of Colonel Tebron's good will, the occupants still could seize him. A hacked-up stump under his throat, a sting at the back of his neck . . .

Then I find out whether the Old Faith or the True Faith is right after all, he thought. *Or if it's all nonsense.*

A couple of centuries earlier, his fellow believers would have cast him out for daring to imagine it might be nonsense. They wouldn't have killed him; they lack the authority to do that. If he'd said anything like that where followers of the True Faith could hear, though, they would have taken care of it.

These days, a good many people, from the Old Faith and the True Faith alike, had trouble believing in any gods at all. As far as they were concerned, man's true measure lay in what philosophers could measure and mages could influence. Either the gods weren't there or dwelt so far from the realm of the senses that they might as well have been absent.

Malk leaned that way himself—most of the time, anyhow. He'd never seen a miracle, which made him have trouble believing in them. Artisanship and sorcery had given people a comfortable way of life, comfortable enough so they didn't need the gods much.

Every so often, though, he wondered whether all the knowledge the modern world enjoyed had actually made people any better. Wondering what had happened to the followers of the Old Faith who'd been taken east and hadn't come back, listening to condemned prisoners singing on their way to meet the chopper—such things left plenty of room for doubt.

"Well, here we are," Sarmel said when they came to the rubbish tip: the first words out of his mouth since the coaches went one way and the junk wagon the other.

"Here we are," Malk agreed; he hadn't said much since then, either. The old man who kept an eye on the tip came up to the wagon, leaning on a stick. Malk raised his voice and forced good cheer into it: "Good day to you, Lescoff! What do you say?"

"Hello, Malk," old Lescoff answered. "And you, Sarmel." When Malk slipped him a silver crown, he acted surprised. He always did. By his manner, he might have been a gentleman once upon a time. He certainly knew how to take a bribe with grace. After the coin went into his pouch, he waved the wagon forward with a gnarled hand.

"Anything new we should know about?" Sarmel asked. He might have been talking about things flung into the tip, or he might have asking for local news.

Lescoff scratched his beard. It was white. He kept it neatly trimmed, even if his clothes were as ragged as everyone else's in Lutesse these days. He said, "One of the Locusts, a captain, got stabbed outside their officers' joyhouse last night. Maybe just a robber, maybe not. Who knows?"

"The Chleuh will come down hard either way," Malk said. Yes, the occupants believed in frightfulness. When one of their men was attacked, they took hostages—and executed them if the killer didn't surrender. As the Quimperi army had, the Chleuh army included priests. Even so, Malk often thought frightfulness was their true faith.

He flicked the reins, then stopped the wagon when the horses got to the edge of the tip. He and Sarmel slid down. Each of them put a feed bag on one of the beasts. Then they pulled on their leather gauntlets and went to see what they could find.

Iron was still easy. Malk took pans and broken tools and anything else of that sort back to the wagon. Colonel Tebron talked about how the Chleuh used it for weapons. That was obvious. Malk also knew, though Tebron didn't talk about it, that wizards used iron to try to extinguish enemy sorceries.

Sarmel waved to him. "Over here! I've got something good!"

Malk waded through rubbish to reach his brother. "By the gods!" he said as he drew near. "Is it just me, or are there more rats than ever these days? Every other step I took, another one scurried away!"

"I was thinking the same thing," Sarmel answered. "The people in Lutesse have less these days, so even the rats need to work harder to make a living. But take a look at this!"

Take a look Malk did. In this part of the tip, rubbish turned to rubble. Work crews had dragged away wrecked housefronts from a dragon raid out of Honter. They must have worried more about clearing the streets than anything else, because they'd left a lot of ornamental bronze and brass still attached to boards and plaster and bricks. The men who'd done the work might have hoped they were keeping the stuff away from the Chleuh. In that, they were likely to wind up disappointed.

"Not bad," Malk said. "No, not bad at all. Let's get it loose."

They did what they could with their gloved hands. After Malk lugged a double armload back to the wagon, he grabbed the toolbox that had sat behind the dashboard between his feet and Sarmel's.

"Ha! You're a clever son of a hound," Sarmel said. With anyone else, he would have said *whoreson* or *bastard*. But he and Malk might have been either of those things, or even both. They had no way of knowing. That made them careful about throwing such names at each other.

Hammers and pliers and pry bars made the job go faster. Nymphs and Sanctified men and women and branches of oak and ivy, all redone in metal, went into the wagon bed. Some were perfect, others broken, others half melted from the destruction that had rained down on them out of the sky. A little dog's panting tongue had drooped onto his bronze jaw.

"I wonder how many people died in that raid," Malk said.

"Better not to think about things like that," his brother told him.

The junkman nodded. "You aren't wrong." He couldn't help worrying at the question, though, any more than he could help worrying at a stringy bit of meat with his tongue when it got stuck between two back teeth.

"Posters these days all blame Honter and Anada for everything that's happened to Lutesse," Sarmel said.

"Of course they do. You think the Chleuh will blame themselves?" Malk said. "Times like this, I'm fornicating glad I can't read." Posters told most of their story without words, but he meant it anyway.

"Your world would be a bigger place if you'd learn," Sarmel said. "I could show you. You're plenty smart enough. You're smarter than I am—I know that—but syllables don't give me any trouble."

"Efa says the same thing. Over and over, Efa says the same thing." Malk rolled his eyes. "Maybe after the war, if there ever is an after the war, I'll think about it. Till then, the world's already too cursed big."

Sarmel looked around. Lescoff had gone back to his caretaker's shack. He probably kept a bottle or two in there, but neither Malkovici cared about that. They only cared about whether he could hear them, and he couldn't. Rats and carrion crows and rooks might, but they weren't likely to report to the Chleuh . . . or the woodsrunners.

Satisfied, Sarmel said, "As far as I'm concerned, any world with King Kangen in it is too stinking big."

"There is that," Malk said, and swung his hammer extra hard. Plaster smashed. He coughed at the dust it threw into the air. Then he picked up the bronze low relief he'd been trying to liberate.

His brother grinned at him. "Shame to melt her down for gears or whatever they'd make of her."

"Keep her if you want her. Put her in your flat." Malk made as if to hand Sarmel the patinaed image of a naked woman. "Chances are she's off the front of a joyhouse, not an apartment block."

"Fair bet, but you can chuck her in with the rest," Sarmel said. "If I brought a live lady back, I'd just have to explain what she was doing there."

"All right, give me some of that flowery stuff, too, then. I'll carry it back with her," Malk said.

He was pleased with himself when he drove the wagon back to the junk shop. He'd made a good start at filling up the hole Tebron had made in his stock. From things he'd heard and pieced together, Chleuh need for warlike supplies wouldn't shrink any time soon. The Muos kept pushing forward in the east. They showed no signs of running short of men or weapons. King Kangen probably wished he could say the same.

When Malk got to the little side street where Sarmel lived, he turned on to it. He stopped in front of his brother's block of flats. Sarmel thumped him on the shoulder and hopped down. He tapped on the door and stood there waiting till the doorwoman let him in. At least she wasn't, or didn't seem to be, one of those people who hated the Old Faith and everyone who followed it.

At the shop, Malk displayed the bronze woman and some of the other nicer pieces of bronzework and piled up the rest, and the scraps of iron and other salable junk he'd hauled back. The racket he made brought Efa downstairs. “Looks like a good haul,” she said, and yawned. She was sleepy all the time.

“I’ve done worse,” Malk said.

“Yes, I see that.” His wife was eyeing the naked woman.

“How are you feeling?” he asked quickly.

“Breakfast stayed down. So did lunch. I haven’t thrown up since day before yesterday. That’s something, anyway.”

“It is,” he agreed, and took off the heavy leather gloves so he could hug her properly. Then he sniffed. An enticing odor was wafting down from the kitchen. “What smells good?”

“Some of the salt cod I found last week, stewing with cabbage,” Efa answered. The cabbage probably came from the rations anyone in Lutesse could buy. Salt cod . . . you had to know someone and have money to spend if you were going to get your hands on salt cod. There would be wine to wash it down, too. Maybe it wasn’t the fancy kind of wine the occupants poured at their feasts, but you could drink it without being sorry you had. In this third autumn after the Chleuh marched in, that was more than good enough.

While Efa cleared up once supper was done, Malk stood and said, “I’m going to go downstairs.”

“Be careful,” she told him. He nodded.

Down to the ground floor he went, then into the cellar where he and his wife had hidden the dragonflyer from Honter. He pulled aside the rug that concealed the trap door set into the floorboards there. Then he descended into the subcellar, carefully closing and latching the trap door after him.

An air elemental was supposed to keep a breeze going in there, but it felt musty and stuffy anyhow. Malk’s shadow jumped and swooped till he set his salamander lamp on a rickety table. Hidden under a paving stone under the table was the crystal that let him listen to emanations from Dreslon, the Honterese capital.

Malk chuckled to himself as he murmured the activation charm no one in Lutesse was supposed to use. It wasn’t really funny; he might wind up in the park near that rubbish tip if a Chleuh wizard caught him at it. But he couldn't help laughing when he thought of the fools all over Quimper attuning their approved crystals to the words of Erol Paki or one of the other liars from Lutesse.

The image of a tall, lean man with a big nose and a thin mustache appeared in the illicit crystal. The fellow wore a Quimperi general's uniform and bicorn hat. "This is Char Tubis, speaking from Dreslon to unconquered Quimper," he said. "Be strong, my friends. Be brave. The darkness *shall* pass."

He talked at people, not to them. All the same, when you listened to the leader of unconquered Quimper, you took what he had to say seriously. "Another Chleuh massacre today," he went on. "Twenty-two heroes done to death in Eckmuhl Park for the crime of loving their own kingdom better than King Kangen. They will be avenged, and sooner than the Locusts think."

So he already knew about the executions in Lutesse! That alone would make the Chleuh want to froth. Char Tubis continued, "We have our lists. We will remember every name on them. Kangen's men keep falling back, running away, in Muosi. Before long, we will cross the Narrow Sea with our allies. Before long, the day of liberation will be at hand. Unconquered Quimper will rise up and be restored. By all the gods anyone follows, I promise this is so. May those gods bless you till then."

His image disappeared. It was a better farewell than *Honter must be destroyed!*, at least to Malk Malkovici. The junkman hid the crystal again. He hid the trap door after going up through it. As he climbed the cellar stairs, he sighed. One more time without getting caught.

VII

Guisa Sachry opened the dressing-room door. The stagehand who'd tapped on it licked his lips before saying, "Master Sachry, General Berhard Stulp would like to see you for a moment. That's what he told me, sir—for a moment."

"How can I say no?" Guisa replied. He knew he couldn't as well as the stagehand did. "Bring him here."

"Is everything all right?" Vonney asked as the young man hotfooted it away.

"I hope so. I myself think so," Guisa said. Stulp wouldn't come backstage in person to haul someone away. Guisa was sure of that. The Chleuh commandant would have Sep Nardand or his own military constables take care of such sordid details.

In came the general. He bowed to Guisa and his wife. "Master Sachry. Mistress Vonney. Good evening to you both," he said in his accented Quimperi. "Another enjoyable performance tonight, as usual."

"Your servant!" Guisa said, bowing a little more deeply than Stulp had. Vonney dropped the commandant a curtsy. Guisa went on, "Your visit honors us."

"Not at all." Stulp shook his head. "I came to congratulate you on something that does not involve tonight's show, though."

"Ah?" Guisa said—a polite noise that, past politeness, meant nothing.

"Yes indeed. I just wanted to let you know that *Among the Villagers* has opened on several provincial stages. People are taking to it, yes they are."

"Are they indeed?" Guisa didn't know how to respond to that. He always wanted everybody to like him and think that whatever he did was wonderful. Since he was sure he himself was wonderful, having anyone else feel differently never failed to pierce him to the root. But he'd done *Among the Villagers* under compulsion, or near enough not to matter. He wished he hadn't had to.

"They certainly are." General Stulp nodded. "The news sheets out in the smaller towns are falling all over themselves with praise."

"Isn't that nice?" Guisa seemed stuck with stock phrases.

"I think so. Count Vurk does, as well. So does the commander of the Watchmen." Stulp didn't seem to want to say Sep Nardand's name. He used such people, yes, but didn't care to acknowledge them. He went on, "That commander had his doubts about putting the play out under Gorec Sembel's name and not your own. To tell the truth, so did Vurk and I. But it has worked out better than we expected."

"I'm glad to hear you say so." Guisa Sachry told nothing but the truth there.

The way Berhard Stulp looked at him said the general understood all his reasons for being glad, too. "That will confuse the woodsrunners, yes," he said. "It has also confused the news sheets. Some of them talk about a newly discovered work of Sembel's, and marvel at how well it mirrors our modern times."

"Do they? Well, sir, I myself must say that that pleases me very much." Guisa seldom tried his hand at pastiche. *Why should I?* was his attitude. *What I write in my own style is always better than just good enough*. But hearing that people liked whatever he did could hardly fail to gratify.

"I thought you might be amused to learn that. I also thought you would be happy to know that your, ah, patrons are pleased with your work. Having brought those messages, I will leave you alone." General Stulp bowed again.

Before he could turn and go, Vonney said, "Thank you very much, sir, for telling us the news in person." Guisa beamed at her, realizing he should have said that himself.

"It is my pleasure, dear lady. And it gave me the excuse to come to the theatre tonight and enjoy the agreeable nonsense you and your husband produce. Good night." After touching the brim of his cap for a moment, Stulp left the dressing room.

Guisa eyed Vonney. "'Dear lady'?" he said. "How dear are you?" He was joking, but the joke lay over worry. If Vonney decided to do something like that, or if the Chleuh general decided he wanted her to, how could a mere Quimperi husband stop them? The occupants made the rules, and enforced them.

That made him remember how, a few centuries earlier, *occupy* had had a much earthier, more vulgar meaning than it carried these days. Any actor who did classic drama knew as much, though you mostly didn't think about it offstage. Guisa didn't care to be reminded now.

But Vonney just waved his words away and said, "Don't be sillier than you can help, dear man." She echoed his phrasing with an actress' precision. "I'm not one of the horizontally occupied."

Guisa had heard that phrase used before, always scornfully. It brought the older meaning of the word back to vivid life. "I wasn't fretting about it," he said with dignity that didn't quite ring true.

"That's nice," his wife said. "As long as I don't need to worry about you and the chorus girls, you don't need to worry about me and the occupants."

"I *said* I wasn't fretting about it, and I'm not." Guisa wanted to leave it right there. He hoped he'd be able to. For the moment, Xya

Fulgine was quietly dancing in the chorus, and dancing well. She hadn't come nagging him about little speaking parts. She hadn't threatened to blab to Vonney if she didn't get them, either.

And he hadn't gone to her and said he'd give her one of those little parts if she went down on her knees again. That he hadn't made him feel smug and virtuous. It also made him feel old; twenty-five years earlier, he knew he would have by now.

He didn't want to think about that. "Are you about ready to head for home?" he asked Vonney.

"Yes." She eyed him sidewise. "Who knows what may happen when we get there?"

"Who knows?" *I am old,* Guisa thought. Eagerness didn't fill him the way it would have half a lifetime earlier. *I'll do the best I can, that's all.*

Rain came down out of a sky the color of corroded lead. It was a cold, nasty rain, the kind that dodged umbrellas and slid under your collar to chill your back as it trickled down. Malk Malkovici hated this kind of rain. He hated it all the more because his slicker was old and patched and leaky.

He had a better slicker. He didn't wear it. Posters that were starting to peel off walls and fences called for Quimperi to donate warm clothes and waterproof clothes to the Chleuh fighting the Muos. They promised extra rations or extra coal in exchange. Malk couldn't read the posters, but the artists who'd done them made sure he didn't need to. The Chleuh didn't always force people to do what they wanted; sometimes they persuaded.

But they had the might to get what they wanted if they didn't persuade. If one of their underofficers saw him in the good slicker, he wouldn't keep it long. This one was shabby enough to keep them from wanting to steal it.

Not many people were out and about. Lutesse's once-crowded

streets had emptied since the occupation began. The bad weather kept more people from going out. Malk wished it could have kept him inside, too.

Here came Bezen the constable. His rain slicker was better than the one Malk had on, but not so good as the one in the junkman's closet. Bezen made as if to tip his cap to Malk, but didn't really take it off. "Hello, you old pussy!" he said. "What are you doing out in this ordure?"

"Trying to make a living. Trying not to wash away while I'm at it." Malk didn't return the constable's genial insult. The old woman at the kiosk could call that Chleuh underofficer such things: he didn't understand Quimperi. And Bezen could say whatever he pleased—he had what passed for the law these days behind him. Malk wasn't so lucky.

Bezen made as if to drop coins from one hand into the other, a gesture men who belonged to the Old Faith had learned not to love. "I thought you were too rich to need to worry about such things."

Malk threw back his head and laughed, even if it meant he got rain in the face. "You're a funny man, you are. You should go on stage. You'd give Guisa Sachry a run for his money."

As a matter of fact, he had a good bit of gold, and some silver, socked away here and there. Even before the war, he and Sarmel had made the business bigger than Efa's uncle ever dreamt it could grow. He'd done better since. The Chleuh weren't the world's wisest merchants. They wanted what they wanted when they wanted it, and they threw money around to make sure they got it. It wasn't as if they had to grub into their own belt pouches to buy.

Of course, the Chleuh had an advantage of their own. They could grab him whenever they wanted and send him to one of those places in the east. Malk's gold and silver might be able to save him from that. Or it might not. He didn't want to have to find out, so he tried to keep the occupants happy with him.

"Guisa Sachry's such a big ham, he needs a caramel-sugar glaze." Bezen stopped short with a sigh. "Gods! I can't remember the last time I had a ham like that—you know, as much as I wanted. How about you, Malk?"

"Has to be back before the war," Malk said, not quite truthfully. "You need to know somebody out in the country who has a farm to get food like that these days, and I don't. We're city people, Sarmel and me."

"If you are rich"—Bezen made that coin-dropping gesture again —"you can buy on the left."

That hadn't been a phrase Quimperi slang used till the occupants took over; it was borrowed from Chleuh. By now, it sounded natural in Bezen's mouth, and Malk naturally understood it, even if someone from a higher class might not have.

"If," Malk said. "You'd better be really rich, though. From all I've heard, the black market sucks silver the way a leech sucks blood." He wasn't about to admit he used it, not to a constable.

"Those dealers, they're bastards, all right." Bezen sighed again. "You can't live with them and you can't live without them. They might as well be women."

Malk laughed in surprise. Bezen didn't usually show so much wit. Officially, the authorities hated the black market. Unofficially, everyone who could afford to bought from it. Unless you did have one of those farmer friends, getting by on ordinary rations meant getting skinny.

The constable gestured for Malk to go on. "You don't have to drown on account of me. I was just passing the time." He made as if to yawn. Walking a beat on a miserable day when nothing looked like happening had to be dull.

When Malk flicked the reins, the horses got going with less fuss than they usually made. They might have hoped he would take them back to the stable or to some other dry place. They were doomed to disappointment. He drove over to the Boulevard of Dreams, then down it toward the Obelisk.

No military band now. No marching troop of Quimperi Popular Party volunteers, heading toward their Leader . . . and then toward whatever fate the sausage-grinder war against the Muos held for them.

No volunteers' kin and friends and sweethearts on the sidewalks, either, to cheer them as they marched toward that fate. No Popular Party members on the sidewalk to spot Malk as someone who clung to the Old Faith and to try to make him sorry for it. Hardly anyone one the sidewalks at all, in fact. The few people who had to go out and about huddled under umbrellas or broad-brimmed rain hats and ignored the junkman's wagon.

He pulled off the boulevard and made his way along smaller side streets to Evets' rag and secondhand-clothes shop. He'd heard a few things here and there the ragman could pass on to the woodsrunners. The more people whose good sides he stayed on, the longer he was likely to live.

Rain poured down harder than ever. When he stopped in front of Evets' place and set the brake, the horses glowered in mute animal indignation. That was their hard luck. He got down from the driving seat and squelched to the door. When he opened it to go inside, the bell rang.

"Hello, you old twat," the ragman said from behind the counter. Three or four customers, a bit younger and more prosperous looking than most who came to Evets' place, pawed through racks of this and stacks of that after something they might want.

"Hello, yourself." Malk furled his umbrella and let water drip down from the tinned brass ferrule. As the worn carpet started soaking it up, he asked the question he asked every time he came in: "And how are things? Besides wet, I mean?"

"Couldn't be better," Evets said cheerfully. "How's by you?"

The ragman sounded so happy and natural, Malk needed a heartbeat to remember that his good humor was a warning. One of the shoppers glanced at him with what looked like a bit more than casual curiosity. He realized he was liable to be playing for his life. "I'm all right," he answered. "Do you have anything worth wearing in the raincoat line? This thing I've got on lets in more water than it keeps out."

"You should have showed up earlier. I sold a couple of pretty good coats this morning, but there's only trash on the shelves now. That's what happens when it rains," Evets said.

"If I could have got here sooner, I would have. What can you do, though?" Malk spread his hands in well-acted disgust. "I'd sooner give you money, but if you can't help me I'll go see what sour Rospor's flogging." The other secondhand-clothes dealer was notorious for his bad temper.

"He'll cheat you," Evets said as the junkman turned toward the door.

Malk laughed. "And you won't?" The bell jangled again when he pulled the door open. He closed it on Evets' curses.

His right hand stayed close to his knife as he used the other to let down the brake lever. How curious had that one customer really been? Curious enough to come out into the rain to ask him some questions? If the man—the Watchman?—did, Malk intended to let the air out of him if he could. One stretch in the hands of Sep Nardand's toughs had convinced him he didn't want another, especially if it had anything to do with the woodsrunners' quiet struggle against the Chleuh.

He gave the reins a flick. "Come on, lazy boys. Get going," he told the horses. For a wonder, they listened to him. The wagon clattered along the street. No one came out of Evets' shop. Maybe it was something as simple as even the Watchmen not caring to get soaked.

Whatever it was, Malk thanked his gods he'd got away. He asked them to help Evets, too, even if the ragman didn't follow them. They might listen. They might, but Malk feared they wouldn't.

Nights were long now. Dragons flying from Honter could visit horror on cities in Chlé and get away without being speared by sunbeams.

The news sheets in Lutesse were full of stories about Honterese and Anadan savagery, and about all the dragons and air pirates the Chleuh had been able to slay in spite of searching by sorcery instead of sight.

Guisa Sachry read the stories with mixed feelings. Blows that fell on Kangen's kingdom meant the Chleuh were less likely to win the war, especially since the Muos still seemed to be moving forward in the east. Then again, blows that fell on Kangen's kingdom didn't fall on Guisa's own home town.

His wife took a somewhat different view of things. "Why do the sheets keep calling the Hontermen pirates?" she asked over breakfast. "The Chleuh did the same thing to Dreslon when they had the chance. They still do every now and then, don't they?"

"I myself haven't been up to the edge of the Narrow Sea to check, but I think they do," Guisa said. "But when our side does it to the enemy, the dragonflyers are heroes. When the enemy does it to us, their men can only be pirates."

She looked at him. "Finish your coffee," she said. "You're grouchier than usual without it."

He did finish. He poured himself another cup, too. He'd managed to get some of the genuine beans for the first time in months. While they lasted, he'd enjoy them. Then he'd go back to the roasted chicory and burnt barley people without connections had endured since the Chleuh marched into Lutesse.

"Guisa . . ." Vonney said, and waited.

"Yes?" He tried not to sound anxious. Had she found out about Xya? If she had, how furious would she be? He didn't want a row right this minute.

She hadn't. But what she did ask next chilled him all the same: "What do we do if the Chleuh lose the war? It looks like they're going to, doesn't it?"

He looked around before answering. He didn't *think* he was important enough in the grand scheme of things for the Chleuh to waste magic and some wizard's time spying on him, but he wasn't sure. "One way or the other, everything will work out all right," he replied at last.

"How can you say that?" Vonney sounded angry. "If they lose, what's going to happen to people who've liked them too much? What's going to happen to people like us?"

It wasn't as if Guisa hadn't worried about that question himself. He had, especially after even the Chleuh admitted things weren't going so well as they wished. "Everything will work out all right," he repeated, trying to convince himself along with Vonney. "Actors aren't big enough for anyone to stay angry at us."

She thought that over, then slowly nodded. "You may be right," she said. "I hope you are."

"Things may not turn out the way you worry about, either." Unlike his wife, Guisa talked around the idea that Chlé might lose the war. If King Kangen's men were beaten, he would have picked the wrong side almost three and a half years ago now. If he had, what could it mean? That he wasn't as smart as he thought he was, an idea he didn't want to face.

"They may not, but we should be ready in case they do," Vonney said. "Do you know anybody who has connections with the wood-srunners?"

"How would I know anyone like that? I—" Guisa broke off, surprised at himself. When he spoke again, it was in an altogether different tone of voice: "You know, I do! That Nea Ennogue, the fellow I ate with not long ago. He doesn't care at all for the way things are now."

"You should find some way to do him a favor, or pass him some news that those people won't have heard anywhere else," Vonney said.

"If he trusts me enough to let me give him a hand, or believes anything I tell him. He's as pigheaded as they come, Ennogue is," Guisa said.

"Send him food," Vonney said. "He may think it's a bribe, but he won't turn it down. Hardly anybody turns food down these days."

"I'll do it." Guisa blew her a kiss. Brasi Robillach had said he gave Ennogue food, too, or Guisa thought he had. Odd how friendships persisted even when politics divided people. Sometimes they did, anyhow. Guisa asked Vonney, "Do you know anyone with connections like that?"

"I'll ask the girls in the chorus. They've been around the block a time or three. One of them will know." Vonney held up a hand before Guisa could say anything. "You don't need to worry—I'll be careful. I know how to play those games."

"I'm sure you do, dear," When Guisa was chasing her, he'd thought she was as innocent as a lamb. It occurred to him, rather later than it should have, that she might have been chasing him, too.

She went on, "That Xya Fulgine you found, for instance, a few of the things she's said make me think she knows everybody in town . . . that way or some other way."

"I wouldn't be surprised," Guisa said, and left it right there. He didn't want Vonney talking with Xya, maybe even getting friendly with her. But if he said he didn't, Vonney would wonder why. Sometimes you had to let things work out instead of trying to force them.

He hoped this was one of those times.

"Send something good to this person you know," Vonney said.

"I will." Guisa still shopped at stores that stayed full of nice things, shops that catered to Chleuh officers . . . and to people like him. He didn't worry about ration books. Nea Ennogue, poor demon, wouldn't be so lucky.

Malk Malkovici and his brother clinked glasses in a little tavern a couple of blocks from the junk shop. Malk sipped his brandy. It was nasty, but he liked getting out once in a while even if he had better at home. He'd been coming here for years. The barman and the regulars took Sarmel and him for granted. He didn't worry about getting thrown out, the way a follower of the Old Faith would have at most taverns in Lutesse.

Sarmel set down his glass and eyed it with not so faint distaste. “Dragon piss,” he remarked.

“Now that you mention it, yes,” Malk said. They both spoke in low voices. If they offended Ullo, the man behind the bar, he wouldn’t take them for granted any more. After a moment, Malk went on, “We could ask him to get out the bottle that’s under the bar, not what he shows.”

“Never mind. He’d charge us three times as much for that. This stuff’ll take the edge off my day.” Sarmel sipped again. He made a face. “And the enamel off my teeth.”

A couple of burly coal heavers arm-wrestled at a nearby table. Skinnier men played backgammon or draughts. The tavern smelled of spirits and sweat, of pipe and cigar smoke, and fried foods.

Sarmel charged his own pipe and lit it with a twig fired by the little lamp salamander on the table. After blowing out smoke, he asked, “No trouble?”

“Not yet,” Malk answered. Whoever those people in Evets’ shop were, they hadn’t asked him who he was or come out to get a look at his wagon. And Evets hadn’t blabbed, no matter what they’d done to him. Malk didn’t think he had, anyway.

“Lucky,” Sarmel said.

“We have been,” Malk agreed. “If we weren’t lucky . . .” He didn’t go on. Sarmel nodded. He’d know what Malk meant. Not many people like them were left in Lutesse. The ones who were, or the ones who were that the Malkovicis knew of, had also found ways to make themselves useful to the occupants. Maybe others who clove to the Old Faith hid here and there. Malk didn’t know. He hadn’t gone out of his way to find out.

He started to say something more. Before he could, bells began to ring all over the city. “A plague!” Sarmel exclaimed. “I thought the Hontermen were leaving us alone while they went after Chlé.”

“Maybe they can do both at once,” Malk said. He rather hoped they could; that would mean their power, and the Anadans', was growing. He wanted the Chleuh to lose, but he didn't want to die to help them do it.

"Come on to the cellar," Ullo said. "We'll ride it out down below." The barman sent Malk and Sarmel an apologetic look. He let them into his tavern, which was risky in itself. Letting them shelter under the place violated orders from the General and from the Chleuh. If anyone down there with them reported the breach, Ullo could land in more trouble than he wanted.

With almost identical flicks of the wrist, Malk and Sarmel knocked back their brandies. They stood together, too. "Stay safe, everyone," Malk said. He was mostly talking to people's backs; the drinkers were heading for the stairs in the back corner of the place. Malk and his brother walked out the door.

Braziers and bodies packed close together had kept the tavern tolerably warm. Out on the street, the night chill slapped Malk in the face. A hundred thousand stars seemed to burn in the sky. He'd never seen so many in peacetime; city lights fought and dimmed them. No lights now. Clouds would have held in some heat and cloaked Lutesse from dragons unless sorcery guided their way.

Focused beams from big salamanders traversed across the sky, seeking to spear raiders. Men painted dragons' bellies black, to help foil searchlights. It did help, too, but not always enough.

"I'm going back to my place," Sarmel said.

Malk shook his head. "Don't do that. They won't let you use the cellar there, either. Come on to the shop with me. I hope Efa's already down below." Sarmel had spoken Quimperi. Malk's reply was in the Nistrian they'd used as boys. It seemed to come out for important things.

"All right," Sarmel said, also in their birth speech. Explosions punctuated the night as they hurried along the street.

When they got to the junk shop, Malk fumbled with his keys. There wasn't enough light to make using them easy. Then the door opened from inside. “Oh, good. It’s both of you,” Efa said. She spoke Nistrian, too.

“You should already be under the floor,” Malk said.

“Hush. Just hush,” she told him. “Come on.” She barred the door behind her husband and brother-in-law. Down into the cellar they went. If the building fell in on the doorway . . . Malk made himself not think about that. He didn’t like going down into the cellar because of the risk there, But tonight it might be smaller than the risk of staying above ground.

Efa went down first, Malk after her, and Sarmel last of all. Malk’s brother closed the cellar door. Malk fed a salamander with scraps of dried meat. The salamander lit up as the food hit its stomach. It didn’t give much light, but a little was plenty.

Booms and crashes outside said the attack from the air went on. Malk waved at the disreputable couch that had held the dragonflyer from across the Narrow Sea. (He hoped again that the Watchmen didn’t know enough to want to do anything particularly horrible to Evets.) “Sit down,” he told Efa. “Lie down if you want to. Sarmel and I can stretch out on the floor.”

“That’s right,” Sarmel said, but with no great enthusiasm.

“We can all sit down,” Efa said. “I’m not going to fall asleep now. I don’t need to sleep all the time, the way I did right after I first caught. And I’m not bulging the way I will be before long.” She was right about that. You couldn’t tell yet that she was expecting when she had clothes on, not if they were loose. Even when she took them off, the bump was still small.

“But—” Malk worried whether Efa wanted him to or not. As a first-time upcoming father, he didn’t see that he had any choice.

“No buts.” Efa sat at one end of the sofa, Malk in the middle, and Sarmel at the other end. *A good thing we all get along*, Malk thought: they weren’t squeezed so tightly as salted smelts in a tin, but also weren’t far from it.

Something came down that made everything shake, as if in an earthquake. Malk remembered earthquakes from his days in the orphanage. He hadn't been through one since he came to Lutesse; the Quimperi were on better terms with their earth elementals than the Nistrians had been.

"That was fun," Sarmel said from his left. From his right, his wife glared at his brother. Stuck in the middle, Malk kept quiet. He tried not to think about what would have happened if whatever that was had burst on his roof. He had as much luck as he would have if someone had told him not to think about a blue monkey.

More booms, more thuds, more shaking. The Anadans and Hontermen were hitting hard tonight. The assault from the sky went on and on. Malk knew time seemed stretched while such things happened, but tonight there seemed to be a lot of it to stretch.

Malk didn't hear any fire crews clanging along the nearby streets. He hoped that meant there weren't any, not that he was behind and beneath too many walls and doors for those sounds to reach his ears.

Efa said, "By the gods, won't it ever stop? What will be left of us by the time the baby comes?"

That struck Malk as much too good a question. He put his arm around his wife and pulled her close. It wouldn't help much, but it might help a little. He didn't tell Efa he often asked himself the same thing even when dragons weren't doing their best to flatten Lutesse. Telling her that, he understood only too well, wouldn't help at all.

The doorwoman thrust three envelopes at Guisa Sachry. "Today's post, sir," she said.

"Thanks, Marsa." As usual, he tipped her. You had to tip such people. They'd find ways to hurt you if you didn't. Marsa got her mean little room and a pittance from the landlord. For anything above the pittance, she depended on the generosity of the people who lived in the apartment block. If they weren't generous enough to suit her, she made them pay in ways that had nothing to do with bronze and silver.

"You're welcome, sir," she answered in tones that said he'd satisfied her. "Isn't it horrible, what the air pirates done to us last night? You can still smell the stink from all the fires they started."

"Terrible, yes." Guisa nodded. He'd had his performance interrupted, which struck him as more terrible yet. He also hadn't enjoyed sharing a cellar with Count Vurk, General Stulp, and several of the leading Quimperi who went along with them.

The Chleuh had done their best to seem wryly amused about what the Anadans and Hontermen were doing to the city they held. So had Odrio Cazh, which impressed Guisa: something to the Leader of the Popular Front after all. Both Brasi Robillach and Erol Paki had a harder time hiding their fear. And the smoke then, after they all came out, had been thick enough to slice, not just to notice.

"You take care of yourself, sir. And you, too, lady," Marsa added for Vonney's benefit. Guisa's wife bobbed her head in reply. The doorwoman opened up for them, then ducked back into her room.

"What have we got?" Vonney asked as they walked to the stairway.

"This looks like a bill from your capmaker. This one's from the cobbler. And this last one . . . Oh! It's from Nea Ennogue." Guisa paused under a lamp to open the third envelope.

"Tell me what he says," Vonney urged.

Guisa opened the envelope. Ennogue's script was as precise as the man himself, every syllable perfect and distinct. *My dear Master Sachry*, he wrote, *I set pen to paper to thank you for your generosity, which, given our differences, is as unexpected as it is welcome. Rest assured that I will remember it. If I ever have the chance to reciprocate, you may also rest assured that I shall. I have the honor to remain, sir, your most grateful servant.* His signature differed not a bit from the rest of the note.

"Good," Vonney said. "That's very good. He understands he owes you."

"Gratitude melts faster than fat in a hot pan. You know that as well as I do," Guisa replied. "A hamper of food isn't so much. Not enough to count on, even if . . . if we ever need to count on things like that." He spoke carefully; Marsa might have pressed her ear to the inside of her door to listen to him.

"Send him another one, then," Vonney said, "and another after that. We can afford it, and if it gets him hooked . . ." She also had the sense not to talk too much there in the lobby.

"Would he do as much for me?" Guisa wondered. Thinking aloud, he answered his own question: "He might. He's that sort."

"So are you," Vonney said.

"Let's go upstairs," Guisa said. He didn't contradict his wife; he liked praise no less than any other man, and more than quite a few. But he knew he was helping Nea Ennogue in the hope of getting something out of him later, not from the goodness of his heart. The teacher and writer might lend him a hand for no better reason than that he thought it the right thing to do.

Guisa admired that kind of goodness without understanding it. Had he been sure the Chleuh were going to walk over the world, he would happily have let Nea Ennogue starve. He wished he were sure of that, the way he had been when the war was new. He wished he were sure of anything these days.

He puffed a little as he came out of the stairwell. He was sure of one thing: that he wasn't so young as he had been once upon a time. When they got back into the flat, Vonney kissed him and said, "You were very smart to turn him into a friend like that."

"I myself think so, too." Guisa still remembered she'd wanted him to send the hamper. If she praised him for doing it a few more times, though, he might start to forget.

She kissed him again, then looked at him with her head cocked to one side. She couldn't have been much plainer if she'd started a bonfire on the floor. "Are you in the mood for . . . ?" she asked.

He was in the mood for sleep. But he answered, "Let's see what happens." He knew the answer to *Can an old man have a son with a young wife?* It was *Yes, if he has a young, handsome neighbor.*

Not much happened, not for him. A man had other ways than

that one to please a woman, though. Guisa used them, and thought he got Vonney where she wanted to go. The happier she was with him, the less likely she'd be to look for fun anywhere else. Xya never once crossed his mind. Men, after all, were entitled to do that kind of thing now and again. They thought so, anyhow.

She put a dark shade over the salamander lamp. "Good night," she said.

"Good night, dear," Guisa answered. Sometimes really sleeping with someone seemed as intimate as the thing that went by that name. It did till you fell asleep, anyhow, which Guisa soon did.

VIII

Snow muted the rattle and clatter of the iron tires on Malk Malkovici's junk wagon. The snow was still falling, too. He wore two ratty wool sweaters under his ratty coat and kept his heavy leather gloves on to warm his hands. Despite all that, he shivered. The wool scarf wrapped around his head didn't do enough to protect his ears, either.

That swirling snow also meant he couldn't see very far. What he could see was beautiful. The snow covered Lutesse's filth and grime, which fewer and fewer people bothered to clean these days. And it softened every harsh angle. It was as if the gods were painting a scrawny, raddled crone as the lovely young thing she once had been —the lovely young thing she still imagined herself to be.

Malk shook his head. He wasn't in the habit of thinking thoughts like that. Well, he wasn't in the habit of going out in the middle of a snowstorm, either. But Colonel Tebron craved scrap metal. The more Malk could get him, the less likely the Chleuh quartermaster was to send him east.

Malk had the streets almost to himself. Too much snow lay on the ground to let scooters make much headway. A few people trudged through the growing drifts on the sidewalks. They looked as miserable as he felt.

He was surprised when a constable stepped out into the middle of the Boulevard of Dreams and held up an imperious (and gloved) hand to halt him. Then a column of Chleuh wagons rolled across the boulevard on a smaller street. The occupants bowed their heads against the weather, just as Malk did. Their greatcoats were in hardly better shape than his.

They could have been freezing somewhere far from here, though, freezing while they fought the Muos. They would have liked that even less than this. No doubt most of them knew it, too.

Some wagons had tarpaulins tied down to protect whatever they carried. Others didn't bother to hide the sheaves of crossbow and death-spitter quarrels in their beds. They crossed the Boulevard of Dreams from south to north. Malk counted twenty-two of them. After the last one passed, the constable waved him forward. He sketched a salute as he got the horses moving. You had to show them you were grateful or they'd make you suffer.

Now he knew something he hadn't known before, something the woodsrunners would want to hear. Arms went east out of Lutesse all the time, bound for the war against the Muos. Arms heading north? That was out of the ordinary.

He'd intended to go north himself, to the rubbish tip at the edge of Lutesse. Now he changed his mind. The wagon kept heading west, toward the Obelisk. After a while, he turned left. This was the corner where those followers of the Quimperi Popular Party had recognized him as a man who belonged to the Old Faith. He'd finished the turn before he was sure: the snow's fault again.

The horses snorted softly and looked at each other. They knew this corner, too—he'd whipped them here. They stayed scared and suspicious till the wagon turned once more.

Malk didn't stop in front of Evets' shop. The door was boarded up, as if the place were quarantined for disease. A sign tacked to the boards said whatever it said. Malk didn't need to know how to read to understand that the ragman had gone out of business, likely for good.

He quietly swore in Nistrian. When he did, his breath puffed out as if he were smoking his pipe. Now he needed to find a new connection to the woodsrunners. He knew he'd be setting his life on the line when he did, too. How could he be sure the fellow he thought he could trust really passed news on to the people who needed it, not to the Watchmen or the Chleuh?

He couldn't be sure. You never could be sure when you played those games. All you could do was play as well as you knew how. Sooner or later, you *would* make a mistake.

He swore again. A mistake now would ruin everything forever, not just for him but for Efa and the baby—the baby they'd given up hoping for. He couldn't do that.

But he couldn't duck out of the game, either. He needed to stay on good terms with the woodsrunners. He didn't think King Kangen's men could win. He wasn't sure, but he didn't think so. There'd be a reckoning if they lost. He had to have markers he could call in.

Sarmel might be able to find someone he could talk to. Malk knew he himself was the Malkovici people noticed. They'd pay attention to what he did. His little brother—who was bigger than he was these days—could go almost anywhere without having anyone pay attention to him.

On rolled the wagon, slowly. The horses didn't like picking their way through snow. Did their feet get cold in spite of their horseshoes? Malk shrugged, which made his sweaters and greatcoat shift oddly. He couldn't very well ask them.

The wagon rolled past a wall on which posters sprouted like toadstools. Anyone with something to say and a bucket of paste had used it. Here was the General, looking grandfatherly. Here were the Chleuh, protecting Quimper from the Muos. And (Malk's mouth tightened) here were the Chleuh again, protecting Quimper from people who followed the Old Faith. The woodsrunners had stuck up posters, too. Here was King Kangen kneeling, his head on a block. Malk wished he knew the people who'd run up those posters. They'd want to hear some things from him.

Those posters wouldn't last long. The Chleuh or some Quimperi flunkies would scrape them off the bricks or paper over them as soon as they realized the subversive things were there.

In the meantime . . . In the meantime, Malk smiled and leaned back a little on the driving seat. He liked imagining King Kangen that way.

"Here you are, my dear." Guisa Sachry handed the cloakroom girl his otterskin coat and his wife's fox jacket. "Cold outside." He slid some silver across the counter, too.

"Thank you, sir. I'll take good care of them." The girl made the money vanish and gave him two brass claim coins. She added, "I really like watching you perform, sir."

"Now it's my turn to thank you." Guisa smiled his professional smile.

"Attractive little thing," Vonney remarked as they went on in to the reception.

"Do you think so?" Guisa did, and didn't particularly want his wife to notice he did. She poked him in the ribs with an elbow, so he wasn't performing well enough to fool her.

Even a prosperous Quimperi like him had trouble getting hold of enough coal and wood to stay warm through what people were calling the hardest winter in twenty years. The Chleuh didn't worry about such things. In Quimper, they grabbed what they needed. The reception hall was crowded, but that wasn't why sweat sprang out on Guisa's forehead. Braziers, fireplaces . . . They all glowed a fiery red.

General Stulp was talking with several other Chleuh officers. Guisa noticed because King Kangen's commander in Quimper usually socialized with the people whose kingdom he occupied. Stulp looked worried, though Guisa understood no more than a handful of words in his language.

"I'm going to get something to drink," Vonney said.

"What a wonderful idea!" Guisa exclaimed. He patted his stomach. "Something to eat, too."

Smoked salmon was part of the spread General Stulp had laid on. Erol Paki had already made a considerable dent in it. He smiled at Guisa. "Get it while you can—before I eat it all up! For I tell you, this lovely fish must be destroyed!"

Guisa laughed hard. The joke was funny, but not that funny. The crystal commentator had caught him by surprise when he mocked his own signature signoff line. Guisa hadn't thought he had that in him.

Paki nodded toward Stulp and his underlings. "Either they're all going to get sent east by this time tomorrow, or they're figuring out how to keep the Anadans and the Hontermen from getting a lodgement up in Carentan."

"I didn't suppose you thought the islanders and their allies could do any such thing," Guisa said.

"I don't suppose they can, because the Chleuh will make sure they cursed well can't," Paki replied. "They'll be sorry if they try."

Guisa reminded himself to send Nea Ennogue another hamper--not one with smoked salmon in it, perhaps, but full of fine food all the same. He wondered whether Erol Paki was making the same kind of arrangements with the people who hadn't accommodated themselves to the Chleuh. He knew he'd go on wondering. It wasn't the kind of question one could safely ask, after all.

He didn't really think Paki would do such a thing, anyhow. The little commentator seemed to wish he were a Chleuh himself. He might worry for the occupants' sake, but he didn't truly believe they could fail. Guisa glanced over at Stulp and tried to imagine how the Chleuh general would respond if Paki told *him* he wanted to be a

Chleuh. His best guess was that Stulp would guffaw himself into an apoplexy.

"You will excuse me," Paki murmured, and made his way towards one of the pretty girls who graced these affairs. Like most of them, she was a good deal taller than he was. He didn't let that stop him. If he had, he wouldn't have had many women to chase.

No more than a minute after Guisa thought of General Stulp, the Chleuh commandant caught his eye and gestured that he should come over. The peremptory wave said Stulp expected no less obedience from him than from one of King Kangen's common soldiers. And Stulp got the obedience he expected. Guisa picked his way through the crowd and presented himself before the general.

He didn't come to attention, as a common soldier would have done, but that was the only thing lacking. "Your Excellency, I want to thank you for inviting my wife and me to this splendid gathering," he said. "How many I serve you?"

"Relax, Master Sachry, relax," Stulp said, as if telling him he might stand at ease. "I just wanted to sing your praises before these officers here. They've come from Chlé to help me consider the situation in Quimper and what's liable to happen when the weather warms up again . . . if it ever does."

"If it ever does, yes." Guisa laughed; any joke the commandant made was witty because he made it. Remembering what he'd been talking about with Erol Paki, the actor asked, "Are you, ah, concerned about an invasion, sir?"

"Of course I am. I would not be doing my duty if I weren't concerned," General Stulp said. The officers with him nodded, nearly in unison. "And one of the things concerning me is Quimper's continued loyalty to King Kangen's authority. Some folk in this kingdom imagine the Hontermen and the Anadans will treat them as something better than tools if they seize a foothold in the north."

"Do they?" Guisa responded, acting on the principle that the less said, the better.

"As a matter of fact, they do." Stulp's voice was as dry as the driest white wine from the far south. "And that is why I wish to sing your praises, Master Sachry. *Among the Villagers* is doing what everyone hoped it would: it is making people laugh at the woodsrunners, and at the enemies the woodsrunners fight for. We need that."

One of the visiting officers spoke to Stulp in Chleuh. The commandant answered in the same language. The other man switched to very bad Quimperi to ask Guisa, "This play, you her write?"

"Yes, sir." Nothing would have made Guisa smile. If the officer's Quimperi was bad, his own Chleuh did not exist.

"Good is. In north help," the officer said.

"Colonel Hrotits is right," Stulp said smoothly. "The closer you get to the Narrow Sea, the more little companies are putting on *Among the Villagers*. We want every villager, every little farmer up there, to see the play and learn its lessons. And you have dipped them in the honey of laughter, to help them go down more smoothly. It is a fine piece of work."

"Real excellently is," Colonel Hrotits agreed. He had to follow more Quimperi than he spoke.

Guisa bowed first to Stulp and then to Hrotits. "I myself thank you both for your kindness, your Excellencies."

"We should thank you. If trouble comes this spring or summer, a quiet countryside will help us deal with it," Stulp said. "Your play helps give us that." Colonel Hrotits nodded. He had a scar over one eye and, Guisa noticed, only three and a half fingers on his left hand.

"Writing in a style not my own was . . . interesting," Guisa said.

The commandant smiled a knowing smile. "And it let you stay discreet," he observed. "Well, only a fool doesn't do what he can to protect himself come what may. As long as you work with me, I don't mind such safekeeping."

Chleuh might not be subtle, not by Quimperi standards, but one thought them stupid at one's peril. "You are gracious, your Excellency," Guisa said.

"Perhaps I am, but here I'm ungraciously keeping you from food and drink. Go on, enjoy yourself," General Stulp said.

Bowing once more, Guisa got away. He headed for the bar; he needed numbing. By the time Vonney made her way to him, he'd gulped a brandy and got a second one. "What was that all about?" she asked, a mild-seeming way of wondering whether everything was all right.

"They admire my dramaturgy. I am a success in the provinces as well as here in the capital," Guisa said.

His wife beamed at him. "I should hope you are! People know your name and your work all over Quimper. Have you heard anything more from that fellow who was interested in translating some plays into Chleuh?"

"No, worse luck," Guisa answered—truthfully, since the fellow in question was another fiction of his. He glanced toward Stulp and the officers from Chlé. They looked serious, even worried. Guisa wondered how he might go about getting his work rendered into Honterese if that turned out to be a better idea.

When Colonel Tebron walked into the junk shop, Malk Malkovici doffed his cap and bent almost double. "I am your servant, sir," he said, looking down at the floor.

"I've told you not to bother with that silly nonsense when it's just the two of us." The Chleuh quartermaster officer sounded peevish, almost angry.

"Sir, it isn't nonsense with you," Malk said, though he did straighten and put his cap back on. "I am in your debt."

"Mine and some other people's, evidently," Tebron said. "You were seen driving your decrepit old wagon past a place the authorities have closed down. Closed down for good reason, by all the signs."

Ice that had nothing to do with the weather walked up Malk's back. He hoped he didn't show it, though Tebron was cannier than he cared to recall. Doing his best to seem natural and unconcerned, he said, "And how many places do the authorities close down every day?"

"Not as many as they should, I'm sure," Tebron replied, which, from the Chleuh point of view, was bound to be true. "But the number isn't small."

"Well, there you are," Malk said. "How can anyone blame me for going past some place I didn't even know was there?"

"You belong to the Old Faith. Anyone can blame you for anything any time, and you know it. You belong to the Old Faith, you still go out and about, and by everything I know you have more silver stashed somewhere than you know what to do with. Of course anyone can blame you."

"I do not have nearly so much silver stashed as you think," Malk said with dignity. He wasn't even lying, not technically. He put as much of what he made as he could into gold. Gold was much less bulky.

"You had enough to give to the Watchmen you sent to me when you got in trouble the last time," the Chleuh said. "I don't think I can pull that trick twice, by the way. Best you remember it. Sep Nardand was not happy."

"I am in your debt again for telling me, and I'll remember," Malk said. If Nardand's bully boys grabbed him again, they'd stick him someplace where he couldn't get out, or else they'd just knock him over the head.

"I understand some of the things you feel you have to do," Colonel Tebron said. "You've made yourself useful enough to me that I don't mind looking the other way. I don't mind too much, I should say. Some of my countrymen might prove less forgiving. There still are people who think we can win this war."

"I think I would be wise to remember I never heard that from you, sir," Malk said. If King Kangen's men seized him, he was even more surely doomed than if the Watchmen did, but he could talk Tebron down with him.

The quartermaster waved his words away. "If it comes to that, everything will be falling in flame and fire anyhow. Who worries about the details of disaster?"

"Anybody who's caught in them," Malk answered at once. "How else can you try to get away?"

"If the disaster is big enough, none of that will matter," Tebron said. "If the disaster is big enough, it will engulf you no matter what you do. If the disaster is big enough, they'll put me in charge of a regiment of horse—of what's left of a regiment of horse, I mean—and command me to stop all the Muos in the world from rolling into Chlé."

Intrigued and horrified at the same time, Malk asked, "Have you ever led cavalry, sir?"

"Not even once." Tebron sounded absurdly cheerful. "I've just worried about whether the riders have enough shields and helmets and lances and arrows. But I know about how to do it from books, and I know how to give orders and sound like I mean it. Some general will have to choose between me and an officer cadet who doesn't even shave yet. And he'll pick me, because he'll see I've been an officer for a long time. If I have a good underofficer to fill me in on what I don't know, he'll think I won't do anything *too* stupid, where the puppy may charge out and get everybody killed fast. And you know what else? Chances are that general will be right."

"You are going to be a hero?"

"Hero?" Colonel Tebron barked laughter as he shook his head. "You're a clever fellow, Malk. Don't sound like a fool, all right? Remember, this is a disaster. I'll do what I can do. I'll get my men slaughtered a few at a time instead of all at once. I'll slow down the Muos as much as I can for as long as I can. And, sooner or later, they'll kill me, too."

"Maybe you should surrender, then. Maybe your kingdom should." Malk was a relentlessly practical man. His whole life had pressed him into that mold. He didn't suppose anything would change his shape now.

"King Kangen won't do that. Chlé won't. If we would, Honter and Anada might let us, but the Muos never would. You don't know what the war there is like. Thank your strange gods you don't. Some of the things we've done there . . . The Muos want revenge. If they get it, our gods will show how much they hate Chlé."

Malk looked at him. "Have you done worse there than you have to folk here who believe like me?"

"Worse? I don't know. Just as bad, anyhow. And you know what a big realm Muosi is. There are a lot more Muos than men who follow the Old Faith. Imagine that kind of thing spread across as much of their kingdom as we could take."

"Gods help you!" Malk couldn't help adding, "If they will."

The Chleuh colonel didn't get angry. He just gave back a somber nod. "Yes. If they will."

Guisa Sachry had an acting award he'd got twenty years—or two wives—earlier. He'd been over the moon when he won the glass statuette. He always thought he performed wonderfully. Other people agreeing with him only made him happier. For a long time after he got it, he'd stared at it for half an hour at a stretch day after day.

Everything palled after a while, though. These days, the statuette sat on an end table, half forgotten and gathering dust. He'd give it a remembering smile once in a while, but more often than not he didn't even notice it.

He got a closer look at it than he expected when he walked into the flat one chilly afternoon. It flew past his head, missing his left ear by the thickness of a fingernail, and smashed against the wall behind him. A sharp ricocheting shard bit him in the back of the neck.

"You *bastard*!" Vonney screeched in a fury he'd never been able to pull out of her as a director. "You stupid, stinking, fornicating *bastard*!" She ran forward after the statuette and swung at him.

He threw up a hand to block the blow, but underestimated the speed such animal rage gave her. A roundhouse slap rocked his head back. He saw stars and tasted blood.

Vonney tried to smack him again. Now his blood was up, too, though. He caught her wrist and hung on hard. "Have you lost all of your mind?" he demanded.

She tried to spit in his face. That went wider than the award statuette had. Then she tried to knee him in the balls. He twisted aside just in time to take the blow on the hip. It still hurt, but not so much as it would have.

"You rancid cockhound!" she shouted, loud enough so Guisa hoped nobody who lived on their floor was home. "That trull, that mattressback, that fleabitten, Chleuh-pawed slut of a *dancer*, that Xya Fulgine! No wonder you hired her! No wonder at all!"

He'd known this might happen. He hadn't cared, not when Xya took him out of his trousers and lowered her mouth to him. He'd figured he could sweet-talk his way out of any real trouble. Which only went to show that a man didn't always think straight when a woman was about to do that for him.

"Now dear, now sweets," he said, still holding tight to his wife's wrist. "It was just one of those things."

"It was *your* thing!" Vonney said, still louder than he wished she would have. "What did you get from her that you couldn't get from me? If you expect me to put up with that manure, you'd better do some new expecting." She stomped on his foot.

"Ow! Stop that, curse it!" He jerked his head back, because she tried to bite his nose.

"I will not! I didn't marry you to get run around on. If you don't like me in bed, you shouldn't have given me a ring."

"I like you fine. You know that." Guisa meant it. Vonney made him as happy as any one woman was ever likely to. Sometimes, though, what he wanted wasn't any one woman but another woman.

"Then why did you have her slobber on your prong?"

Vonney knew, all right. Guisa wondered how. Asking her didn't seem to be the smartest idea he'd ever had. Instead, he repeated, "It was just one of those things." After a moment, he added, "If I let you go, will you hold off on trying to murder me?"

"Maybe," Vonney said, but she relaxed a little, so he did turn her loose. To his relief, she stepped back. Her glare, though, her glare stayed hot as dragonfire. "The whole company's been laughing at me behind my back for gods only know how long. Since that poxy twat started dancing with us, probably."

That went some way toward telling Guisa how Vonney'd found out. He'd thought Xya wasn't the kind to blab. He'd been wrong, though. He'd been wrong about women before, more often than he cared to remember. He said, "As you wish, my dear. I myself shall let her go."

"Oh, no, you won't," Vonney answered. He stared at her in surprise. She explained: "I already did it. She didn't even seem upset. She just smiled and sashayed out the door."

"She'll land on her feet," Guisa said unwarily.

"On her back, you mean," Vonney snarled. Guisa winced; he'd left himself open for that. His wife continued, "And now, Master Sachry, you'd better tell me why I shouldn't sashay out the door myself. Convince me if you can."

The obvious answer was that she'd suddenly turn poor if she did. But she had to know that herself. Right this minute, she seemed angry enough not to care. Better to try something else. "Because I love you?" Guisa suggested.

"Then why did you feed her your sausage?" Vonney held up a hand. "Don't waste my time with lies. You think I don't know what men are like? You did it because she was there and because you didn't worry about whether I'd find out. A stiff prong doesn't worry about anything, does it?"

"Not . . . as often as it should." Guisa half-admitted what he wanted to deny.

"So what are you going to do about it now? How am I ever going to be able to trust you again? Why should I? How do I even know this was the first time?"

Those were all good questions. Guisa had an answer for only the last of them: "By the gods, Vonney, it was!"

"You say that. You're good at saying things. You make lies sound true all the time. You get paid for it. Why should I believe you? Why should I believe you about anything?"

"Because I love you!" he exclaimed again.

"Really? You have an odd way of showing it. Why with her and not with me?"

Because when you and I do things, we're doing them because we feel like it, that's why. Because I could get away with it. Because I was making Xya do something she didn't much want to do, and I enjoyed that. Those thoughts flashed quickly through Guisa's mind. A working sense of self-preservation kept him from coming out with any of them. Instead, he said, "I would have let Xya go if you hadn't done it for me."

"I'll bet you would. Probably with a nice chunk of side money so she'd keep her mouth shut—unless you wanted her to open it again, I mean."

Guisa didn't just wince this time; he flinched. "You're not being fair. You're not being reasonable."

"Too cursed right, I'm not! I just found out you cheated on me, in case you don't remember. I don't care a fart about fair or reasonable. All I want to do is roast you over a slow fire like the swine you are!"

He didn't think she meant it literally. He wasn't sure enough about that to take a chance on finding out. "Give me one more chance, Vonney, I . . . I beg you," he said, surrendering. "I swear by all the gods I won't slip again. I swear it!"

Guisa watched her thinking it over. Not for the first time, he realized he had no idea what was going on behind her eyes. His cheek stung. He raised a hand to it. Yes, it was swelling, and probably red as flame. Extra makeup tonight, then. Thinking about himself again comforted him, the way it always did.

After more than a minute, Vonney nodded. "*One* more chance. That's all. Anything like this, anything even close to this, and I'm gone. You'd better believe that, because I mean it. I'll be hungry for a while—I know I will. But I don't think I'll starve before the Chleuh get driven out of Lutesse, out of Quimper. And the whole world will turn new then."

He didn't think it would be as quick or as easy as she made it sound. Again, though, he wasn't sure. Besides, she *had* said she would stay. That mattered more than he'd thought it would. Leaving a wife was one thing. Having a wife leave him turned out to be something else again.

"Thank you, dear," he said.

"Make me glad I'm doing this. Don't make me think I'm doing something stupid. Do you understand me?"

"Oh, yes. I understand you." *Much too well*, Guisa thought gloomily.

~

Bossed by an underofficer, ordinary Chleuh soldiers carried scrap metal out of Malk Malkovici's shop and tossed it into their wagons. Every bang and clatter was music to Malk's ears.

To his brother's ears, too. As the wagons rolled away, Sarmel said, "I never dreamt we'd make money like this!"

"Neither did I," Malk said. "We wouldn't be, either, if the Anadans and the Hontermen weren't doing their damnedest to knock Lutesse flat. Everything we're selling the Locusts these days stinks of other people's misery. It bothers me—I'd be lying if I said anything else."

"It bothers me, too. It feels like blood money," Sarmel said. "But I'll tell you who it doesn't bother. The Chleuh, that's who. It doesn't bother them even one little bit. Other people's misery? That's their stock in trade."

"I only wish I could say you were wrong," Malk answered. "But I can't, because you aren't. They're cruel for the sake of being cruel. I don't know what worse I can say about them."

"More heads have gone up in the park," Sarmel said, changing the subject not at all.

"Have they?" Without noticing he was doing it, Malk touched the back of his neck. "Not our heads, not yet."

"Not yet," his brother agreed. "How bad will they get if they start losing the war? I mean losing it so they can't even pretend everything is fine any more. If the Hontermen and Anadans start moving down from the coast toward Lutesse, for instance."

"I don't know. I just don't know," Malk said unhappily. "The way they think is, if they're going to die, nobody else deserves to live, either." He dropped into Nistrian halfway through that. He didn't realize he had till the words were already out of his mouth.

Sarmel caught the switch, and sent him a sharp look. "If they lose like that, Lutesse won't be their city any more. They won't care what they do to it, or to the people here—people like us."

"That's crossed my mind, too," Malk said. "I wish I could do something about it, but. . . ."

"Yes, but." Sarmel nodded. "The Chleuh don't listen to anyone but themselves very often. As far as I know, they don't listen to people who follow the Old Faith at all."

"Some of them do," Malk said, thinking of Colonel Tebron. "Once in a while, anyhow. And a lot of them listen to money. If spending some of ours helps keep Lutesse in one piece, I don't mind spending it."

His brother surprised him by using the coin-dropping gesture he'd seen from Bezen the constable. "You'd best watch yourself, you know," Sarmel said, smiling a twisted smile. "If anybody who hates the Old Faith heard you, he'd be sure you couldn't really belong to it."

Malk wanted to laugh and cry at the same time. "The only difference I've ever found between us and the folks who belong to the True Faith is which gods we worship, and how. Good and bad, smart and stupid, brave and cowardly, honest and crooked? Some of each in both faiths."

"You forgot something," Sarmel said. Malk hoisted an interrogative eyebrow. Sarmel went on, "Lots of them want all of us dead. King Kangen's giving them what they want, too."

"Mm, yes, there is that," the elder Malkovici replied. "But do you know what? If we ruled the kingdoms and there were only a few people who clung to the True Faith, chances are we'd treat them the same way."

Sarmel gnawed at the inside of his lower lip, then gave his brother a grudging nod. "Well, you've gone and ruined my afternoon for me," he said. "I think I'll head over to Ullo's and see if some brandy will wash the taste of that out of my mouth." Muttering to himself, he left the junk shop at something close to a run.

Malk wanted brandy, too, to wash the taste of the whole world out of his mouth. The only trouble was, he didn't think anyone brewed stuff strong enough to do it.

He'd thought of Tebron. Early the next morning, just after he'd opened up, the Chleuh quartermaster walked into the shop. Even as Malk started to doff his cap in the required gesture of respect, Tebron waved for him not to bother. "I didn't look to see you again so soon, sir. Your men cleaned out the shop yesterday."

"I'm not looking for scrap metal now," Tebron said, and stopped.

"What are you looking for, then, sir?" Malk asked after a moment, realizing he had to.

"Absolution," the Chleuh said. Malk frowned; the notion was more at home in the True Faith than in his own. Colonel Tebron went on, "I was at the East Station before dawn on some business—never mind what. And while I was there . . . While I was there, Malk, a train full of people who believe the way you do, people they must have hauled in from all over Quimper, pulled out on an eastbound track. Gods help them all. Absolution, you see?"

He wasn't drunk. He would have been less alarming if he were. Slowly, Malk said, "Sir, thanks to you my wife and my brother and I weren't on that train. We're in your debt because we weren't. Not much absolution, but what I can give."

"Scraps. Crumbs," Tebron said, which was bound to be true. "The cake gets eaten, but a few crumbs stay on the serving tray. I'm not the only man from my kingdom who thinks so, either." He stared at Malk as if waiting to be called a liar.

But all Malk said was, "One of these days, sir, I may ask you for a name or two."

"I may even know which days you mean. And I may even give you those names. That would do . . . something to cleanse me, wouldn't it?" Tebron sounded pleading.

"You are as clean as anyone from your kingdom." Malk meant it.

"That's what I'm afraid of," Tebron said. "Gods help us all!"

IX

On the stage, everything between Guisa and Vonney was fine. She was a trouper. No doubt she'd worked with other people she was angry at. Not a bit of that showed in her performances. She stayed smiling and friendly behind the scenes, too, and in public generally.

But back at the flat, Guisa felt as if he were walking through a field of the devilishly clever sorcerous weapons that the Honterese and Anadan dragonflyers had taken to dropping on Lutesse. Most of those delivered their energies right away, as anyone would expect. Some few, though, had cunning magics cast over them so they lay quiet for hours or even days. Then they'd go up in gouts of fire, catching the crews who'd come in to battle blazes or the city dwellers who thought it was safe to come home.

Guisa never knew which word, which gesture, would make Vonney burst like one of those wicked weapons. Whenever she did, she scarred him. He'd taken too long to realize how bright she was. Now he was paying for it.

Some of the lines she used on him, he would have written into the play he was working on—if they hadn't hurt too much and cut too deep. The way things were, he tried to forget them as fast as he could.

At last, having stood as much as he could, he asked her, "Do you want me to leave you and not the other way around?"

"Do as you please," she answered. "You will anyhow. That's all you know how to do, isn't it?"

A hot flush mounted to his cheeks. He didn't leave, though. He wasn't always sure why he didn't; regret at showing he'd made a mistake came as close as anything he could think of. Little by little, she got milder. But winter was giving way to spring before she let him take her to bed again.

"I had to make up my mind whether I ever wanted to let you touch me that way again," she told him. "I suppose I can try, anyhow."

"I'm very glad to hear it," he said truthfully.

"Of course you are. Abstinence makes the heart grow fonder," Vonney said. Delighted by the line even more than by the sight of her in the dim lamplight, Guisa did everything he knew how to do to please her before worrying about himself, which was anything but his usual style. Everything he knew how to do must have been enough, because she told him, "Well, you still remember what you're up to, anyhow."

"I myself am glad you think so," he answered. In a different tone of voice, that would have been meant to wound. But he sounded grateful even in his own ears, something he didn't commonly do when he wasn't onstage.

"So am I," Vonney said, and then, "What else have you got in mind?"

Because he'd gone without for some time, he performed like a much younger man. And then he rolled over and went to sleep, something his much younger self would have laughed at.

When he woke the next morning, Vonney was propped on pillows next to him reading a romance. He managed a crooked smile.

"You see? You wore me out," he said, a moment later adding, "Are we friends again?"

With what he thought of as regrettable precision, she said, "We have a chance of being friends again, anyhow. Believe me, that's more than I thought we could be after I found out what a polecat you are."

"I do believe you," Guisa said, wishing he didn't.

On their way to the theatre, he and Vonney saw a junk wagon. The wagon looked as if it were made from bits of junk itself; the horses pulling it couldn't have been more than two steps from the glueworks. But the driver tipped his cap as the wagon rattled past and said, "I enjoy your performing, Master Sachry," in rhythmically accented Quimperi.

"Why, thank you!" Guisa said. He worked to sound surprised at praise; people expected modesty even when he felt none. Here, he didn't have to work hard. The junkman didn't seem the kind of fellow who came to the theatre. In fact, what he looked like was someone who clung to the Old Faith, and not many folk like that were left in Lutesse these days. But he'd known who Guisa was and what he did.

"'Malkovici Brothers Salvaging.'" Vonney read the sign on the side of the wagon. "Those are the people who bought our brass saltcellar and pepper mill, Guisa. I don't know if he's the one who got them or if it was his brother. But do you remember what I said about the one who came up to the flat?"

"I do," Guisa replied. "You're right. Even fewer of those people around now than there were last summer."

"I wonder what happens to them," Vonney said.

Guisa clicked his tongue between his teeth. "So do I, but not enough to try very hard to find out. Otherwise, it might happen to me, too."

"Yes." Vonney looked back over her shoulder at the receding wagon. Because she did, so did Guisa. Though the day was clear and mild, the driver's back seemed hunched, as if he were moving ahead into the teeth of a blizzard. *If you cleave to the Old Faith, every day probably seems like that,* Guisa thought. He shivered himself and did his best to forget about the Malkovici brother.

Getting ready for the performance, familiar work, helped with that. And everything went off well that evening. Afterwards, a stage-hand slipped Guisa an envelope. When he opened it, he found a note from Artak Shmavon. The Chleuh who supervised publishing in Lutesse invited him to a gathering. *And your charming wife, of course,* Shmavon finished.

Guisa showed Vonney the note. "Shall we go, charming wife?" he asked.

"We probably should," she said. "He'd wonder if we didn't. And we can eat our fill." Even for Quimperi who cozied up to the occupants, being able to do that grew ever less certain.

Though Artak Shmavon's spread couldn't compete with the epic feasts higher-ranking Chleuh laid on, he did set out plenty. In Lutesse these days, quantity had a quality of its own. Erol Paki was there, and made no bones about filling his plate to overflowing. The little commentator bobbed his head at Guisa. "And I say to you, these sausages must be destroyed!" he declared.

"Nicely done!" Guisa gave back silent applause. If Paki could laugh at his own signature line about destroying Dreslon, there was more to him than Guisa had thought.

But then Vonney murmured, "Oh, by the gods!"

"What is it, my dear?" When Guisa's eyes followed his wife's, though, he saw what it was. There stood Xya Fulgine, a glass of wine in her hand. She was laughing and joking with a tall young Chleuh: one of Artak Shmavon's assistants. "Do you want to leave?" Guisa asked, also softly.

Vonney stood very straight. She lifted her head and stuck out her chin, as if she were a soldier hearing the trumpet blow the signal to attack (a stage soldier, of course; Guisa knew real soldiers hunched over when they went forward like that, to make themselves smaller targets for arrows and crossbow quarrels). "Curse me if I do! I'm not about to let that mangy trull run me off!"

"All right," Guisa said, hoping against hope that it would be.

Then he got distracted. One of the Chleuh at the gathering was from a publishing house in Trufknarf, Chlé's leading center for such enterprises. When he found out who Guisa was, he really did seem interested in putting out translations of some of his plays.

"This would not be immediate, sir—you must understand as much," he said.

"Oh, I do, Master Malkhaz. I do indeed," Guisa said. "Nothing in publishing is ever immediate, at least not in Quimper. I myself would be surprised if it were different anywhere else."

Papag Malkhaz laughed. "It isn't, not in that regard." He spoke excellent Quimperi, with only a vanishing trace of a Chleuh accent.

"How is Trufknarf holding up, if I may ask?"

"Pretty well." The way the laugh cut off all at once said Malkhaz wasn't telling everything he knew. "Some of the raids have done damage, but not nearly so much as the defeatists want people to believe. My firm remains very much in business, and expects to go on even after the war ends. You may rely on us to bring your wit to our folk, come what may."

"I'm glad to hear it." Guisa wanted to ask the Chleuh official more questions, but found he didn't have the nerve. If he read Papag Malkhaz's words right, Malkhaz was saying the war was lost and he hoped his house would survive the disaster.

If he read Papag Malkhaz's words wrong, though . . . A knock on the door in the middle of the night, two or three hatchet-faced Chleuh to haul him away, and whatever they did after they got him where they wanted him. It had happened before, once or twice to actors he knew who'd thought, or said they'd thought, they were on good terms with the occupants.

So he didn't ask those questions. He didn't even ask about money. He asked who might do the translation and how well qualified the person was to turn clever, sophisticated Quimperi into

Chleuh. He didn't quite say *into the hogs' grunting you people use among yourselves*, but he came closer to it than he might have.

His luck stayed in—either Papag Malkhaz didn't notice his scorn or let it pass. "I have just the perfect man in mind," Malkhaz said. "Sahak Levond taught our language and literature in one of your provincial towns before . . . well, before the war. He is fully at home in both tongues, and I happen to know how much he enjoys your work. He is also, sadly, at leisure—he came back from the fight against the accursed schismatics with his left arm gone halfway between elbow and wrist."

"Oh." Guisa's stomach did a slow lurch. "I am very sorry to hear that."

"So was everyone who knows him," Malkhaz said. "But he can do the job, and would be glad to gain the gold."

"That seems an excellent arrangement, then." Guisa happened to look up. Vonney's expression said she'd been waiting longer than she liked to catch his eye. "Do please excuse me," he said quickly. "My wife—"

"*Now* we can leave," Vonney said when he went over to her. She sounded pleased with herself.

"What did you do?" Guisa was sure she'd done something.

And she had. "I asked Master Shmavon why he invited a certain person to this gathering when everyone knew she'd been visiting Doctor Rivoal every other day for the past month."

Dr. Rivoal had built a sizable practice in Lutesse, fighting the pox, the gleets, butterflies of love, and other intimate misfortunes. Guisa had seen him a time or two, in between wives. He asked, "Did Shmavon know who old Rivoal is?"

"Do you see that Fulgine piece here any more?"

When Guisa glanced around the room, he didn't. He sketched a salute. "Let's go home," he said. Home they went.

~

A man walked into Malk Malkovici's junk shop. He wasn't anyone Malk had seen before, or the junkman didn't think he was. Not tall, not short. Hair between brown and sandy. Eye-colored eyes, a face-shaped face. Clothes no more stylish and in no better repair than anyone else's in Lutesse these days. As ordinary as ordinary could be.

"Good morning!" Malk said. "Looking for anything in particular? If I've got it, I'll help you find it."

The stranger looked around. He was the only person in the place besides Malk. Casually, he asked, "You knew Evets the ragman, right?" His voice was as nondescript as the rest of him.

His question, though, wasn't. "Name sounds familiar. I may have met him," Malk said. "What about it, though?" Was this ordinary fellow a woodsrunner or a Watchman? *How can I tell?* Malk wondered. *Can I?*

"People come. People go. The struggle, though, the struggle always moves forward," the man said.

"I've never seen you before. I have no reason to trust a stranger. These days, only fools trust strangers. So you can give me some reason to trust you or you can go look for scrap somewhere else," Malk said.

"Evets trusted you," the stranger said.

Malk laughed harshly. "Evets didn't trust his own mother. If she was anything like the son she had, I don't blame him."

"Heh, heh." The nondescript man laughed, too: more from courtesy, Malk judged, than from amusement. Then he said, "You follow the Old Faith." He held up a hand. "Don't waste your time calling me a liar. It's written all over your face. You'd better keep a connection with people who fight for liberation, or else your connection with the Locusts will cost you when purification comes. And it will."

"Someone from that side would say such things. So would someone from the other side, looking to dig me a grave so I can jump into it myself." Malk spread his hands. "So you see how things are, eh, my friend?" Outside of his little stint in the Watchmen's jail, he'd never felt less friendly towards anyone.

"You'd better figure it out pretty cursed quick." The stranger didn't sound threatening. He sounded altogether matter-of-fact. That made his words more intimidating, not less. "This isn't dice or draughts. This is life and death. Things happen to people who can't figure that out."

Anyone who belonged to the Old Faith understood that things happened to people. "A horse's cock up your back door," Malk muttered in Nistrian. No, the ordinary man didn't follow that. But it didn't do Malk any good past salving his feelings, either. He said, "Will you take a walk with me? It isn't far—only a block and a half or so."

The stranger considered, then nodded. "I'll go. You won't like what comes next if anything happens to me, though."

"No, I expect not. But you'd say that no matter which side you're on." Malk stepped out from behind the counter and walked to the door. "Come along if you're coming."

"I said I was." The ordinary man went outside with Malk. He waited while the junkman locked all three locks, then ambled along with him. They might have know each other for years. They might have, but they hadn't. That was the rub. When Malk's steps slowed and then stopped, the ordinary man chuckled at the sign over the door. "'Pests Disposed Of'? Didn't I tell you not to play those games?"

"Is that what it says?" Malk didn't worry about the words on signs. He opened the door. A bell clanged when he did. He waved the stranger in ahead of him. Nodding to Batz Kergrist, he said, "I've got some work for you, maybe."

The skinny wizard nodded back. "Well, I can use some, the gods know." He dipped his head to the nondescript man. "I don't think we've met, sir. I'm Batz Kergrist, vanquisher of vermin, very much at your service. And you are . . . ?"

"You can call me Guer." The man didn't even bother pretending it was his real name.

Batz saw that as plainly as Malk did. "However you please," he said, and then gave his attention back to Malk. "And what is this work you have in mind?"

Malk jerked a thumb at his companion. "You're a wizard. Have you got a spell that will tell us if Master Guer here is worth trusting?"

"That's not my usual line of work, you know." Batz pointed out the obvious.

"Yes, yes," Malk said impatiently. "But can you do it?"

"Let me think." The wizard made a point of it, almost as if he were on the stage. Then he said, "Yes, I expect I can. With Master Guer's consent, of course." He sounded as sardonic about the obvious alias as Malk had a moment before.

"Go ahead," said the ordinary man with the equally ordinary false name.

"Right you are." Batz Kergrist rummaged in the drawers behind his counter till he triumphantly held up two chunks of what looked like rusty iron, one in each hand. When he brought them close together, they clung to each other like lovers, so he needed a grunt of effort to pull them apart again. "Lodestone," he explained.

"I've seen it before. I deal in iron, after all," Malk said. The man who called himself Guer nodded.

Batz walked up to him. "I will hold one chunk to either side of your head while I incant," he told him. "If you are true, they will stick to you, each on its own side, as if the distance of your noggin were not there. If you have deception and betrayal in mind, though, they will fall to the ground like ordinary pebbles."

"Go ahead," Guer repeated.

Batz did as he'd said he would. The spell was in the old language followers of the True Faith still used in prayer. The wizard brought it to a rhythmic climax, at the same time jerking his hands away from the pieces of lodestone. When he did, they stayed in place on either side of the nondescript man's head.

"I can feel them," Guer said. "I'd bet I look silly."

He might have looked dead if he'd failed the wizard's test. Malk thought Batz Kergrist would have helped him cover up the crime . . .

if he'd been able to commit it. He had the feeling Guer might be someone who'd take a deal of killing. But he didn't need to worry about that now. "What do I owe you?" he asked Batz.

"Oh, a crown and a half should take care of it," the sorcerer replied.

"I keep telling you, you'd have some meat on your bones if you charged more." Malk gave him an extra crown and pretended not to hear his protests. Turning to Guer, the junkman said, "Let's go back to my shop and talk about this."

"Yes, let's." The ordinary man looked at Batz. "I wasn't here. You've never seen me."

"How strange! It almost seemed as if the air talked to me," Batz said to Malk Malkovici. Malk snorted. Guer let out another couple of syllables' worth of laughter. He and Malk left the wizard's establishment and retraced their steps of half an hour earlier.

Once they were inside again, Malk wasted no time: "All right, tell me what you think I can do for you."

"I was trying to. You didn't want to listen." Guer held up a hand before Malk could tell him why he hadn't wanted to. "Never mind. I know how hard it is to believe anyone who you haven't known for your whole life. Even some of those people can knock you down, let alone strangers."

"That's all true," Malk said, and then, "How's Evets?"

"Dead," Guer answered bluntly. "We think he managed to take care of it before they pulled too much out of him."

"A blessing on his memory," Malk said, and covered his eyes with one hand in the Old Faith's gesture of mourning.

"We're still here, though," Guer said. "You won't be amazed when I tell you the thrust across the Narrow Sea is coming soon. If the Hontermen and Anadans don't all die on the beaches, the Chleuh are in more trouble than they know what to do with. They don't have enough men or dragons or horses or wizards to fight here and against the Muos at the same time."

Malk nodded. "Some of them think the same way you do."

"They aren't stupid. That's not what's wrong with them." Guer paused to light a smelly little cheroot the color of boot polish. "But that's what we want from you. Whatever you hear from the Locusts, we need to know about it. It doesn't have to seem important to you. Whatever you hear. We'll fit the pieces together. That's our job."

"I can do that. Now that Evets' place is gone, though, how do I get word to you?"

"There's a rock wall in a park where you can leave a note. The Chleuh don't know that one of the stones is loose, and—" the nondescript man broke off. "What's wrong?"

"No notes," Malk said. "I don't know the syllables. How can you know so much about me and not know that?"

"Bugger me blind! *That's* what you meant when you said 'So that's what it says.'" Guer sounded disgusted, at Malk or himself or both of them together. He blew an angry cloud of smoke at the ceiling. Then he said, "There's a fish market on a little avenue three blocks up from General Limerzel's Street, not far from the Obelisk. Maybe there."

"I know that place. The fellow who runs it has red hair and whistles all the time."

"That's the one," the ordinary man agreed.

"I didn't know he worked with you people. When he sells on the left, he doesn't gouge as hard as a lot of shopkeepers do. I will say that for him."

"You weren't supposed to know who he works with. If you did, too many others would, too." Guer pointed out the obvious.

"True enough," Malk said. "How will he know to believe anything I tell him from now on? And what signal will he give me if things go wrong? Evets saved my stones when he warned me under the Watchmen's eyes."

"He'll know. We'll make sure of that. As for the other, you work it out with him. You don't need to tell anybody else about it. The less outsiders know about those things, the better off everybody is."

"You make sense." Malk's smile lifted only one side of his mouth.

"As long as you're here, do you want to buy some scrap iron? If I sell it to you, the Chleuh won't get it."

"We want them to buy from you," Guer said. "We want them coming in here all the time and running their mouths. That one Locust you were talking about, the fellow with the wit to see what's coming . . . We need to hear about those things."

"Him? For a Chleuh, he's pretty decent." Malk didn't name Colonel Tebron. The quartermaster officer was the best protector he had. He didn't want anything bad to happen to Tebron.

"Decent? Who cares? He's in the wrong uniform—nothing else matters," Guer said. That was bound to be sensible from his perspective. He wouldn't see it was much less so for Malk. He touched a finger to the brim of his cap and started for the door. Over his shoulder, he added, "Liberation coming soon, by the gods!"

"May it be so," Malk said. When Guer left, the junkman wanted a big knock of brandy, and he wasn't someone who drank in the morning.

At least he'd been to the fish market before. The Chleuh wouldn't frown and scratch their heads if they saw him there again. He assumed they kept an eye on him. He assumed the Watchmen did, too. They might be more dangerous to him than the occupants were. Being Quimperi themselves, they understood Lutesse and what went on in it better than foreigners ever could.

As far as the Watchmen are concerned, I'm a foreigner, too, Malk reminded himself. He wasn't an admirable foreigner, either, the way King Kangen's men were. The Watchmen wanted Lutesse cleansed of people like him. They might have been even more eager about that than the Chleuh were.

Colonel Tebron came to the junk shop a couple of days later. Malk wondered whether Guer and the other woodsrunners had known beforehand that he would. Wonder or not, he wasn't about to ask. Questions were dangerous. He knew that.

Because Tebron had a couple of men with him, Malk jerked off his cap and went through all the submissive rigmarole the Chleuh required of people who clung to the Old Faith. The quartermaster acted the conqueror, too. "I require your brass, your copper, your bronze," he snapped. He didn't require Malk's absolution, not with a couple of underofficers listening and watching.

"Yes, exalted sir. I have a fair bit." Malk waved toward the ruddy scrap metal.

"What is the weight? I will pay you at the usual rate," Tebron said. By the way the underofficers eyed Malk, they would sooner just have confiscated it. You could do that . . . once. If you did, though, you wouldn't find much waiting for you when you came back.

Malk exaggerated the weight a bit—not too much, because the Chleuh had scales they could use if they thought he was out of line. A little cheating wouldn't bother Tebron. Like Malk, the quartermaster seemed to think cheating was as much a part of war as fighting.

"I'll take all of it," Tebron said. "Ashusha, go back to the depot and tell them to send, mm, four wagons. The usual paperwork, and the payment, too."

"I obey, Colonel." The man called Ashusha put his right fist over his heart and hurried away.

To Malk, Tebron said, "I'd haggle harder and check more if we didn't need the stuff so bad. The next few months will tell the tale."

"However you say, exalted sir. May all prosper for you and for your kingdom." Malk Malkovici meant the first part of that rather more than the second. Tebron, of course, hadn't had to tell him anything at all. Malk, a man trying to play both sides at once, wondered if the Chleuh officer wasn't another.

By the time the wagons rattled up, the junkman had got word to his brother to come and check the Chleuh papers. "Everything looks all right," Sarmel said, so Malk made his mark on the lines where he was supposed to. The young lieutenant in charge of the work crew paid him what he was owed, down to the half-copper. The wagons rolled away, leaving blank space on the shop floor that would have to be filled. If Tebron didn't get what he wanted . . . Malk shivered. That didn't bear thinking about.

The next day, Malk stopped at the fishmonger's on his way back from the rubbish tip in the southern part of the city. Sure enough, the redheaded owner stood behind the counter in a leather apron. Just because he whistled all the time didn't mean he did it well.

"Good day to you, Camaret," Malk said. "Master Guer told me you had crabs."

"Just because Guer has them, he thinks everybody else does, too," Camaret answered, which made Malk chuckle. The fishmonger went on, "But he also has a way with news, Guer does. He tells me you do, too, eh?"

"Isn't that interesting?" Malk looked around. He didn't see anybody else, so he plunged: "Somebody I know—a name you may have heard of—thinks we'll know what we'll know in the next few months. He's putting all the coppers he has on it." He did his best to get his meaning across without saying what he meant.

"Nothing I haven't heard before, but still interesting—especially if you're talking about the fellow I think you are," Camaret said.

Malk nodded. "I expect I am."

"All right, then." Camaret reached into a bin behind the counter and took out four green crabs. They didn't pinch his fingers; the spell that preserved them as if fresh from the sea also slowed them down so they couldn't fight. "As a matter of fact, I do have these. They'll cost you, though."

"How much?" Malk asked, and flinched when the fishmonger told him. He haggled harder than Tebron had. He beat Camaret down some, though less than he'd hoped. Then he paid.

"Tell your wife to be careful when they go into the pot," Camaret warned. "Boiling water breaks the spell. They'll get lively till cooking kills 'em."

"Not the first time I've bought crabs from you," Malk said. "Gods willing, it won't be the last, either."

"That would be good. As long as you pay me, you can come around any old time." Camaret winked at him. "Some of the girls in the officers' joyhouses tell the Chleuh the same thing."

He surprised a laugh out of Malk. Even one of the occupants might have laughed at that. You could joke about them, as long as you didn't joke about politics or allegiance. You could if you were lucky, anyhow.

~

Living in his own flat had turned strange for Guisa Sachry. He felt as if he'd lost a war, and his victorious opponent was keeping him on a leash so tight, it choked him whenever he did the least little thing. He felt, in other words, much as Quimper had since the Chleuh paraded down the Boulevard of Dreams.

It was the first time he'd felt that way since King Kangen's men marched into Lutesse. He'd done well for himself these past nearly four years. Oh, the Chleuh pinched him now and again, but that was political. However little he cared for it, he understood it.

This? This was personal.

It wasn't as if Vonney lorded over him the way the Locusts lorded over Quimper. She didn't even go out and make free with his money, as the occupants did with everything they wanted in the occupied kingdom. But she had the upper hand in ways she hadn't before she found out about Xya Fulgine.

Guisa wasn't used to anyone holding a moral advantage on him. He didn't like it, not even a little bit. He couldn't complain to his wife, though. She'd say something like, *Well, you shouldn't have fed her your part in exchange for her part, then.* In one of his bedroom farces, a line like that would have brought down the house.

When you were living it instead of acting it, it didn't seem so funny. He couldn't grouse to any of his theatre friends, either. They'd listen sympathetically, but they'd laugh behind their hands and behind his back. He knew they were laughing behind his back now.

Then, one day, Vonney said, "I've got a question for you."

"Do you? What is it?" Guisa thought he'd sound apprehensive. His voice recognized her tone before his brain could. She'd really tried to learn from him back in the days before . . . *Before you got caught*, he reminded himself. She said this the way she had then.

"I heard a line of poetry, and I don't know what it's from. Somebody out in the street told his friend, 'The autumn viols' long wailing breaks my heart with a boring languor.'"

"That's Laup Lervain, from a long lifetime ago," Guisa said at once. "'Fall Song' is the name of the poem. How funny!"

"I don't think it's funny. I think it's sad," Vonney said.

"Of course it is. I myself didn't mean that." Yes, he enjoyed teaching her again, even if only for a moment. It put things back the way they had been, the way they were meant to be. He thought of it so, at any rate. Quickly, he went on, "But why would anyone recite a sad autumn poem here when spring's moving toward summer? It makes no sense."

"Things don't have to make sense. They just have to happen," his wife said. "I was there. I heard it."

He wagged a finger at her. "You act in plays. You don't write them. Everything there has to make sense, or the audience walks out on you."

"Plays turn reality neat. They've got to. You go to a play, you want to be able to understand what's happening." Vonney made a face. "Nobody understands what's happening in the real world. I don't think even the gods understand what's going on these days."

"Neither do I." Better than his wife did, Guisa understood how much trouble they would have been in with the priesthood two or three hundred years before had anyone overheard them saying such things. People didn't take the gods so seriously now, perhaps because of how thoroughly they'd shown they didn't understand what was happening in the real world since those days.

If they'd asked him to clean up the drama for them . . . But they hadn't. The gods, alas, didn't do such things.

Vonney said, "Well, anyhow, thanks. I didn't have any notion who wrote that, and I would have gone crazy trying to find out."

He bowed to her, as low as his belly would let him. "I am your servant." Had he thought more before speaking, he wouldn't have put it just that way. Luckily, she didn't agree with him out loud.

And then, two days later, in a coincidence he himself never would have allowed to enter one of his plays, he heard the line himself. Two ragged men sitting on a bench were passing a single rank stogie back and forth. The one who didn't have it at the moment quoted Lervain to the other.

After blowing out smoke, his friend replied, "May we hear them soon!"

"That would be good," the first man agreed.

Guisa almost asked them what they were talking about. But there were two of them and only one of him, and he was as obviously prosperous as they were poor. They didn't have to be Muo schismatics to want to hit him in the head with a rock and carry off whatever they thought worth stealing.

And he never had been any braver than he had to be. As often as not, he wasn't even as brave as he should have been. So he just kept walking, and looked back over his shoulder once or twice to make sure they weren't following him. They weren't; they just kept sharing that black, twisted cigar.

Whatever the autumn viols' long wailing meant, it meant nothing to Guisa Sachry. He never did find out what that was all about.

X

Malk Malkovici anxiously eyed Efa. Her time was very close; her belly bulged more every day. "Will you be all right if I go down into the cellar under the cellar for a while?" he asked. "Something interesting may happen." He didn't name the unauthorized, illegal crystal hidden down there. If a Chleuh wizard was spying on him, let the fellow think he was shooting dice or something of the sort.

His wife sent him the kind of look wives send uncommonly stupid husbands. "Of course I will," she said. "The baby won't fall out while you're down there. And if it does, I'll catch it before it bounces on the floor." She made pushing-away motions with both hands.

Ears afire, Malk fled the bedroom. He went down the stairs to the shop floor, opened the door to the cellar, and latched it behind him. Only the small salamander lamp in his hand shed any light down there, and it didn't give much. Enough to let him find the hidden doorway that led to the deeper level, though.

Once in the subcellar, he freed the illicit crystal from its hiding place and whispered the activation charm. He could have recited it out loud; no one would have heard him if he had. But it seemed more secret spoken softly.

Light filled the crystal. It wasn't Char Tubis' image that formed inside it: the tired-looking man Malk saw was only a commentator, a free man's equivalent of Erol Paki or one of the other Quimperi who made their living lying for King Kangen.

"Hello, friends who can't admit you're listening—here I am again, Douar Brug, talking to you from Dreslon," the man said. Camaret the fishmonger had told Malk to be sure to listen to him tonight.

Douar Brug went on with the usual business of his hour: giving Quimper the kind of news that wouldn't find its way into the news sheets here. Prisoners beheaded. Hostages killed. More hostages imprisoned in Chlé. Food and weapons stolen from Quimper by the Locusts. A joke about King Kangen, one filthy enough to make Malk wince and giggle at the same time.

Mixed in with all that, Douar Brug spoke phrases and sentences that sounded like nonsense. To anyone who didn't already know what they meant, they *were* nonsense. If the gods were kind, the Chleuh who were bound to be listening to the emanation from Honter didn't already know their meaning.

Malk muttered to himself. Douar Brug's time was almost up. He still hadn't heard what Camaret'd told him to listen for. If he didn't hear it tonight, another month might go by before he needed to listen again. As far as he was concerned, too many months had already gone by.

Then, in the same bored-seeming voice he'd used for the rest of his meaningless sentences, Douar Brug intoned, "The autumn viols' long wailing breaks my heart with a boring languor." And then he started talking about more of the iniquities of the Chleuh. Passion filled his words when he did that.

Passion or not, Malk deactivated the crystal though the commentator was still going on. He'd heard what he'd come down here to hear. He hid the crystal, left the subcellar, did his best to make sure no one could guess there was any subcellar down there to leave, and climbed out of the cellar.

Sure enough, Efa was still extravagantly pregnant when he walked back into the bedroom. The baby hadn't escaped. She put down the romance she was reading and asked, "Well?"

"A day," Malk said. "Maybe two."

His wife's pupils widened, like a cat's when it spied a mouse. "Are you sure?"

"I'm not sure of anything. That's what they told me. That's what they think. Or else that's what they want me to think."

"We'll find out, then—in a day or two," Efa said.

"Or else we'll find out there was nothing to find out," Malk said. If they'd played him for a fool . . . He could go to Colonel Tebron if they had. He knew enough to do some damage if he chose that path. He'd sold the Chleuh tons and tons of scrap metal. Selling them men, though? He snarled silently. No, he hadn't fallen that low yet.

Bells woke Efa and him later in the night. The Anadans and Hontermen were paying another call on Lutesse, then. At first, with Efa great with child, it was an annoyance, a fear, he could have done without. Then he remembered what he'd heard on the crystal. Maybe those dragons had reason to come tonight.

"Shall we go down?" his wife asked as the first bursts and blasts began off to the north.

"Yes, we'd better," Malk said. He held on to her hand as they went down the stairs to the ground floor, and again as they descended to the cellar. If he could stop her, she wouldn't fall.

He listened till he closed and latched the cellar, which muffled the direction from which noises came. Carefully, he said, "I *think* they're mostly staying north of the city."

"I don't much care right now," Efa answered irritably. "With the baby kicking and thrashing in there, I have enough trouble sleeping anyhow. It's rude of them to wake me after I finally did start getting a little rest." She yawned, as if to prove her own point.

Even so, Malk began to feel they'd wasted the trip down here. He kept that to himself. Maybe, just maybe, before too long, he could stop worrying about the Hontermen and Anadans flattening Lutesse. Then, of course, he'd need to start worrying about the Chleuh.

When Guisa Sachry started for a kiosk to buy a morning news sheet, a constable pointed at him with a white-gloved hand and blew a shrill blast on a brass whistle. "Get back inside, you stupid son of a whore!" the uniformed man shouted. "Don't you know there's a curfew on?"

"No, I myself did not know that," Guisa replied with dignity. "At whose order?"

"At the order of the Chleuh commandant for all of Quimper, General Stulp himself," the constable replied. "So get your fat, flabby arse back behind closed doors where it belongs, or I'll make you sorry."

"No need to be crude about it, I'm sure," Guisa said, but he retreated.

When he walked back into the flat, Vonney said, "You don't have the sheet. Did you forget what you went out for?"

"Don't *you* start," Guisa snarled. She looked at him in surprise—he hadn't snapped back at her like that since she found out about Xya Fulgine. He went on, "A nasty vulgarian of a constable ordered me home. He said there's a citywide curfew on."

"Oh," Vonney said in a different tone. "Maybe we should activate the crystal, then, and find out why. There've been plenty of worse attacks on Lutesse where they didn't do anything like that."

"True." Guisa went over to the crystal and murmured the charm. He didn't listen to it all that often. It told even more lies than the news sheets, which was really saying something. Well, people like Erol Paki didn't get invited to Chleuh gatherings for telling what was truly going on in Quimper. *And why do* you *get invited to those gather-*

ings? Guisa asked himself. As usual, he fought shy of answering his own question.

A pompous-looking man appeared in the crystal. He spoke pompously, too: “All inhabitants of Lutesse are required to obey the curfew ordered by the occupants’ commandant in Quimper, General Berhard Stulp. Those flouting this order are liable to summary punishment, and no mercy will be shown. Furthermore, Count Vurk, King Kangen’s minister to Quimper, assures the populace that the attempted landings in the north are foredoomed to failure, and that the barbarous invaders assuredly will be thrown back into the sea. I repeat—”

Guisa didn’t listen to him saying the same thing over again. He turned away from the crystal. Before he could find anything to say, Vonney beat him to it: “So it’s happened at last.”

His head bobbed up and down, seemingly of its own accord; he didn’t think he’d told it to do that. “It has,” he said. “Now we see if they can make it stick.”

“What do you think?” his wife asked.

“I . . . just don’t know.” Guisa didn’t usually say anything like that, but he wasn’t usually so confused, either. “The Chleuh can’t be taken by surprise. They’ve been getting ready for this for a couple of years now. But the Hontermen and Anadans wouldn’t have crossed the Narrow Sea if they didn’t think they could push on from the beaches.”

Vonney nodded in the same distracted way Guisa had a moment earlier. “If they do get a foothold in the north . . . Are there enough Chleuh to fight against the Muos and here at the same time?”

“Stulp and Vurk are probably asking themselves the same question right now,” Guisa said. “King Kangen is probably asking his generals right now, too.”

“You’d think they would have asked themselves a while ago,” she said.

“Yes. You would.” A while ago, though, Chlé hadn’t had to worry about what its enemies could do. Quimper had fallen. The

Hontermen were driven off the mainland and back to their cold, rainy island. And even Muosi looked like falling when the Chleuh first stormed eastward.

"What do we do now?" Vonney seemed less sure of herself dealing with invasions than with husbandly infidelities.

"Right now?" Guisa wasn't certain what tomorrow or the day after would bring, either. For today, though, or at least for this morning, he had no doubts. "Right now, we stay where we are. The constables are jumpy."

"They should be," Vonney said. "These past four years, they've done whatever the occupants told them to do. If the occupants aren't occupying any more, somebody will ask them questions about that."

"I wish I thought you were right, but I don't believe it," Guisa said. "When Quimper ran its own affairs, the constables did what the people set above them told them to do. When the Chleuh took over, they still did what the people set above them told them to do. If the Hontermen and Anadans get here, the constables will still do what the people set above them tell them to do. They aren't political, any more than actors are."

"If the Hontermen and Anadans get here, people will ask actors those questions, too," Vonney replied. Guisa started to answer, then realized he had nothing to say. He also knew they'd ask those questions. Why was he sending Nea Ennogue parcels, if not to give himself answers when they did?

After a moment, he did murmur, "I wonder what people like Erol Paki and Brasi Robillach are thinking right now."

"And people like Sep Nardand and Odrio Cazh," Vonney added. "Some people have been talking for the Chleuh. Some people have spilled blood for them, their own blood and their enemies'."

"If everything gets remembered, we'll have hard times ahead," Guisa said.

Now his wife didn't answer. All she'd done was perform as she'd performed before the war. Well, that and go to Chleuh gatherings, and anyone would wanted a full belly would have gone to those. She hadn't stood on a reviewing stand with Odrio Cazh. She hadn't written a play that poked sly fun at the Quimperi who resisted the occupants. And she was a woman, and a pretty woman at that. She wasn't in much danger.

It's unfair, Guisa thought. But even if it was, he couldn't do anything about it. If he had to suffer for his art, well, wasn't that what art was all about? People said so. He had noticed they said so much more often than they willingly suffered for their art.

Willingly. Yes, that was the word. If the Hontermen and Anadans—and the rebels who'd refused to acknowledge the General's yielding to King Kangen—came to Lutesse, *willingly* wouldn't have much to do with it. They'd be looking to punish, and to avenge.

Vonney walked over to the crystal and activated it again. "We may as well know what's going on." A moment later, she amended that: "What they want us to think is going on, anyhow."

"Yes," Guisa said. Little children kicking a ball around in the empty streets sang a nasty jingle: *Lutesse Crystal lies! Lutesse Crystal lies! Lutesse Crystal belongs to the Chleuh!* If that was obvious to them, it was obvious to everybody.

The pompous-looking announcer who'd told of the landings had given way to another cut from the same cloth. This fellow appealed to the people of Lutesse and to all Quimperi for order, discipline, and obedience. "Obey the occupants as you obey your beloved parents, and all will be well," he said.

"How much food have we got in the flat?" Guisa asked, not quite out of the blue.

"Enough for two or three days—maybe a little more if we stretch it," Vonney said. "After that, they'll have to let us go out and get to the market . . . won't they?"

"I myself would think so. They're likely keeping us in so we don't get in the way of soldiers moving through the city," Guisa said. Most people here, he knew, had a lot less food than that stashed away. Most people in Lutesse were hungry most of the time. Suppose the

Chleuh did let the locals leave their flats and houses, only the markets held nothing.

How much would the occupants care? Not much, not if Guisa was any judge. Unless the people of Lutesse started rioting, that is. There'd be a bloodbath if they did; Guisa had no doubts about that. The war had come back to Quimper at last. With real fighting in the north, the Chleuh wouldn't want to waste men and weapons putting down city folk.

Which didn't mean they wouldn't do it, of course. Though the flat was comfortably warm, Guisa shivered.

Char Tubis looked out of the crystal in Malk Malkovici's cellar. The tall, bony officer looked uncommonly pleased with himself. "Dear people of Quimper, I have returned to my homeland!" he said. "With the help of my allies from Honter and faraway Anada, I shall liberate this beloved land from the Chleuh and from the pestilence of occupation!"

Malk wondered what the Anadans and Hontermen thought of that. How big a part of their army were Char Tubis' Unconquered Quimperi? Most of the kingdom's fighting men on land and sea had stayed loyal to the General. They didn't fight for the Chleuh—men who did that belonged to the Quimperi Popular Party and other little outfits like it. But they didn't fight against the occupants, either. Some kept order in the provinces. Most had accepted paroles, lain down their swords and bows and lances, and gone home.

Then again, numbers of warriors might not matter here. If Char Tubis was back on his homeland's soil and in the fight to help free it from the Chleuh, he and his men would draw Quimperi to them the way a lodestone drew nails.

Back into its hiding place went the illicit crystal. Malk went up into the cellar, then unlatched the trap door that opened up onto the shop floor. He was surprised to see Efa coming down the stair from the apartment above it. "Are you all right?" he blurted.

"It depends on what you mean," she answered. "My waters just broke."

"Are you sure?" he asked foolishly. He had only the vaguest notion of what that meant. He was not equipped to have waters, let alone to have them break.

His wife made a face at him. "It isn't something I'm likely to be wrong about. There was a snap inside me, and then I was dribbling. I might have been pissing myself, only I couldn't stop. The bedding's wet—I'm sorry. But the labor pains started for real then." She made a different kind of face, one that said she was feeling a pang then.

"You . . . could have picked a better time," Malk said.

In spite of the labor pain, her face shouted, *You stupid man!* All she said, though, was, "It's not as though I've got much choice."

"I suppose not." After a moment, he added, "Shall I fetch the midwife?"

"That's the first sensible thing you've said since I set eyes on you," Efa said. "Yes, why don't you?"

She winced again, which sent Malk out to the street even faster than he would have gone otherwise. No one else was out there, no one except Bezen the constable. He pointed an accusing forefinger at Malk. "Get back inside! Right now! Absolute curfew. No exceptions."

"Efa's time has come. I'm just going to bring the midwife," Malk said.

"I don't care what you're doing. Get back inside!" Bezen snapped. "If anybody in a uniform who isn't me sees you, he'll kill you before he asks you questions. I mean it. The Locusts aren't joking about this."

It was the first time Malk had ever heard him use that name for the Chleuh. As the junkman walked up to the constable, he was digging in his belt pouch. "Here," he said. "You never saw me, either." He pressed two gold crowns into Bezen's hand.

The constable quickly made them disappear. Then, out of the

side of his mouth, he said, "Give me another one." Without hesitation, Malk did. Bezen walked off. "I could have sworn I heard a voice," he remarked to no one in particular. "Guess I'm losing whatever wits I had."

Iliz Plou, the midwife, lived four blocks away. Malk did his best to walk them invisibly. Before he dealt with her, he had to take care of the doorwoman. Fixing him with a fishy stare, she said, "Are you asking to get a bolt through your brisket?"

"I'm not asking for anything except Mistress Plou to come for my wife." Malk used another gold crown. He didn't care about money now.

"Well," the doorwoman said, and then disappeared. The front door opened a couple of minutes later. There stood Iliz Plou. She was a handsome woman perhaps ten years older than Malk; she might have been a beauty in her younger days. She carried a cloth bag with whatever she thought she might need to aid a childbirth. Malk didn't know, or want to know, what all it held.

"She's ready, is she?" she asked him.

"She is, ma'am. Her, uh, waters broke a little while ago, she told me."

"Did they?" Iliz Plou nodded in what looked like approval. "That will speed things up. Let's go, then." After they got out of the doorwoman's earshot, she asked, "You've settled things so greedyguts Bezen won't bother us?"

"It's taken care of," he answered, and she nodded again.

Sure enough, the constable ignored them when he passed them on his beat. All the same, Malk let out a long, relieved breath when he got back inside the junk shop.

Efa wasn't on the shop floor any more. He called up the stairs: "Are you in the bedroom?"

"Of course not. I'm off climbing a plane tree in the park outside of town," his wife answered. One of Iliz Plou's eyebrows twitched. She started up toward the apartment.

"Can I do anything to help?" Malk asked.

"Stay down here. Stay out of my way. If I need you, I'll call you. I don't expect to need you till the baby's out," the midwife said. Malk gave back an unhappy nod. Iliz Plou had a good name in the neighborhood, but everybody said she didn't put up with any nonsense.

She went upstairs. Malk stayed where he was and brooded. He wondered if he ought to go down to the cellar so no one could watch him coming to pieces. After a moment, he shook his head. He wouldn't get any customers now anyway. The Chleuh and the Quimperi constables who followed their orders had Lutesse locked down tight.

Then he wondered what would happen if Colonel Tebron chose this exact moment to come buy scrap metal. He shrugged. Tebron was a decent man . . . for a Locust. That Malk made the qualification said everything that needed saying about what the Chleuh had become by following King Kangen's lead.

Malk paced back and forth, a traditional thing for an expectant father to do. A couple of clocks ticked so he or anyone who came in could track the hour at a glance. He didn't look at either one of them. He didn't want to know how slowly time crawled by. Iliz Plou would be up there with Efa for hours. She might stay up there a whole day, or even longer.

And what if something went wrong? "Gods forbid!" Malk exclaimed, first in Quimperi and then in Nistrian. Begging his gods was all he could do. The midwife couldn't have been plainer about that.

Of course, men and women who clung to the Old Faith had been hurling prayers at their gods since this accursed war began. Yes, they'd prayed before it started, too, but all the more—and all the more desperately—since that day. And how much help had the gods given them?

Every train stuffed full of Malk's coreligionists that left for unknown places in the east, every trainload of believers in the Old Faith that vanished without a trace, answered that question. Malk ignored the answer. He was not a pious man in any common sense of the word, but now he needed to believe in gods who helped people who believed in them. Gods like that might keep Efa safe from harm.

Malk shook his head again. Gods like that *would* keep Efa safe. If anything happened to her . . . He'd asked Guer for a vial of poison in case the Chleuh or the Watchmen grabbed him. A quick end would be better, far better, than the one they'd give him.

A quick end also might be better than the endless anguish of going on without Efa. Along with Sarmel, she anchored his life. He couldn't remember a time when he hadn't known her. They'd been skinny, hungry kids at the orphanage together. Together . . . They'd been together all that time. He wanted her with him as long as he lived.

He remembered when he first noticed her as something more than just another skinny, hungry kid at the orphanage. He'd been twelve, or maybe just eleven. His life had never been the same since. He was lucky—he had the sense to understand how lucky he was.

They'd always wanted a child. They'd always grieved because it seemed they couldn't have one. And now they were about to! Now, when the world was barking mad and only his utility to the ogres from Chlé, who hated all his kind and Efa's, kept him alive.

Why hadn't the baby come? Hadn't Iliz Plou climbed up there weeks ago? Why wasn't she coming down with his son or daughter in her arms? Or calling him up to see what Efa and he had made together?

Not quite by accident, his eyes found one of the clocks. He stared at it in pained disbelief. Only an hour and a half had gone by? Impossible! Something must have gone wrong with it at this worst of all possible times! But when he turned to the other one, it said the same thing.

Had it broken, too, or . . . ? Addled as he was with prefatherhood jitters, he wasn't addled enough to believe in two clocks broken exactly the same way. He came close, but he wasn't.

A turtle with rheumatism, a snail with a sore foot—they both moved far faster than time just then. He'd wait six or eight hours, then check one clock or the other and find a quarter of an hour had gone by. It would have been funny if it hadn't made him want to shriek.

Somewhere up in the north, the Chleuh were battling the Hontermen and Anadans who'd crossed the Narrow Sea to try to take Quimper away from King Kangen. It was the most important thing in the world . . . unless your wife lay upstairs, trying to push out a baby.

Then Efa screeched or groaned or made some kind of purely animal noise or did all of them together at once. The sound was full of effort and pain to a degree Malk had never imagined, much less felt. A few minutes later, she did it again.

He couldn't help himself. He ran to the bottom of the stairs and called up: "Is she all right?"

"Shut up, you idiot," Iliz Plou explained. Shut up Malk did.

Efa made that astonishing, dreadful noise once more. Malk wanted to stuff his fingers into his ears so he wouldn't have to hear his wife hurt so. Then she fell silent again, and not hearing her terrified him, too.

A little later, he heard another sound, one he'd never thought he'd hear coming from his flat: the high, thin cry of a baby very new to the world. Wonder and awe tingled through him, but dread remained. "Is she all right?" he called again.

This time, the midwife sounded friendlier. "Yes, she's doing as well as anyone could hope for," she answered. "And congratulations, Master Malkovici. You have a little girl with a fine set of lungs."

"A little girl!" Malk exclaimed. He'd rather hoped for a son, but a daughter was wonderful, too. "Can I come up and see her?"

"In a few minutes," Iliz Plou said. "Let me set things to rights here a little." She took hardly longer than she'd promised before summoning Malk like a queen calling for a servitor.

The bedroom smelled of sweat and blood and other, earthier, things. Blood stained the sheets, too. Efa looked as if she'd fought harder than the Quimperi army had against King Kangen's warriors. She was pale as milk and greasy with sweat, her eyes enormous and bulging. The baby in her arms was almost as purple as she was pink. The shape of her head alarmed Malk. "Should she look that way?" he blurted.

"Of course she should, you fool of a man," Iliz Plou said scornfully. "She got a little squashed coming out, that's all. They mostly do. She'll be fine. She's fine now."

"All right." Malk felt a little squashed himself.

"Your wife says you're going to call her Lillat. Nothing wrong with that," the midwife said.

"It was my mother's name," Efa said. "I hardly know anything about her, but I know that."

Malk hadn't remembered Efa's mother's name till they started talking about what to name the child. He didn't know the names of his and Sarmel's own parents. That made going with hers easy. He said, "I hope she wears the name through a long, full, happy life."

"That's a good wish any time," Iliz Plou said, and Efa added a weary nod. The midwife went on, "It's especially good the way things are now." Efa nodded again. So did Malk.

Guisa Sachry gave a boy a copper for a copy of *I Am Everywhere.* Brasi Robillach's news sheet had never been printed on good paper. Good paper was for books, not for something you'd pitch into a rubbish bin as soon as you finished it. *I Am Everywhere* still got paper; Count Vurk and the other occupants liked it. But this sheet seemed ready to crumble even before Guisa got done with it.

KING KANGEN'S WARRIORS DRIVE TO THROW BACK INVADERS! a headline shouted. *I Am Everywhere* and the rest of the Chleuh-approved news sheets had been saying to same thing for more than a week. They talked about fierce fighting, vicious fighting, savage fighting. If you took them at face value, the Anadans and Hontermen had spent the past week and more getting smashed again and again.

If! None of the news sheets talked about the invaders getting thrown back into the Narrow Sea. In the story under that vaunting headline, the writer told of desperate fighting in and around the town of Bocaj.

That might not have meant much to many people in Lutesse. Guisa Sachry, though, had played in Bocaj several times. It wasn't a big place, but it had a well-run theatre with some of the best lighting he'd seen outside the capital. It also wasn't a seaside town. It lay fifteen, maybe even twenty, miles inland.

If the Hontermen and Anadans had pushed that far forward in nine or ten days, the Chleuh weren't going to be able to force them out of northern Quimper. The question was more like, how long could Kangen's soldiers keep their foes from bursting out of their beachhead and driving all before them?

The Chleuh weren't driven out yet. One of their officers strode up the sidewalk toward Guisa. As he drew near, he touched a finger to the bill of his cap. "You're the performer, aren't you?" he said in good Quimperi. "Sachry, that's the name."

"Yes, sir, I myself am that man," Guisa replied. "You have the advantage of me, I'm afraid."

"No reason you should know me, Master Sachry. My name is Roupen Tebron. I'm just a quartermaster, not even a fighting soldier. No glory sticks to me. But do you mind letting me glance at your news sheet there for a moment?"

"Of course not!" Guisa handed him *I Am Everywhere*. A tiny scrap of brownish paper flaked off the edge of the sheet and fluttered to the ground.

"My thanks." Tebron's eyes said he too was looking at the story under the hopeful headline. By the speed with which he read, he was indeed fluent in Guisa's language. When he gave the news sheet back, he asked, "What do you think of all this?"

"What can I possibly think?" Guisa had a well-developed sense of self-preservation. "If the powers that be allow the sheets to say what they say, then whatever they say must be true."

"Yes, it must be, mustn't it?" Roupen Tebron's smile didn't reach his eyes. He looked tired and worried. He probably had to guess less than Guisa did to read between the lines. He'd probably heard other Quimperi not telling him everything they were thinking, too. "Stay safe, Master Sachry. We aren't beaten yet." He touched his cap again and went on his way.

Guisa couldn't decide whether to be pleased by what seemed a show of optimism or worried at that *yet*. He ended up feeling both ways at once, which would have been hilarious if he were mugging on the stage but was only confusing in real life.

Some new posters had sprouted on walls and fences. They showed King Kangen and the General striking martial poses side by side, both looking stern and resolute. Beneath them, the posters declared TOGETHER, WE DEFEND QUIMPER!

The posters didn't say what the Chleuh and the General were defending Quimper from. People who read them could think of the Muos. Anyone comfortably well off would hope the schismatics who hated wealth stayed far away. The Hontermen and Anadans, who were actually fighting on Quimperi soil? Fewer folk were likely to want to see them lose.

A constable held up a white-gloved hand, stopping Guisa and a handful of other people from coming any farther. A troop of Chleuh horsemen and what looked like at least a regiment of foot soldiers marched up the cross street, heading north. Guisa didn't know for sure, but guessed that before long they'd try to stop—or at least slow down—the invaders from across the Narrow Sea.

They weren't prime soldiers. A good many of them were in their thirties or even their forties. Some were fatter than they should have been; one or two limped. They were the kind of men who could hold down a conquered kingdom, not the kind who'd go out and conquer another one. They looked nothing like the tough, virile warriors who'd marched into Lutesse when the war was young.

They seemed to know their own shortcomings, too. If they were eager and excited to go into battle against the new invaders of Quimper, they hadn't told their faces about it. They looked as glum and worried as Guisa would have in their boots.

Someone behind him started whistling the mournful tune often played at Quimperi funerals. The Chleuh soldiers probably didn't recognize it. The constable, a Quimperi himself, did. He pointed at whoever that was in back of Guisa and blew a long blast on the brass whistle that hung from a rawhide cord around his neck.

Running footsteps said the local was making a getaway. "Stop that son of a whore!" the constable bawled. "Stop him, I say!"

Guisa was in no position to stop the subversive whistler. No one else seemed to want to try it, either. Cursing a blue streak, the constable pounded after the fellow. The uniformed man wasn't young or thin. He couldn't catch the man who'd musically suggested the Chleuh soldiers were marching to their deaths. Panting and shaking his head, he came back to his place before King Kangen's soldiers had finished trudging past.

He did manage a small spark of élan as he waved pedestrians forward once the way finally cleared. Guisa hoped he wouldn't be late for his own appointment with a backer, or that the man would understand if he was. Lutesse had become a town full of inconveniences these past four years.

Someone else who crossed the street after he did had other things on his mind. "Somebody will know who that swinehound of a constable is," the man told his friend. "Things like that, people like him, they get remembered."

"Bet your arse," the friend replied. "All these things, all these people. They get remembered, and they get paid back. You'd best believe they do."

The longest day of the year was nearly at hand to usher in summer. Just the same, Guisa shivered as if a frosty breeze had slithered under his tunic and were stirring up gooseflesh on his shoulders and back. He reminded himself to send Nea Ennogue another parcel, and to make it especially good. He didn't care for the stiff-necked teacher and writer, but his own neck? He was very fond of that.

XI

"Ah, Sarmel," Malk Malkovici said around an enormous yawn, "I wish I were sleeping at your flat. Then I'd be sleeping, if you know what I mean." He yawned again.

His brother grinned at him without much sympathy. "More fun being an uncle than a papa, you tell me? And you don't even have to stagger out of bed in the middle of the night to feed the brat. Never mind you—how's Efa doing?"

"You know how you hear about people falling asleep standing up? I always thought that was rubbish, but I know better now. I've seen it," Malk answered. At least he and his wife had enough food so Efa could nurse Lillat. Women who were too worn and hungry to make their own milk abandoned their children, scoured Lutesse for wet nurses, or tried to feed their babies on milk from cows and goats—which was also in desperately short supply. Next to nothing came into the Quimperi capital these days. The occupants had other things to worry about.

Sarmel changed the subject: "Were you listening to the crystal last night?" Rattling along in the junk wagon, he could ask dangerous questions like that as long as he didn't shout them.

"Whose?" Malk returned.

"Think you're funny," his brother said, tossing his head. "Shows what *you* know. The real one, of course."

"I wondered if maybe the Locusts or their stooges were telling even bigger lies than usual. Every time you think, *Oh, they can't top* that *one!*, they go and surprise you."

"Except they do it so often, you're hardly surprised any more. Or you'd better not be," Sarmel said, and Malk nodded. Sarmel went on, "Anyway, word is that the Muos have started some big attacks off in the east. To celebrate the anniversary of when King Kangen invaded them, the story goes."

"Isn't that . . . interesting?" Malk said thoughtfully. "I don't think there are enough Chleuh to stop big attacks there *and* the Hontermen and Anadans here, not all at the same time."

"Looks that way to me, too," Sarmel said. "How much do you want to bet that's no accident?"

"What makes you think I want to give you my money?" Malk asked. His brother laughed. Malk wondered what Colonel Tebron would think of the news. If it was true, he didn't expect the Chleuh officer found it so funny. He remembered how Tebron had talked about leading a cavalry attack against the Muos because the other choice would be a cadet still wet behind the ears. Then he'd thought Tebron was bound to be joking or exaggerating. Now he began to believe the quartermaster'd been a prophet.

"What do the Locusts do if everything starts falling apart on them all at once?" his brother asked. "What *can* they do, except surrender on the best terms they're able to dicker?"

"If Kangen were an ordinary sensible person, he might try to do that," Malk answered. "But if Kangen were an ordinary sensible person, he never would have started this war to begin with. And I don't know about the Anadans, but my guess is that the Hontermen and the Muos won't let him give up. They'll want to smash Chlé to ruins so they never have to worry about it again."

"I know how they feel—do I ever!" Sarmel said. Malk nodded

once more. Sarmel hadn't finished: "Most of the Quimperi feel that way, too. All the Quimperi who aren't—"

"—aren't in bed with the Chleuh," Malk broke in.

Now Sarmel's head bobbed up and down. "Not exactly what I was going to say, but by the gods close enough."

"If you and I can see that, bet your arse King Kangen can, too," Malk said. "He isn't stupid—that's not what's wrong with the Chleuh." He remembered Guer, or whatever the woodsrunner's real name was. "What's wrong with them is, if they can't run everything, they'll want to break everything so nobody else can run it, either."

"If they want to break Chlé, that's fine by me. Better than fine, in fact," Sarmel said. "But they still hold big chunks of Muosi, and most of Quimper, too. Do you think they'd smash Lutesse like a nasty little boy throwing a fit because his mother won't let him have a candied apple?"

"It's crossed my mind. Hasn't it crossed yours, too?" Malk replied. "Winning or dying: that's about all Kangen's got in him, looks like. He wants other people to give up. He'd never do it himself. Or do you think I'm wrong? I'd love it for you to tell me I'm wrong and make me believe it."

"I can't. I don't think you are."

"Too bad!" Malk said with heartfelt sincerity.

They rattled past a wall poster of two steely-eyed Chleuh soldiers escorting captured Hontermen and Anadans. It showed King Kangen's warriors as young and fit and strong, with neatly trimmed whiskers and clean uniforms. It showed them as they'd presented themselves to the world when they marched down the Boulevard of Dreams, in other words.

Their foes, by contrast, were dirty and bedraggled. A couple had bandaged wounds. A couple of others were black fellows from one or another of Honter's tropical colonies. The legend at the the top was in big red syllables. "What does it say?" Malk asked.

"'Protect civilization! Help Chlé beat the savages!'" his brother answered.

Malk sighed. "The Chleuh mean it, too. I'm sure of that. They never have learned now to look in the mirror."

Guisa Sachry studied himself in the dressing-room mirror. He'd always been a handsome dog—he knew that. But time was having its way with him, as it had its way with everybody. His jowls sagged more and more. Makeup kept that from showing too much to the audience, but not to him. Makeup also helped hide the dark pouches under his eyes . . . again, from a distance. People in the seats wouldn't—might not—know he dyed his hair. At least he still had hair to dye. Too many performers his age clapped on wigs to hide their shiny scalps. You could always tell, too.

Vonney set a hand on his shoulder. "You look splendid," she said. For a long time after she found out about Xya Fulgine, she hadn't paid him those little compliments. He hadn't known how much he missed them till he had them back.

"Thank you, my dear. Thank you so much." Guisa sounded more sincere than he commonly did. He looked her up and down. "So do you."

"I bet you say that to all the girls." Vonney could have put a scorpion's sting into the words. Lately, she had put that kind of sting into her gibes. Now, though, she was just teasing. Guisa hoped so, anyhow.

A stagehand tapped at the door. "Five minutes!" he said through it, and went down the hall to tap and warn at the next one.

"Shall we?" Guisa said grandly.

"We'd better, don't you think?" Vonney answered. They took their places in the wings. The house lights were still up. Guisa could get a quick look at the audience. It was the same kind he'd seen for the past four years: Chleuh officers and soldiers (mostly officers down close to the stage), Quimperi who got on well with the occupants for political or business reasons, and the women who kept such men company.

As the lights dimmed and the music swelled, he wondered how much longer he'd keep putting on shows for this kind of crowd. Even sheets like *I Am Everywhere* couldn't deny that the Hontermen and Anadans went on moving forward, moving down toward Lutesse from the north. Guisa never doubted that he'd keep putting on shows. The idea that no one would want to watch him was unimaginable.

Then he was on. He stopped thinking about everything that wasn't part of the play and the audience's response to it. He noticed where the laughs and the applause were louder than he'd looked for, and where they fell short. He could worry about how to tweak a line or make a dance routine more interesting at the same time as he spouted bawdy silliness. He'd put on this comedy since the days before the war. He could do it in his sleep (unkind critics—and what other sort were there?—had been known to suggest he sometimes did).

But the performance got interrupted in a way it wouldn't have in those long-gone peacetime days. Bells all through Lutesse clanged out a warning of attack from the sky.

The house lights came up again. Guisa Sachry went from performer to host in an eyeblink. "Your attention, please!" he said in a commanding voice. "This is a modern theatre, and was built to double as a shelter. Its cellars boast most sturdy roofs. Please take the stairs down to them in a quick but orderly fashion."

He gestured to an actress who played a woman too blind to find him attractive. She said more or less the same thing in Chleuh, for the benefit of the occupants who'd come to ogle pretty girls and didn't know enough Quimperi to follow the action. Guisa thought the announcement sounded better in his own language.

Stairs down do the cellars also ran from the wings. Performers and stage crew hurried down them. Guisa wasn't even halfway down when dragonflyers started pounding Lutesse. The stairway shuddered under his feet. A chandelier hanging from the sloping ceiling swung from the force of the blasts of energy, making shadows swoop alarmingly. One of the dancers in the chorus yipped—not a scream, but close. A couple of people laughed nervously.

Count Vurk gave Guisa an ironic bow as they both hid from the Anadans and Hontermen whose dragons seemed to rule the night sky above Lutesse. "I had not planned to watch you from such close range, sir," said the Chleuh minister to Quimper—in effect, King Kangen's viceroy here.

"Such is life. Such is war." Guisa spouted clichés, not least to keep from showing how nervous he was himself.

He seemed to create the proper impression on the Chleuh nobleman. "Just so," Vurk replied. "Your spirit does you credit. Do not despair of our cause, either. The secret sorceries our sovereign's wizards are readying even now will yet lay Dreslon waste and give our mad and wicked foes everything they deserve. Yes, everything, I assure you, and more besides."

Before Guisa could answer, more unleashed energies made the ground shake under his feet and Vurk's, made mortar dust drift down from the roofs whose strength he'd praised on stage, and briefly startled the salamanders into going dark. Several people, women and men, squawked in the sudden blackness. Luckily, it lasted only a few heartbeats.

Vurk managed a dry chuckle. "All things considered, I would sooner have seen the end of your play."

"All things considered, your Excellency, I would sooner have given it." Guisa looked around. He would have liked to finish the comedy down here, but there just wasn't room.

"I was going to invite you and your lovely lady to a gathering after the performance, but. . . ." The Chleuh minister spread his hands. "Tonight, the thought will have to do duty for the deed."

"A kind notion, your Excellency, most kind." The deed would

have filled Guisa's belly, and Vonney's, too. The thought, no matter how kind, did rather less along those lines. One of Guisa's thoughts escaped him: "The air pirates grow bolder."

"So they do," Vurk said, and not another word.

Most of the time, Guisa would have taken the hint and talked about something else. But, with one possibly dangerous thought already running loose, he freed another, asking, "Ah, how do things up in the north fare, your Excellency?"

"What? With all the reports in the news sheets and over the crystal, you don't already know everything there is to know about the war?" Even in a crowded cellar, even under assault by dragonflyers who hated his kingdom and everyone in it, Count Vurk didn't lose his sardonic aplomb. Guisa admired his consistency. After a moment, the Chleuh noble continued, "If things were better, we would have driven the enemy back into the sea. If they were worse, we would have surrendered by now. Somewhere in that middle range, sir. Somewhere in that middle range."

"I see," said Guisa, who didn't. Vurk was, and no doubt meant to be, as uninformative as he could. Guisa tried one more time: "Your Excellency, could you be a bit more precise?"

"I'm sure I could, but I don't care to." In case Guisa Sachry still didn't take the point, Vurk added, "If you'll excuse me—" and limped away, pushing past people who didn't dodge fast enough to suit him.

Vonney's breath was warm and moist in Guisa's ear as she murmured, "Did he tell you anything worth hearing?"

"Not a word. But he told me nothing with great grace and cleverness," Guisa answered. "He writes his own part skillfully, I must say."

His wife rolled her eyes. "Only a playwright would talk that way." She might have said, *Only a lunatic would* . . . For all practical purposes, she had.

The attack from the air went on for three hours. Now, Guisa realized, the Anadans and Hontermen would have dragons here on the mainland. They wouldn't have to fly across the Narrow Sea to reach Lutesse. Neither the dragons nor the men who flew them would be nearly so worn as had been true before. If they felt like flattening the capital of Quimper, what could stop them?

Chleuh dragons and searchlights and bolt-spitters ran through Guisa's mind. But King Kangen's warriors hadn't done very well against this attack. Would they—could they—perform any better next time, or the time after that?

For the sake of his wish to grow older than he was, Guisa hoped so. Whether what he hoped had anything to do with what was real . . . he'd find out soon. So would the rest of Lutesse.

The air still stank of sour smoke. Some of the men clearing rubble wore wet cloths over their mouths and noses to try to keep from breathing in the filth. Malk and Sarmel Malkovici both did. Malk didn't think it helped much, but he didn't suppose it could hurt.

Wet cloths did only too little against another reek that grew by the day (indeed, by the hour): the stench of death. Whenever workers uncovered another body or opened the way down to a cellar that had turned into a death trap for the people who'd sheltered inside, his stomach wanted to turn over.

He wasn't the only one. After a while, Sarmel said, "We're getting lots of scrap, but you can buy things at too high a price."

"Colonel Tebron wants us here." Malk touched the brassard on his tunic front that showed the Chleuh he wasn't a looter and was authorized to paw through the wreckage of Lutesse for the occupants. His brother wore an identical brassard. Another one, larger and gaudier, adorned their wagon. Malk went on, "If we disappear, he'll hear about it before we get home. Do you want that to happen?"

"I want it not to matter," Sarmel said.

"Maybe, before too long, it won't," Malk said. "But it still does. You've got to remember, the difference between bad and worse is a lot bigger than the difference between good and better."

Sarmel's bushy eyebrows, so much like Malk's, came down and

together while a vertical line between them trapped shadow and perhaps soot with it: as much of his brother's frown as the older Malkovici could see. "You're especially annoying when you make sense," Sarmel said.

"If you think I'm glad to be here . . ." Malk's voice trailed away. The only thing he cared about was keeping Tebron sweet. Without a protector, no one who clung to the Old Faith could last long here.

Sarmel looked over his shoulder. The way his eyes widened made Malk's gaze follow his.

Stepping out of a carriage was a Chleuh general. It wasn't Stulp, King Kangen's commander in Quimper. This fellow was younger and sprier. After a moment, Malk recognized him as General Tritzkhol, the officer in charge of defending Lutesse. If the woodsrunners rose in revolt or if the Anadans and Hontermen neared, he would be the fellow who gave the local garrison its orders.

He looked like a worried man as he strode through the streets kicking rubble out of the way. Neither the destruction itself nor the mingled reeks it left in its wake seemed to trouble him. No—if Malk was any judge, what bothered him was that the devastation had happened at all. He might have been happy had his kingdom dealt it out. That Chlé and Chlé's clients had suffered it and hadn't been able to stop it . . . *that* worried him.

He missed very little. He certainly noticed the brassarded junk wagon and, a moment later, the brassarded junkmen. He recognized them for what they were right away. That alarmed Malk. Then the general changed course and came over to them. That alarmed him even more.

As Tritzkhol neared, Malk and Sarmel yanked off their caps and bowed their heads. Followers of the Old Faith had to seem servile toward Chleuh they didn't know. "Who gave you your safe-conducts, you two?" Tritzkhol asked in good but throatily accented Quimperi.

Not raising his eyes to look the general in the face, Malk answered, "Sir, may it please your Excellency, sir, we had the honor and privilege to receive them from the estimable and honorable Colonel Tebron." Surfeit of honorifics aside, he told the truth. Beside him, Sarmel nodded, also without looking up.

"Ah," Tritzkhol said. "From what I've seen of him, Tebron is a sound man. He must think the same of you both, or he wouldn't have given them to you. Carry on." He started to turn away, then caught himself. "And if I run into you again, don't bother with this silly play-acting. It wastes my time, and I'm sure it makes the two of you feel like idiots." This time, he did stump off, a couple of aides in his wake.

Sarmel spoke in quiet Nistrian out of the corner of a mouth that barely moved: "Well, he could be worse."

"He could. He really could." Malk answered the same way in the same language. Growing up in that orphanage had taught them a lot of the tricks people learned from five or ten years in prison.

"Think he'll check us?" Sarmel asked, still as far under the rose as he could go.

"Of course he will," Malk said.

"He didn't ask who we were."

"So what? He knows what we look like and what the wagon looks like. Tebron won't sell us out."

"How can you be so sure? He's a Locust, after all."

"I know. But if he wanted us dead, he could have had us killed any time since the Chleuh came down the Boulevard of Dreams four years ago. Nobody would have said a word. It's keeping people like us alive that starts tongues wagging." For a moment, Malk let his bitterness show.

Sarmel grunted as if he'd taken an elbow in the belly. "There is that, sure enough." He stooped and threw aside a big sheet of plastered board, one Malk hadn't cared to try to lift. "Ha! Look what we've got here!" his brother exclaimed. "Pipes and taps and who the demon knows what all else?" He seized some of the loot and threw it into the wagon bed.

Malk grabbed more of the metal. It would make Colonel Tebron happy . . . for as long as Tebron stayed in the scrap-collecting business in Lutesse, anyhow.

Another gathering, this one at General Stulp's. In a way, nothing seemed to have changed: Chleuh officers and officials; the inevitable snoop in a tarncape, trying to be completely invisible in a gloomy corner; Quimperi who clung to the Chleuh for a free ride, the way suckerfish clung to sharks; pretty women to amuse Chleuh and Quimperi alike. Plenty to eat, something even the Chleuh had trouble guaranteeing these days. Plenty to drink, in case thought got in the way.

But fewer officers and officials were here than there would have been before the landings in the north succeeded. Guisa noticed that right away. Some of the warriors who weren't here were bound to be up there, doing their best to act like heroes, or at least to stay alive till the war ended.

Not all the Quimperi who would have been at an affair like this a couple of years before were here now, either. Most of the ones who were had no way back if King Kangen's men lost. Odrio Cazh stayed close to the bar, soaking up spirits like a rag. Erol Paki was trying to eat from a plate piled high with food and chat up a striking brunette at the same time.

And Brasi Robillach was deep in conversation with a tall, handsome Chleuh captain. The women at the gathering did nothing for him, but he still found ways to entertain himself.

Eyeing the crowd, Guisa found the obvious question. *What am I doing here?* he wondered. His own plate held steamed prawns and fried crabs. A golden wine he couldn't have found or afforded anywhere else filled his goblet. *I am an animal. I enjoy the animal pleasures,* he told himself. *No one enjoys hunger.*

He also enjoyed looking at the women Stulp had laid on. He didn't do anything but look at them, not with Vonney looking at him. He didn't like to admit she still held the upper hand, but couldn't very well deny it.

He didn't see Xya Fulgine among the women. Maybe the general hadn't asked her to come. Maybe he had, and she didn't care to. Maybe she felt the new wind blowing down from the north. Maybe she thought it would rise to a gale that swept all this away.

Maybe she was right.

A glass of wine in his own hand, General Stulp pushed his way through the crowd toward Guisa. The performer bowed. "Your Excellency," he murmured, and then, "As always, I find myself indebted to your kindness, sir, for this generous invitation."

"My pleasure, Master Sachry," the Chleuh commandant said. "With you, I mean that more literally than I do with most of your countrymen. You will know I often come to the theatre to watch your lovely lady and you. Whatever you're in, I don't go away unhappy. That is no small boon you've granted me, especially in these hard times. I hope food and drink and perhaps even a bit of pleasant company help even the balance a bit."

Guisa bowed again, more deeply this time. "I am delighted to hear you've enjoyed my silliness and Vonney's, sir. Playing to an appreciative audience is the greatest pleasure an actor has."

"Can't speak for the rest of the house, but I like what you do, sure enough." Stulp's mouth twisted. "And I thought I'd take advantage of the occasion to get you here and tell you so, because I don't know how much longer I'll be able to keep throwing this kind of bash here."

"Your Excellency is . . . forthright." Guisa paused before picking the last word. He wanted to make sure he used the right one. Then, taking advantage of the general's frankness, he asked, "Are things truly so bad as you seem to make them sound?"

Before answering, General Stulp drained his glass and set it on the snowy linen enrobing the table. "By no means. They're much worse than that," he said. Guisa must have stared, for the Chleuh commandant let out a harsh chuckle. "They cursed well are, Master

Sachry. You may gossip as widely as you please—I doubt what you say will surprise anyone. And you may rest assured that King Kangen, the gods bless him and keep him, knows my views in far greater detail than you do. We've been futtered for fair ever since the Anadans and Hontermen established themselves on the mainland."

"That is not the story the news sheets and the crystal tell, or even his Excellency the minister," Guisa said.

"Yes? And so?" Berhard Stulp waited. When Guisa didn't say anything, the Chleuh nodded like a mechanism that badly needed oil. "We try not to advertise our disasters too loudly, sir. That doesn't always work, but we do try. We still would stand some kind of chance, I think, if the gods-despised Muos weren't biting great chunks out of our armies in the east. We might bring more men here—if we had more men to bring, I mean. As is . . ." He shook his head as jerkily as he'd nodded.

"The crystal and the sheets haven't talked much about that, either," Guisa said carefully.

"As little as they could," Stulp agreed. "But just because you don't talk about something doesn't mean it isn't happening. I wish it did. Life would be simpler." His chuckle didn't signal amusement—anything but, Guisa judged. The general went on, "I daresay you didn't look for me to drop the woes of the world on your shoulders. That's what you get for having a friendly face." There was something few people had accused Guisa of before. With a final sad shrug, Stulp strode away.

Guisa headed straight for the bar. He needed numbing. Three men worked there, but the lines were still long. A lot of people seemed to feel the way he did. Maybe he wasn't the only one on whom the Chleuh commandant had unburdened himself. Or maybe it was just getting easier for the Quimperi who followed King Kangen to see they'd chosen the wrong side.

"Yes, sir?" asked a bartender whose hands built perfect drinks whether he watched them or not.

"Brandy over ice. A double," Guisa said. The thin little man poured spirits and used tongs to pluck chunks of ice from a bucket chilled by a small ice elemental who dwelt in the thick base.

"Here you are, sir," the barman said. It was nearer a triple than a double, but Guisa didn't mind. On the contrary. His tip made the man eye him as if to ask whether he was sure. He waved aside the unspoken question. The barman gave him half a bow.

"I hope you are well, Master Sachry." Odrio Cazh's glass held brandy, too. By his grand manner, the Leader of the Quimperi Popular Front had started pouring it down some time before. He raised the glass. "Here's to victory! Victory swift, victory sure, victory complete!"

After listening to General Stulp, Guisa didn't see that victory coming. But he wasn't an actor for nothing. "To victory!" he said, not missing a beat, and clinked glasses with the occupants' Quimperi hunting hound. They drank together. Even iced, the brandy started a fire in Guisa's gullet.

"We've got the Hontermen and Anadans where we want them now," Odrio Cazh declared. "They can't shelter behind the Narrow Sea any more. They're finally close at hand, so we can reach forth our strong right arms and kill them in swarms."

"I trust you've given General Stulp the benefit of your warlike expertise and insights." Guisa didn't even sound sarcastic: sure enough, an actor to the marrow.

Odrio Cazh sniffed loudly. "Sir, I'm sure I've said it before, but the Chleuh who serve King Kangen don't deserve him. And he deserves better than they give. I am loyal to his Majesty unto death and beyond!"

Guisa almost asked him how he proposed to manage that. Brandy or no brandy, at the last instant he held back. Odrio Cazh might be looking for a quarrel—or might repeat anything he said to the Watchmen. In Quimper, Kangen's locals were more dangerous to their own countrymen than the Chleuh were.

Earnestly, the Quimperi who seemed to wish he were a Chleuh went on, "Kangen, gods bless him, he'll win in spite of everything, you know. He really will. He has that unstoppable will, and it *will* triumph. Nothing can hold him back. Nothing, do you hear me?"

"Of course I hear you," Guisa answered; Odrio Cazh was shouting in his face. He added, "No one could possibly deny that King Kangen is a remarkable man."

"Remarkable? You don't know the half of it. In truth, Master Sachry, you don't," Odrio Cazh said. "I've had the pleasure—no, the privilege—of meeting him. The ancients spoke of demigods, beings halfway between men and the great gods in the heavens. That never made any sense to me till I met King Kangen and clasped his hand. Now I understand!"

As someone who worshiped only himself, Guisa Sachry had always found trying to penetrate someone else's mysticism a mug's game. "Isn't that interesting?" he said now, and added, "Excuse me, but I think Vonney's waving at me." She wasn't, but it gave him an excuse to get away. He wondered whether he'd ever come to another affair like this. The way things were, he doubted it.

Malk Malkovici opened his shop an hour earlier than usual. For one thing, it was the season where the sun went to bed late and got up early. For another, after Lillat started yowling like a cat with its tail caught in the door, he knew he had no chance of going back to sleep himself. And so, rubbing his eyes, he put on some everyday clothes and went downstairs to try to do something useful himself.

So he found the body in front of his shop before Bezen the constable did.

By his uniform, the dead man had belonged to the Watchmen. Somebody'd shot him in the back of the head at close range. There was a hole in his head behind his right ear, with blood puddling under it. Half the crossbow quarrel stuck out above his left eye. More blood ran down his face and pooled between cobblestones.

Closing the door behind him, he hurried down to the corner

kiosk that sold news sheets. The old woman who ran it raised an eyebrow at him. "You're up beforetimes today," she remarked.

"I am, Mistress Quilly," he agreed. "Tell me, have you seen Bezen on his rounds yet?"

She shook her head. "I haven't. You're the first one who's asked after him in a demon of a long time, too—I'll tell you that."

"I believe you. Even so, today I need him."

Before he could say anything more, the gray-whiskered Chleuh underofficer who'd been a regular at the kiosk since the occupation was new ambled up and bought a news sheet in his own language. "Here you go, you old pussy," Mistress Quilly said, not unkindly, as she handed it to him. "They haven't shipped you off somewhere to get killed so far, eh?"

The man smiled vaguely and left, sheet in hand. He never had learned any Quimperi, not in these past four years. He wouldn't last long if he actually had to fight; anyone could see that. Since he didn't seem a bad fellow, Malk hoped he'd stay out of danger.

"Why on earth would anybody need Bezen?" Mistress Quilly asked. "Chances are even his mother doesn't, if they didn't just take him out of a crate and wind the key in his back."

In spite of everything, Malk laughed. But he answered, "I need him because there's a body in the street right in front of my place. It isn't there on account of me, and I don't want him thinking it is. It's a Watchman's body, you see."

"Oh." That sobered her. She gave back a slow nod. "There's a reason, by the gods." Her narrow eyes swung right, toward the main street. "Well, you're in luck, if it is luck—here he comes now."

Sure enough, Bezen strode up to the news kiosk, a parade of one. "Good morning, Mistress Quilly," he said, and then, "What do you know, Malk?"

"Constable, I know someone murdered a Watchman right in front of my door, and I know it wasn't me," Malk said.

That rocked Bezen back on his heels. "Bugger me blind! Another one!" he said, which was . . . interesting. He visibly gathered himself. "You'd better take me back to him, eh?"

"Come along with me, then, sir," Malk said.

In front of the shop, Bezen stared at the corpse without touching it. He didn't want to do anything that might make the constabulary's forensic sorcerers unhappy. "Do you know this fellow?"

"No, sir. He isn't one of the ones I had anything to do with when they grabbed me," Malk answered.

"One or two of those, maybe you wouldn't care if they came down with a sudden case of loss of life?" Bezen suggested. Malk didn't answer. A constable could say whatever he wanted. A man talking with a constable didn't want to aim the headsman's axe at the back of his own neck. Bezen rubbed his chin. "He's been hanging around here? Asking people in the neighborhood questions about you?"

"Not that I know of. I'm either in the shop or out getting stuff for it, though. Have you seen him while you're walking your beat?"

"Like you said, not that I know of." Bezen rubbed his chin again. "I don't suppose you'd fall over dead from surprise if I told you the woodsrunners are rubbing out Watchmen whenever they find the chance?"

"No, I expect not," Malk said. Then he took a chance of his own: "The way things are right now, it looks like maybe the Watchmen didn't pick the right side. You make a mistake like that, chances are you wind up paying for it."

"There is that," Bezen—agreed? "Me, I'm lucky. I just kept doing the job I was doing already. No one can say anything different about me, neither."

"You haven't changed a bit," Malk said. That wasn't quite true, but Bezen could have got much worse than he had.

"Who wants change? Change is bad. Go on the way you are for as long as you can. Everything else is worse and hurts more." The constable eyed Malk. "You'll give a statement that this fellow's a stranger to you and just happened to wind up dead on your doorstep, you don't know how?"

"Yes, sir. I won't even be lying when I do it."

"All right. I'll go back to the station and have 'em bring the meat wagon. Nobody will get real upset at a dead Watchman, not the way things are right now." Off Bezen went, officious as ever. Malk watched him around the corner. Was *this* how the Chleuh grip on Lutesse loosened and fell away? Maybe it was.

XII

"Move!" the wizard said, and waved angrily at Guisa Sachry. "Yes, you! The old one with the big belly! Get out of my line of sight!"

He was a Chleuh, of course. The way he talked and his uniform both told Guisa as much. He was also a walking demonstration of why King Kangen's folk made all their neighbors love them so much. A Quimperi wizard at least might have politely asked Guisa to move.

Because the Chleuh was a clot, Guisa looked back at him and said, "I'm sorry, but I can't understand a word you're saying."

The occupants might not be having a happy time in Quimper, but they'd lost none of their arrogance. And antagonizing a wizard was seldom a bright idea. This fellow pointed a forefinger at Guisa—a forefinger, he saw with a sudden rush of apprehension, whose nail put him in mind of an eagle's talon—and chanted in his own language.

A sudden thin line of fire burst from that clawlike nail and made the very tip of Guisa's right shoe smoke and start to flame. He yipped and hopped and stomped out the little blaze with the sole of his left shoe. And he got out of the wizard's line of sight.

"You understand me now, Turds-for-Brains?" the Chleuh asked, and peered down the middle of the almost empty Boulevard of Dreams toward the distant Obelisk.

"Yes, yes." Guisa wanted nothing so much as to get away.

But the Chleuh wizard didn't feel like letting him escape, not yet. "You better understand me, Dogface," he said, a hate-filled grin stretching his mouth wide. "You Quimperi, you think, *Ha! Ha! The Hontermen and Anadans come! We don't got to pay attention to Chleuh no more!* You think that way, fat man?"

"As a matter of fact, no," Guisa replied.

"Tell me more lies, hey? Hontermen and Anadans, they not in Lutesse. We, King Kangen's men, we are. We knock this worthless city flat before we let them have it. What you think of that, lard tub?"

"You can't!" Guisa blurted. Lutesse was one of the most famous, one of the most beautiful, cities in the world. Deliberately damaging it would be a horrible crime. But how many horrible crimes had the Chleuh already committed wherever their power reached? How much did they care? What would one more atrocity be, among so many?

"Can. Will." As if it were a crossbow, the wizard aimed his clawed index finger at the Obelisk. "Knock that fornicator down. Knock it flat. Block a whole swarm of streets that way. Whole bunch of other places to wreck. We maybe leave one of these days, but you remember us once we're gone."

Guisa didn't argue with him. Arguing with a lunatic, he'd always heard, was a waste of time. He did hurry away now, straight to the Chleuh ministry, from which Count Vurk had ruled Quimper the past four years. People there knew him, recognized him, treated him with the respect he was sure he deserved.

And they passed him on to the minister. In less than half an hour, he sat in Vurk's comfortable if heavily furnished sanctum. "What can I do for you, Master Sachry?" the Chleuh noble asked. "Would you care for something to drink? You seem a bit green around the gills, if you don't mind my saying so."

"In a moment, maybe. First, your Excellency, please tell me straight out—does Chlé intend to ruin Lutesse to keep her enemies from using it after her own forces leave the city?"

"Where on earth did you hear that?" Vurk said—which, Guisa noted, was not a denial.

"It doesn't matter. What matters is whether it's true."

"I love this city. Anyone who knows me at all knows I love this city. You, for instance, will know I love this city," the Chleuh minister said, and Guisa had to nod, for he did know that. Count Vurk continued, "My job, from the moment I got here, has been to do everything I can for Lutesse in the circumstances in which the city, your kingdom, and my kingdom find themselves. You will know that, too."

"Yes, your Excellency," Guisa replied, for that was also true. But a lifetime on the stage and four years of Lutesse's news sheets had also left him as sensitive to what wasn't said as to what was. "Then why won't you just come out and tell me Chlé means Lutesse no harm?"

Something tightened for a moment under Vurk's pouchy eyes. Guisa knew what that meant—something on the order of *Curse it, you're not quite so stupid as I thought you were*. The count said, "Before I am anything else, I am King Kangen's servant. You will also know *that*, Master Sachry. When the king gives an order, what can his servants do but obey?"

"Even if it's a stupid order? Even if it's a wicked order?"

"To answer these questions admits the possibility that King Kangen could give a stupid, wicked order. Since I do not and will not admit this possibility, there's really no point to further conversation, is there?"

"I'm afraid not, your Excellency," Guisa said sadly. Knowing dismissal when he heard it, he stood to go. But he wouldn't leave without adding, "I thought better of you, sir. By the gods, I did."

"If I were the monster you make me out to be, I'd clap you in the dungeon for that, and no one would see you again or dare admit he'd ever watched you perform. You might live a while after that, but you would cease to exist. As things are, I expect to sit down front the next time you tread the boards, and to enjoy myself. Good day till then."

Guisa left. Guisa, in fact, fled. That wouldn't have saved him were Vurk less civilized. But he was sure down to his marrow that a civilized monster remained a monster still.

As far as Malk Malkovici knew, Iliz Plou had never borne a child of her own. With the midwife, he wasn't sure how far he knew. She was uncommonly good at keeping her own business to herself. But he was sure she knew everything about babies worth knowing, much more than he did and more than most mothers ever would.

Day by day, sometimes hour by hour, Lillat began to turn into, well, a person. The stump of the cord that had connected her to Efa dried up and fell off, leaving her navel as a mark of where it had been. Together, Efa and Malk burned the stump in a brazier with fragrant sandalwood chips, murmuring prayers and charms as the little flames consumed it. No one would ever be able to use it to work magic against their daughter or against Efa through it.

And, as Iliz Plou had prophesied, Lillat's head began to take on a shape more like that of most people. Malk ran a hand over the back of his own noggin. "Good thing she isn't kind of flat there, the way I am," he said.

"A very good thing," Efa agreed. "Of course, we haven't dropped her on her head half a dozen times, the way you got treated when you were tiny."

"Me?" Malk's voice dripped mock surprise and fury. "And all this time I thought that was Sarmel!"

"Him, too, I'm sure," Efa said.

But Sarmel denied everything when Malk told him the story while they were out scavenging a couple of days later. "They just kicked me around like a football. Everybody could already tell I didn't have any brains worth scrambling. You, though, you might have been dangerous if they hadn't made sure to stupid you up."

Malk retained a lingering hope he might yet be dangerous. He retained some other hopes, too, hopes that were starting to flourish, not just to linger. Seeing a boy flogging *I Am Everywhere*, he pulled the junk wagon to the curb and bought a copy.

"What did you do that for when you don't have your syllables?" Sarmel asked.

"You've got yours. Maybe they didn't drop you on your head all the time after all. Maybe," Malk said. "So read to me. Tell me what's going on. It's getting to the point where the Chleuh can't hide how bad things are in the north."

"Or in the east," Sarmel put in. "The Muos are kicking them even harder than they kicked Muosi three years ago. All that rubbish about straightened lines and improved defensive positioning, that's all it is—rubbish."

"Read, then."

"All right, all right. Here's a statement from General Stulp, saying large numbers of Chleuh soldiers have broken out through the Lafeiz Pass and are regrouping farther south. He says he's confident they'll keep fighting strongly."

"If you listen to the other side, they say they've got the Locusts trapped there, and the Anadans and Hontermen are tearing them to pieces," Malk remarked.

"Who would ever listen to the other side? You might get in trouble if you did that," Sarmel said. "Besides, it's taken them six weeks to get down to the Lafeiz Pass. When will they start rolling the way the Muos are? Kangen must be shitting himself over how things are going there."

"Here's hoping," Malk said. His brother laughed.

They had good luck at the rubbish tip. A part of their good luck was other people's bad; the tip was one in the northern part of Lutesse, which Anadan and Honterese dragons had been pounding to make it hard for the Chleuh to move more reinforcements and supplies through the capital. They'd smashed up the railway lines and the main highway leading north . . . and everything close to them. Assault from the sky was often devastating, seldom precise.

The horses complained about all the extra weight they had to haul back to the shop by going even slower than usual. "You're lucky you've got me sitting back here," Malk told them. "The way you slack off, a lot of people would whip you to dog meat."

Sarmel snorted. "Have you ever touched them with the lash?"

"Once. I told you about that."

"Oh. You're right. I forgot about that time," Sarmel said.

"I wish I could." The looks on the faces of those friends and loved ones of the Quimperi Popular Party volunteers when they recognized him as someone who belonged to the Old Faith would live forever in Malk's memory. He hoped he'd stop seeing it in nightmares one of these years. He'd been at the zoological gardens once when a keeper was throwing the wolves chunks of cut-up meat. . . .

The horses did speed up for a little while after he snapped the whip above their bony backs. They still remembered that dreadful day, too. To them, it was the day their driver went raving mad. They didn't understand why he had. They were only horses, after all. *They don't know how lucky they are*, Malk thought.

Boys were screeching to get people to buy their afternoon news sheets. Having bought a morning one, Malk ignored the treble shrieks till a particularly shrill one slithered past his ears and into his brain: "King Kangen escapes murder try!"

"What?" the junkman said, and steered the wagon over to the edge of the street.

"They've been yelling that for a while now. I just thought you didn't care," Sarmel told him.

"I don't—but I do. You know what I mean." Malk hopped down from the wagon. His aching back and shoulders reminded him he wasn't so young as he had been once upon a time. He bought a sheet, took it back, and thrust it at his literate brother. "Here. Tell me what happened. What they say happened, I mean."

"I understood you," Sarmel said. Malk had some trouble getting the horses going again. They seemed offended he wasn't giving them the break they were sure they deserved. Sarmel went on, "Kangen was at the headquarters out in the east, the one they call the Bear's Den, trying to find a way to stop the Muos. One of his generals pulled out a ceremonial dagger and tried to stab him or cut his throat. The guards and the other officers killed him before he could. Kangen has a wound on one arm and another one in his leg, but the story says he'll be fine."

"Of course he will," Malk muttered darkly. Then he said, "One of Kangen's generals tried to do him in? What about the rest? The ones who maybe didn't help the bodyguards finish the fellow with the knife?"

"Hang on. I have to find that." Sarmel opened up the news sheet to get at the continuation of the story. "Here we go . . . 'A plot against the person and the reign of his glorious and triumphant Majesty, King Kangen, is suspected. All officers at the Bear's Den are being rigorously interrogated to learn how far it stretches. The same holds true in Hashtéankh.' That's the capital of Chlé, you know."

"Yes, yes," Malk said impatiently; he *did* know that. "I wonder how many generals will keep their heads once Kangen's butchers get done torturing them." The news sheets could call it interrogation, but he knew better—and what he'd got in the Watchmen's jail was pretty mild, as those things went.

"All right," Sarmel said. "It finishes, 'In spite of this vile, unholy treason, nothing will stop King Kangen from bringing the war to a victorious conclusion and ensuring Chlé's rightful place in the world. The struggle goes on! Forward!'"

"'Forward!'" Malk echoed, and flicked the reins. The horses paid no more attention than they had to.

"Some of the Chleuh are seeing there is no way forward," Sarmel said. "You don't try to kill the king if you don't see that. Unless he's having fun with your wife or your daughter, I mean, and for all the things I've heard about Kangen, I've never heard he takes women who aren't his."

"No, neither have I." Malk felt oddly reluctant to grant King Kangen any virtue, even one so mild and so common.

"They're going to fight as hard as they can. Even harder now, I bet, on account of this," his brother said.

"Probably, yes." Malk looked around. Even with the stench of sour smoke still fouling the air, Lutesse was a beautiful city, unless you were in a neighborhood that had just burned. It was still beautiful for the moment, anyway. "You've heard the stories about what the Locusts will do if they have to pull out of here, haven't you?"

"Everybody has, I think. Those were going around before this thing at the Bear's Den," Sarmel said. "I didn't pay much attention to them, mostly because I didn't want to."

"Same with me. But I don't think they care what they do any more. They never cared much. When you don't care at all . . ." Malk's imagination let him see Lutesse in ruins. He pictured it very clearly, much more so than he wished he did.

There were plays about wreckage and devastation, about people living in the aftermath or in the middle of destruction and despair. Guisa Sachry had performed in several of them. Every once in a while, he enjoyed giving the audience a good cry instead of a laugh.

Playing that kind of role was one thing. Living it turned out to be something else again.

Chleuh soldiers filled the streets of Lutesse, waiting their turn to go forward to try to stop or at least slow down the Anadans and Hontermen. They always traveled in groups and always kept weapons ready. Now that Char Tubis and his little force were back in Quimper, too, the woodsrunners had grown bolder than ever. Any Chleuh they caught wound up dead, and his sword and crossbow joined the other side.

The Watchmen were even jumpier than the Chleuh. They knew most of their countrymen hated them. If they hadn't known, wall scrawls would have told them. So would the frequency with which they got murdered.

A note smeared with what was probably fowl's blood wound up in Guisa's post box, there in the secure lobby of his peaceful block of flats. Marsa the doorwoman handed it to him with the rest of the mail one afternoon. All it said was, *You're next, Sachry!* He didn't show it to Vonney or even tell her about it. He just burned it. If it had a curse attached, he could hope that would take it off.

Every night, on the crystal, Erol Paki kept insisting that Dreslon had to be destroyed. Guisa ran into the little commentator when they both walked into a café at the same time. "Want to join me?" Paki asked.

No, Guisa thought. But he said, "All right." Insulting people the occupants fancied wasn't the kind of thing a sensible man did. After a waiter led them to their seats, though, the actor couldn't help asking, "Do you really think Dreslon will be destroyed?"

"Of course." Paki showed no doubts; he was an actor of sorts himself. A performer, anyhow. "The magics King Kangen will rain down upon Honter with leave it a smoking ruin of its former self." He eyed the menu with an unhappy sneer. "Rather like the bill of fare here."

"Yes, I see," Guisa said. More than half the choices were scratched out—things the kitchen couldn't get any more, no doubt. Prices for what was left had doubled, sometimes tripled.

As he might have in in happier days, the waiter came back with pen poised over notepad. "What can I bring you gentlemen today?"

"Real food would be good," Paki said.

"I'm sorry, sir. We're doing the best we can. Times are hard for everyone." The waiter didn't pretend to misunderstand.

"Let me have a bowl of stew," Guisa said. "That will fill me up no matter what's in it." Before the war, he'd never heard cats called roof rabbits. There weren't many of them in Lutesse these days.

"I'll do the same," Paki said. After the waiter left, he leaned forward to whisper to Guisa: "If it barks when I stick a fork in it, I'll throw the bowl at that fellow."

"I was guessing it would meow," Guisa answered. They both laughed.

Whatever went into the stew, it was about good enough to finish. "Isn't life grand?" Paki said with a rueful shake of his head.

"Lovely," Guisa said. He'd poured down the indifferent house wine, too, to try to distract himself from what he was eating. Maybe he shouldn't have, for it left him franker than he might have been: "How can you keep thinking the Chleuh will smash Honter when they won't even hold on to Lutesse much longer?"

"It doesn't matter," Erol Paki replied, patting his lips with the napkin.

"What do you mean, it doesn't matter? Do you think Char Tubis will kiss you on both cheeks if he gives orders here?"

"I don't care about that tall, troublesome, tuber-nosed fool. If the Chleuh have to pull out, I'll go with them, even into Chlé if I have to. When things work out the way they're supposed to, I'll come back and pay off all my debts." Paki smiled unpleasantly. "I won't be the only one, either. Oh, no."

"I admire your optimism," Guisa said—the most polite thing he could come up with on the spur of the moment.

"I have faith in King Kangen. Everybody should have faith in him. People who don't will be sorry," Paki said. "And those people who schemed to murder him? Roasting over a slow fire's too good for them, way too good! They should pay, their slimy children should pay, and the ugly grandchildren they don't even have yet should pay, too. Kangen never should've been born a Chleuh. The gods should've given him to us. We Quimperi can appreciate him the way he should be! It's not quite like seeing a god on earth, but it's the next best thing."

Odrio Cazh had said much the same thing. Guisa remembered the poster of King Kangen on the wall in General Stulp's headquarters. It showed a man intent on what he was doing and desperately in earnest at its importance. Did that make him godlike? If he got enough other people to feel the way he did and to work to do what he wanted, maybe so.

No matter what Erol Paki said, most of the Chleuh still followed Kangen wherever he led. So did Paki himself, Sep Nardand, Brasi Robillach, and the rest of the Quimperi who thought like them, along with their ilk in other kingdoms Chlé still occupied. In the face of assaults from the Muos, the Hontermen, and the Anadans, would they be enough?

"What will the Chleuh think if you go with them to their own realm?" Guisa asked.

"That we're the only Quimperi left with any sense—what else?" Doubt never troubled Paki.

"Will you be welcome there? They'll have their own troubles." Guisa didn't say, *They'll be losing the war. They won't have time for puppets that have taken to following them even without strings.* That was in his mind, though.

If Erol Paki understood, he didn't care. "I got on this coach because I thought it was going in the right direction," he said. "I still do. I regret nothing. I'll ride it all the way to the end, whatever that is."

"I admire your consistency," said Guisa, who did not share it.

Here and there in northern and western Lutesse, the Chleuh set up little forts that covered the roadways leading into the heart of the city. They hadn't bothered when the Quimperi were the only folk on their minds. Now, though, they realized they'd have to fight soldiers, not just a handful of woodsrunners. They were getting ready . . . after a fashion.

Whenever Malk spotted a new street fortification, he got word to Camaret the fishmonger. Not coincidentally, he and Efa ate more seafood than they'd been in the habit of doing. That got expensive, but he was lucky enough not to have money on the long list of things he fretted over.

"This Tritzkhol bastard, he looks like he wants to make a real fight of it here," Camaret said one hot, sticky afternoon. "That could get bad for everybody. He can't hold Lutesse, not for long, but he can tear it down around our heads."

"Have you talked to him?" Malk asked. The man behind the counter in the leather apron gave him an odd look. Ears heating, Malk went on, "I don't mean you, *you*. I mean you, the people you're with. For a Locust, Tritzkhol could be a lot worse."

"I suppose you know this personally, because you've met him." Camaret leaned hard on the sarcasm.

But it didn't faze Malk. "As a matter of fact, I have." He told the fish dealer how Tritzkhol had come through the burnt-out part of the city after the attack from the air. "He knew what my brother and I are. It didn't bother him. I don't think he's one of the *We'll fight here till we're all dead* Chleuh. I think he's someone who'd make a deal, if he had a decent deal to make."

"What kind of deal?" Camaret asked, his tone not quite so sardonic now.

"How should I know? I'm just a junkman," Malk said—reasonably, he thought. "But suppose you say something like, 'If you don't rip the city to pieces, we'll let you pull your soldiers out without giving you any trouble.' I bet he'd tell you yes, not because he loves you or anything, but because it gives him something he needs."

Camaret looked thoughtful, but he said, "I can't decide anything like that, you know. I'm just—heh, heh—a little fish."

"Heh, heh," Malk agreed: as much laughter as a joke like that deserved. "All right, fine, you can't decide. But you can pass it along with the rest of my news, right?"

"I can do that much." By the grudging way Camaret said it, he'd make sure everybody understood the scheme came from the crazy fellow who stuck with the Old Faith, not—gods forbid!—from him.

A few days later, the man who called himself Guer showed up in Malk's shop. He eyed the stuff in there and waited patiently till the woman who'd come in before him bought three flower pots and a skillet with a broken handle. Only then did he stop pretending to shop and say, "So you know Tritzkhol, do you?"

"I don't know him. I've met him," Malk answered. "What I know is, he could have spit on my brassard and had his men grab Sarmel and me and send us off to wherever they send people like us. He could have, but he didn't. He respected it, and he even said we didn't need to bother with Chleuh ceremony for him. That's somebody you can bargain with."

"Interesting," Guer said, and then, "So you know, you aren't the only one who talks about him like that."

"Maybe he's worth talking to, then. I wouldn't trust him too far, but I don't trust anyone too far these days." Malk looked straight at Guer.

"You're sensible," said the anonymous-looking man with the ordinary alias. "Very sensible. Believe me, that blade cuts both ways."

"Of course I believe you. People who cling to the Old Faith suck that understanding in with their mothers' milk. Lillat's probably doing that upstairs right now."

"Why *do* you cling to it?" Guer asked with what seemed genuine curiosity.

Malk shrugged. He'd asked himself the same question a good many times. He'd never found an answer that fully satisfied him, but did the best he could for the woodsrunner: "I suppose because all my ancestors, back for I don't know how many generations, believed the way they believed. If I changed, I'd be breaking a long, long chain, and I don't want to do that."

"Your life would be easier if you did."

"Maybe. Maybe not. The way things look, the Chleuh are taking people who were born into the Old Faith whether they still hold to it or not. They don't care. And besides, people like me have a name for the ones who join the True Faith."

Guer waited. Malk didn't say anything. The silence stretched. At last, Guer murmured, "Ah?"

Thus prompted, Malk gave the name: "Traitors."

"Ah," Guer said again, on a different note.

The way he said it and the way he looked at Malk when he did made something else occur to the junkman. Cautiously, he said, "May I ask you a question?"

"Of course," Guer said. "One may always ask."

"How important are you in the woodsrunners' scheme of things?"

"Everybody who works to throw the Chleuh out of Quimper is important." Guer chuckled with the air of a man who'd made the same comment a great many times.

Malk gave an irritated snort. Since he was a patient man, he tried again: "If the woodsrunners were an army, what rank would you hold?"

"Me? Troublemaker." Guer touched a casual hand to the bill of his unremarkable cap. It wasn't a salute. It was nothing like a salute.

When Malk did the same thing, his gesture was much more like one. "Sometimes," he remarked, "you can answer a question by not answering it."

"Isn't that interesting? I never would have guessed! Did you learn such wisdom from the books of the Old Faith?"

"Of course not. I can't even read, remember? I learned it from getting as old as I am and keeping my eyes open. How else does anybody ever learn anything?"

"A point, my friend, a point. Well, do you have any other questions for me, or shall I be on my way?"

"You'll do as you please. You would anyhow."

This time, Guer laughed as if he'd said something really funny. "If only it were true!" the woodsrunner replied. "But I do thank you for your view of the city commandant. I don't know many people who've actually met him."

Which other people would he know? Clerks or secretaries at General Tritzkhol's office? A woman in one of the joyhouses Chleuh officers visited? Those were Malk's first guesses. He didn't ask. He was sure Guer wouldn't tell him, and he didn't want to find out anyway. Things you found out, other people could pull from you. Ignorance made a shield of sorts.

By Guer's small smile, not asking meant he'd passed a test. "Maybe I'll see you again before Lutesse is free," the woodsrunner said. "Or maybe I'll see you afterwards."

"I hope so. I can hardly remember what being free felt like," Malk said.

The smile disappeared. "Too many people will be like that, the ones who've sucked up to the Locusts and the ones who've just quietly gone along. Having someone big and strong ordering you around all the time is like drinking brandy laced with poppy juice. When you stop all of a sudden, you'll hurt. A lot of those people will want to head right back to that." Guer's voice was soft, but deadly serious. "It won't happen. We'll make sure it doesn't happen. We won't go back to a world with a few rich, powerful fools telling too many poor people what to do."

Malk didn't know the details of the message the schismatic Muos preached, but that sounded as if it might be cut from the same cloth. Again, he didn't ask. For one thing, he wasn't a poor person himself. For another, he didn't want the old way of doing things to come back, either. All he said was, "May it be so!"

"Yes, may it. We live on hope. What else have we got?" Out Guer went. As the front door opened and closed, the bell attached to it jingled, then fell silent.

There was a story in the Old Faith about a man who'd beaten a god at an archery tournament. The point was, he'd been able to do it only because he hadn't known his opponent was divine. If he had, he would have been too flustered to shoot straight. Looking at the little brass bell that wasn't jingling any more, Malk felt a lot like that man. Guer could have . . .

He could have, but he hadn't. Maybe he wouldn't. Maybe.

"Master Sachry, I am very sorry." The theatre manager sounded humble but determined. "This house will be closed for the indefinite future. Things are simply too unsure for us to go on. The attacks from the air, the killings so close by . . ." He shook his head. "I am sorry."

Two Chleuh, an officer and an underofficer, had been murdered two nights before, just after they left the theatre: one shot at close range, one knifed from behind. "Is this at the order of Count Vurk?" Guisa asked. If it was, arguing with someone doing as he was told only wasted time.

But the manager shook his head again. "No, sir. It is at my order. When we know how things will go, we'll have some idea of what we can do."

He didn't say, *After the Chleuh get run out of Lutesse* . . . He didn't say anything like that, certainly nothing Guisa could take to the Chleuh if he were so inclined. He wasn't, but why should the theatre manager take chances? He wouldn't even open up his building. "How do I change your mind?" Guisa said.

"You don't, Master Sachry. Haven't I been plain enough?"

"If Vonney and I perform for free, so you just have to pay the rest of the company?" Having cash socked away made it easier for Guisa to offer that. But he knew he would have said it even were he stony broke. He needed to be admired, to be *seen*. When he wasn't, he soon began to doubt he was there at all.

"If the whole cast performed for free, the house would stay dark," the manager said. "This is in our best long-term interest, believe me."

Guisa threw the dice one last time: "Have you told the occupants what you've decided to do?" The Chleuh let him go on with his chosen life. How could he not have a certain regard for them just on account of that?

"I don't think they care a quarter copper one way or the other right now," the theatre manager answered. "They have bigger things to sweat about than whether my building opens."

He was much too likely to be right. Guisa had played in half a dozen deathbed scenes, as everything from mourner to celebrant to corpse. He'd been in a few real ones, too; no one approaches sixty without losing loved people. Now Chleuh rule over Lutesse, over all of Quimper, lay on its deathbed, and even he could see it wasn't long for this world.

Not knowing what else to do, he gave up, much as his kingdom had when the Chleuh raced through its defenses. "You will do me the courtesy of informing me when your policy changes?"

"Of course, Master Sachry," the manager said, with transparent relief at getting Guisa out of his office and out of his hair. He couldn't help adding, "I think you'll have a pretty good notion of the right time yourself."

Guisa didn't rise to that. He just left. As he went outside, he glanced up into the sky to check for dragons. Anadan and Honterese dragonflyers had started appearing over Lutesse in broad daylight and flaming any group of Chleuh they saw. They didn't go after Quimperi on purpose, but that wouldn't matter if you happened to be standing near some Locusts and the dragon missed its mark.

The headline on *I Am Everywhere* was REVENGE SORCERIES SMASH DRESLON! Guisa didn't buy a copy. He did wonder if Erol Paki had written that headline, or, if he hadn't, whether he would have believed it. Of his own opinion, he had no doubt.

He saw no dragons—and, for that matter, only a handful of Chleuh—on the way back to his apartment block. When he walked into his flat, he told Vonney, "Well, we don't have to worry any more about that chorus girl who's always half a step ahead of the beat."

"You gave her the axe?" she asked.

"No. I didn't have to. We aren't going on tonight. Gods only know when we're going on again." He explained what the theatre manager had decided.

"I know which way he thinks the wind is blowing," Vonney said when he finished. After a moment, she went on, "He's probably right."

"He probably is," Guisa said with a sigh. "But shuttering a theatre! Closing a production! We had a good show. Now people won't be able to see it!" *Now people won't be able to see me!* lay not far under his words.

"We have to let everybody know," she said. "Some people will need to start scrambling sooner than we do."

"True enough." He nodded. Money in hard times like this was like soothing salve on a burn. It eased pain and healed hurt.

"I wonder what things will look like in a few months." Vonney spoke in musing tones. "Without . . ." Her voice trailed away. She didn't name the name.

"Without them." Guisa didn't, either. "It's been more than four years now. You take them for granted. They're just . . . there. They're everywhere, like their news sheet." Guisa had taken the Chleuh so much for granted, he hadn't given more than a moment's thought to what Lutesse might be like without them. It would be different—he was sure of that. Would it go back to the way it had been before the war, before King Kangen's men paraded down the Boulevard of Dreams? Or would the play have a whole new act?

"This hasn't been . . . such a bad time." Vonney's eyes sparked. "Except when you got stupid with that tart, I mean."

He spread his hands. "It's over now. It was never anything much anyway."

"Is that what she thought?"

Guisa mimed taking a crossbow bolt in his ample midsection. No, he hadn't thought he'd married a woman with such a wicked wit. But he had, and now he was stuck with it—as the Chleuh were stuck with losing Lutesse. How hard would they fight to hold it, though?

XIII

When Malk Malkovici opened the junk shop early on a bright, clear morning, he found a crossbow quarrel in the door. He had no idea when it slammed home. He thought he would have heard it, but with the baby in the house he slept like the dead when he slept at all. So did Efa. If Lillat heard, she hadn't said anything about it.

He tugged at the quarrel, but it was embedded in the oak too deeply and tightly for him to pull it out. He thought he might manage with pliers, and wondered where he'd put the putty he needed to fill in the hole.

Before he could do more than wonder, someone came dog-trotting up the street toward him. Sarmel, he saw a heartbeat later. His brother waved. "It's started!" he called.

"What has?" Malk asked—foolishly, he realized later.

As Sarmel stopped, he pointed at the crossbow quarrel. "What do you think? The rising against the Chleuh, that's what!"

"Really? So soon?" Malk knew the Hontermen and Anadans (and Char Tubis' Quimperi) were getting close to Lutesse, but he hadn't thought they were *that* close.

"So soon. From what I hear, the constables attacked the Watchmen, and that set everything going," Sarmel said.

"The constables? The same constables who've done everything the Locusts told them for the past four years?" Malk both was and wasn't astonished. Like anyone else, the senior constables would be making their own guesses about how things were going. If they figured the Chleuh couldn't hang on, wouldn't they be smart to jump to the other side instead of sticking too long with the losers?

No more than half a minute after that thought crossed Malk's mind, Bezen came around the corner. The way he strutted was as self-important as ever. So was his uniform, with one exception: his left arm bore a green-and-white armband. He'd been a Quimperi while he did the Locusts' bidding, too, but he hadn't worn his kingdom's colors to brag about it then.

He stopped a few feet from Malk and Sarmel. "What shall I do with the two of you?" he asked, sounding at least half serious. "Tell you things will be better now for folk who cling to the Old Faith, or jug you for being too cozy with the Chleuh?"

"*You* should talk," Sarmel said.

Malk clicked his tongue between his teeth in warning. To Bezen, he said, "If you just leave us alone and let us get on with our lives, we'd be grateful for that."

"No one's ever grateful. I'm a constable. By the gods, I ought to know," Bezen said. "And nobody just gets on with his life, either, not when the world keeps kicking him in the nuts."

That matched Malk's own way of thinking much too well. He said, "How much can you tell us?"

"When we jumped the Watchmen, they yelled to the Chleuh for help, and they got it. That was when the Chleuh started having problems of their own," Bezen said.

"Are they going to pull out of Lutesse, or will they fight to hold the city?" If the Chleuh meant to fight, Malk planned on spending as much time as he could in the subcellar with Efa and Lillat. As long as the shop and living quarters didn't burn over it, it was the safest place he knew.

Bezen only shrugged. "Your guess is as good as mine." The way he eyed Malk reminded the junkman that, while he was annoying and venal, he wasn't stupid. He went on, "If you have friends on the left, your guess may be better than mine."

"Friends on the left? Black-market friends?" Malk touched the bill of his cap. "You have a way with words."

"That's me," Bezen said smugly. He didn't touch the bill of his own flat-crowned cap. He touched his armband instead, as if to remind the Malkovicis that he was a proper Quimperi—or maybe that he was a proper Quimperi *again*. If Malk and Sarmel did have friends on the left, what they thought of a constable might matter much more than it usually did.

Somewhere not far away, someone started screaming and didn't stop. Malk had rarely heard noises like that in Lutesse before the war: only in a couple of horrible work accidents. They'd become far more common after the Chleuh marched in. If he hadn't been lucky, he would have made noises like that himself after the Watchmen seized him.

"You going to do anything about that?" Sarmel asked Bezen.

The constable considered for a moment, then shook his head. "I don't think so. Stuff like that, it'll just have to sort itself out till we see what's going on and which end is up. Take care."

Away he went. Yes, his walk seemed confident enough and to spare, but he kept checking right, checking left, and checking behind his back. Did someone have a score to settle with him? By his manner, he wanted no nasty surprises.

"He's a piece of work," Sarmel remarked.

"Yes, he is. But you know what? He could be worse. Too many people right now you can't say that about." Again, Malk remembered the faces of the friends and relatives of the Quimperi Popular Party's warriors. What they would have done to him had they caught him made what he'd got in the Watchmen's hands seem loving by comparison.

"If only you were wrong." Sarmel cocked his head to one side, listening to the anguish around the corner. "Whoever's making that racket, I hope he deserves every bit of it."

"He's really clanging on a teakettle, isn't he?" Malk spoke in Quimperi, but used a Nistrian expression for making a lot of noise. And not just a Nistrian expression, but one commonly in the mouths of people who belonged to the Old Faith. He got a startled laugh from his brother.

He didn't open up the shop after all. He sent Sarmel back to his flat and stayed inside himself, behind a barred and triply locked door. Two different groups of shouting people ran along the street, one up, one down. Nobody tried to get in.

Then, someone knocked on the door—politely, not the way a constable would have. "Who's there?" Malk asked through it. He had a knife in his hand in case he didn't like the answer.

"Tebron."

Malk hesitated. If they found him sheltering a Chleuh . . . His back stiffened. What if they did? He owed Tebron his life. He could hope he wouldn't have to pay it, but he couldn't turn his back on the debt. He opened the door.

The Chleuh was alone. He stepped into the doorway to make sure Malk couldn't slam the door in his face. At the same time, he waved to someone at the corner—Malk couldn't see who. A moment later, though, the junkman heard a wagon (no, wagons) coming toward the shop.

With what sounded like genuine apology in his voice, the Chleuh colonel said, "Very sorry, but we have orders to pull out of Lutesse, and I'm going to take whatever you've got that my kingdom needs with me."

"Suppose I say no?" Malk didn't use the knife he held, but he was ready to.

Tebron shook his head, slightly, just once. "You can kill me. I don't think you can kill all my men. I don't think you'll like what they do to you and to your family if you're foolish now, either."

He was bound to be right. Sighing, Malk stepped aside as the first wagon stopped in front of the shop. "Well, come all the way in. You will anyhow."

"You're a sensible fellow. I'm glad." Colonel Tebron spoke to the wagon crews in his own language. They hurried in and started wrestling with all the scrap iron and brass and bronze and copper and even lead Malk had. It clattered and clanged as it went into the wagons.

"Do you think you'll be able to get that stuff out of town? Will the woodsrunner let you?" Malk asked.

Tebron eyed him shrewdly. "You might know that better than I do." He held up a hand. "Never mind. I ask no questions. But I can tell you that your bandit chiefs have agreed to let General Tritzkhol take his men out of Lutesse peacefully if he doesn't wreck the city the way . . . certain people in Chlé might want him to."

"What's all the fighting about, then?"

With a shrug, Tebron answered, "Some people don't get the word. Some people have to show how big their cocks are. Some people are like dogs—they think anyone moving away from them is running and so fair game. We have to show those people it doesn't work that way. We're pulling out, yes, but we aren't beaten yet. And we wouldn't be beaten by the gods-cursed woodsrunners in a thousand years." He made as if to spit. "If you happen to see any of them—just by chance, you understand—you can tell them I said so, too."

"I have no idea what you could be talking about," Malk said.

Tebron snorted. His men seemed to be taking anything that wasn't nailed down, and to be thinking about prying up the nails. "Do you really think Quimper will be able to stand on its own feet once we're gone?" he said. "You'll belong to Honter and Anada the same way you've belonged to us these past four years and more."

Now Malk was the one who shrugged. "I'll take my chances. The whole kingdom will, I mean. But I'll tell you one thing—the Anadans and Hontermen won't want to kill me because of the gods I follow."

"There is that," the Chleuh officer admitted. Malk gave him credit for sounding sorry about the things his kingdom had been doing. Some credit, anyhow: Tebron had dodged the worst of King Kangen's horrors, but he hadn't done anything to try to stop them. None of the Chleuh had, not that Malk knew of.

Something else occurred to the junkman. "You aren't going to pay me for what you're taking this time, are you?"

"On the contrary, Master Malkovici," Tebron said with a crooked smile. He'd never called Malk that before, not in all the time they'd known each other—a time now coming to an end. "On the contrary. I'm going to let you live, and your wife and little girl, too. What payment could be greater than that?"

Malk opened his mouth, then closed it again. After a couple of heartbeats, he managed, "You could have killed us any time for the past four years."

"Oh, but you used to be useful to my kingdom. Now? No." Tebron seemed to pause for thought himself. "You may possibly be useful to me, though. If by some accident I live through what's coming, tell people the truth. Let them know whose fault it is that you're still breathing."

"Fair enough." Malk would have thought it fairer yet had he got cash for what the Chleuh were taking, but not enough to make a fuss about it. One man against a squad of soldiers was bad odds—Tebron had that right.

By the time the Locusts finished, the shop floor was barer than Malk ever remembered seeing it. The colonel sketched a salute as he turned to leave. "Good luck. Remember—not all your enemies hate you as much as they should, and not all your new friends will like you as well as friends ought to."

"Good luck to you, too." On the whole, Malk meant it.

Tebron climbed aboard the lead wagon and nudged the underofficer at the reins. The junior Chleuh flicked them and got his team going. The wagon rattled away, followed by the others. Malk watched till they were out of sight. Then he shut the door again, locked all the locks, and set the bar in its brackets.

~

"I think they're really leaving," Guisa Sachry said to Vonney after another look out the window. He could hear the wonder in his own voice. The Chleuh had been part of Lutesse for so long now, he could hardly imagine what things might be like without them.

"Let me see." His wife shoved in beside him. The block of flats lay on a small street, but only half a block away from an east-west avenue. Chleuh soldiers kept marching and riding along it, sometimes on horseback, sometimes in wagons, and always to the east. She looked back at Guisa. "They really are!"

"It's . . . a new world, or it will be soon," Guisa said. He hoped the new world would have room for him, but didn't mention that. He was realistic enough to take prophecy and jinxes seriously.

Vonney nudged him. "Let's go out! I want to watch them scurrying away! I won't scream at them or anything, I promise. No matter what I'm thinking, I won't show it."

She's bolder than I am, Guisa thought. It was not a new realization, and he knew a good many people were. "If they yell at us to go inside again, we will," he said.

"All right," she agreed. Too easily? He'd find out when the time came. Meanwhile, he had to hope when the time came it wouldn't be too late.

They weren't the only Quimperi on the sidewalk. Other people wanted to watch the occupants abandoning Lutesse, too. A skinny man clutching a bottle of something strong hoisted it at Guisa and Vonney before he swigged from it.

Guisa had seen the Chleuh marching into Lutesse. They'd been splendid then, young and strong and clean, all in new uniforms in good repair. As he'd noticed before, now they looked almost as shabby and threadbare as the folk they'd lorded it over for the past four years. They didn't look proud, either, the way they had then. Some held their faces blank, as if they were playing cards and didn't want to give anything away. Others looked worried. A few, looked frankly scared.

That didn't surprise Guisa. Wherever King Kangen and his generals send them, they'd be going to a place worse than Lutesse. (Guisa patriotically refused to believe any places were better.) Would they march into battle against the Anadans and Hontermen outside the city? Or were they bound for the grinding war in the east, where even news sheets like *I Am Everywhere* admitted the Muos had pushed a long way toward Chlé?

Vonney strolled along the sidewalk, as if at a peacetime promenade. Guisa perforce went with her. More than one Chleuh noticed her. No matter how downhearted they might be, soldiers noticed attractive women. They kept tramping along; discipline in their ranks still held.

A couple of Chleuh sentries still stood at either end of a bridge over a dry wash. They carried crossbows and swords; they looked ready for anything. But Quimperi walked past them as if they weren't there. The men couldn't look every which way at once.

Vonney and Guisa paid them no more attention than any of the other locals on the street. Once over the bridge, though, Vonney murmured, "Those poor, sorry dogs! As soon as the rest of their army is gone, they're dead men. How can they not know it?"

"They probably do. I've talked with soldiers," said Guisa, who'd never been one himself. "It's a lot like acting—you have to pretend to be what you aren't, and to make yourself believe it along with everybody else. Only when you're fighting, what you have to pretend to be all the time is brave."

"It won't do them any good," Vonney said, and she was bound to be right.

Around the corner a couple of blocks farther on, they found an open café. Three Chleuh officers sat at one table, as if nothing had changed. No, not quite: two of them had set their ceremonial daggers next to their plates, so they could grab them in a hurry if they had to.

The man who didn't have his dagger at hand touched the bill of his cap to Guisa. "If I am lucky, I see you again after this cursed war is over," he said in passable Quimperi.

"One never knows," Guisa said. He and Vonney chose a table as far from the Chleuh as they could; seeming friendly to the occupants —the almost ex-occupants, now—wouldn't do. Someone would notice. Someone would remember. And everything remembered was liable to be paid for. Every single thing.

After that one greeting, the officers left them alone. They had to understand how things were, and how they'd be. And, of course, they had their own fears.

A waiter came up. "We can make sandwiches—cheese and onions on bread. We have white wine. It isn't great white wine, but it won't kill you."

"I think we've just ordered," Vonney said. Guisa nodded.

When the sandwiches came, the cheese was nasty, the onions eye-wateringly strong. Guisa was sure the bread had barley flour in it, and maybe ground peas and beans, too. The white wine could have been worse, but not much worse. He ate without complaining. Things had been like this for a while. The bill came to almost three times what it should have. He didn't complain about that, either, any more than the Chleuh at the far table had. They'd got out of the eatery in one piece. How long they'd stay that way lay in the hands of the gods.

"Shall we go back?" Guisa asked.

"Let's," Vonney said. "We can come out again after . . . after the change. I wonder if those sentries are still alive."

Guisa left a good tip, to show that, although he was an important person, he remembered those who weren't. He and Vonney walked back out onto the sidewalk again and started home. He didn't know how his wife felt, but the flat seemed a fortress to him.

Those two Chleuh keeping watch on that worthless bridge while their countrymen abandoned Lutesse hadn't survived. Guisa shook his head; he wasn't much surprised. Somebody was spreading sand over the pool of blood where one had fallen. The other still lay there, the blood soaking into his tunic and trousers. He didn't have any weapons now. The woodsrunners did, or maybe some freelancer who'd grabbed a chance to strike at the occupants.

Vonney seemed no more upset at the body than Guisa was. "Before the war, I think I would have fainted if I'd seen anything like this," she said. "We've been pretty lucky, the two of us, but we've both seen enough by now that we just . . . go on."

"We've been pretty lucky, the two of us." Guisa echoed the words, but gave them a different slant.

"We would have been luckier if you'd never run into that Fulgine mattressback," Vonney said. "Or would it have been somebody else if it wasn't her?"

It probably would have been, but Guisa wasn't foolhardy enough to say so. He did say, "I made a mistake," which wasn't something he admitted every day. Not the smallest part of the mistake was thinking Xya would keep her mouth shut when he didn't want her to open it.

A man coming the other way carried a crossbow and wore a green-and-white armband. People were quick to get out of his way, Guisa and Vonney no less than anyone else. He strode—almost marched—past them as if the last four years had never happened, as if the only Chleuh who'd ever visited Lutesse were scholars and wanderers and pleasure-seekers.

King Kangen's warriors were still draining out of the city like dirty rainwater running down a gutter. They paid no attention to the armed and disciplined Quimperi man. Lutesse wasn't their problem any more. As long as he didn't start shooting at them, they didn't care what he did.

Vonney looked back over her shoulder at him. "That didn't take long," she said. "The people who've been sneaking around at night are already coming out into the open."

Guisa nodded. "They are. He looks like he thinks he can do whatever he wants, too. I hope the Anadans and the Hontermen get here soon. They won't want to murder everybody who ever had anything to do with the Locusts. I don't think they will, anyhow."

"If they do, there won't be more than a hundred people left in Lutesse three weeks from now," Vonney said. "Not everybody who sticks an armband on his sleeve will live, either."

"You're bound to be right," Guisa replied.

He didn't let out a sigh of relief when he got back inside the flat, but he felt as if he had. He made sure he locked all the locks. Vonney was watching him as he did—to make sure he remembered to take care of it, he judged, not because she thought he worried too much.

When the place was as secure as it could be, she went to the window. "I don't see any more soldiers marching by," she said. "That has to mean they're gone—most of them, anyhow."

"One way or another," Guisa said, remembering the sentries who'd stayed at their pointless post until people finally got around to killing them. "That major in the café may come back to Lutesse one of these years, but a lot of those fellows never will."

"They thought they had the whole world roped and tied. For a while there, everybody thought they did, too. But it didn't work out that way, did it?" Vonney laughed, maybe at her own foolishness back when the war was new, maybe at the way things *had* worked out.

"I myself wonder what sort of audience the Hontermen and Anadans will make," Guisa said. "Hontermen are cold fish, and most of them speak Quimperi like a Chleuh cow. Anadans . . . The only Anadans you ever saw here before the war were the rich ones. Crossing the ocean isn't for anybody with no silver in his pouch. The ordinary soldiers, the ones who could never afford it if they weren't at war, I have no idea what they're like."

"Neither do I," Vonney said. "Back before we got together, there was one of those rich Anadans who was crazy about me. His family made . . . what was it they made? Caps, that's what! They must have made a lot of them, and sold a lot, too, because he had more money than he knew what to do with. I was sad when he had to go back home."

"Sad because you cared about him or sad because he had more money than he knew what to do with?" Guisa asked slyly.

"Meow," Vonney said, and then, "Sad. I was sad. He was a nice man. I wonder if he's with their army now. He'd be a colonel or something, I bet."

"All right," Guisa said, wondering if it was. Stories about war—both romances and histories—insisted it was full of chance meetings that twisted coincidence's arm to the breaking point. He could do without this one.

"I wonder who's running the city now. I wonder if anyone is," Vonney said.

After a moment's thought, Guisa answered, "The constables. They were here before the Chleuh came, they were here under them, and they're still here now that the Locusts have flown away. They'll find some way to make people think they helped drive King Kangen's men off."

"I wouldn't be surprised," his wife said. "Do you think they're all gone yet?"

"Except for a few who somehow never got the order, like those sorry sentries on the bridge. Maybe they'll take the ones who're left prisoner, or maybe they'll cover their bloodstains over with sand, too." Guisa liked that phrase after he'd said it. He pulled a little notebook out of a pouch and wrote it down. One of these days, he might find a way to make money from it.

"Activate the crystal," Vonney said—he stood closer to it than she did. "Let's see if we can find out what's going on."

"All right." Guisa put his hands over the sphere and murmured the activation charm. A light sprang into being inside the crystal—it wasn't just an inert globe of polished quartz any more. But the light didn't turn into anyone's image. No clear voice came from the crystal. It was all mutter and garble and nonsense. With a disgusted mutter, he spoke the charm that darkened it again. "The emanations are all tangled up. Both sides are trying to talk to us, but neither one can."

"That tells us something, anyway. Even yesterday, we could listen to Lutesse Crystal," Vonney said.

"Only a matter of time now," Guisa said. "I wonder what's happened to Erol Paki and Brasi Robillach and all those people. Did they really pull out with the occupants? They wouldn't be happy there. But they wouldn't be happy here with the Chleuh gone, either."

"Sep Nardand, too."

"Sep Nardand especially! Erol and Brasi wrote things, but Nardand and the Watchmen killed people. I wonder how many of *them* have thrown away their uniforms and are trying to pretend they never had anything to do with that."

"It won't work," Vonney said.

"Of course it won't. They'll try anyway. What else can they do?" Guisa said. "The same with the men who belong to—belonged to, I mean—the Quimperi Popular Party and the other outfits like that. Odrio Cazh won't want to say hello to Char Tubis."

His wife change the subject, at least a little: "Do you suppose Char Tubis will make himself king?"

"It probably depends on whether the Hontermen and Anadans let him. I don't know that much about him, but I have heard he always had trouble getting along with other officers in our army."

Vonney nodded. "I've heard the same thing."

"If he rubbed them the wrong way, he probably annoyed the foreigners, too. And they're bound to have more soldiers than he does, because. . . ." Guisa paused to find a polite way to say what was on his mind.

Before he could, Vonney did: "Because most of our men went with the General, not with Char Tubis."

"That's right!" Guisa made as if to salute her. "I wonder what will happen to the General now, too."

"He meant well. He tried to do whatever he could to keep the Chleuh from hurting Quimper too much," Vonney said.

"True," Guisa said. But the Chleuh had been the ones who gave the orders, and the Quimperi, under the General, the ones who carried them out. That got more and more obvious and more and more odious as days and months and years went by. Not long before, a bitter joke had made the rounds in Lutesse. King Kangen and the General were talking. Kangen told him, *You give me your clock, and I'll tell you what time it is.* Sure enough, the Chleuh took whatever they wanted. Why else did people call them Locusts?

"I can imagine some people running off with the occupants. I can't imagine that the General would. Can you?"

"No, I don't think so. He's too brave for that. And he always *thought* he was doing the right thing," Guisa said.

"But will Char Tubis think so? Will the Hontermen and the Anadans?"

"My dear, I myself am only an actor and a scribbler. Gods be praised, I don't have to answer questions like that." After speaking, Guisa wondered if he was telling the truth. Whoever wound up giving orders in Lutesse now that the Chleuh weren't might wonder about some of the things he'd done. He was suddenly very glad he'd written *Among the Villagers* under a name that didn't belong to him. If he had a bit of luck, no one would be able to trace it back to him.

That was as naive as Watchmen thinking they could shed what they'd done along with their uniforms, but it didn't seem so to Guisa then.

"I hope you're right," Vonney said in a tone that suggested she wasn't sure he was.

"I am not an important enough person for anyone to get excited about." As Guisa often overplayed vain glory, he overplayed modesty, too.

Politely, Vonney talked about something else: "I wonder if we can ever get back to the way things were before . . . well, before everything."

"That would be wonderful. It would be a lot better than the Muos taking over and stealing everything everybody's spent years working to get." Guisa laughed self-consciously. "Though maybe I shouldn't say that, not when Honter and Anada are allied with Muosi."

"You shouldn't say it where anyone but me can hear you, that's certain sure," Vonney said.

Guisa sighed. "I'm used to the way things have been lately. I guess I'll just have to get used to the way they turn out to be."

When Malk Malkovici drove the junk shop's wagon toward the rubbish tip in the southern part of Lutesse, it was almost the only moving thing on the road. Sarmel felt the stillness, too. "Doesn't seem right. Doesn't seem natural," he said.

"It's early in the morning yet. Things should liven up by the time we head back." Was Malk trying to convince himself as well as his brother? He knew too well he was.

Every now and then, the wagon rattled past a corpse or a couple of corpses: Chleuh and Quimperi, in numbers more or less equal. Malk hardly noticed them, especially since they hadn't started to stink yet. Neither did Sarmel. His attention was more on the white road signs with black, angular syllables that remained behind though the occupants who'd put them up were gone. "They're funny," he said, "like shadows with nothing left to cast them."

Malk made a sign with the fingers of his left hand that the kids in the orphanage were sure turned aside evil. He'd seen too much since really to believe that, but he did it anyhow. *It can't hurt*, he told himself.

And then Sarmel said, "Hello!" and pointed ahead.

"Uh-oh!" Malk said. A man with a crossbow cradled in his arms came up the street toward the wagon. He wore a uniform of unfamiliar color—halfway between leaves and mud—and a helmet that looked like a pot jammed low over his eyes. Two more men in the same gear followed half a bowshot behind, and four or five more came after them.

"That's Anadan kit," Sarmel said.

Malk nodded. "I don't think those are Anadans in it, though," he said, and pulled over to the edge of the street. As the horses stopped, he waved to the approaching soldiers.

The point man waved back, brusquely. As he drew near, Malk spotted the green-and-white armband above his left elbow. And, when he spoke, he spoke like a young tough from a rough quarter of Lutesse: "Who the demon are you bastards?"

"Junkmen," Malk answered. "We're out after junk—besides dead Chleuh, I mean."

When the soldier grinned, he showed off a mouthful of bad teeth. "There you go! Most of that junk already cleaned itself out, right?"

"Sure did," Sarmel answered before Malk could speak. "Who are you people, anyway?" More soldiers were coming up. Their uniforms had seen hard use. They were whiskery and smelly, and looked ready to dive behind a tree or into a doorway like spooked cats at anything they didn't like.

"We're Char Tubis' Unconquered Quimperi," the point man said proudly. "Lutesse is *our* city. We're the ones who came first, to take it back from the Chleuh. The Anadans and Hontermen, they can wait a bit." His comrades nodded.

One of the other soldiers had Quimperi captain's badges on the sleeve of his Anadan tunic. He said, "You men haven't seen any Locusts hanging around, have you? Live Locusts, I should say. Char Tubis himself isn't very far behind us. He wants Lutesse so bad, he can taste it, but nobody wants anything to happen to him."

"No, sir. Some dead ones, but none alive," Malk said. "They're pretty much gone by now. The Watchmen, the Popular Party people, I can't tell you about them."

"Those turds." The captain's lips skinned back from his teeth in a fierce smile. His teeth had seen better care than the point man's. "We'll take care of them soon enough. Oh, you bet we will."

Somebody behind the knot of soldiers gathered around the junk wagon let out a shout that carried a long way on the otherwise silent street: "He's coming!"

"You see?" the captain said. Both Malkovicis nodded.

A couple of minutes later, around a corner strode Char Tubis himself, several lower-ranking officers in his wake and a couple of worried-looking guards trying to stay ahead of them all. He stood out in the crowd, being at least half a head taller than anyone else.

A woman called to him from a window. He doffed his cap at her, waved, and kept moving on. Soon he neared the junk wagon.

As the Chleuh commander now gone from Lutesse had before him, Char Tubis immediately recognized Malk and Sarmel for what they were. Curiosity on his face, he came over to the wagon. The junior officers and bodyguards eyed him as if sure he'd gone out of his mind. Taking no notice of them, he nodded to Malk. "You are something out of the ordinary," he observed.

"Yes, sir," the junkman replied. "After these past years, sir, so are you, if you don't mind my saying so."

"It seems so now. But the four black years just past, they are what was out of the ordinary for Quimper. Our freedom before them, our freedom afterwards, that is what we should have. As time goes by, we will all do our best to make as if they never happened." Char Tubis spoke with complete assurance.

That surprised Malk not at all. The officer who'd believed in Quimper even when the General didn't always sounded self-assured. He had to believe in himself; for a long time, hardly anyone else had. Malk said, "By the gods, sir, I hope you're right."

"Your gods of the Old Faith, mine of the True Faith . . . By all the gods, I shall do everything in my power to help make things right." Char Tubis cocked his head to the side to study the two Malkovicis. "And you men, what did you do to keep yourselves safe when so many of your kind were lost?"

The question could be dangerous. Malk saw that at once, but answered it anyway: "What we had to, sir, as long as it didn't mean selling anyone out to the Chleuh."

"A good response. I hope, for your sakes, a true response." With another nod, Char Tubis went on. He had more on his mind than two immigrant junkmen and a ramshackle wagon.

XIV

Guisa Sachry stood on the sidewalk along the Boulevard of Dreams. He held the staff of a small Quimperi flag in his right hand and waved the flag over his head. Vonney stood beside him. She was waving a flag, too. They both cheered for all they were worth.

Everybody on the sidewalk seemed to wave a green-and-white flag. Men, women, and children all cheered at the tops of their lungs. Guisa wasn't cheering just to be cheering. He was cheering so other people could see and hear him cheering.

Char Tubis and the Unconquered Quimperi had paraded down the Boulevard of Dreams three days before. Guisa and Vonney had been there for that parade, too, again to be seen celebrating the departure of the Chleuh from Lutesse. Guisa was pleased with himself for making that appearance, for it had been a little dangerous. Not quite all the Locusts had fled the city, and the Watchmen and others who'd backed their cause still made trouble.

Not any more. Now the allies who'd done most of the hard, bloody work of driving the Chleuh away were staging their own triumphal procession. They wanted to show Lutesse—to show the whole world—King Kangen's men were never coming back.

They knew how to get what they wanted, too. Regiment after regiment of Hontermen and Anadans tramped past, all of them armed, all of them ready for anything anybody might throw at them. The Hontermen, whose uniforms had more dirt and less leaf in their hue, and whose helmets were more soup plates than pots, looked like soldiers whose kingdom had been fighting for years: tough and proud, but also worn and tired.

Not so the soldiers from across the Western Ocean. By the grins on their faces, everything they'd done might have been a game. All their uniforms and gear looked clean and new. Some of them would have seen hard fighting after they crossed the Narrow Sea, but no one would have known it by their appearance.

Such a show of abundance was daunting. Always suspicious, Guisa wondered how much was just a show. Some, he judged, but surely not all.

Leaning down to put his mouth next to Vonney's ear, he shouted (in effect, whispered), "Have you seen your rich Anadan capmaker?"

"No, and I've been looking for him, too," his wife answered. She winked at him. He managed something of a smile in return. He'd teased her, and she'd teased him back. He couldn't even complain.

A lot of the women in the crowd were eyeing the Anadans and Hontermen as if the warriors were the most delicious treats they'd ever seen. And that might well have been true. Defeat had made their own men seem unmanly. Not all of them would have cared to lie down with the Chleuh, and the occupants' own growing shabbiness was anything but a love philtre. These fellows, though . . .

Any of them who can't get laid tonight aren't half trying, Guisa thought. He waited for the stab of jealousy he was sure he should feel. It came, but it was slow and weak. He sighed theatrically—the only way he knew how to sigh. *You're getting old,* he told himself. Himself didn't argue.

A dragonscreech overhead was plenty loud enough to pierce the crowd's racket. The new conquerors guarded the air against the old conquerors' return. Quimper . . . was acted upon but had not the strength to act, no matter what Char Tubis thought.

Someone only a few feet from Guisa yelled, "Next thing we do is, we settle everybody who licked the Locusts' arses!" The cheers that rang out then sounded full of bloodlust, at least to Guisa. The people shouting might have been at a pancratiasts' battle, when one bruiser's buffet flattened his foe's nose and sprayed gore over the spectators close to the circle. That was what people who went to those brawls laid their silver down for.

"String 'em all up!" somebody else bawled.

"By their stones!" a woman added. That won more applause. Most of the time, Guisa felt angry at fate when no one recognized him. Here this afternoon, anonymity felt like armor.

He turned to Vonney again. "Maybe we should head for home."

"Maybe we should," she said. She would have heard those cries, too. They might not put her in much danger—it wasn't as if she'd been sleeping with a Chleuh captain or anything like that—but she would understand that Guisa could find himself in an embarrassing predicament.

Getting out of the crush along the Boulevard of Dreams was harder than getting into it had been. Everyone wanted to see the new foreigners, the fierce fighters who'd forced the old foreigners to flee. People swarmed toward Lutesse's main thoroughfare. Pushing against the current seemed even harder than it would have in a swift-flowing stream. Guisa used the buffer of his ample belly and a sly elbow or two to force his way out of the crush. Vonney stayed close behind, traveling in his wake.

At last, in a little side street, things eased up. "Whew!" Guisa said. "I've done a lot of things I enjoyed more."

"Not so many people around when Kangen's men marched in," Vonney agreed.

"No," Guisa said. Lutesse had been eerily silent that late-spring day. Now everyone was full of joy. Well, almost everyone: everyone who hadn't had too much to do with the Chleuh while they were here. Once more, Guisa hoped nobody would look too closely at him.

"I think we're wasting our time," Sarmel Malkovici said as the wagon rattled along. "We've lost our best customers."

Malk put a hand on the back of his neck, as if to shield it from a falling axe. "Can't say I'm sorry," he answered. "But the new folks will need junk, too. Everybody needs junk. And working is good any which way."

"If you say so." Sarmel didn't sound convinced. It wasn't that he wouldn't work. Malk understood as much. Sarmel did everything his brother asked of him. But the older Malkovici was the one with the relentless drive that had built the business from its small beginnings under Efa's uncle to what it was now.

Two Anadan soldiers gaped at the battered old wagon and at the battered old horses pulling it. One of them pointed. They both laughed; the one who hadn't pointed said something in their language. They laughed some more. Anadans spoke their own dialect of Honterese. It sounded harsher in Malk's ears than it did coming from the mouths of men who lived in the island kingdom across the Narrow Sea.

Hardly any Anadans spoke Quimperi or Chleuh or any other language besides their own. They were strangers in Lutesse and always would be, even more than King Kangen's soldiers had been. But they were strong strangers and rich strangers, so they could do pretty much as they pleased here.

A couple of blocks farther on, Malk saw just how true that was. A constable was doing his best to make a company of Anadans wait while traffic on a cross street went through the intersection. He held up one white-gloved hand while pointing with the other, at the same time blowing furiously on the brass whistle he wore on a lanyard around his neck.

Those Anadans laughed at him the way the others had laughed at the junk wagon. Half a dozen of them trotted forward. They grabbed him, picked him up, and, laughing still, carried him out of the middle of the road and plopped him down on the sidewalk. Then the whole company swarmed across the avenue, and damnation to cross traffic.

Two or three men in the last rank of soldiers turned and blew the constable a kiss. He looked as if he wanted to kill them or to burst into tears, or maybe both at once. Since he couldn't do either, he went back to his proper station. But the way his shoulders slumped said he was a beaten man.

"I wonder if he'll ever hold his head up again," Malk said.

"He's a constable. He'll be fine in an hour." Sarmel was a realist.

Malk laughed. "You're bound to be right. I'll tell you something, though—if he'd told a bunch of Chleuh to wait, they would have done it."

"Oh, you bet they would," Sarmel said. "One thing about the Locusts: they do whatever anybody set over 'em tells 'em to do."

"Don't they just?" Malk shivered a little, remembering the trains full of followers of the Old Faith that had gone east from Lutesse.

"Hullo, young fellows," said the white-haired tip guard when they got where they were going. "Wondered if I'd see the two of you again now that the city's changed hands."

"We aren't going anywhere," Malk said, and shivered again. No, he'd never get those trains out of his memory, however much he might wish he could. "And everybody needs junk." The way he said that, he might have been reciting part of the Old Faith's litany. He believed the one almost the same way he believed the other.

The old-timer waved the wagon in. Laughing, he said, "Hope you find yourselves some good stuff."

Pulling on their leather gloves, Malk and Sarmel went to see what kind of good stuff they could get. Less scrap metal from the fronts of houses and blocks of flats was mixed in with the rubbish than had been true before the Chleuh pulled out. Now that the

Hontermen and Anadans had taken Lutesse, they weren't trying to knock it to pieces. King Kangen's dragonflyers were, but he had fewer of them than his foes did, and most of those he did have were in the east, trying to slow down the rushing Muos. The schismatics were drawing near to what had been the border between their kingdom and Chlé before Kangen's invasion. Between their push from the east and that of the Anadans and Hontermen from the west, the Chleuh were getting squeezed as in a vise.

Through the thick leather protecting his hands, Malk felt something square and solid and smooth. His fingers closed on it. He grunted when he pulled it up; it was heavier than he'd expected. "Hello!" he said when he got a good look at it.

"What did you find?" Sarmel asked from a few feet away.

"Strongbox, I think." Malk pitched his voice so the old tip guard wouldn't overhear.

"How about that?" Sarmel also spoke quietly. Neither he nor Malk sounded very surprised. It wasn't the kind of thing you could count on, but it happened every now and then. Men clearing rubble were often careless, shoveling it into wagons to get rid of it. They just wanted to make it go away, and didn't pay attention to everything they were disposing of.

Before Malk took the strongbox to the wagon, he wrapped some drapery around it. He could sell the embroidered cloth, too, and he didn't want anyone besides his brother knowing how lucky he'd been. He always tipped the guard when he and Sarmel drove away. This time, instead of silver, he crossed the old man's palm with gold.

The fellow gaped at the little gleaming coin. "You don't got to do that, Master Malk!" he exclaimed.

"I didn't do it because I had to, Jehan. I did it because I wanted to," Malk answered. "Call it a freedom gift if you want to."

"Gods bless you and keep you. I'll buy me a choice cut of mutton, and something nice for the missus, too," Jehan said.

Once they got rolling, Sarmel chuckled. "He doesn't know why you're keeping him extra sweet."

"That's all right. I do," Malk replied.

He chose a secondary street, the Avenue of Admiral Morzen, to head back to the junk shop. It ran parallel to the Boulevard of Dreams, three or four blocks south of the main road. These days, a lot of soldiers crowded the Boulevard of Dreams, some men looking for a good time, others marching to or from the train station not far from the Obelisk.

Naturally, something clogged the Avenue of Admiral Morzen, too —some kind of parade or procession. Malk swore resignedly, thinking, *Nothing ever works*. Then he saw what kind of procession it was, and the words clogged in his throat.

Cheering, jeering people were chivvying half a dozen naked women up the street toward the wagon. They weren't just naked, either; they'd had their heads shaved. They'd had them shaved roughly, too—two or three of them had trickles of blood on their bare, shiny scalps.

Somebody'd written something in big syllables on the bare belly of one of the women coming toward the wagon. As Malk pulled over to the edge of the street, he asked Sarmel, "What does it say?"

"The usual," his brother answered. "'I screwed a Locust.' You really should learn to read, Malk. I keep telling you."

"Yes, yes," Malk said as a rotten squash splashed on a woman's back. This wasn't the first such procession he and Sarmel had seen. The women forced through the streets weren't whores; whores had lain down with the Chleuh in the line of duty, as it were. These were women who'd slept with the occupants from love or lust or hope of gain. Now that the rest of the Quimperi could, they were punishing them for their betrayal. That was what they claimed, anyhow.

He didn't say anything as the weeping women shambled past in shame. Neither did Sarmel. It wasn't as if they hadn't trafficked with the Chleuh themselves. And it wasn't as if the mob wouldn't turn on them if they protested. It wasn't as if the Quimperi wouldn't turn on them later, either, maybe under something that looked like the cover of law, maybe not.

After the women had gone by, Malk muttered, "It's a good thing we just sold Kangen's men scrap metal."

"What was that?" Sarmel asked. Malk said it again, a little louder this time. His brother nodded. "I wish I could tell you you were wrong, but you aren't."

"I know. Let's get out of here." Malk flicked the reins. Reluctantly, the old horses started moving again.

Guisa Sachry paid a boy for a news sheet. This one was the *Lutesse Spark*, which had published while the Chleuh ruled Quimper and for a couple of lifetimes before that. The *Spark* looked the same as it always had: the colophon had the spark of knowledge lighting up the world. What was in it, though . . .

Back in the days before the Chleuh marched into Lutesse, the sheet had despised them. After they took over, it parroted whatever King Kangen's officials wanted it to say. So did every news sheet, except for the ones the woodsrunners put out on the sly. A lot of the writers had stayed the same, though.

Guisa glanced at the front page now. Sure enough, a lot of the bylines seemed familiar. As long as the writers got paid twice a month, they didn't worry much about what they said, or for whose benefit. The same applied to the wizards who used the laws of similarity and contagion to make sure the newsboys had enough sheets to hawk every day.

Not everything was the same as it had been, of course. *I am Everywhere* was nowhere to be found, its offices closed by order of Char Tubis. Guisa hadn't seen or heard about Brasi Robillach since the Chleuh left Lutesse. He wondered if the writer and editor had gone with them. He hadn't tried to find out, though. Asking such questions seemed unwise.

The same went for Erol Paki. Guisa rather missed the little crystal commentator. Paki could laugh at himself. Brasi Robillach? Much less. The closest he came to mirth was a kind of cold smirk.

By what the *Lutesse Spark* said these days, the Chleuh were falling back toward their own kingdom through eastern Quimper. They were falling back against the Muos, too, much faster and in much worse disorder than the news sheets admitted while the Locusts told them what to write.

How much of what the *Spark* claimed these days was true? Occupation and the nonsense that came with it had made Guisa better able to read between the lines than he had been, or needed to be, before. As best he could judge, there were fewer lies in there now than the sheet had printed over the past few years. Past that, he wasn't ready to say.

Someone called his name. He looked up from the new sheet. A middle-aged man, very erect, in clothes that had been good but were now frowzy like everyone else's, a limp when he walked . . . "Master Ennogue!" Guisa said. "How are you these days?"

"One breathes," Nea Ennogue answered. "By the gods, one breathes." A smile stretched across his skinny face.

"Yes, indeed. I myself suffered greatly when the theatres closed," Guisa said, not grasping that the author and teacher might have something larger in mind.

He got lucky: Nea Ennogue didn't call him on it. Coming near with that stiff, hitching gait of his, Ennogue touched a finger to the bill of his cap. "I must tell you, Master Sachry, that I know myself to be in your debt," he said. "Though we agree on nothing, you were generous to send me those parcels. They helped tide me over when things were worst."

"It was my privilege, sir, believe me." Guisa said nothing about sending food exactly so he could get on Nea Ennogue's good side. He wouldn't have been amazed to learn Nea understood just why he'd done it. The man was no one's fool, no matter how stiff-necked he was.

But a good part of politeness involved what you *didn't* say. Like other kinds of good manners, silence smoothed dealing with other people.

All Ennogue did say was, "You do me too much honor. If ever you find yourself needing a favor, you know where to look for one." He touched his cap again and stumped down the street.

"I am your servant, sir." Guisa had trained his voice to carry to the back rows of upper balconies. He was sure Nea Ennogue heard him. But the teacher didn't respond. He kept on walking, with determination if not with grace. He wasn't any less difficult now that the Chleuh had fled.

Guisa started to throw the *Lutesse Spark* into a rubbish bin. He checked the motion and left the news sheet on a curbside bench instead. Trams were beginning to run again. Somebody sitting down to wait for one would find something to read.

He laughed at himself. Even he knew he wasn't in the habit of generosity large or small unless he hoped to get something out of it, the way he had with the parcels he'd sent to Nea Ennogue.

"Oh, by the gods!" he exclaimed. Wry horror was an emotion he'd never felt before, but he did now. Was Ennogue rubbing off on him?

He blamed his lapse into whatever this was—altruism? perish the thought!—on the theatres' having been closed so long. From everything he'd heard, they'd soon open again. He longed for that the way a man who smoked poppy juice longed for his next pipe.

Can't come soon enough, he thought. He sometimes took a sort of pride at having kept his temper as well as he had. He'd done his best not to take things out on Vonney. That might have been natural goodness welling to the surface of his disposition. Then again, it might have been a well-founded fear that she'd stick a knife in him while he slept if he did anything to her she really didn't like. The latter seemed more likely.

When the theatres *did* open up again, he wouldn't have to worry about it any more. He threw back his shoulders and tried to suck in his gut as he promenaded up the sidewalk. He could hardly wait.

~

Lillat smiled up at Malk Malkovici as he held her. She didn't have any teeth yet, but that didn't matter. She knew who he was, and she knew she was all right when she lay in the crook of his elbow. *That* mattered.

The smile turned the junkman to jelly, the way it did every time she aimed it at him. He wasn't the only one who fell under its spell. It did the same thing to Efa. A lot of the time, babies seemed to do their best to drive their parents mad. The gods must have given them those irresistible smiles to keep their father and mother from pitching them across the room when they wouldn't shut up no matter what.

Then Lillat's heavenly smile disappeared. She screwed up her face. Squelching noises came from her other end. Malk wrinkled his nose, though she didn't stink nearly so much when she fouled herself as an adult would have.

"Dear!" Malk called. "She's made another mess in her drawers!"

His wife's voice floated back from the kitchen: "Can you deal with it, please? I've got three pots on the stove, and I don't want to ruin supper." Efa sounded harassed.

"All right," Malk said, though he felt on the harassed side himself. He laid a towel on the bed, folded double. It was old and ratty, so he didn't much care if she dribbled onto it. Practically everything he and Efa had was old and ratty. Even people who'd done well for themselves had had trouble getting anything new while the occupants held Lutesse.

We did very well for ourselves. We lived, Malk thought. He kept Lillat in the crook of his left arm as he used his free hand to gather what he'd need to set her to rights. He couldn't just lay her on the towel, the way he would have before she learned to roll over. She hadn't fallen off the bed yet, but only a desperate grab had saved her once. Malk didn't want to do that again.

He cleaned her off and powdered her bottom and put a fresh

wrapping around her middle. No, she didn't smell *too* bad. Someone who went guddling around in rubbish tips for whatever he could find got used to worse.

After he'd got the wrapper folded, he consciously noticed what a neat, accurate job he'd done. That was his hands working without his mind engaged. Practice. Lots of practice.

He slid the new wrapping under Lillat's backside. Then, of course, she started to wiggle. "Hold still, you miserable thing," he growled under his breath—he didn't want Efa to catch him saying anything unkind to the baby. But pinning the wrapper wasn't something he could do automatically. He was always afraid he'd stick Lillat while he was at it. He hadn't yet, and didn't want to start.

The job done and his daughter unstuck yet again, he set her on the rug at the foot of the bed while he cleaned up. He threw the nasty wrapping into a big glazed pot with a tight-fitting lid that held most of the odors inside. The changing gear went back on the dresser. That taken care of, he got to wash his hands.

He didn't get to finish drying them before Lillat started crying. She didn't wail, as she would have if she'd hurt herself. But she wanted the world to know she realized she'd been abandoned and she wasn't happy about it.

"I'm coming, I'm coming!" Malk said. He scooped her up, patted her, and dried her tears on his tunic sleeve. She decided she hadn't been forgotten forever and smiled again.

As he carried her into the kitchen, he was struck by how little he'd known about how demanding babies were before he'd had one. Whenever Lillat was awake, she needed somebody paying attention to her. And, of his wife and himself, he knew he was the luckier. She was the one who nursed the baby, and she was still getting over bringing Lillat into the world. Work also meant he got away from the shop and the flat more than she could.

The interesting smells coming from those pots on the stove reminded him that she did still buy the food. "What have you got going there?" he asked.

"Mostly Anadan rations, perked up with fresh vegetables and some spices," she said.

"Oh?"

Efa nodded. "That's right, they're showing up on the left. As far as I can tell, the Anadans don't try very hard to stop it. They don't care. I don't think anyone over here started to understand what a big, rich kingdom Anada is till now."

While they ate, Lillat lay in a little wooden reclining chair that rested on the table. Malk had found it in the wreckage of a smashed block of flats while Efa was carrying their daughter, and brought it home in the hope it would prove useful. He'd put a canvas belt across the middle of the chair to keep the baby from rolling out. Holes in the wood suggested it had had such a belt before, but it didn't when he chanced upon it.

He and Efa hadn't been eating long when she made an unhappy face and said, "If the Anadans have so much food, why don't they have better food?"

"You can't really judge from soldiers' rations," Malk replied. "They have to keep for a long time. Even the best preservation spell will fade and then fail sooner or later. Remember the stories from when the war was new, how our men in the border forts were eating meat the wizards had treated at the end of the last war? Dead Donkey, they called it."

His wife smiled. "I didn't till you reminded me, but I do now. Some of the Chleuh rations went back that far, too. Didn't they call theirs Old Man?"

"I think they did," Malk said, and then, "I wonder what Colonel Tebron had to say about that. For one of those people, he wasn't that bad."

"From the little I saw and everything you've told me, he could have been a lot worse," Efa said.

"That's true. But he followed King Kangen's orders, even when they bothered him. If he's still alive, he's still following them the best way he knows how. And anybody who follows Kangen's orders could be a lot better. The whole point of this war was to make it so the Chleuh could tell all their neighbors what to do for the next thousand years."

"And so they could kill off everybody who follows the Old Faith," Efa added.

Malk hadn't intended to say anything about that. He hadn't wanted to upset his wife. Not for the first time, though, nowhere near for the first time, he discovered she was tougher-minded than he gave her credit for. "Yes. And so they could do that," he said, nodding.

"I've seen soldiers in the Anadan army who believe the way we do. A few in the Honterese army, too, but not so many. With the Anadans, the other warriors treat them like . . . like anybody else." Efa might have been reporting a miracle from the pages of a prayer book.

"Men who belong to the Old Faith fought for Quimper, too." Malk said as much as he could for the kingdom where Efa and he lived. He didn't claim the Quimperi who followed the True Faith—which was to say, almost all of them—

treated the men who believed differently the same way they treated one another. Lying to your wife was never a good idea, obviously lying to her worse yet.

Efa said, "We could still be back in Nistria."

"There is that. I thank our gods—I even thank the True Faith's gods—we aren't," Malk said. Nistria had more people who clung to the Old Faith than Quimper did. Perhaps because of that, the majority who belonged to the True Faith treated them worse than Quimperi did.

"We're just . . . people. Lillat's just . . . a baby. Why should anyone care which gods we worship? What difference does it make, anyway?" Efa sounded troubled, and well she might have.

Like anyone who followed the Old Faith, Malk had banged his head against those questions more often than he cared to remember. "I don't know why anybody should care about our gods. I know just about everybody *does* care, though," he said. "The difference it makes is, there are more of them than of us. They can murder us a lot more easily than we can murder them."

She smiled a crooked smile. "You always did know how to cheer me up, didn't you?"

Malk laughed. That sounded like something he would have said. They'd rubbed off on each other, the way couples who'd been together a long time always did. "I love you!" he exclaimed. Before Efa could answer, Lillat started to fuss—she wanted supper. He cleaned up while his wife nursed the baby.

"Another opening! Another show!" Guisa Sachry spoke in a low voice, but he sounded as excited as if he were going out in front of an audience for the very first time, not for the gods only knew how many thousandth.

He and Vonney stood in the darkness of the wings. The house lights were still up. He could see about a third of the crowd. In the lower level, a lot of the people he could see were wealthy Quimperi and their wives or (usually more decorative) lady friends.

The rest were Honterese and Anadan officers, some of whom also had lady friends beside them even if they hadn't been in Lutesse very long. These past four years, Guisa'd got very used to playing in front of men in uniforms. These weren't the uniforms he'd got used to, but the principle didn't change.

How much of the night's play would the newcomers understand? While many Chleuh spoke fluent Quimperi, thinking it the language of culture and refinement, Anadans and Hontermen were notorious for scorning any tongue not their own.

Well, if those fellows couldn't follow, too bad for them. They'd paid for tickets, which was all that really mattered. And they could always ogle the dancing girls. Some things didn't need words.

"Two minutes!" a stagehand called in a low but penetrating voice.

Guisa turned and gathered up his fellow performers with his eyes. "Let's make it good," he said. "I know we're rusty. I know we haven't been able to run through things as much as we should. Let's make it good anyway. Let's show the foreigners what we can do!"

He hadn't talked about the Chleuh like that, even when the theatres reopened after they marched into Lutesse. Like almost everyone else then, he'd assumed they'd stay a long time, maybe forever. Like almost everyone else now, he assumed the Hontermen and Anadans wouldn't. It made a difference.

"Ready?" he asked Vonney as the house lights faded and the stage lit up. Lighting technicians were handling shades and feeding salamanders and swearing under their breath the way they always did when they were trying to take care of too many things at once.

At his wife's nod, he took her arm. They promenaded out to where the crowd could see them. They didn't get the hand he thought they deserved. After a moment, even as he was going into his first speech, he realized why. The Quimperi were applauding. To them, he and Vonney were familiar, reliable, first-class performers. They were glad to see them back on the boards.

But to the foreigners? Vonney was a pretty woman to them, but what was he? Just an aging man in funny clothes spouting off in a language most of them wouldn't speak well. No help for it, though. The show was on. Nothing would stop it now, not unless the Chleuh sneaked some dragons through the cordon the new occupants had sat up around Lutesse.

Some younger actors said you couldn't give your best unless you actually felt the things you were showing onstage. Guisa thought that was nonsense—interesting nonsense, but even so. Why did they call it acting unless you were showing things that weren't real? That was where the skill, the artistry, came in, as far as he was concerned.

And so he had no trouble worrying about the size of the house and about what the Honterese and Anadan officers would make of the show even as he and Vonney pledged eternal love to each other and kissed to show they meant it. The whoops from the crowd while that was going on sounded reassuringly normal.

When he and Vonney went off, she said, "I think it's going to work."

"Don't jinx it!" Guisa exclaimed. But he felt the same way, even if he never would have said so out loud.

They didn't get all the laughs they might have, but they got enough, and all the people in the seats seemed to blister their hands when the cast came out for bows after the curtain fell.

Guisa and Vonney took theirs last, of course. Then, as he straightened, "Now let us applaud you, the brave warriors who have freed us after these last four long, hard years!" Along with everyone else up on stage, he clapped for the men from Anada and Honter.

He'd suggested doing that while the company ran through things earlier in the day. No one had said no. Who wouldn't want to keep the powerful, dangerous foreigners happy? Those four years of life under the Chleuh had taught everybody in Lutesse how important that could be. And, like all the best bits of stagecraft, it seemed more natural than it was.

Back in the dressing room, he scrubbed off his makeup and got into ordinary clothes. "It really did go over pretty well, didn't it?" he asked Vonney—he thought so, but he needed to hear it from her, too.

"It did. It truly did," she said. "I think—"

He didn't get to find out what she thought. Someone knocked on the door before she could tell him. When he opened it, he found three hard-faced men with crossbows standing in the narrow corridor. He stared. "What's all this about?"

One of them aimed a bolt at his brisket. "Come along with us. You're under arrest. You'll answer questions, not ask them."

Guisa did ask another one: "On what possible charge?"

"Dancing at the end of the occupants' strings. What else?" the man said. "Come on." Helplessly, Guisa came.

XV

Malk Malkovici bought a *Lutesse Spark* from the kiosk. As he paid the old woman who ran it, he said, "You don't call me 'you old pussy,' Quilly."

She laughed. "You'd know if I did. I wonder what ever happened to that fat fool. I wonder if he's still breathing. He wasn't much more of a soldier than I am."

"I've thought the same thing. For a Locust, he didn't seem like such a bad fellow." Malk reflected that he'd said that more often than he'd ever expected to. Maybe the Chleuh seemed less horrible the farther away they got both in distance and in time.

Quilly spat on the cobblestones by the little kiosk. "He did what Kangen told him to do. He wouldn't have been here in Lutesse if he didn't. He might've been fine back in Chlé. Not here."

"Can't argue with you. I said almost the same thing to my wife about another one." Malk touched the brim of his cap and ambled back to his shop and the flat over it.

When he brought the sheet up to the flat, Efa was just sliding Lillat into the cradle for her morning nap. He stood there quietly till his wife straightened; any little disturbance might make their daughter decide she'd sooner fuss and squawk for the next hour than sleep.

Efa let out a soft sigh of relief when the baby stayed quiet. "She was up enough in the night. I hope she gets a good nap now." Malk's wife held out her hand. "Let's see what happened in the world while I was—or mostly wasn't—asleep."

"Here you go." Malk handed her the *Spark*. "What does it say?"

"I *am* going to teach you to read, so help me I am, if only so you can read to me while I'm holding Lillat," Efa said, and then, glancing down at the sheet, "Hello!"

"What is it?" Malk remembered—remembered only too well—the days when the news was always bad, except when it was worse. This *Hello!* didn't sound quite like that, but it came close enough to make him worry.

"They've caught Brasi Robillach," Efa answered.

"Who?" Malk knew he'd heard the name before, but couldn't put a mental finger on where.

"The son of a whore who put out *I Am Everywhere* for the Chleuh."

"Oh. Him." Though he didn't have his syllables, Malk knew *I Am Everywhere* spewed out hate against the Old Faith, Honter, the Muos, and anyone else King Kangen didn't care for. From things he'd heard, Robillach hadn't just done Kangen's work for him: he'd enjoyed doing it, too. The junkman asked, "Where was he?"

Efa's lip curled. "Hiding in an attic—an attic in a rich man's house, by the address." Malk nodded, unsurprised—the more money people had, the more likely they were to think the Chleuh a better bargain than the Muos. His wife went on, "He got sold out anyway, you'll notice. And do you know what he said when the constables broke down the door to his hidey-hole?"

"No, but you're going to tell me, aren't you?" Malk replied. By the look on Efa's face, it would be something worth hearing.

"You bet I am. He said, 'The scum who follow the Old Faith

closed themselves up in attics, so I thought it would work for me, too.'"

"He may have run a news sheet for the Locusts, but he's an idiot anyway," Malk said. "It mostly *didn't* work for us." A handful of men and women who clung to the old Faith had come out of hiding after King Kangen's men abandoned Lutesse, but only a handful. Far more had made some fatal mistake or been betrayed as the war ground on. They were somewhere in the east now . . . if they were anywhere on earth at all.

"It didn't work for Robillach, either." Efa seemed savagely delighted.

Malk understood that; he felt the same way. "What are they going to do with him? To him, I mean?"

She had to check the news sheet again before she could answer. "Char Tubis says he'll get a fair trial. The charge will be aiding Quimper's enemies and treason against the kingdom. If he's guilty—" She tapped the back of her neck with her right index finger.

"That's what he deserves." Malk didn't have much doubt Brasi Robillach would get it, either. Too many Quimperi had helped King Kangen's men hold the kingdom down. They'd spent four years tormenting everyone on the other side. For the first two, at least, they'd been sure they were on the side that was bound to win.

They'd been sure, but they'd been wrong. Though revenge had held off for a long time, here it was at last. Malk shivered, remembering the naked women with shaved heads shambling along the Avenue of Admiral Morzen. Next to someone like Robillach, they hadn't done much. Their hair would grow back; their humiliation would fade. The editor and writer was facing punishment more permanent.

Efa took him by the arm and guided him into the dining room. She sat him down at the table and moved the other chair on that side next to his. "I mean it. By the gods, I really do this time," she said. "You're going to learn to read, you stubborn lump."

"All right," he said. She gaped at him. "All right," he repeated.

"I've been thinking for a while now it would come in handy. I'd sooner learn from you than Sarmel. He'd never let me forget he knew first and he was showing me."

"The two of you . . ." She shook her head. "But never mind that." She sat the news sheet on the table between them. "See? This first syllable says 'Lu.' This is the character for syllables that start with 'l,' and this little tick above it means the syllable has an 'u' sound after it. This next mark stands for 't.' The tick down in the line over it shows it has a following 'e.' The last mark shows 'ss.' The curlicue in the line above means there's no vowel sound at all after it. Are you with me?"

"I think so. All together, it makes 'Lutesse.' I see how. Keep going. I'll learn." Malk meant it. If he set his mind to something, he could figure out how it worked. He'd finally decided to do that.

Guisa Sachry had been in jail cells several times on stage, and once for real when he got into a drunken brawl as a young man. Even then, though, he'd spent only a night. Longer exposure didn't make him like this cell more.

At the moment, he had it to himself. They were grilling his cellmate. The cell wasn't big enough for two. It wasn't really big enough for one. He would have complained had he thought it would do any good. Since he thought complaining would only get him slapped around, he kept quiet. They hadn't started any rough stuff yet. He didn't want to give them an excuse to.

He used the slops bucket. Doing that without his cellmate watching was a small pleasure. He savored it; he'd had no big ones lately. When he finished, he put the lid back on. At least the bucket had a lid, even if it fit badly.

A key went into the lock on the other side of the thick oaken door. The door swung open on rusty, raspy hinges. He'd got that right in one of the plays he'd directed. The props man had grumbled but gone along.

Four constables stood in the hallway, two with loaded crossbows, the other two with shortswords. One of the men gave his cellmate a shove, growling, "In you go, traitor."

"And whose orders did *you* follow when the Chleuh ran the city?" Brasi Robillach inquired sweetly.

Instead of answering, the constable slammed the door closed. The lock clicked as he or one of his friends shut it. Footfalls faded as the constables walked down the corridor.

"You won't make them treat you any better if you get them angry," Guisa remarked.

"Those shambling sheep! They don't deserve my respect," Brasi answered. "The Chleuh, now, the Chleuh were worth admiring. They still are, by the gods! They fought the whole world and almost won. But Quimperi constables who trim their sails to go however the wind blows? A pestilence take them all!"

Guisa cupped a hand to his ear and pointed up at the ceiling. Didn't Robillach know listening spells were easy to cast? Maybe he didn't care what the constables thought of him, but their opinion mattered to the actor.

Brasi's careless wave said he didn't give a fig. Sighing to himself, Guisa said, "Well, it doesn't look like they've started knocking you around so far. What kind of questions are they asking you?"

"About what you'd expect—who my bosses were, and my colleagues, and my underlings, and why was I wicked enough to betray Quimper." Brasi spat on the stone floor in vast contempt. "I gave them an earful about *that.*"

"What did you say?" Guisa asked, apprehensive and morbidly curious at the same time.

"That I wasn't the traitor, of course. That Char Tubis was. After the king and his family died, the General was Quimper's rightful ruler. He surrendered to the Chleuh. He chose to work with them, and had the kingdom do the same. I didn't do anything he didn't do. Char Tubis was the one who disobeyed him."

"That's interesting. It's even clever." But Guisa couldn't help adding, "I don't think it will do you any good, though."

"Oh, neither do I," the writer and editor said, with what sounded like genuine good cheer. "One of the men asking me things was too smart to be a constable, and spoke too well. He's bound to be a flunky for our new lord and master. I didn't want him to doubt where I stood."

"This isn't a game, Brasi. If they don't like what you tell them, they'll take your head for it," Guisa reminded him.

"They'll take it anyhow. They have four years' worth of reasons. *I Am Everywhere* makes a good start. And I went to Chlé and talked with King Kangen's writers and journalists. And I haven't exactly made a secret about thinking the maggots who cling to the Old Faith deserve everything they've got, and more besides. So I have got nothing left to lose. I may as well enjoy myself."

Guisa shook his head. Unlike his cellmate, he still had hopes of saving himself. He hadn't got so deeply involved with the Chleuh as Robillach had. *And no one,* he thought, *could really want to hurt* me.

Lunch was the same as breakfast had been, and all the meals the day before: a sandwich of some nasty almost-ham between slabs of hard bread—all Anadan rations, from what the constables said—along with some wine a short step up from piss. Not only was it bad, there wasn't enough of it: one more thing Guisa didn't have the nerve to complain about.

Not long after lunch, the door opened again. Another party of four armed constables stood outside. One of them aimed an index finger at Guisa as if it were a crossbow bolt. "Come along with us, you fat tub of goo."

"I am merely well fleshed, sir," Guisa replied with dignity. All four constables laughed at him. Even Brasi Robillach snickered softly. That hurt more. Since his other choices were worse, Guisa went with the men in blue coats with brass buttons.

He'd been questioned before, but they took him to a different room this time. They shackled his ankles to the legs of the heavy chair in which they sat him, and his wrists to its arms. That didn't seem a good sign.

He hadn't seen this interrogator before, either. The man looked more like an archivist than a constable. He puffed on a pipe. Guisa wouldn't have been surprised if he was the fellow who'd questioned Brasi earlier in the day.

"You are the writer, director, and performer Guisa Sachry." The man sounded as mild as he looked.

"That's right. I'm afraid you have the advantage of me, sir. You are . . . ?"

"Yes. I do have the advantage of you. You would do well to be afraid, too. Traitors had better fear me. And you don't need to know my name. *Sir* will do."

"However you please, of course." Guisa tried to sound light, even relaxed. It wasn't easy, not when he couldn't move, not when a cold lump of fear was growing in his guts.

The man who was questioning him took out a small pen knife and trimmed a fingernail or two with it. He didn't put it away after he finished. Guisa did his best not to look at the blade. Still mildly, the man remarked, "Lutesse has been hungry these past four years. You haven't lost much meat, though. How did you manage that?"

"I kept performing. And I always knew how to save money. Actors and writers had better learn to do that, because they never can tell when they'll go without." Guisa wasn't even lying, though he also wasn't telling all of the truth.

"You performed with the consent, with the permission, of the occupants."

"Sir, I could not have done so without it."

"True. Some did not, because of that. But never mind. Not all who performed, for instance, also stood on the reviewing stand with Odrio Cazh as men from the Quimperi Popular Party marched past on their way to make war against King Kangen's enemies."

"I was coerced into making that appearance. Count Vurk made it very plain that severe consequences would follow if I did not."

"Ah, Count Vurk." The interrogator held up his little knife so the blade flashed red in the salamanderlight. "You knew the Chleuh minister well?"

"Not very. We would see each other at gatherings, that's all."

"Is it? How interesting you should say so. And yet I've heard you also wrote a play at his urging: his and General Stulp's, I mean. A clever piece—I've read it. But would you say it puts those who opposed the occupants in a good light?"

Guisa licked his lips. They knew too much. They knew much too much. Still working to sound as if everything were fine, he answered, "Sir, it is a comedy. It laughs at everyone and everything. No one, and no point of view, comes out of it unscathed."

"You wrote it for the occupants. They ordered it shown in places where those who stood against them had some strength. Do you think the Chleuh hoped to make their foes stronger or weaker when they did that?"

"How can I speak for them?" Guisa asked—sensibly, he hoped.

"Perhaps you were doing that when you wrote it." The interrogator held up his hand. "'Perhaps,' I say. I am here only to ask questions. We are not the Chleuh, to hurt or kill for the sport of it. You will have a trial. Someone else will decide your guilt. You will have justice."

He stepped outside. Flunkies came in to unlock Guisa's bonds and take him back to his cell. Right at that moment, justice was the last thing, the very last thing, he wanted.

An Anadan officer walked into the junk shop. Malk Malkovici bowed, not quite so deeply as he would have to a Chleuh. "Good morning, sir. How may I help you?" he said.

"You speak Honterese?" the officer asked in that language.

"I am sorry, sir, but no," Malk said in Quimperi. He was starting to pick up bits and pieces, as he had with Chleuh, but he was nowhere near fluent. Talking Honterese would put him at a disadvantage—and a sensible man tried not to show everything he knew.

"Damnation," the Anadan said in his own tongue. Then, a bit to Malk's surprise, he switched to Quimperi: "Can you follow me in your lingo?"

"I can, yes. You speak very well." Malk buttered him up, the way he would have with any possible customer. The Anadan had an accent thick enough to slice and a barbarous turn of phrase, but Malk did understand him. His own Quimperi wasn't perfect, either. People in Lutesse noticed, though the foreigner might not.

"Learned in school. Ain't hardly used this talk in thirty years since, not till I got over here," the fellow said. "So chances are I ain't that great. Don't see no old clothes or rags."

"I don't deal in them." Malk spoke slowly and carefully. "I knew a man who did, but the Chleuh took him away. He helped the woodsrunners, you see."

"All right. Looks like you got a fair bit o' stuff anyways. What can you do to me—uh, do *for* me—about cookpots and trays? Not big ones. The kind a soldier'd use to boil up somethin' and eat it off of? Don't got to be pretty or match or nothin'. Just got to be there."

Pots were easy. Malk found some in his pile of copper and among the scrap iron. "These copper pots will need to be retinned. You understand 'retinned'?"

"Sure do. Our wizards can take care of that," the Anadan officer said. "How about them there trays?"

Malk searched. Trays could be made of several types of metal or of wood. As he looked, he said, "If you will want more, sir, tell me now, so I can watch out for them."

"I'll be looking to buy whatever you can get along these here lines. What all we got here?" The soldier looked at the pots and trays Malk had found for him. Counting on his fingers, he muttered in his own language. "For this lot, I'll give you—" The price he named was close to three times what Malk could have hoped to squeeze out of Colonel Tebron. The Anadans had to be so rich, they had no notion of how rich they were.

Cautiously, Malk said, "That may be enough." He'd never had anybody try to throw money at him before. He went on, "May I ask your name, sir? If we'll do more business, I should know it."

"I'm Genry Spith," the officer replied, as if surprised Malk didn't already know. "And it says Malkovici Brothers out front, but I don't know which Malkovici Brother you is, uh, are." What he did to Malk's family name was bad, but no worse than the way some Quimperi pronounced it.

"I'm Malk. I live over the shop. Sarmel has a flat not far from here."

"Right pleased to meet you, Malk." Genry Spith held out his hand. By the standards Malk was used to, he was overfamiliar, but the junkman had heard Anadans were like that. The officer continued, "Now you got to tell me—you ever sell stuff to the Chleuh while they was here?"

Malk looked at him. He only wished the question surprised him. "Of course I did, Master Spith. If I hadn't, I would be dead now, and my brother and my wife with me. Chances are my baby girl never would have been born. We belong to the Old Faith, you see."

"Well," Spith said, and then, "Well," again. His harsh accent made the word sound like something to be carved on a grave marker. "I ain't supposed to have nothin' to do with nobody who worked with them folks."

"Good luck in Quimper, sir!" Malk exclaimed.

Genry Spith smiled crookedly. He might talk like a savage, but Malk got the feeling he was nobody's fool. "Yeah," he said. "Tell you what—I'll buy this here lot now, on account of I need it, and make like I forgot to ask you if I get gigged for it. But sooner or later, we're gonna have to work somethin' out."

"However you please, of course." Malk sounded as obsequious as if he were talking with Tebron while other Chleuh could overhear.

But, if the Anadan officer was willing to skirt the rules to work with him, now he had a hold on the man. That might prove useful.

Willing Spith was—even eager. He set gold on the counter. It was Anadan gold, so Malk weighed the coins. Sure enough, they were the equivalent of the price in Quimperi crowns Spith had quoted. Then the Anadan took a small crystal from a belt pouch, activated it, and talked into it in Honterese. As he stowed it away, he spoke to Malk again: "Wagon'll be here pretty quick for pickup."

Malk did his best not to show how impressed he was. The Chleuh used crystals more than the Quimperi army had. Being able to talk among themselves at a distance was part of the reason they'd beaten Quimper so easily. For an officer to be casually able to call a wagon this way, though—Malk had never seen anything like that. Anadan wealth again, now used to change how wars were fought.

The wagon showed up even sooner than Malk had expected. Two Anadan soldiers loaded Genry Spith's purchases into it. Then it rolled away. Spith went with the men he'd summoned. They laughed and joked together as if they all belonged to the same class. Watching them, Malk suddenly understood why so many rich Quimperi had preferred King Kangen's rule to . . . this.

Guisa Sachry didn't keep Brasi Robillach as a cellmate for very long. The man who'd so enjoyed running *I Am Everywhere* for the Locusts went to trial, was swiftly convicted and condemned, and got carted away to another prison outside Lutesse to await the headsman.

From things the guards and other captives here said, that prison was reserved for people like Robillach, people who'd liked the Chleuh much too well for much too long. Not many of those people were expected to come out of that prison in one piece. A guard felt at the back of his neck as he gave Guisa that news.

"Wonder when they'll send you there," the man added—much too cheerfully, as far as Guisa was concerned.

They didn't send him away. They didn't try him, either. They kept him in the cell, by himself now, and went on questioning him. After a while, the interrogator who looked like an archivist didn't bother having him shackled any more. Guisa took that as a small good sign.

He never did get to call the man anything but *sir*. That was not such a good sign, not to him. No one cared about his opinion even so much as a housewife might care about a dried-up cat turd. He wasn't used to being thought of no account. He didn't care for it.

Again and again, the interrogator kept coming back to *Among the Villagers*. "Why didn't you use your own name for it?" he asked.

"Sir, I wrote it in the style of Gorec Sembel. Pastiche has its own challenges, its own rewards. I wanted to see if I truly might be taken for him—and I was." Guisa spoke with more than a little pride.

"And the idea that you might hide from punishment behind a false name never occurred to you?"

"If we've come to the point where writing a play calls for punishment . . ." Guisa shrugged expressively. He also didn't answer the question.

The man who looked like an archivist took out his little knife. Even though Guisa could move, that still chilled him. The man didn't do anything with it, not now, but Guisa knew props shown were props ready to be used. After a moment, the interrogator said, "Well, that depends on why you write them, for whom you write them, and what's in them, wouldn't you say?" He paused again. "It *is* a good pastiche. Whether that makes things better or worse for you may be a different question, eh?"

Guards took Guisa back to his cell not much later. He felt oddly cheered as he went with them. The dusty little man who questioned him spoke like someone who could appreciate the fine points of writing. Surely someone like that wouldn't be too harsh on an artist.

Surely, Guisa thought again. That he had to repeat the thought meant he wasn't sure at all, not that he really grasped that.

He got to see Vonney twice, the two of them sitting on opposite sides of a thick metal mesh that made her dim and blurry to him (and, no doubt, made him the same to her) and that made sure neither could pass anything to the other. After the conventional things about how much he missed her and how he wished he were home, the first question out of his mouth was the same both times: "Will they let me have a lawyer?"

She shook her head the first time. The second, ten days or so later, she answered, "Now they say they may. Pevar Forsen won't take your case, though. He told me he wouldn't touch it for all the gold the Chleuh stole from Quimper."

Forsen had handled Guisa's legal affairs for more than twenty-five years. "A pestilence take him! I myself never thought he was a coward till now," Guisa said. "You'll have to find someone else."

"I've been looking. I haven't found anybody willing yet," Vonney said unhappily. "One fellow flat-out told me he wouldn't stand up for anybody charged with getting too close to the Chleuh. He said people would think that meant he'd been cozy with them, too, and no one would want anything to do with him then."

"Ha!" Guisa said. "Six gets you a dozen he was thick as thieves with the Locusts and doesn't want it coming out now. Even more than actors, lawyers had to be if they were going to work at all while the occupants ran things."

"Dear, I'm sure you're right, but it doesn't help you," Vonney said.

"Gods only know what will." Guisa shook his head. "At least they haven't taken me off to that prison where they're keeping Robillach. I'm still here, still in Lutesse. That has to be good, or at least better than it might be. But I'm going mad—mad, I tell you!—because I can't perform."

"I'm sorry." Vonney had the actor's madness, too, if less severely than Guisa. When no one was watching you, admiring you, applauding you, how could you be sure you were there? Wouldn't you just . . . disappear after a while?

Trying to take his mind off the fear that felt so real, Guisa asked, "What's the news in the outside world?"

"The Anadans and Hontermen have taken back most of Quimper. They're almost to the Chleuh border. In the east, the Muos are over the border. Nistria switched sides. Their Golden Guards turned on the Chleuh in their kingdom, and now they're fighting for King Ninel."

"I'm sure they'll have joy from that." Four years of war and more had honed Guisa's already-sharp cynicism. He added, "Ninel will take care to see that they fight to the very last Nistrian, too."

His wife nodded. "Chances are."

A guard on her side of the wire mesh came over and said, "Time's up. You've got to leave."

Vonney got off the stool where she'd perched. Guisa blew her a kiss. She gave it back to him, not that that did him much good. Men on his side of the mesh returned him to his cell. He sat on the hard cot that was the only furniture he had and buried his face in his hands.

An hour or so later, someone down the hall started screaming. The prisoner didn't sound as if the guards or an interrogator were torturing him. He sounded more as if he'd gone out of his mind. Guisa found himself more interested than irritated. Lunatic ravings, at least, were something out of the ordinary.

They went on for a while and then stopped, quite suddenly. Two guards came along the corridor, their boots thumping almost in unison. "Gods-cursed crackpot," one of them said.

"We cracked *his* pot for him, all right," the other replied in tones of satisfaction. "He won't make trouble like that again any time soon."

"Not if he knows what's good for him, he won't," the first man said. They both laughed.

Time dragged on for Guisa. Fall gave way to winter. He was cold for a while. Then he wasn't—they issued him an Anadan blanket, as thick as any he had in his flat if a good deal scratchier. It was dyed the same drab color as the uniforms the men from across the ocean wore.

One of the guards said, "The Anadans, they've got so much stuff, it must fall out of their arseholes. They've got so much, they can even dish it out to treasonous scum like you."

"Thank you for your kind words." Guisa had never learned to let bad reviews slide off his back. He knew he was wonderful—why couldn't the blind fools out there see it, too? But he'd also learned, painfully, not to show he was hurt. They only nipped harder if you did that.

He did hope the Anadan capmaker's son who'd admired Vonney in the days before she met him wasn't in Lutesse. That could prove awkward, or worse than awkward.

The guard looked at him, frowning. The fellow suspected he'd just got the glove, but couldn't work out how. Chances were they didn't hire prison guards for brains. Still looking back over his shoulder, the man slammed the cell door before locking it. He wasn't too stupid to forget that, alas.

Word came that Char Tubis declined to commute Brasi Robillach's sentence. By all accounts, the editor died well, walking to the block without faltering and wearing a red scarf the headsman had to unwind before he did his job. Brasi'd even cried "Long live Quimper!" as the axe fell.

None of which left him any less dead, of course. They still hadn't summoned Guisa to trial. He hoped that meant they feared their case was weak. Nobody told him anything. No one cared what he thought. And if that wasn't the worst unkindness, what could be?

Malk and Sarmel Malkovici stacked coins for easy counting. "This is madness," Sarmel said. "The Chleuh didn't haggle very well, but they did try. These people don't bother."

"It's true. They don't care what they spend, not even a little."

Malk picked up an Anadan goldpiece. One side showed their emblem, a plump bird with a tail that spread out behind it like a fan. The other held the portrait of a man with a strong chin who wore a crown. Malk tried out what Efa'd taught him: "'King He-orge, bless-èd by gods.'" He read the motto under the image, too, though the syllables were very small: "'To-geth-er, we are strong.' It's Honterese, so who knows what it means, but that's what it says."

His brother made as if to clap his hands. "You've really got it! Can you manage news sheets and romances, too?"

"I'm slow. It's like anything else, I guess—it takes practice. The more I do, the easier it seems to get. It's a handy thing to know how to do. I won't say it isn't. I should have learned a long time ago. If you want to go, 'I told you so,' be my guest."

"I told you so." But Sarmel grinned to take away the sting. "And I'll tell you something else—I won't be sorry not to have to come over to make sure a contract is the way it's supposed to be. I lost a lady friend on account of that a couple of years ago. Your timing was terrible."

"I'm sorry. But if something like that could make her walk away, chances are she wasn't worth keeping."

"Who said anything about keeping her? She was really pretty, though, and she knew how. Did she ever!"

Malk wished his brother would find a woman who was worth keeping, latch on to her, and settle down. He'd done it himself, so why couldn't Sarmel? Because he'd done it so thoroughly, he didn't see it wasn't always easy.

Once they worked out what they'd made for the week, Malk took some of the coins down to the subcellar and stashed them where he'd kept the illicit crystal, which he could show openly now. He could and he did; it sat on the counter in the shop, a couple of feet from the cash box. The Quimperi gold from the strongbox he'd found in the rubbish tip was in that hole, too.

Gold . . . Gold was a complicated story. Unlike a lot of people who'd done well for themselves while the occupants were here, he'd never shown off his good fortune. For one thing, flaunting wealth was even more dangerous for someone who clung to the Old Faith than for an ordinary Quimperi. And, for another, he understood in his bones how the bush that poked up tall was the one that got chopped down.

Sarmel understood it, too, even if it chafed him more than it did Malk. Having started with nothing, Malk was content with plenty to eat and a comfortable flat. His brother wanted to show the world he wasn't somebody with nothing any more. He couldn't do that with King Kangen's minions calling the shots. Now he was thinking about it.

Even Malk was thinking about it, though he was sure he wouldn't do it. Another year like this—maybe just another few months—and he'd never need to worry again about anything money could take care of.

When he came up into the shop again, he reached under the counter and pulled out a bottle of apple brandy from the north. The cork popped when he pulled it out. Raising the bottle, he said, "Here's to the Anadans, gods bless 'em!" and swigged.

Sarmel held out his hand. "I'll drink to that!" When Malk gave him the brandy, he did.

From the top of the stairs, Efa said, "I just got Lillat down, gods be thanked. Who's drinking what? I want some!"

"Come on down. Maybe Sarmel's left a couple of drops in the bottom of the bottle," Malk said.

"My brother is a funny man. Such a funny man. Funny like a truss," Sarmel said with no particular anger. He held out the brandy bottle to Efa.

"Ahh," she said after she drank, and then, "If that goes on through to Lillat in my milk, she's sure to sleep through the night tonight."

"Does it? Go through, I mean?" Sarmel asked.

"I'm not sure, but I think so," Efa said. "I don't like to drink enough to get drunk—I always feel horrible the next morning when I do—but she seems to sleep better when I have an extra glass of wine after supper."

"You sleep better when you have that extra glass, too," Malk said.

Efa laughed at him. "I always sleep as if somebody hit me over the head with a rock. I'd better! I'm always sleepy and tired while I'm awake, gods know. That's one of the things babies are for—wearing out their mothers, I mean. You always hear that, but you have no idea how true it is till it happens to you."

"Too many things are like that," Sarmel said. "We always heard about how most people felt about folks who follow the Old Faith, folks like us, but we didn't get our noses rubbed in it—"

"—too badly," Efa broke in.

"Too badly," Sarmel agreed. "We didn't get our noses rubbed in it *too* badly till the Chleuh marched in."

"And we're lucky. We're still here to talk about it. Those places the Muos are finding . . . They make me wish you didn't teach me my syllables, sweetheart. Then I wouldn't know so much." Malk shuddered. He thought he'd been hardened to everything worshipers of the True Faith did to his own coreligionists. But the encampments King Kangen's men had set up were charnel houses, abattoirs. No wonder no one came back from them. The wonder was, the Muos had found a few starving survivors to rescue.

XVI

The judge peered at Guisa Sachry over the tops of his gold-framed half-spectacles. His eyes were black and cold, the eyes of a bird of prey. He had a hawk face, too, long and narrow, with a hooked beak of a nose. "The accused will rise," he said in a voice that gave nothing away.

Gulping, Guisa said, "Yes, your Excellency," as he got to his feet. The mouthpiece he'd finally found sat to his left. Vonney was behind the lawyer—and behind the railing that separated participants in the proceedings from the audience. Most of the spectator seats were empty, which irked Guisa; he always thought he deserved a full house. A handful of scribblers for the Lutesse news sheets waited to see what the Purification Court would do to him.

"There can be no doubt that you cooperated with the Chleuh during the occupation now just past, cooperated to a degree much greater than anything that might have been required merely to continue in your occupation. Witnesses have made this abundantly clear," the judge said with distaste, as if he were scraping Guisa off the sole of his shoe.

Guisa stood mute. One of the witnesses had been Xya Fulgine, who told of how many gatherings at Count Vurk's ministry or General Stulp's headquarters or the establishments of other Chleuh leading lights she'd seen him at. He could scarcely deny that; too many other people knew he'd been to those places, and the news sheets even recorded his presence at some of the events. Luckily, the judge didn't ask Xya how she'd come to pay attention to him.

After a moment, the man resumed: "It also cannot be doubted that you wrote a perfidious play, *Among the Villagers*, intended to aid the occupants and scorn their foes. That it appeared in the style of and under the name of Gorec Sembel does not relieve you of responsibility for it. Do you understand me?"

"Your Excellency, I am afraid I do." Guisa hoped no one would ever know how afraid he was. He didn't think he could die as bravely as Brasi Robillach had.

But the judge hadn't finished. "There are, however, certain mitigating circumstances in your case. No one has ever claimed you denounced or betrayed people to the occupants. On the contrary: you were known to be generous to those who suffered through what has come to be known as internal exile."

He meant the people who'd stayed silent through the occupation and had had as little to do with the Chleuh as they could. Sure enough, the food packets Guisa'd sent to Nea Ennogue hadn't gone to waste. Ennogue had even spoken of them here a couple of days before.

"Others who were generous in a similar fashion nevertheless received the ultimate penalty. It is a mitigating factor, not an exculpatory one," the judge continued, and Guisa's heart sank. After a moment probably intended to make him sweat, the hawk-faced man said, "But there is less to mitigate in your case than in theirs. Are you ready to receive the sentence I am about to impose on you?"

Whatever Char Tubis' minions were about to do to him, they didn't seem to plan on killing him. He managed a nod. "Yes, your Excellency."

"Very well. You are plainly guilty of undue cooperation with the

Chleuh during the occupation recently past. As plainly, your guilt, unlike that of some, does not require your head to atone for it. And so, after consulting with certain colleagues and associates, I have devised for you a sentence fitting your offense—fitting it quite well, I might add."

Guisa bowed his head and waited. They would do what they did, and he would bear it as best he could. *But I'll live!* Relief filled him.

"All too often, Master Sachry, when you opened your mouth or dipped your pen in ink, you did so in service to the occupants, not to the people of Quimper. Your private life, on the other hand, was irreproachable," the judge said.

Somehow, even without turning around to see, Guisa knew Vonney would be stirring. He knew exactly what expression her face would wear. He knew he'd earned it, too.

But the judge kept rolling along, as unstoppable and resistless as a landslide rolling downhill: "This being so, I order for you the worst sentence I can devise while still leaving your head on your shoulders. Guisa Sachry, you are *silenced.* From this time forth, until I or some other judge may reverse my decree, you may not perform in public. No work of yours first produced after the General's unfortunate surrender may be shown, again until or unless my decree is reversed. This applies regardless of whether the work was written or produced under your own name or some other one. Should you violate this decree, you become liable to any and all punishments not imposed now. Do you understand all that?"

"Yes, your Excellency," Guisa said once more. Part of him—not such a small part, either—wished the judge had ordered his head struck off. The man was more clever, and more cruel, than Guisa had given him credit for.

"Do you accept it?"

"Have I a choice, your Excellency?"

"Certainly. Up till the end, one always has a choice. But yours here would very quickly bring you to that end."

"Then I accept," Guisa said. "And I thank you, sir, for . . . as much mercy as you've shown." Try as he would, he couldn't swallow that small pause.

He was sure the judge noticed it, too. But the man affected not to, saying only, "Very well. You are no longer required to remain imprisoned, but may leave the custody of the free men of Quimper and live quietly in your own home hereafter. *Quietly*, I repeat. Once more, do you understand and accept?"

"Yes, your Excellency." The words of the formula tasted like ashes in Guisa's mouth.

~

When winter was at its worst, King Kangen's warriors counterattacked in the west, pushing back into eastern Quimper. The stroke caught the Hontermen and Anadans by surprise; they'd looked for defense from the Chleuh, not offense. And it was cleverly timed. The bad weather kept dragons from flying, and from doing much harm if they did.

In Lutesse, the news sheets shrieked of doom. Eyeing the panicky stories in the *Lutesse Spark*, Malk Malkovici told Efa, "You never should have taught me to read, curse it. Now I worry about everything I see. The sheets make it sound as bad as it was four and a half years ago."

"It probably isn't," his wife replied. "They make it out to be terrible so people will buy more copies to find out how terrible it is."

"That's a filthy way to do business." Malk thought about it for a moment. "But it does make sense if you're trying for as much money as you can grab. If I ran a news sheet, I might run it that way."

"I don't think so," Efa said. "If you were like that, you would have let Uncle Ory starve years ago."

"He would have deserved it." Malk wasn't fond of Efa's uncle.His wife understood that as well as he did. "Watching you do well—and even more so, eating food you bought—has to be bitter as wormwood to him."

"I know. Sometimes that makes me happy, sometimes just sad. As for wormwood, the Quimperi used to mix it into their brandy. Then they decided it made people crazy, so they stopped. Or they said they stopped, anyway."

Efa nodded. "You can still get it if you know where to look, and if you want to pay that kind of money."

"Not me. For one thing, I'm cheap. For another, I'm already crazy."

"How long have I lived with you? You think I don't know that? Just means I must be crazy, too."

Before Malk could answer, someone knocked on the door down below. He frowned. He'd closed an hour before; supper was almost ready. He stayed where he was, hoping whoever was out there would go away. Whoever it was didn't. The knock came again, louder and more insistent this time.

Scowling, he headed for the stairs. He didn't open the door. He called through it instead: "Who's there?"

"Men who love freedom," came the answer from outside. "Let us in, or you'll be sorrier than you can imagine."

Malk unlocked locks, took down the bar, and threw the door wide. He hadn't known this moment would come, but he'd feared it would. The four men outside were all young and tough looking. They all carried weapons. The clothes they wore were an odd mix of things ordinary people might put on, old Quimperi uniforms, and fresh Anadan gear. The one who'd spoken before said, "You're Malk Malkovici?"

"That's right." Malk knew denying it would do him no good.

"You're going to come with us. You're one of the people who got chummy with the Locusts and stayed chummy with them as long as they were here. People like that are paying for what they did, the way they're supposed to."

Malk wanted to scream. Didn't they know he and everyone he cared about would have died if he hadn't done business with the Chleuh? Didn't they know the Watchmen had hauled him off to prison once? Didn't they know he'd passed on what he'd learned from Colonel Tebron to the woodsrunners?

Looking at them, he saw that, if they did know, they didn't care. He also saw they'd hurt him or maybe kill him if he annoyed them. So all he said was, "Will you let me talk to my wife, tell her what's going on?"

One of them growled and shook his his head. But the fellow who'd done the talking, and who seemed to be their leader, answered, "Yes, go ahead. We aren't savages—not unless someone pushes us and makes us savages, I mean."

Malk called Efa. She paused on the landing when she saw the men with swords and crossbows. He waved for her to come down. Slowly, she did. He said, "They're going to take me away for what they think I did while the Chleuh were here. You know the people to talk to." He hoped she knew the people to talk to. "You know where the strongbox is. You'll be fine. Everything will work out all right." He really hoped he knew what he was talking about.

"It's all nonsense!" Efa said angrily. She rounded on the fellow who fronted the . . . *the enforcers* was what came to Malk's mind. "You know it's all nonsense, too!"

He took it from her, where he probably wouldn't have from Malk. "We're doing what we have to do, Mistress. This city wants cleansing," he answered. "Your man, he'll have a trial. If it turns out he hasn't done anything bad, he'll walk free. It's happened." By the way he spoke, it hadn't happened very often.

Efa wanted to spit in his face—Malk could see it. He shook his head, warning her not to. He thought he had a decent chance that nothing too bad would happen. He had money. He had connections.

Up in the flat, Lillat started to cry. That took Efa's attention away from everything else. She hurried up to see what the baby needed. "Didn't know you had a brat," the chief enforcer said.

"Well, I do," Malk said. He didn't think it would make a difference.

He was right. "It's stinking cold out. Grab a mantel and come along," the man told him. "We've got to do what we've got to do."

Luckily, Malk had one on a nail behind the counter. He didn't think his captors would have let him go upstairs to get one. He wrapped it around himself.

Cold it was, and darker than dark. Lutesse had been pitch black at night for years, first to foil Chleuh dragons, then those from Honter, and now Chleuh again. King Kangen's men didn't have many left, and used most of the ones they did have against the Muos, but nuisance raiders still appeared in the skies above the city every few days.

They hadn't tied his hands. One of them had hold of his shoulder, but that was all. He could have broken away and run. In the all-engulfing blackness, he might well have got free. But then what? Efa and the baby were hostages for his good behavior. He went with the men.

Even in the depths of night, he had a fair notion of where they were taking him. When he went up the stairs and into the building, he started to laugh. He knew he shouldn't have, but couldn't help himself.

"What's so funny, curse you?" one of the enforcers growled.

"I've been here before. This is where the Watchmen jailed me." Malk also couldn't help adding, "I hope I get a nicer cell than I did then. You'd have to work to give me a worse one."

"This place isn't as filthy as it was then," the leader said. "Some of *us* started scratching all the time."

They took him to the fellow in charge of dealing with new prisoners. Malk wondered whether they were using the same forms Sep Nardand's hounds had. He hadn't been able to read them then, of course. Now he could, not that it did him any good.

This cell was cleaner than the one he'd had before. It smelled some of the slops bucket, but not of mold or rot or fear. Instead of a nasty straw pallet, it boasted a cot with a blanket. Malk recognized them at once—Anadan military issue. He'd had that kind of stuff pass through his shop a time or three the past few months.

He sat down on the cot. It creaked when he did. He ignored it. He wondered if he could fall asleep. He also wondered if they'd let him. The Watchmen had hauled him out to question him in the middle of the night. These people might be on Char Tubis' side, not King Kangen's, but he didn't expect their methods to be much different.

Guards walked up and down the corridor, their shoes thumping on the stone flooring. One fellow wore wooden soles. He clacked instead of thumping.

Eventually, Malk used the bucket. He took off his shoes and slid under the rough wool blanket. He still didn't think he'd sleep. But, probably because he had nothing else to do, he drifted off almost as fast as he would have in bed with Efa.

Guisa Sachry poured himself a shot of apple brandy, then knocked it back at a gulp. It was a terrible way to treat such a noble spirit, but he didn't care. Scowling, he poured himself another one.

"It's the middle of the afternoon," Vonney said, alarm in her voice. "Do you want to get drunk so soon?"

"Would I be doing this if I didn't?" Guisa drank again—half the shot this time, not all of it at once. He would have needed a copper-plated gullet to gulp twice so quickly. After a pause, however, he finished what he'd poured. Then he filled the little glass once more. He wanted to drink enough to stop thinking.

Vonney understood that—this wasn't the first time since his release he'd drunk hard and early. She proved she didn't understand why, though, by saying, "Everything is fine, dear. You're here. You're home. They won't come after you any more."

"Nothing is fine!" Guisa shouted, loud and furious enough to make his wife flinch. He'd never been one of those men who knocked around the women they loved after taking a few on board. He'd always despised men like that. Always . . . till now.

"Yes, it is. You're here. You're with me. We're safe. We have plenty to eat. We have plenty—more than plenty—to drink." Vonney spoke calmly, reasonably, as if to calm a dangerous lunatic.

Even with a couple of slugs of fierce brandy in him and another ready to go, Guisa recognized that tone. "I'm just as much in prison now as I was when they hauled me away." He, on the other hand, sounded like someone trying to explain to an idiot child that two and two really *were* four.

"This isn't prison. This is our flat. If you don't want to stay in here with me, you can go anywhere in Lutesse you please and keep whatever company you want to—except you'd better not go looking for that Xya Fulgine trull."

No, she hadn't the faintest idea what was gnawing at his liver. Seeing that she didn't made him drink more brandy. Then he spelled it out in simple syllables: "I can go anywhere in Lutesse I please—except up on stage. I can keep whatever company I want—except a performing company. I can do anything I like—except the one thing that really matters."

"Oh," Vonney said, and then, "Oh," again, on a lower note this time. She couldn't very well mistake what he meant when he put it as plainly as that. After a moment, she went on, "It won't last forever, sweetheart. It can't last forever. Think of it as a holiday, that's all."

Guisa started on the new shot. "It's not a gods-cursed holiday," he ground out. "A holiday is something you do because you want to. This is a *sentence*. This is what that whoreson judge is making me do in exchange for keeping my head attached to the rest of me. I didn't know how high a price he'd set till I started serving it."

"You don't have to treat it that way. You can sit and write. Think of how much you'll have ready to roll out when they finally decide enough is enough. The war won't last much longer. It can't. Did you see in the news sheet yesterday that Odrio Cazh is dead?"

"I saw," Guisa answered. Like others loyal to King Kangen to the end, the leader of the Quimperi Popular Front had gone to southern Chlé as their chosen sovereign's soldiers fell back and the Party proved not so Popular after all. In a little town there, they'd set up a sort of occupied-Quimper-in-exile.

But the war went no better for them than it did for Kangen. Odrio Cazh had been riding outside the hamlet when a Honterese dragon swooped down and flamed him and his handful of companions. *He died a hero's death for the cause he held dear*, his fellow exiles said.

"Well, then!" Vonney didn't care about Odrio Cazh. She was just trying to get Guisa out of his funk.

Guisa didn't care much for Odrio, either. Alive, the younger man had scared him. Fanatics always did. Guisa had worked with the occupants because that seemed the easiest, the smartest, thing to do. Odrio Cazh, by contrast, wanted nothing more than to make Quimper over the way King Kangen had in Chlé.

He'd never have the chance now. And made-over Chlé was invaded from east and west. As Vonney said, the war couldn't last much longer. Without Kangen's mad determination to fight as long as any Chleuh still stood, it wouldn't have lasted as long as it had.

None of which had anything to do with why Guisa shook his head. "I've always written because I wanted to, or because I needed the money. I don't want to now. It would remind me I was doing it because I can't do what I really want to. Some of the people I'd write about wouldn't be happy at what I think of them, either."

"Write it for yourself, then. Write it to get it out of your system. By the gods, that has to be better for you than filling yourself full of rotgut every day."

"Apple brandy isn't rotgut," Guisa said with dignity.

Vonney just snorted. Anything the other side of coffee was rotgut to her right now. She said, "Try it, though. I mean it. That has to be better medicine than anything out of a bottle. And you can enjoy getting even with everybody who's done you wrong."

"Ha! There's not enough paper in Quimper for that. There's not enough paper in the whole *world* for that!" Like many performers, Guisa remembered every critic who'd ever been unkind. He couldn't have said why, but stinging reviews stuck in his mind much better than kind ones.

"Try," Vonney urged.

He rubbed his chin. "Well, maybe I will. Tomorrow. Today—" Today, he poured another shot of brandy.

Malk Malkovici cuddled Lillat. Being home again felt wonderful. He hadn't asked Efa how much she'd spent, or with whom, to get him out of that cell. She'd had it to spend, which was what counted. Maybe it had come from the gold in the subcellar, whether from the Anadans or the strongbox he'd found, or maybe from somewhere else; that didn't matter, either.

Lillat looked up up at him and said, "Bwee."

He laughed. "Bwee to you, too, little one." She was making more and more noises these days. They weren't words yet, but some of them sounded as if they wanted to be.

"She says 'da-da-da' all the time. She hardly ever says 'ma-ma-ma,'" Efa said. "That doesn't seem fair. I take care of her more than you do. I'm the one who feeds her, by the gods. Why doesn't she go 'ma-ma-ma' more?"

"I train her to do it, just to drive you mad." Malk sounded convincing enough to make his wife give him a horrible look before she realized he was joking and stuck out her tongue at him. He went on, "Relax. 'Da-da-da' doesn't mean me. It's a sound she likes to make, that's all."

"It *will* mean you," Efa said darkly.

"I'm taking care of her more now, too," Malk said. As part of the terms of his release, he'd had to accept a geas that let him go no farther from his shop than the kiosk on the corner or Ullo's tavern. A bored constabulary wizard had slapped it on him, and it seemed to work.

He suspected a top-drawer sorcerer could give him the freedom to wander more widely through Lutesse. He hadn't tried to find out, and didn't plan to. A wealthy man who followed the True Faith might get away with something like that. Somebody who clung to the Old Faith? If the authorities caught him, chances were they'd put a crossbow bolt through him on the spot.

So Sarmel went scouting and scavenging for scrap metal and other junk by himself. He grumbled about it, but not very hard. Malk grumbled, too, more for form's sake than anything else. Sarmel was probably glad to get out from under his eye, and from under his thumb. And Malk . . . Malk wasn't sorry he had an excuse to stay home with Efa and Lillat.

His wife said, "It's so stupid. You did everything you could to help the woodsrunners. We had that dragonflyer hidden down below there, and we passed him along to them, too. What do they want?"

"They want all the time between when the General surrendered and when Char Tubis came in never to have happened." Malk had had too much time to brood on such things. "A lot of the ones giving orders now, they were in Honter, in exile, themselves. They don't know what things were like here when Kangen's men told everybody when to jump and how high to go."

"They should find out before they start throwing people into cells," Efa said.

"Yes, they should. They won't," Malk said. A lot of the people Char Tubis' men had seized deserved everything that would happen to them. Some who didn't had been acquitted at their trials. Some . . . hadn't.

Purification, the new rulers called it. They wanted no one who'd stuck by the General or got too friendly with the Chleuh to have any place in their Quimper, the Quimper that would go forward when the war did end. If they were too harsh sometimes, they trotted out the old chestnut about omelettes and eggs.

Not quite out of the blue, Malk said, "I wonder how Tebron's doing these days."

"We're still here mostly on account of him," Efa said.

"I know. We were useful to him. I made cursed sure we were useful to him, and the other side jugged me on account of it." Malk shook his head. He'd been stuck in the middle, and tried to play each side against the other. He'd done it well enough that he was still here, still breathing, still worrying about what would happen when he stood before a judge. He continued, "Tebron was about as good as you could be if you were King Kangen's man first."

"Is that good enough?" Efa asked.

"Good enough for what? He knew what his king was doing to people like us. It bothered him. It didn't bother him enough to make him try and stop it, or to leave his service to Kangen, or to stick a knife in him. But—well, you said it. He could have made that happen to us, too, and he didn't. I owe him something there, anyhow. I wonder if I'll ever have the chance to pay it back."

Was Tebron still alive? If he was, was he leading a cavalry troop in a desperate charge against the Muos, the way he'd talked about? Malk didn't particularly want him dead . . . but wouldn't generally mind if he perished, any more than the junkman would have minded any Chleuh dying. He wasn't filled with forgiveness toward the recent occupants. The only reason they hadn't done worse to people like him was, they were losing the war.

Efa said something. Lost in his own thoughts, Malk realized he had no idea what it was. "I'm sorry, dear?" he said.

She looked at him, one of those wifely looks that declared she had no idea why she put up with his nonsense. "I *said*, would you speak for him if he gets called back here to answer for what he's done?"

"Oh," Malk said uncomfortably. Yes, that marched too closely with what had been going through his own mind. He scratched the side of his jaw, considering. At last, with a reluctant nod, he went on, "Yes, I suppose I would. He could have been plenty worse, and you can't say that about too many Chleuh."

"All right." Efa nodded, too. It was a serious question, and she'd got a serious answer. "I never had much to do with him."

"I didn't want you to," Malk said, and left it there. She was a fine-looking woman. If she'd caught Tebron's eye . . . If the man who was keeping Malk alive decided he wanted to bed Malk's wife, what could the junkman have done about it without putting Efa's, Sarmel's, and incidentally his own neck on the block? *Cut my throat*, was the first thing that occurred to him.

"Of course," she said, so she was probably thinking along with him again. She could do that even better than his brother could. Well, he was with her more than he was with Sarmel, and in more intimate settings.

Not wanting to think about Tebron and Efa, he said, "I saw in the *Spark* that an Anadan army is getting close to Tsawdek."

"The town where the Quimperi traitors are pretending they still count for something?"

"That's right," Malk said.

Efa smiled at him, almost the same way she sometimes smiled at Lillat. It was a pleased smile, a maternal smile, an amused smile. "Look at you! Anyone would think you'd been reading your whole life, not just a few months."

"It's a good thing to know, and it's not that hard. I should have learned a long time ago." Malk held up a hand. "I should have, but I didn't. I got along well enough. Now I finally have. Thanks for showing me how."

"I was glad to do it," Efa said. One of the many reasons he loved her was that she didn't go *I told you so!* . . . too often. Then she asked, "What do you suppose they'll do if they catch them?"

"The news sheet said Char Tubis has asked the Anadans to turn them over to his men, to bring them back to Lutesse for trial and for whatever happens after trial. He says they're Quimperi, and ought to have Quimperi justice." Malk tapped the back of his neck, to show what kind of Quimperi justice he thought they'd get. He hoped he wouldn't get that kind of justice himself when the authorities finally put him in front of a judge.

"I'm surprised Anada and Honter don't laugh at him for pretending his army's as big and strong as theirs."

"It's bigger than it used to be," Malk said. Char Tubis' recruiting posters were plastered all over Lutesse—likely all over Quimper. Many woodsrunners had joined the hard core of fighters who'd come with him across the Narrow Sea. Many Quimperi who'd lived quietly under the Chleuh wanted to pick up a sword or a pike or a crossbow and pay the occupants back.

They carried Anadan, or sometimes Honterese, swords and pikes and crossbows. They wore Anadan uniforms with Quimperi emblems. They flew Anadan dragons. Char Tubis talked a lot about Quimperi freedom and glory. If the Honterese and Anadans laughed, they laughed quietly, between themselves, not where any Quimperi could hear them.

"Guisa Sachry!" a voice behind Guisa exclaimed.

He turned. He had been about to cross a street, but being recognized made him pause. "Oh, hullo, Pornic," he said. Pornic Theron was an actor of an age not far from Guisa's own. He'd kept working down the years, but he was nobody special. *Not like me*, Guisa thought.

"Good to see you, by the gods! It's been much too long," Theron said. "I was starting to wonder whether, well, whether something'd happened to you."

He meant *Whether they'd chopped off your head and I somehow didn't hear about it.* He was at least polite enough not to say it that way. "I myself am still here," Guisa said, acknowledging the thought behind the words. "Still here, but between roles right this minute." He'd be cursed if he intended to admit he'd been muzzled. Pornic plainly didn't know that, though it had been in the news sheets.

"You?" The other man looked at him in surprise. "You never had trouble finding gigs, no matter how things were, ah, going." He'd performed enough to keep eating while the occupants ruled Lutesse, but not much more than that. Guisa had no idea what his politics were. While the occupants held sway, you didn't ask such questions.

"Things are harder now," Guisa said. "I myself wish they weren't, but you get what you get, not what you wish for."

"Ah." Pornic eyed him again, in a different way this time. He might not be such a great actor, but he was smart enough to read the words between the lines. "Well, good luck to you. Take care." He scooted away as if Guisa were on fire.

Guisa swore under his breath and kicked a pebble down the sidewalk. Even if people didn't know he'd been silenced, they didn't have any trouble figuring it out. He wondered how long the new authorities in Quimper would need to decide he was harmless. Longer than he needed to go mad? He hoped not.

"What was I supposed to do?" he muttered, throwing his arms out wide and making someone coming by skip smartly to one side to keep from getting smacked. The Chleuh had *won*. People had to get along with them, didn't they? Almost five years ago, it had seemed obvious. Which only went to show . . . what, exactly?

For every question, there's an answer that is simple, obvious—and wrong. Guisa couldn't remember where he'd heard that, but he had. He'd gone along with the occupants. Oh, not the way people like poor Brasi Robillach and Erol Paki had, let alone people like Odrio Cazh and Sep Nardand, but he had. He'd kept working. He'd done well for himself. And he'd taken much too long to realize his choice was liable to have consequences.

He'd laughed at Nea Ennogue and the handful of others like him. He'd thought they were fools for not recognizing which way the wind blew. Nea hadn't even held a grudge. Or, if he had, those strategic food parcels had softened it. *If he hadn't spoken for me, gods only know what that scrawny old judge would have done*, Guisa thought.

What he had done was bad enough. Guisa knew he would have had trouble finding work even if he were allowed to go on. Directors and producers knew who was in good odor with Char Tubis and his henchmen and who wasn't. No one had said a single word about keeping Vonney off the stage, but she also hadn't landed a single part since his own ban came down. People wouldn't take the chance of hiring her.

Guisa kicked at the sidewalk again. "Well, good," he said, not quite so quietly as he meant to. There was a name for men who lived off what their women earned. It wasn't a nice name, or one Guisa wanted attached to him.

A woman walked by. She wasn't far from his own age, with a lined, sad face and gray hair. She took no more notice of him than she had to, just enough to keep from running into him and to make sure he didn't run into her, either. That was all he was to her: a possible obstruction. A younger man whose clothes and pathetically eager expression said he might be a commercial traveler gave Guisa equally short shrift.

I am Guisa Sachry! You're suppose to pay attention to me! I make you laugh! I make you cry! I make you sit on the edge of your seats! You can't take your eyes off me! He wanted to scream it.

But he wasn't in a theatre now. Without his being up there, he was nothing, no one. And nobody cared about him at all. He couldn't stand not being cared about. He wondered what would happen if he walked past a mirror. Would he show any reflection at all?

Vampires didn't show a reflection in the mirror. There weren't any vampires closer to Lutesse than in half-barbarous, faraway places like Nistria—there weren't supposed to be, anyhow—but everybody knew that. Was it because nobody paid attention to them? Guisa wouldn't have been surprised.

He walked past a shop window that wasn't boarded up. Little by little, Lutesse was shedding its protective shell. And there in the glass was his image, dim, dusty, and a little distorted, but unmistakably there. He sighed on seeing it. Even his stabs at melodrama fell flat.

Two Anadan soldiers came—no, reeled—around a corner. They'd been drinking for a while, plainly. One of them said something to Guisa in his own language. Guisa shook his head and spread his hands. He didn't, and didn't want to, speak Honterese.

The man made a stab at Quimperi: "House of tolerance?"

"Oh." Guisa understood that, all right. With simple words and lots of gestures, he gave directions. When the soldier tried to tip him, he shook his head again. He hadn't dreamt he could be more disgusted with himself than he was already, but he'd been wrong.

XVII

"Here you go." The old woman at the corner kiosk thrust a copy of the *Lutesse Spark* at Malk Malkovici before he could even ask for it. More extraordinary still, she waved away his copper. "On me. You've earned it. He's dead. The big pussy, the pussy of all pussies, the king pussy, he's dead. It's a day, all right!"

Malk looked at the headline. Now he was glad he could read it, because it said **KANGEN CUTS HIS THROAT!** "Oh, by the gods!" he exclaimed.

"Yours or mine?" Quilly knew he belonged to the Old Faith, sure enough.

"Any of them. All of them. I don't know. I don't care, not right now," he said. "It's over, isn't it? Chlé can't go on without Kangen. It's a wonder the Locusts went on as long as they did with him."

"They should get everything they've given all their neighbors, and some more besides," Quilly said.

"If even half what your news sheets say is true, the Muos are giving them every bit of that and then some. If they weren't laying siege to the citadel at Hashtéankh, Kangen wouldn't have killed himself." Malk remembered how glad the Chleuh stationed in Lutesse had been not to have to go fight the swarms of schismatics coming at them from out of the east, and how glum—even despairing—they got when they had to go fight instead of occupying.

A poster slapped on a wall said TOO MANY RICH MEANS TOO MANY POOR. Someone who sympathized with the schismatics must have stuck that up in dead of night. Char Tubis didn't want that branch of the True Faith spreading through Quimper. Whether he wanted it or not, he was liable to have it.

Before Malk got back to the junk shop and the flat over it, Bezen the constable waved to him. Bezen had walked this beat while King Dalad still ruled Quimper. He'd walked it while the Chleuh strutted through Lutesse. And he was still walking it now that they were gone.

After waving, he pointed an accusing forefinger at Malk. "What kind of magic has Batz Kergrist cooked up for you?" he demanded roughly.

"I don't know what you're talking about." Malk lied to Bezen whenever it was to his advantage, as one did with constables, but he told the truth here. He went on, "I haven't seen him in weeks." That was also true; Kergrist's studio lay farther from his home than the geas let him go.

But Bezen said, "Likely tell! They hauled you in a while ago now. Then they turned you loose. They don't do that with people they think were too friendly to the Chleuh. They just don't."

"They must not have thought I was too friendly, then, because they haven't called me in or come for me," Malk said.

"And then you wake up!" Bezen retorted. "Don't play games with me, Malkovici. How many times did the Locusts bring their wagons by your joint? How much scrap did they haul away? How much did they pay you for it?" He made money-counting motions, the way followers of the True Faith did when they wanted to scorn people who clung to the Old Faith. Maybe he was joking, maybe not. You never could tell with Bezen.

Malk just shrugged. "I don't know what you want me to say to you. If they decided to charge me with something, they will. I can't run away—my geas won't let me. So far, gods be praised, they haven't."

Bezen made a discontented noise, down deep in his throat. "You aren't scared of them. Bugger me blind if I don't think they're scared of you. My own captain, he told me to be careful around you. You see how well I listen to him, right?"

"But of course!" Malk looked down at the *Lutesse Spark* so the constable would have a harder time reading him. Naturally, he'd spread money around after they let him out of his cell, as Efa had before they did. One of the places they'd spread it was among the constabulary higher-ups. That bit of bribery seemed to have done what he wanted it to do. Holding up the news sheet, he changed the subject: "Kangen's out of the picture. Who's going to miss him?"

"A swarm of Chleuh. The only thing they'll be sorry for is, he lost." Cynical as ever, Bezen was also bound to be right. He continued, "And some of the rich whoresons here. To people like that, Kangen was a shield against the schismatics." He spat in the gutter to show what he thought of that.

"There's a Muo poster back beyond the kiosk." Malk pointed in the direction he'd come from.

"I haven't seen it yet. I probably won't see it any time soon, even if I walk right by it. I am *not* everywhere," Bezen said pointedly, mocking the name of the pro-Chleuh news sheet that had thrived under the occupants and died when they fled.

"I've got no idea what you mean," Malk said. They both laughed. Bezen made as if to elbow Malk in the ribs, but didn't follow through. He might have listened to his captain after all.

When Malk brought in the news sheet, Efa asked, "What kept you?"

"I was talking with our great protector," Malk said in Nistrian, rolling his eyes. In the land they'd come from, constables were even more venal and even more brutal than they were here. Not wanting to remember Nistria, he switched back to Quimperi to tell her, "Kangen's gone." He showed off the *Spark*.

"Give me that!" She grabbed it from him and read the story. Then she shook her head. "Too quick. The only thing I can hope is, the gods give him everything he deserves for the rest of time."

"And an hour longer," Malk said. Efa laughed. So did he, but sourly. The older he got, the more horrible the world got, the more trouble he had believing in the gods of the Old Faith, or in any gods at all. This had to be humanity's fault. If there were gods, wouldn't they have done a better job with it?

Guisa Sachry scowled at the manuscript in front of him. It wasn't going the way he wanted. Nothing seemed to go the way he wanted these days. Nothing had gone the way he wanted since that stinking judge silenced him.

Vonney came in clutching a news sheet and a stringbag with some carrots and parsnips in it. "They won't take the General's head," she announced without preamble.

"No?" Guisa said, interested in spite of himself. The Anadans had captured the old man along with the other Quimperi who'd followed King Kangen to—and beyond—the bitter end. As Char Tubis asked of them, they'd turned them over to his revived Quimper. Guisa went on, "Didn't that court condemn him to die?"

"It did," Vonney said, nodding. "But Char Tubis commuted it." She tapped the news sheet. "He did it 'in recognition of the General's heroic services to the kingdom in the days before this latest war,' he says. The old boy will live on an island off the coast for however much time he's got left."

"I wonder if that's doing him a favor," Guisa said. From things he'd heard, the General hadn't had all his oars in the water for a few years now. Guisa dreaded that more than anything else about getting old. If you were shambling around inside your carcass without even being able to remember your name, were you truly alive? Wouldn't the headsman's axe be more merciful?

Only half his age, Vonney didn't worry about such things. "The Purification Court says Erol Paki's going to get the chop," she said.

"Can't say I'm surprised. You go around shouting 'Dreslon must be destroyed!' night after night for years, no one will feel sorry for you after your side loses," Guisa said.

"Till we met him, I never imagined he was a little short fellow," Vonney said. "He had such a big, booming voice coming out of the crystal."

"He was nobody much till the Chleuh marched in—just a scribbler from the provinces," Guisa said in musing tones. "But he had the kind of voice they wanted and the kind of ideas they wanted, and he grew like a weed while the occupants were here. Not physically, but you know what I mean."

His wife smiled. "Oh, yes." Then the smile blew out. "From now on, it won't be smart to admit we ever knew him, will it?"

"Not smart at all. How many people out there right now don't want to admit they ever knew us?" Guisa didn't bother trying to hide his bitterness. If the world wouldn't acknowledge how wonderful he was, that had to be the world's problem, not his.

And Vonney's mouth puckered, as if she'd bitten down on a citron. "Before I got the vegetables, I stuck my head in at the Luxe. You know how often we filled that place—and killed the crowds, too. They wouldn't even talk to me. They just said, 'Nothing for you here,' and almost threw me out. If I hadn't walked away on my own, they would have."

Guisa stood up and set a hand on her shoulder. "I'm sorry, my dear. I know how you can get as many parts as you want, though."

"That's more than I know. How?"

"Divorce me, of course. Then you won't be tied to somebody whose politics smell like fish that's gone off. Politics!" He made it into a swear word. “I didn’t even know I had any politics till the Chleuh got here. After that, everybody had ’em, like it or not. You’d be a hero to all the booking managers for dropping me.”

After he spoke, he wondered if he should have. He hadn’t thought Vonney would look so thoughtful. After a few heartbeats that stretched longer than they had any business doing, though, she shook her head. “If I didn’t walk out on you because of that dancing slut, I don’t suppose I will now. It’s not as if we’ll starve to death soon.”

“No, that’s true.” Guisa had spent a good deal while the occupants held Lutesse, but he’d also made a good deal. He’d hung on to what he could. And money did still come in. Nobody here in the capital wanted to put on even his older work. Out in the provinces, though, people didn’t know how bad his reputation in Lutesse was. They still enjoyed his shows, and still mounted them. The money he made from that trickled back to him. It wasn’t enormous, but it was something.

“Sooner or later, things will loosen up,” Vonney added.

“They have to.” After a moment, Guisa amended that: “They’d better, anyhow. Oh—and thank you. I myself am sensible to know when I’ve found a good one.”

Had Vonney felt predatory, she might have asked him if he’d said the same thing to his first two wives (as a matter of fact, he had, though he would have denied it convincingly). All she did say, though, was, “We’ll get by.” In her own way, she was a trouper.

“Of course we will. We’re better off than the people who’re back from Tsawdek. Poor Erol!” Guisa sighed. Even more than Brasi Robillach, who’d had a nasty streak, Erol Paki was a decent enough fellow aside from his infatuation with King Kangen. He’d got ahead because he had that; he’d made something of himself he never could have in peacetime. But his choices didn’t pan out in the end, and he’d pay for it.

Incautiously, Vonney asked, “Did you get any work done while I was shopping?”

"A little," Guisa said. It wasn't quite a lie, but it stretched a point.

"You've been fighting it a bit, haven't you?"

"More than a bit. I want to tear it all to pieces and pretend it never happened. I want to hire a wizard to conjure up a demon to do the writing for me. It can pastiche me, the way I pastiched Gorec Sembel for Stulp and Vurk. I don't know what it is. Usually, I just sit down and the words come out."

"I've seen you. I don't know how you do it. Most people who write have to fiddle with it much more than you do."

That gratified Guisa, but not enough to throw him off his own train of thought. "It's not working this time," he said. "I may as well have mud between my ears, not brains. I don't want to be doing this, is the trouble. I want to be out there. I want to hear people cheering."

"I know you do," Vonney said patiently, as if to a small boy with a skinned knee. Guisa realized she knew him uncomfortably, even alarmingly, well. He hadn't meant that to happen, but it had. She went on, "You didn't want to write for the Chleuh, either. I remember."

"Of course I didn't!" Guisa said. "Who would have—who would have except for somebody like Erol, somebody who really believed? Anyone with a dram of sense could see something like this would happen. Something like this or even worse."

"But you did it anyway. You did it well, too."

He shrugged. "What choice did I have? The Chleuh would have . . . I don't want to think what the Chleuh would have done to me. Something horrible, I know that much. Say what you want, but they weren't—aren't—cultured people."

"Maybe you aren't seeing something," Vonney said. From anyone else, that would have made him bristle. Somehow, he took it from her. He just raised a questioning eyebrow, as if to ask what he was missing. And she told him: "What choice have you got now? You can't go on stage—they won't let you. The only way you can pay them back is putting it down on paper. Think of it that way, and the syllables may come easier."

He started to wave her words away, but didn't go through with it. "That's . . . not the worst notion I've ever heard," he said after a pause he noticed but hoped she didn't. "If I concentrate on that judge's sour, scrawny face while I'm writing . . ."

"The fellow who brought Char Tubis' charges looked like a thick slice of lamb stuffed with liver forcemeat," Vonney said helpfully.

"He did!" Guisa laughed. "He really did! How did he stay so fat under the Locusts unless he sucked up to them while they were here?" Altogether unselfconscious, Guisa forgot about his own ample contours, which hadn't got any less so while the occupants held Lutesse.

He forgot about everything, in fact, except the play on the writing desk. With his tormentors' faces burning in his head, he began to see how it might come to life after all. When it did—how they'd howl when it did, and when he could put it on!

He kissed Vonney. For now, he remembered doing it like that was her suggestion. How long he'd keep remembering . . . *I'll worry about that later,* he thought, and sat down to see if the words would flow.

Malk Malkovici helped Sarmel lug scrap into the shop. "I'm sorry you've got to go out by yourself. I really am," he said. "If you want to hire somebody to help you lug things, I don't mind. Gods know we can afford it."

"I'm all right," his brother answered. Sarmel liked spending money he didn't have to no better than Malk did. He wiped his sweaty forehead with the sleeve of his tunic. As he tugged his cap back down again, he added, "Stinking hot."

"It is," Malk said. "Just about a year now since Char Tubis came back to Lutesse. I don't know whether it seems like yesterday or a hundred years ago, but it doesn't feel like a year."

"Sure doesn't." Sarmel held up a gloved forefinger. "Oh! that reminds me! Did you hear Sep Nardand is shorter by a head?"

"I hadn't, no. That wasn't in the morning news sheets. Can't say I'm sorry." Malk laughed to show how sorry he wasn't. "I'm only lucky the Watchmen didn't get their teeth into me harder than they did."

"Too many people weren't that lucky. But he's dead now. The short-pants kids were flogging their sheets with the news while I was coming back here." Sarmel had a copy of one of them on the wagon's driving bench. He held it up. "Says Nardand had the nerve to write to Char Tubis—'as one soldier to another,' no less—trying to keep himself away from the block. Says Char Tubis wrote back, too, and told him no."

"What else would he tell him?"

"Nothing. But I would've told him a lot more than just no."

"When the next thing after no is the axe falling, you don't need much talk."

"Mm, something to that, sure enough." Sarmel opened the news sheet to an inside page. "Says he went to his death with courage. Smoked a stogie and laid his head on the wood himself. They didn't have to force him or anything."

"Most of those people have died well. Being cowards wasn't their trouble. As long as they die, I don't care how," Malk said.

"That's fine by me, too." Sarmel pointed to another story on that same inside page. "And the Muos have caught the Chleuh bastard who was in charge of killing people from the Old Faith at the Locusts' biggest camp in the east. Says he has the blood of hundreds of thousands on his hands."

"Hundreds of thousands!" Malk mournfully shook his head. It wasn't that he didn't believe his brother. No, the trouble was that he did. "Isn't our modern age wonderful? In the old days, nobody could kill so many people all by himself. There's progress, if you like."

"I don't like it one cursed bit. And this Colonel Dolvech didn't kill them all by himself. He had good help—you know how the Chleuh are when they set out to do something. But he ran the camp. Ran it pretty well, too, I suppose, if you like such things."

"Not so you'd notice." Malk shuddered. "What was he doing when they caught up with him? Not still running the camp, I'm sure. That's out of business now, gods be praised."

"He was"—Sarmel checked the news sheet—"a greengrocer in a town not far from the one he grew up in. He had the place in his own name, too. He must've been sure the people there wouldn't turn him in, and he was right. The Muos tracked him down on their own."

Muosi held about a third of Chlé: the eastern part that its armies had overrun. The rest of the kingdom was divided among the Anadans (who had the biggest chunk), the Hontermen, and, at Char Tubis' loud insistence, the Quimperi. He had a large score to settle against the Chleuh. King Kangen's former realm wouldn't be a going concern again for years to come.

Malk said, "If somebody grabbed him, can't say I'm sorry it was King Ninel's men. They'll try him, they'll give him the axe, and they'll stick his head on a pike somewhere till it gets too black and smelly and disgusting to make a good lesson for the rest of the Chleuh any more."

"That's about the size of it," Sarmel said, nodding. "The only thing I'd like better would be for the Muos to stake him down somewhere and let all the people who believe the way we do file by and kill him a quarter of an inch at a time. Even that would be less than he deserve—he can only die once, curse him."

"Hundreds of thousands," Malk repeated in a low voice. Like the True Faith, the Old Faith preached against taking vengeance into your own hands. Most of the time, in most circumstances, Malk thought that was only sensible. Now . . . "I'd stand in a line like that, and hope something was still left for me when I finally got to the front of it. For me and Efa, I should say. She'd be right there, too."

"What about me? You think I don't want a crack at somebody like that?" His brother sounded indignant, even irate.

"You might," Malk said. Sarmel stuck out his tongue at him. The older Malkovici went on, "Bound to be just as well the Muos will handle it themselves. There'd be riots from all the disappointed people who didn't get to carve a chunk off--what was his name again?"

"Dolvech."

"Dolvech, that's right. Off Colonel Dolvech. Some people would probably buy their way to the front of the line to make sure they got a lick in, too." Malk knew he would have done that in a heartbeat. "The guards could make a pile of goldpieces selling places, I bet."

"Muos aren't supposed to do such things." Sarmel wagged a finger. "Profit is wicked—they say so, anyway. And they've got priests and deacons and acolytes and I don't know what all preaching it to the Chleuh, too."

"Good luck with that!" Malk said. He and his brother both laughed. It was funny, and then again it wasn't. If he hadn't made a good profit off the Chleuh and known when and where and how to spread it around, odds were someone like Colonel Dolvech would have killed him, too.

Guisa Sachry carefully moved the last page of his manuscript out of the way. Only after he'd taken care of that did he throw down his pen. "There!" he said. "The cursed thing is done!"

His wife clapped her hands. "Huzzah!" she said. "It's some of the very best stuff you've ever written, too!"

"It's your fault, you know," he said.

"Mine?" Vonney shook her head. "I'd never make a playwright, not in a million years. I can deliver lines, I can play with them to make them go over better, but I can't put them together like that."

"Who told me to write it as if I were sticking my finger in that gods-despised judge's eye? Somebody who looks a lot like you, unless I remember wrong."

"All right, I said that. But you did all the hard work afterwards," she said.

"When somebody gives you credit, take it," Guisa said. *When I give you credit, you'd better take it, because I don't do that very often.* Even he heard the words behind the words he did say. If he could hear them, he was sure Vonney could, too.

She gave no overt sign of it. "I just hope you get to put it on one of these days," she said. "It will be a hit. A smash!"

"How many years will I have to wait? Will I still be alive when they decide the things I've done aren't poisonous any more?" Guisa had lost more sleep than he cared to remember worrying about things like that. So far as he knew, he hadn't admitted them to anyone else till now. But finishing this play brought his worries into focus, as a crystal ball did with emanations.

Vonney took his fretting in stride. "You know what you ought to do? You ought to see if you can put this out on the left."

That startled a laugh out of him. He hadn't heard *on the left* in weeks, probably for months. The black market wasn't dead—far from it—but its Chleuh name was dying.

He put on a heavy's voice: "Melodrama on the left! Get it here, 'cause you won't find it nowhere else!"

Vonney laughed, too, but she also nodded. "That's right. That's just right. It *is* good work. Maybe being forbidden will make people want to see it even more. Everyone's wondering why you aren't working these days."

"Well, some people are," Guisa allowed, remembering Pornic Theron. "The ones who don't pay attention to the news sheets or don't remember them for more than a day after they read them."

"Most people, then," Vonney said, and Guisa couldn't very well tell her she was wrong. She went on, "Talk to some theatre managers. What have you got to lose? The worst they can tell you is no, and how are you worse off if they do?"

"You have the right attitude. Anyone would know you're a performer," Guisa said. People who wanted to go on stage and people who wanted to write for the stage heard *no* all the time. If you didn't harden yourself against it with a sardonic shell, it would crush your spirit and your career.

"Go on, then," Vonney told him.

Go Guisa did, the next morning. He stayed away from the bigger, more prominent, more prosperous places, the kind he'd played in before the war started . . . and after the Chleuh seized Lutesse. The capital had been a theatre hotbed for two or three hundred years, far longer than anywhere else except perhaps Dreslon. There were plenty of the other kind.

At the first place he walked into, the secretary giggled when he told her who he was. Giggling still, she ducked into the manager's office. By the look in the man's eye as he came out, he was ready to give a fraud the bum's rush. But his jaw dropped when he saw Guisa.

"I will be cursed!" he said. "It really *is* Master Sachry! Ruz, beg the gentleman's pardon for doubting him."

"I'm so sorry, Master Sachry. Please forgive me," Ruz said, all embarrassed confusion.

"It's all right," Guisa said. It wasn't really, but he was in no position to push. He nodded to the manager. "Can we talk in privacy, Master Locmar?"

"By all means, sir. By all means." Larz Locmar stood aside to let Guisa into his office and closed the door behind the two of them. He waved Guisa into a chair whose creak reminded him of the one his prison cot had made. Locmar sat down behind his battered desk. "What's on your mind?"

"I've written a new play. It takes a hard look at how cruel and unforgiving this modern world can be. Without false modesty, I myself think it some of my finest work." Guisa contrived to preen without moving. "I would be interested in exploring ways and means of putting it into production and performing in it. Money is not my first concern, and I wouldn't fuss if it appeared under a pen name."

"Isn't that . . . intriguing?" Larz Locmar was about forty. The way his jacket hung on him said he hadn't had an easy time under the occupants. So did the harsh lines gullying his cheeks. After a moment, he went on, "You tempt me, Master Sachry. You tempt me more than I dreamt you could. To put on a new work of yours—who wouldn't jump at that? But the thing's impossible, as I'm sure you must understand."

"If I thought it impossible, sir, I should not have brought it to your attention," Guisa said stiffly.

"Yes, of course. Let's go through it point by point, though. The way things are now, it could not come out in your name and you could not act in it no matter how wonderful the role might be. I don't know just what they'd do to me if I were a party to that. I don't care to find out, either."

"All right," Guisa said again. Again, it wasn't, but he couldn't do anything about it. "Anonymity, then."

"If possible. I doubt it's possible. One knows the hedgehog by its spines and the writer by his pen," Locmar said. "I would have to be taken for a silly fool for not recognizing your authorship, and no one could be in a position to give me the lie. I trust Ruz out there, but I don't know that I care to trust her so far."

"How much would you have to pay her to make sure she keeps her mouth shut?" Guisa was experienced, and cynical enough, for all ordinary use.

Larz Locmar's smile said he was, too. Well, not many who'd gone through four hard years in Lutesse weren't. But the manager answered, "Even that might not do it—she's a Quimperi patriot, you see. During the war, she did this and that. I don't know the details. They were none of my business at the time, and I haven't cared to ask since."

"I . . . see." Guisa fought not to grimace. So the secretary had worked with the woodsrunners, had she? By the way Locmar spoke, he might have, too. No, they couldn't be counted on to keep that kind of secret. Guisa heaved himself to his feet. The chair creaked again when he did. He made as if to bow. "I do thank you very much for listening to me, sir. Perhaps one day, if those in power chance to recall how little separates them from those who acted differently on the spur of the moment, we can speak of this some more."

"If that happy time should come, Master Sachry, nothing would please me more. I know, admire, and respect your talents, sir, regardless of how you may have acted on the spur of the moment." Larz Locmar didn't try to talk Guisa into staying longer now, as the actor had hoped he might. Managing another almost-bow, Guisa stumped out of the cramped office and out of the theatre.

He wasn't a man who gave up easily. No one who was could hope to make a go of it as a performer or a writer. But he had no better luck at the next couple of small theatres he tried. One of the managers was as polite as Locmar, and as unaccommodating. The other fellow sent him a fishy stare over the tops of his reading spectacles and said, "If you're silenced, you're silenced. See you." He jerked a thumb at the door.

Out Guisa went. He took the tram home and got drunk.

"Book!" Lillat plopped a picture book in Malk Malkovici's lap. "Read book!" She was only a year and a half old—a year and a half new—but she had a firm idea of what she wanted.

"That is a book," Malk agreed.

"Read book! Read!" his daughter said.

"Now I *don't* think I should have let you teach me my syllables," Malk said to Efa. "See all the trouble you cause me?"

"Oh, hush," Efa said, and then, "Read to her."

"How am I supposed to do both of those at once?" Malk asked—logically, he thought. Before his wife could answer, he scooped up Lillat and opened the book. "This is a dog. Dogs are your friends. The dog says—?" He waited.

"Woof!" Lillat knew what dogs said.

"Woof. That's right. That's good!" He turned the page. "This is a—"

"At!" Lillat said. She knew a cat when she saw one, even if she couldn't pronounce the word correctly yet.

"Right again! It's a cat, sure enough. Cats kill rats and mice, and good for them, too. And what do cats say?"

"Meow!" His daughter was as shrill and squeaky as a kitten.

The next page showed a parrot in a brass cage. A lot of those cages had gone through the shop in the past few years. "What have we got here?" Malk asked.

"Birdie!" Lillat knew what was what.

"Very good! If that isn't a birdie, I don't know what it would be. And everybody in the whole wide world knows that a birdie says, 'Moo!'"

Lillat's face clouded and threatened to storm. "Urp!" she said, that being as close as she could come to *chirp*.

"Malk . . ." Efa said, with the air of someone working hard to hold on to her patience. "Dear, you know she doesn't like it when you do that."

"Yes, yes. Well, *I* don't like it when I do it right all the time. I've already read this book eleven hundred times. Saying the exact same thing over and over and over gets boring. It's already got boring, as a matter of fact."

Efa exhaled through her nose. "Remind me again—which of you is the grown-up, and which one is the little tiny child?"

"Big!" Lillat held her arms out wide.

"There! You see? She told *you*." Malk laughed.

His wife laughed, too. So did Lillat. She didn't know what she'd said that was funny, or why it was, but she'd go along with it. She was the kind of audience actors prayed for. After a moment, Efa said, "You *can* do it right. I've read that one more than you have, and I manage."

"You've got more sense than I do. I've got more . . . more I don't know what than you do." Malk paused to think. "More crazy, maybe."

"I wouldn't be surprised," Efa said.

Lillat tugged at Malk's tunic sleeve. "*Read!*"

"Oh, is that what we're doing here? I thought we were knitting."

Malk turned the page again. The next picture was of a fat pink pig. It looked so stupid and smug, Malk felt sure it deserved to turn into sausages and bacon and pigskin gloves. "What have we got here?"

"Hig!" Again, Lillat scored a near miss.

"There you go! And I remember now—the pig's the one who goes, 'Moo!'"

His daughter shook her head. "No! Hig say 'oink!'" People who had older children said they said *no* all the time when they got closer to two. Lillat hadn't started doing that yet, but Malk could see it on the horizon like a far-off cloud warning of rain on the way.

"Maybe you'd better read the rest of the book the way it's supposed to go." Evidently, Efa saw trouble coming, too.

"It's a lot less interesting that way," Malk said sadly.

"It is to you. Not to the person you're reading it to." By her expression, Efa was sorry she had to point out the obvious, but she was doing it anyhow. She would have made a fine diplomat if she'd grown up on a nobleman's estate, not in an orphanage. Idly, Malk wondered what he might have become if he'd grown up as the pampered son of some count or duke.

He would have got rich sooner had he grown up like that. He would have started out rich, in fact, instead of starting with nothing. But he might not have wound up as rich as he had. Money wouldn't have been so interesting or so important to him if he'd always had it and always taken it for granted.

Of course, if he'd grown up a nobleman's son in any realm King Kangen's armies overran, chances were he'd be dead right now. Out in the east, there were some nobles who clung to the Old Faith. Not many, but some. Or there had been. From the stories coming out of that ravaged part of the world, few still lived. As one of their sons, Malk wouldn't have had the chance to learn the gutter skills that kept him and his family breathing.

"Read!" Lillat said, which made him realize he must have been woolgathering for a while now.

"All right." He turned the page. "This is a chicken. A chicken says—"

"Neighhh!" Lillat broke in, and laughed and laughed. She knew she was doing it wrong.

Malk laughed, too. So did Efa, till tears ran down her face. "Sure enough, she's your child," she said, and laughed some more. Malk hadn't doubted that, but he was extra sure it was true now.

XVIII

The doorwoman had keys to everyone's postboxes. She picked up the day's mail and handed it out as she saw people. She gave Guisa his when he and Vonney came in. "Thanks, Marsa," he said, and tipped her a little. He hadn't performed or published for almost two years, so he wasn't particularly prosperous himself, but those coins helped keep her sweet.

"What have we got?" Vonney asked as they started up the stairs.

He shuffled envelopes. "Grocer's bill, advertising flyer, bootmaker's bill . . . Hello! Here's a letter from that fellow in Ylon!"

"What fellow in Ylon?"

"Oh." Guisa realized he hadn't told his wife everything he'd been up to. "Cresc Mamzer is a producer and theatre manager down there. He has . . . the kind of politics that mean he doesn't care whether someone's been silenced, as long as that someone is the kind of someone who has something to say. I myself, he believes, may fall into this category."

"You'd go out to the provinces to work?" Vonney said it the way she might have said, *You'd eat with your fingers, like a savage?*

"It won't be so bad. Ylon's Quimper's second city. I toured down there, back in the days before I knew you. They'll be all the happier to see me because I haven't left Lutesse for quite a while. And"—Guisa paused to open the door that connected the stairs to the hallway on their floor—"I'm so eager to be seen again, I'd go on stage out in the middle of the Narrow Sea."

"That might be safer than this," Vonney said. "You haven't been unsilenced, have you?"

"Well, no," he admitted, "but it's been so long now! And things are loosening up. People who wouldn't have dared show their faces in public right after the war ended are writing pieces in the news sheets and signing their names to them. Cresc Mamzer says everyone down in Ylon will be panting to see me. He wouldn't tell me anything like that if he didn't mean it."

"You hope he wouldn't."

"Do you think I—we—shouldn't go? I hate to tell him no, especially when I'm the one who got hold of him to begin with."

Vonney scratched the side of her jaw as she considered. "No, you're probably right, dear. People aren't getting as upset as they did right after the Chleuh pulled out. I suppose you can have your fill of anything, even revenge."

By then, they were standing in front of their door. Instead of opening it, Guisa kissed Vonney. "I love you!" he said, by which he meant, *You're telling me to go ahead and do what I want to do anyway.* "I'll write back to Mamzer. The world has done without my talents for too long!"

One of Vonney's eyebrows quirked, but not very much and not for very long. She was used to the way Guisa thought and talked. "Of course, dear," she murmured, and Guisa didn't worry about what she wasn't saying.

His letter to the southern producer went into the corner postbox half an hour later.

Two weeks after that, he and Vonney boarded a train for Ylon. "This should take a while," Guisa said resignedly. People complained about Quimper's railroads all the time. The Chleuh had pilfered a lot of the kingdom's rolling stock and made off with almost all of the younger, healthier dragons that powered the engines. The one that boiled water for this train was so ancient, it looked as if it would have trouble breathing enough fire to light a cigar.

The second-class car, by contrast, was new and clean. The seats were bearable if not comfortable: pretty good for second class. And the labels screwed into the backs of those seats were in Honterese. "It's from Anada," Vonney said.

"Shame the Anadans couldn't have sent some dragons over, too," Guisa said.

"They are doing that. There was a story about it in the *Spark* the other day. We just don't happen to have one," Vonney said.

"Oh." Guisa subsided, feeling vaguely punctured.

Slowly, the train pulled out of the station. Trains always moved slowly till they built up momentum. This one never got going very fast. "Well, you were right, dear," Vonney said. "I hope that poor dragon doesn't die of old age before we get to Ylon.

"Who would notice if it did?" Guisa said. Vonney laughed, for all the world as if he'd been joking.

Ylon lay two hundred fifty or three hundred miles southeast of Lutesse. Once, Guisa had known which, but he'd long since forgotten. It hardly seemed to matter. The landscape slowly slid past the windows. Farmers were busy in the fields; it was getting close to harvest season. Every once in a while, the train clattered through a small town (as far as Guisa was concerned, every Quimperi town save Lutesse was small). Sometimes it would stop to let passengers on and off; sometimes it would just keep going.

Either way, Guisa started to get bored—till the train rolled through three towns in a row that looked as if the gods had stomped on them and kicked them. But the gods hadn't had anything to do with it. The Chleuh had tried their best to hold those towns against the oncoming Anadans and Honterese, but their best hadn't been good enough.

Here and there, carpenters and stonemasons were repairing old buildings or running up new ones where the old had been totally destroyed. Most of the damage remained raw, though, like a wound just beginning to scab over.

Quietly, Vonney said, "At least Lutesse was spared this."

"Some of this," Guisa answered. "The dragons did what they could from the air." But she wasn't wrong. Instead of fighting block by block and house by house in the capital, King Kangen's warriors had pulled out. Most of Lutesse remained intact when it might have been a stretch of wreckage miles across.

The dining car was Quimperi. The waiter—gray-haired, erect, formally dressed, impassively sardonic—was so very Quimperi, Guisa knew critics would have called him a walking cliché in a comedy. The food seemed to be Anadan rations perked up with Quimperi skill and spices.

They got into Ylon as the sun was setting. "I hope someone's going to meet us," Guisa said as he and Vonney stood up to get out. "I haven't been here enough to know my way around."

People who'd left ahead of his wife and him were already embracing friends and loved ones on the platform. He nervously looked up and down. Somebody? Anybody?

A tall man with a swarthy southern face waved and called, "Master Sachry?" When Guisa nodded, the fellow went on, "So glad to meet you, sir. Cresc Mamzer, very much at your service. I have a carriage waiting to take you and your lovely wife to the hotel."

"That would be wonderful!" Guisa introduced Vonney. Mamzer clasped hands with each of them in turn. Controlled strength filled his grip. He had a nasty scar on the back of his hand.

The hotel was a hotel, the room a room. Guisa and Vonney ate dinner with Cresc Mamzer at the restaurant there. It also seemed to be serving Anadan rations, but did better disguising them than the dining car had. Wine helped everyone relax.

"I look forward to putting on *Justice for Some*. I truly do," Mamzer said. "We've seen too much hypocrisy since . . . well, since the Chleuh left, to be frank. Quimper is ready for some plain truth. When

Char Tubis squats on the pot, what comes out isn't perfume. It isn't even toilet water."

Guisa had had enough wine to laugh more than the joke deserved. He'd also had enough loneliness and isolation. "Getting back on the boards will feel so good!" he said. "Thank you so much for giving me the chance!"

"Thanks for writing the play," Cresc Mamzer replied. "Only a sour fool would imagine we don't need to hear your voice. I've started doing the casting. When you come to the theatre tomorrow, you'll meet some of the people. They've told me how thrilled they'll be to work with you."

"That's very kind," Guisa murmured, meaning *You're telling me what I most want to hear.*

"Oh, but I mean it," Mamzer said. "I truly do. The theatre will be full, I promise you. Full night after night. Ylon loves your work and you, Master Sachry. You can play here as long as you like. If we have better taste than Lutesse, that's the capital's fault, not ours."

"I myself like the way you talk, Master Mamzer. I truly do," Guisa said, beaming.

He liked the way Cresc Mamzer acted, too. The producer picked up the tab for dinner without thinking twice. He waved away the protests Guisa didn't really mean, understanding Guisa didn't really mean them. And he said, "We'll go to work in the morning. For now, you and your lovely lady should rest. I know what a train trip is like these days."

"Thank you!" Vonney said. Her yawn wasn't at all feigned.

Mamzer walked out into the night. As Guisa and Vonney went back toward the stairs, a clerk called, "Excuse me, sir, but someone left a note for you here at the desk. I didn't see who—I'm sorry." He held out an envelope.

Sure enough, it had Guisa's name on it in neatly printed syllables. Guisa took it and tipped the young man. He felt easier about doing that since dinner was on Mamzer.

Up in the room, he opened the envelope. The message inside was in the same hand as his name. It was short and to the point: *If you know what's good for you, you'll remember you're supposed to keep quiet.*

"What will you do?" Vonney sounded worried.

He crumpled up the note and threw it in the wastebasket. "I've come this far. I won't back down now."

"All right," she said, and then, "I hope it's all right."

"It will be. And I'll sleep like a stone tonight."

He did, too. So did Vonney. After coffee and a roll in the hotel restaurant, they went over to the theatre. It was only a couple of blocks away; Cresc Mamzer had chosen their lodging well. It sat on a prominent square. In the center of the square stood a larger-than-life statue so new, the bronze hadn't weathered to green. It was of a determined-looking man in ragged clothes holding a crossbow. The plaque on the base said TO THE HEROES WHO FOUGHT BACK AGAINST THE CHLEUH.

Vonney clicked her tongue between her teeth. "Not everyone here has politics like Mamzer's."

"Some people want to keep Char Tubis happy, that's all," Guisa sniffed. "Everything will be fine."

Everything was fine at the theatre. COMING SOON! a poster outside shouted. GUISA SACHRY'S FIRST ROLE SINCE THE WAR! *JUSTICE FOR SOME!* Inside, Cresc Mamzer and the performers he'd hired fussed over Guisa and Vonney, and made much of them. That softened him like butter . . . till the run-throughs started. Then he was all business. So were the Ylonese actors and dancers. They might have that southern twang in their voices, but they knew what they were doing—which meant Mamzer did, too.

"I think this is going to work," Guisa told the producer when they took a break.

"So do I," Mamzer said. "How does it feel to see the new one coming to life at last? Not that you haven't done it before, but still . . ."

"I'm pleased with it. I think it will go over well," Guisa said. "You always wonder till you go up there and find out what you've got. It never feels quite real while it's just on the page." He'd meant to mention the note to Mamzer, but it slipped clean out of his mind, which was full of more important and more enjoyable things.

They had only a few days to rehearse before the play would open in front of an audience. As performers will, they egged one another on to learn their lines and movements. The locals chaffed Guisa whenever he fluffed. "You wrote it—why don't you know it better?" one of them said.

He clasped his hands, as if begging for mercy. "Patience, please? Don't you know what writers are like?" They laughed with him, not at him. If he'd got up on his high horse, they would have hated him. He'd been in the trade a long time. He knew how these things worked.

Then it was opening night. Cresc Mamzer put new posters out front. Instead of COMING SOON!, they said HERE AT LAST! Guisa smiled when he saw them; he appreciated attention to detail.

Peering out at the crowd from the wings before the house lights dimmed, he thought it looked strange. He had trouble putting his finger on why. Then all at once he did: nobody out there wore a uniform. Not Anadan or Honterese. Not Quimperi. Not Chleuh, either. He hadn't seen that since before the war, and before the war was a long time ago now.

The lights went down. The play got going. He wasn't on at the opening. When he made his first entrance, the burst of applause stopped the show in its tracks. He stepped out of character for a moment to acknowledge it with a bow. They liked him! They remembered him! They wanted him back! After basking in that for a few heartbeats, he started acting again.

Justice for Some was about the accommodations ordinary people had had to make for the occupants, and about how little the Quimperi coming back from Honter, who hadn't been here through the black years and hadn't needed to make them, understood what life under the Chleuh had been like.

Here and there, some people booed and even hissed at his

sharper lines, but fewer than he'd expected. More cheered to drown them out. The audience was lively, interested, *involved*. Guisa always wanted audiences like that, and hardly ever got them.

A few people booed when he came out for his bows afterwards, too. He heard them through the applause and shouts. You always did. They made him remember the man who'd left the note at the hotel. *A plague on him*, he thought. You couldn't please everybody. If you tried, you just turned out pap.

After cleaning up, the cast went with Cresc Mamzer and the stage crew to a tavern all the theatre people in Ylon seemed to know. It got drunk out. Everyone kept telling Guisa how wonderful he was. He soaked up the praise like a sponge soaking up water. He felt he'd been dry far too long.

Mamzer guided him and Vonney back to the hotel. A bright moon beamed down on them. *A dragons' moon*, Guisa thought, as he would have in Lutesse during the war. But he didn't have to worry about that now, gods be thanked.

"I did it!" he exclaimed when Vonney and he got back to the room. Then, remembering she was there, too, he added, "We did it!"

Before she could answer, someone knocked on the door. "Who can that be?" she said. "It's late. I want to go to bed."

"Maybe it's Cresc." Guisa opened the door. When he did, he thought for a moment no one was there. Then he noticed how the wallpaper across the hall shimmered and blurred. Somebody—no, two somebodies—in tarncapes stood in the corridor.

He should have slammed the door then. By the time he realized that, it was too late. One of the almost-invisible somebodies hit him in the stomach. He folded up like a concertina and sat down, hard, on the floor. Then they were in the room. One of them shut the door. The other pulled back his cape enough to show a small crossbow, drawn and ready to shoot.

"Don't scream," the man barked at Vonney. "Nobody gets hurt as long as you behave. You'll come along with us and do what we tell you."

"Who—are you?" Guisa choked out as he struggled to his feet.

"We're the people who told you not to put on your stinking show, that's who," said the fellow who was still all but invisible. "We're the people whose good names you shat on when you wrote it. We're the people who'll make you pay for it."

"When we get going, the two of you'll walk downstairs. You'll act natural in the lobby, or we'll kill you and get away while you're croaking," his friend said. "You'll go to the monument in the middle of the square."

"Then what?" Vonney asked.

"You'll find out when you get there. Now move!"

Numbly, dull with joy and pride all at once turned to despair, Guisa moved. So did Vonney. Her hand found his. It was cold from fear. So, no doubt, was his own. Down the stairway they went. He could feel the two woodsrunners—what else could they be?—behind them, and hear their footfalls on the stairs.

But for a dozing night desk clerk, the lobby was empty. The clod didn't even stir as the performers and their tarncaped escorts went by. Was he worn out, or had he got paid to seem sleepy? Either way, he was useless.

Out into the night. Across the cobbled square in the yellow moonlight. When they got close to the monument, Guisa realized three or four more men in tarncapes stood there. He wondered where they'd got those light-bending cloaks. Civilians weren't supposed to own them, for all kinds of obvious reasons. From friendly soldiers? The Chleuh, before the war ended? The black market? He didn't dwell on it; right now, it was the least of his worries.

"Stand in front of the warrior for liberty, both of you," one of the men behind him said.

As Guisa and Vonney obeyed, one of the other woodsrunners opened up his cape enough to show a crystal. Where the emanations from it would go, who would see them . . . Again, Guisa didn't wonder for long, this time because someone he couldn't see yanked his trousers down to his ankles.

"Repeat after me," said a voice from a tarncape. "Repeat exactly. Make no mistakes, not if you value your neck—and your lady's. 'I, Guisa Sachry—'"

"I, Guisa Sachry—" Guisa brought out the phrases one by one: "—though silenced for loving the Chleuh too well—broke my silence to mock—the men who fought for Quimper's freedom.—I am sorry for what I did—and I pray pardon to—the gods of the True Faith—and the gods of the Old Faith—and any other gods there may be. I understand that if I break my silence again—my life is forfeit."

He started to pull up his trousers. He didn't get the chance. An unseen foot kicked him in the backside. He went to his knees, and scraped them both on the cobbles. Off the woodsrunners trotted. They disappeared as soon as they got more than a few feet from him.

Vonney helped him to his feet and yanked his trousers up somewhere near his middle. "Are you all right?" she asked.

"I'll live," he managed after a moment. "But *Justice for Some*, curse it, will only have a one-night run. This miserable, stinking world seems not yet ready for my genius."

The hawk-faced judge eyed Malk Malkovici over the tops of his gold-framed half-glasses. "The accused will rise," he said in a voice as empty as if he were a piece of animated machinery, not a man.

Rise Malk did, trying not to show anything himself. He'd spread more money around than he cared to remember, trying to get Quimperi justice to forget all about him. He'd fogged its memory for better than two years, but not forever. He did hope delay would help some. Hatred didn't run so high as it had right after the Chleuh left Lutesse. Jeering mobs weren't parading shaven-headed women stripped naked through the streets any more. And he'd got the geas lifted so he could come to the courtroom.

Then again, while those women would have given King Kangen's warriors more comfort than he had, he'd given them distinctly more aid. He'd got more money from them than those women had, too. He didn't think the judge had any idea how much more, which was bound to be just as well.

"Are you prepared to hear the verdict of this Purification Court?" the judge asked.

"Yes, your Excellency," Malk said. *I hope so, your Excellency*, was what went through his mind.

"Very well. Your case is complex, even by the standards of the others that have passed through these chambers. There can be no doubt of how much help you gave the occupants while they held Lutesse. The matériel you provided them assisted their war effort more than the actions of many people who suffered the ultimate penalty because of what they did. Do you deny that?"

Malk wanted to, with all his heart. He'd fry himself in his own grease if he did, though. He shook his head instead. "No, your Excellency," he said, as expressionlessly as he could.

"Let the record show the accused does not deny the assertion," the judge said. A clerk or secretary or reporter or whatever the right term was scribbled furiously. The judge's attention swung back to Malk. "Some people cooperated with the Chleuh out of political conviction, for the sake of personal advantage, or for reasons that can only be described as frivolous. That foolish actor who came before me, for instance . . ." He scowled. "He broke my order to stay silent, and he paid for it. The punishment was extra-judicial, but seemed to fit the offense. You are familiar with this, Master Malkovici?"

"Yes, your Excellency. Most people are, I think," Malk said. Guisa Sachry's humiliation had been the talk of the town when this trial started a couple of weeks before. Comics could get a laugh in coffeehouses by making as if they were going to drop their trousers, or by kicking or pretending to kick someone else in the rear. Sachry'd come home to Lutesse, but was lying very low.

"Indeed," the judge said with a thin smile: the only kind that fit on his narrow face. It disappeared as he went on, "Do any of the motivations I mentioned apply in your case?"

"No, your Excellency." Malk said as little as he could. If the judge ruled he'd worked with the Chleuh for the sake of personal advantage, he knew he would have a hard time refuting that. He'd brought out his reasons during the trial. Whether the man in the green robe believed him . . .

"You, your wife, and your brother belong to the Old Faith," the judge said. It didn't sound like a question, so Malk nodded instead of speaking. The hawk-faced man continued, "Had you not made yourself useful to the occupants, you and your family surely would have been transported to the murder camps in the east, as so many of your coreligionists were. And it is likely none of you would have come back to Quimper from them, is that not correct?"

"It is, your Excellency," Malk said.

The judge nodded. "Self-preservation will drive a man to do things he would not do otherwise. Testimony has also established that, in addition to dealing with the Chleuh, you provided significant information to the brave patriots who opposed them under the occupation. You also rescued Dragon Officer Chim Leynords of the Anadan Army Dragon Force and turned him over to those patriots, enabling him ultimately to be returned to Honter and resume his service. Is *that* not correct?"

"Yes, your Excellency." Till the trial, Malk hadn't known the dragonflyer's name or what finally happened to him.

"Very well. Some people deliberately helped patriots to some small degree while still cooperating with the occupants. That actor fellow again. Playing both ends against the middle." The judge scowled. "I believe it has been established that you never hoped for or expected a Chleuh victory."

"Your Excellency, that's true." Malk wasn't so sure about *expected*—in the dark days right after Lutesse fell and Quimper surrendered, almost everyone had expected King Kangen's men to win. But no one who clung to the Old Faith could have hoped they would. He added,

"If they had won, they would have disposed of me sooner or later. Sooner, I think."

"Speaking in my own person and not from the bench, I agree with you," the judge said. "Now hear the verdict of this court. While you did cooperate with and assist the Chleuh, you did so under compulsion and fear of death. Your dealings with Quimperi patriots show where your true affiliation lay. This being so, the court finds you not liable to punishment relating to your actions during the war. The geas holding you close to your home shall not be reimposed. So ordered!" He slammed down his mace of justice. "Master Malkovici, you leave my courtroom a free man."

"Thank you, your Excellency." Malk bowed to show the judge his respect.

When he turned, there sat Sarmel in the first row of the spectators' gallery, bringing his hands together without making any noise. Had the judge imposed a sentence on Malk, both Malkovicis were sure the authorities would have gone after his brother next. As things were, Sarmel was probably safe. Probably, because not everything that happened in Quimper these days made logical sense—and because nobody who clung to the Old Faith was ever more than probably safe. If the war hadn't proved that, what had it proved?

"Efa!" Sarmel mouthed, and flashed a thumbs-up.

Malk grinned and nodded. His wife was back at the flat with Lillat. However well behaved the little girl was, she wasn't up to sitting through long, boring courtroom sessions. And they had no one with whom they could leave her. Efa's uncle wasn't up to it, and probably wouldn't have done it had Efa asked. And he and Sarmel were all the family Efa and Malk and Lillat had.

Outside the courtroom, a reporter for one of the news sheets asked Malk, "How do you feel about hearing your case compared to Guisa Sachry's?"

"He's a fine actor," Malk said. "Back in the days when I could go to the theatre without worrying about the Chleuh, I enjoyed watching him. But the judge was right—he had less to worry about when he worked with the occupants than I did."

"What would you tell him if you could tell him anything?"

"That your choices stick with you, whether you want them to or not." Malk shrugged. "I know that isn't very wise or very deep. And I'm sure Master Sachry doesn't need to hear it from me."

"See what a famous fellow you are? Your words of wisdom will be in a news sheet tomorrow morning," Sarmel said.

Malk's brother was unlikely to have the depraved attraction to a diseased cow that the older Malkovici attributed to him. When Sarmel laughed, Malk added, "And somebody will spread my words of wisdom on the floor of his spare room so his puppy that isn't housebroken can shit on them. That's what they're worth."

"I knew that. I didn't know you did," Sarmel said. Malk mimed throwing a punch at him. This time, they both laughed. Sarmel went on, "Care to stop at Ullo's for something wet before you go home?"

"Thanks, but I don't think so," Malk answered after no more than a heartbeat's consideration. "I just want to get back and let Efa know they won't do anything horrible to me . . . this time." Yes, he belonged to the Old Faith. He understood down to the ground that dodging one disaster didn't mean others weren't on the way.

Sarmel did, too. "Fair enough, when you put it like that." He thumped Malk on the back. "And the Anadans are still doing business with us."

"If they weren't, their equipment would be. The Honterese stuff, too," Malk said.

Neither Anadan soldiers nor Hontermen had left the mainland after the war ended. Officially, they were making sure conquered Chlé didn't revive and turn vicious again, and helping the kingdoms the Chleuh had conquered and looted get back on their feet. Unofficially, they were trying to make sure the Muos' hatred of wealth didn't spread any more than it had already. It alarmed them almost as much as it had King Kangen, though they didn't want to fight Muosi to stamp it out. They said they didn't, anyhow.

"They have so much, they don't even bother keeping track of things," Sarmel said.

"Somebody's going to make money off them. Somebody's bound to. Might as well be us," Malk said. A Muo schismatic who heard him would have screamed that he was an enemy of holiness. He didn't care. The black market that had sprung up in Lutesse under the Chleuh had only grown after the allies replaced King Kangen's men. If you had the money, you could get anything.

But when hadn't that been true? Ever?

The sky was blue, the sun bright. A lazy breeze stirred the leaves on the plane trees lining the boulevard the courthouse stood on. Malk couldn't see any war damage, though he knew there was some not far away. If he pretended to forget that for a moment, Lutesse seemed as magical as it had before anyone dreamt King Kangen's bluster would set the world ablaze for five years.

As if plucking that thought from his mind, his brother said, "This isn't such a bad old place, you know?"

"Could be worse," Malk agreed.

When he and Sarmel got back into their neighborhood, there was Bezen, walking his beat. "So they didn't drop you in the jug and bang home the stopper, hey?" the constable said.

"Not this time," Malk said.

"You always know how to cheer people up, don't you?" Sarmel asked Bezen.

Sarcasm rolled off Bezen's thick skin like water off well-greased chainmail. "It's a gift I have," he replied. "A natural gift. Sort of like my natural gift for the ladies."

He left himself open to any number of retorts. Malk swallowed all the ones that occurred to him. He would have stepped on Sarmel's foot had his brother let fly. But Sarmel knew better than to poke a constable too hard.

"Well, I won't tell you I'm real sorry you'll stick around the neighborhood a while longer," Bezen said to Malk.

Of course you won't. I'm good for a touch whenever you need one.

Malk didn't care to tot up just how much he'd slipped Bezen over the years to take care of one thing or another. The constable generally had given him his money's worth, though; he did have to admit that.

He said his goodbyes and went on to the shop and the flat over it. Sarmel set a hand on his shoulder, saying, "I'll be on my way. You'll have things you want to talk about with Efa without me around." He might have meant *talk about*, or he might not.

When Malk walked in, his wife was behind the counter in case a customer came by. Lillat was happily playing with a crate of brass door latches and knobs. You still had to keep an eye on her, but she didn't always stick everything in her mouth any more.

She was also on her way toward learning to use the pot. *Another step toward civilization*, he thought, and then, *Or as much of it as any of us have. Gods know that isn't enough.*

Efa came out and around and hugged him. She felt wonderful in his arms. Lillat hurried over and grabbed each of them by one leg. "Mama!" she said. "Papa!"

"That's us," Malk agreed. "That's me."

"You're here. Does that mean everything's finally over?" Efa asked.

"I think so. The judge had sense enough to see I needed to work with the Locusts more than somebody like Guisa Sachry did. Sachry passed through his court before me, as a matter of fact," he said.

Efa sniffed. "Him! If you want to know what I think, he got less than what was coming to him down in Ylon."

"It could be. For people like that, though, getting embarrassed so the whole world is laughing at you may be worse than sitting in a cell," Malk said. Efa sniffed again, which told him what she thought of that. He went on, "I wasn't fair to the judge, either. Very sharp fellow."

She nodded against his chest. "You've said that before."

"It's still true. I wouldn't want to go up before him with a conscience dirtier than the one I've got." A stickler for detail, Malk didn't claim his conscience was clean. He knew better. He knew his wife knew better, too. He continued, "He's not the type you can soften with silver, either—I'm pretty sure of that."

"Good thing you didn't have to, then."

"A very good thing. If the gods can give me one more favor—over and above living through the war, I mean—I hope it's that I never see the inside of another courtroom for the rest of my days."

"May it be so!" Efa said in Nistrian; they'd been using Quimperi up till then. She went back to it to ask, "What if you need to testify for Colonel Tebron?"

"I'd still do that," Malk replied. "If I can pay him back, I will. He even felt bad about what the Chleuh were doing to people like us. Not bad enough to try to stop it, you understand, but bad."

"Huzzah!" his wife said sourly.

"Huzzah!" Lillat echoed in much more cheerful tones. "May it be so!" she added. She soaked up Nistrian as readily as Quimperi; Malk wasn't sure she knew there was any difference between the two languages.

"I know," he said to Efa. "He was King Kangen's man first, last, and always. He just happened to be a pretty good fellow anyway. I don't *think* I'll have to speak for him. If I needed to, it would have come up by now. Either he died fighting or he managed to give up without getting his throat cut. That's how it looks to me."

"Loose ends," she remarked.

"Life isn't as tidy as your romances," Malk answered, and she poked him in the ribs. Jerking, he went on, "You know it isn't. The two of us were loose ends. We never would have wound up in that orphanage if we weren't."

"That worked out all right. Didn't it?"

By the ominous way Efa asked the question, Malk knew how much trouble he'd land in if he said no. Since he didn't want to say no anyhow, that was all right. "Oh, pretty much," he allowed, and she poked him again. He didn't jerk so much this time; he'd expected it.

"Maybe when Lillat takes her nap . . ." Efa said.

"Don't want nap!" Lillat sounded ominous, too. In a few hours, though, she might not.

Malk nodded. "Yes, maybe then," he said. It wasn't as if they didn't have anything to celebrate, after all.

~

THANK YOU FOR READING CITY IN CHAINS

We hope you enjoyed it as much as we enjoyed bringing it to you. We just wanted to take a moment to encourage you to review the book. Follow this link: City In Chains to be directed to the book's Amazon product page to leave your review.

Every review helps further the author's reach and, ultimately, helps them continue writing fantastic books for us all to enjoy.

Want to discuss our books with other readers and even the authors?

JOIN THE AETHON DISCORD!

You can also join our non-spam mailing list by visiting www.subscribepage.com/AethonReadersGroup and never miss out on future releases. You'll also receive three full books completely Free as our thanks to you.

Don't forget to follow us on socials to never miss a new release!
Facebook | Instagram | Twitter | Website

www.ingramcontent.com/pod-product-compliance
Lightning Source LLC
LaVergne TN
LVHW041531240525
812134LV00001B/47

* 9 7 8 1 9 6 4 5 0 5 1 3 8 *